HUNTER'S HEART

BY

SLOANE MURPHY

Hunter's Heart
The Shadow Weaver #2
Part of The Seven Realms Saga

Published by Hudson Indie Ink
www.hudsonindieink.com

Hunter's Heart/Sloane Murphy – 2nd ed.
ISBN-13 - 978-1-915118-05-9

Grief is the price we pay for love

- UNKNOWN

ONE

FALLON

"I need you to keep this a secret," I plead, my hands trembling.

"What is it with you mortals and your secrets?" Morgan sighs as she sits. "So be it. But we need to do something about it."

"What can we do?" Deacon asks as I sit, gnawing on my bottom lip. I knew it was possible, but I hoped that I was delusional. I hoped that despite everything, that Azriel wouldn't have done this to me. Attaching one soul to another… it has dire consequences for the living soul. At least most of the time.

Except, it hasn't been done in so long, that the only

times I've heard of it are from the journals of my ancestors. Removing his soul from mine means shredding my soul again.

I'm not sure I'll survive it. Putting myself back together was hard enough the first time, I don't know if I'm strong enough to do it again if Morgan can't put me back together this time. I swear, if Azriel was alive still, I'd wring his goddamn neck. How fucking dare he do this to me? I'm so mad I could spit.

I never meant for this to happen, love. It was just a precaution.

I swipe my hand at the angry tears falling down my cheeks, ignoring the voice in my head and trying to turn my attention back to the conversing Demons around me.

"Do it. Whatever it takes. Just do it."

Their voices stop as my words register. I guess they weren't expecting me to be so demanding, or so resolute. I know there are consequences, and everyone has a lot going on, but I need to be able to use my power. Especially if Michael won't give Remy back without a fight. That's not something I'm going to just sit out of.

"What you ask, Witchling, is not so simple. And you have a lot going on back at home," Morgan says to me. "Remy is missing in Avalon, and the factions are on the brink of war yet again because of it."

It takes everything in me not to roll my eyes. I know

exactly what's at stake, exactly what's going on. Granted, she probably has a better idea of just how much shit we're in, and she could probably turn me to ash with a look, but still. "I'm aware of all of it, but having his soul connected to mine… the possibility of giving him the power to hurt them again, I won't have it. Do what you must to me, but I will not have my friends and family suffer because of him."

"This won't be easy…" Morgan starts but then shakes her head. "And it's going to really fucking hurt."

"I get that, but I've survived pain. I can survive it again. I just need it gone. Knowing the truth of why he's inside of my head… I feel violated in the worst way. I can't have him attached to me like this." I try to not sound as desperate or as angry as I feel.

"This could kill him, too."

"I have absolutely zero issue with that," I tell her honestly, the venom in my voice isn't as hidden as I would like. Morgan frowns at me, but she must see how determined I am because she doesn't push further.

A woman pops into the room as if summoned, and I let out a small squeal. Her eyes are completely black—which is at odds with her pale white skin—but there's no denying she's a Demon. The black markings under her eyes that go down her cheeks and the white horns kind of give it away.

"Can I have him yet?" the woman asks, her long white

hair flowing around her as if it has a life of its own.

Caleb glances over at me and must see the look on my face because he chuckles. “No need to worry, Fallon. This is Korrìn, but everyone calls her Kori.” The woman stands there, somehow looking both bored and excited. It’s so freaking bizarre. “No, you can’t have him yet. We still don’t know how long it’s going to take.”

“I’ve wanted him for a while. Are you keeping him here? Or is he going somewhere else?” Kori asks, and I just blink. They might as well be speaking Japanese for as much sense as this all makes to me.

“No idea yet. I’ll call you when I know.” Morgan dismisses her with a wave of her hand, and the woman sucks her teeth.

“Fine. Fine. Not like he can escape death for long,” is all she says before she disappears just as quickly as she showed up.

“She’s a soul collector. Well… I mean, technically, she’s Death, but I digress. She’s here for Azriel. Though, it would’ve been useful if she’d told us before that she hadn’t reaped his soul.” Morgan lets out a sigh, glancing at Caleb before focusing her attention back on me. I have so many questions, so freaking many, but now probably isn’t the time. “Enough about all of that, though. We can do this, but are you sure now is the right time? I can’t say what repercussions it will have for you.”

"My friends need me to be whole, to be healed. Hell, I need that. So do what you have to," I tell her, sounding braver than I feel, but that could just be the anger that's still simmering inside of me.

"Okay, we'll go to my chambers. Somewhere we won't be disturbed. Caleb…"

"Yeah, I'll sort everything out around here and let the guys know where you are," he says with a smile before kissing her softly and disappearing before my eyes.

"Come on, we should get started. I don't want to be too distracted in case Levi needs a helping hand with Michael and those other asshole Angels," she says with a glint in her eye. I think she'd enjoy the chance to tear off a few wings.

"Fine by me, I'd like to get rid of this Demonic parasite sooner rather than later."

You don't need to do this, pet. Please. I can help you.

Don't ignore me, love. I hate being ignored. You don't need to do this. They're trying to poison you against me. I've been helping you, I'm not trying to destroy you.

You'll regret this. You don't hate me. You know I'm not

what they all think I am. You know me better than anyone. Please love, don't separate us. They're trying to kill me once and for all.

I ignore the pleading in my mind as I walk further into Morgan's private rooms. I'm flip flopping between being angry that he did this to me and feeling guilty for cutting him out of my life. Even after everything, I still feel guilty because I know he wasn't all bad. I mean, yes, he was a giant asshole; but even so, that's not all he was. He showed me that time and again, even while he held me captive. I mean, he showed me plenty of his shittier side then, too. Man, my head is reeling. I want it over with... but I'm almost unsure. What if he's right and they're wrong?

I shake my head. No, there's nothing Morgan stands to gain from this. She's Remy's friend; she wouldn't put me through this if it wasn't needed. Hell, she tried to talk me out of it. I need this to be done, completely over with. I want to get my life back, get back to who I was. We have too much shit going on for me to be the problem yet again. I just want this taken care of quickly and quietly without causing a fuss. Look at what happened the last time I wasn't strong enough.

People died. So many people. And look at what happened to Creek.

No, there's a reason I want to keep this between me

and Morgan. I don't want to be a burden, and I don't want anyone to think I'm not capable. Especially considering the people I find myself surrounded by. I am not some damsel in distress… Okay, right now I might be, but I refuse to be a pawn any more. All I've ever wanted is my own freedom, the option to choose my own fate and not be ruled by everyone else's wants and needs. Selfish maybe, but the title of heir comes with a lot of responsibility.

"Are you ready?" Morgan looks toward me. There's pity in her eyes, and that slays me. Pity is the last thing I want, especially after everything I've been through.

"As ready as I'm going to be." I take a deep breath and step out of the robe she gave me, into the pool of water.

"The water will help the conduction of my power. It will make this less painful... well as much as it can." I wince as the icy water washes over my bare skin as I move to lie down in the shallow pool. The swimsuit isn't exactly warm and protective, but it's better than being naked.

"Like I said, this could leave permanent damage. Your soul could tear beyond repair. I can't say what the consequences of that would be," Morgan utters as she kneels beside the pool, placing the tips of her fingers on my temples.

"I know the risks," I say, my voice starting to shake from the cool temperature. "But if he's been playing nice in my head while knowing that he can take over my body...

never warning me about the consequences of accepting the help he's been offering...then I was wrong. There was never a good part of him. He's a parasite that's attached himself to me and I want him gone."

Come on now, love. Let's talk this through.

"Okay, then we'll begin, I'll try to heal you as much as I can, but it's likely we won't know the true extent of any damage for some time. Once you go back home and try to use your power..." she pauses and I nod, letting her know I understand.

"This is going to hurt." At her words, it's like my veins are filled with ice as the world turns dark. My skin feels as if it's on fire, and yet I'm so fucking cold.

You don't need to do this.

You stupid bitch, if you'd have just waited, I could've been free. We could have both been free.

You made a deal. You bound yourself to me. You'll regret this, do you hear? Fucking whore. I'll make sure you regret this. Even if it's the last thing I do.

I try to blank out the screaming voice in my mind, but his vitriol only gets worse as the pain increases. I feel myself thrashing in the water, as the white-hot pain takes over my body. I can't hear anything then.

And then... I feel like I'm floating. Like I might be dead. Until white light, so bright I can't really see, appears, and I see Azriel. He yells at me, but I can't hear him. As quickly as he arrives, he disappears, being yanked backward by an invisible thread.

Then the darkness creeps back in as the pain washes over my body in waves again.

"Come back to me, Fallon. Don't get lost out there." Morgan's voice filters in, and I try to speak, but the pain is unbearable. I've never known anything like it. As if my body has been pulled to pieces and is being stitched back together excruciatingly slowly.

"That's it. I've got you. We're nearly done." Her voice is so soothing, like a warm balm over the icy cold pain, and I feel myself drifting away. But this time, I know I'll be okay.

I wake up in the softest sheets, feeling lighter than I have in longer than I can remember. I open my eyes, blinking at the foreign surroundings, and it takes a second before I remember where I am. Everything hits me, and it's like I can't breathe.

We really did it. Morgan severed Azriel's soul from

mine. She's not here, and neither are any of her Horsemen, so it must have gone okay. At least I hope that's the case and this isn't some nightmare I can't wake up from. But I can feel it, deep within me.

He's gone, and I'm free.

I don't feel like anything went wrong, but then, I probably won't know until I go home and try to use my power. Morgan's repeated warnings about it play through my head as I sit up and try not to think about the fact that I'm in silky soft pajamas or how I got into them. I just tell myself that magic is a wonderful thing.

Guilt pangs in my stomach, though, and I try to ignore it. Azriel should have died already. It's not my fault he's dead or that his soul is probably with the soul collector woman now. His own decisions and actions laid the path he ended up going down. I just wish I'd said something earlier, maybe then I wouldn't feel like I need to scrub myself in a scalding hot shower, inside and out.

I find my clothes over the back of a chair, freshly cleaned and pressed, so I grab a quick shower—much quicker than the one I'd like—and get dressed before making my way down to the throne room. I have no idea what time it is, but there's always someone there. By the time I get there, I've passed more people than I think I've ever seen on this level of the Shadow Realm before. When I finally reach the throne room, it's teeming with people, but I spot Bryce near the door.

"Glad to see you're awake," he says, his eyebrows pinched as he looks me over. "How are you feeling?"

"I feel… okay. I think. I feel kinda floaty if I'm being honest," I say with a shrug. "How long was I out?"

"That's to be expected," he says, his gaze flickering over to Morgan. "We've got a lot going on over here, but I can call Deacon to take you home if you'd like? You were only out for an hour or so, nothing too alarming."

"Okay, well that's something at least. Is there anything I can do to help?" I ask, taking in the sheer amount of people shifting in the space. They look like they're gearing up for war.

I guess Morgan wasn't joking when she said she'd storm the gates of Avalon if Levi didn't find a way to get Remy back.

"No, we have it covered. It's chaos, but it's organized chaos," he chuckles, and I can't help but smile. All things considered, this might be the most relaxed I've seen the guy. It might also be the most I've heard him speak.

"Okay, well yeah, if Deacon can take me home, that would be great. Thank you," I say, feeling more awkward than I should. Really I'd like to ask Morgan a few more questions, maybe have her check if there is any damage… But looking around, I already know that's not going to happen. I'm sure she'd have let the guys know if she'd thought anything was wrong. At least that's what I tell myself, mainly because I don't want to think otherwise.

"Awesome," Bryce says, smiling again, and then his gaze goes distant. I try not to freak out as his eyes go glassy. But a few seconds later, just when I start to think about panicking, he comes back to me as if nothing happened. "He's on the way. If you want to wait just outside so he doesn't have to come in here…"

"Yeah, I know he's not exactly a fan of this place," I agree, wondering if Bryce will give me any details on why. But he smiles knowingly, and I know I'm not going to get a thing. I head out of the throne room, leaving him to the chaos, and wait for Deacon. It takes less than a minute before he appears at my side. The stress lines on his face make my stomach drop.

"Are you okay?" I ask, even though he obviously isn't.

"I will be," he says, taking my hand. "Let's get you home before anyone freaks out about you being gone, shall we?"

Crap. I hadn't thought about that. Though I imagine with Remy being gone, everyone's plenty distracted.

"Yeah, that's probably best." I give him a small smile, wishing that things weren't so strained between us. He nods, relaxing a little, and squeezes my hand.

"Then home we shall go."

TWO

When I make it home, it's the middle of the night.

"Thank you for getting me home," I say with a smile to Deacon, who looks very comfortable hanging back in the shadows.

"Fallon," he says, gripping my hand, "we need to talk."

"No, we really don't," I sigh. I knew something like this was coming.

"Fallon, I know what we went through, what *you* went through was the worst kind of thing, but I can't just ignore how I feel. There's something between us, and I don't *want* to ignore that." He looks down at me, reaching to cup my jaw. I pull back, taking a step away from him.

"Deacon, I don't want to hurt you, but what happened when I was held captive… the things you did to me, forced to do or not. I'm not sure that's something I can get over. Whatever is between us… Maybe in another life, or under different circumstances… Plus, I have other people to think about, too."

"You mean the Hunter?" he asks, and I nod. "I'm a patient man, Fallon. You don't live as long as I have and not develop a deep kind of patience. We can get past it if you're open to it. I'm not giving up on this, Fallon. No one has made me feel the way you do in at least a few hundred years." I blink up at him, shocked by not just his words, but his age as well. I mean, I know he's a Demon, but still totally not something I expected.

"I don't know what to say to that," I tell him with a sad smile, and he takes my hand again.

"You don't have to say anything. Just know my truth, Fallon Laveau. Our story isn't over yet." He leans down and kisses my hand before disappearing before my eyes.

Well shit.

Not exactly how I expected this all to go. Like I don't have enough going on in my warped mind as it is.

I take a deep breath and turn to face the back door of the house. The whole place is dark, so at least I know no one is panicking about me. I check my phone just in case, but there's nothing other than a message from Mama saying goodnight.

I manage to sneak in the house while everyone else is

sleeping. Maybe I can just pretend I had a super late night with Colt. Mama doesn't need to know where I spent the last day, and since time moves more slowly here than in the Realm, I might just get away with it.

I change out of my clothes and into some pajamas, then tuck myself into bed. I'm not even remotely tired, but I know I'm going to need to get some sleep. I need to check in with Creek tomorrow about the whole Remy thing. Fuck knows what's been going on, but I'm tired of being kept out of the loop. She's my friend, and I want to know what's being done to get her home. I flick the television on quietly and lose myself in some ass-crack-of-dawn shitty TV until the sun rises. Wishing I'd been able to sleep at least a little because I can just tell today is going to drag ass.

Colt: Morning, Beautiful. Give me a call when you get a minute. I need your help with something, and I'd really like to hear your voice.

I smile at the message. Now, without Azriel inside my mind, maybe we have an actual shot of making things work. Goddess knows Colt's been trying ever since everything came to light with Remy. I'm almost proud of how he's managed to put his prejudices behind him, especially since they were ingrained over half a dozen or so lifetimes.

Some might think I'm foolish to believe I can hold a

Hunter's heart. They live lifetimes over, and as a Witch, I only get one life… In this Realm at least. But I think it's better to follow my heart, no matter where it leads. So even if I only have his heart for this life, it's better than never having had it at all.

I jump from my bed and dive in the shower again, scrubbing myself until my skin almost hurts, and I almost feel clean. I finish brushing my teeth and fixing my hair just as Rebel knocks on the door, demanding to use the bathroom.

"There you go, I'm all done," I tell her with a smile as I leave the room.

"You look pretty. Where are you going? Are you going to see a boy?" she coos like the little girl that she is.

"I'm going to go and see Colt today, yes," I laugh, sticking my tongue out, glad that my red lip-stain is practically indestructible.

"Boys are so gross." She shudders, and I can't help but laugh.

"And I expect you to remember you felt this way in like three years, little miss." I smile widely at her, basking in her innocence.

"You seem happier today. That makes me happy. Maybe boys aren't so bad," she says glibly, and I sigh.

"I am happy, sweet girl. Come here." I wrap her in a tight hug and then kiss the top of her head. "Get cleaned up and dressed, and I'll make you some pancakes if Mama is still in bed."

"Yes!" She does a little fist pump and shoos me from the bathroom, requesting chocolate chip pancakes in the same breath. I smile the entire way to the kitchen.

After I got Rebel sorted out and checked on Mama, I dropped Colt a text to let him know I'd head over this morning, which is how I find myself portaling into his front yard. Being here is so weird now. Knowing that Colt is the only Bennett Hunter left, that this place is his and his alone. That his brother and his dad aren't just going to rock up and blow up the potential of what we're trying to build here. I try not to picture the possibilities of our future, but it's impossible not to.

Though, I'm pretty sure there's never been a faction hybrid. I wonder if the Hunter or Witch genes would win out or if we'd have a true hybrid.

I shake my head, clearing the thoughts. Totally not what I should be focused on right now. Really, I should tell him about what happened with Azriel, but the whole thing makes me feel kind of dirty, so I'm hesitant. I don't want him to judge me or think that the progress we've made is tainted in any way. But I don't want to move too fast either, despite my errant thoughts of what could one day be.

And yet, I feel myself falling harder and faster for Colt than I ever have for anyone else. I can't control it, and it fucking terrifies me. But at the same time, it's exhilarating and I can't wait to see where it takes us. I know secrets aren't the best way to start this, but I don't know that I can cope with how he'd look at me if he knew.

I'll tell him. Just not yet…

I climb the steps and head into the house. It's finally back in one piece, so I guess Kain's Dracul finally finished helping him put it back together. You can't tell that anything happened here just a few weeks ago.

"Colt?" I call, not hearing a sound other than my own footsteps.

"Hey, babe, I'm up here." I look up and see him smiling down at me from the railing of the third floor.

I head up toward him, unable to stop a grin so wide it almost hurts my cheeks. This, with him… It feels so normal. So right.

I reach the third floor, and he sweeps me into his arms, kissing me with so much heat my toes curl. He steals my breath away, but if he keeps making me feel like this, he can have it. He can have it all. Every breath and every other part of me, too.

"I missed you," he says quietly as he pulls back a little, though still close enough that his lips brush mine as he speaks. "Sorry I've been so absent. I've been trying to stay on top of Hunter crap. Plus there's everything with Remy. I feel like I've barely seen you since she was taken."

"It's okay, you've been busy. How's the stuff with Remy going? Any updates from Levi or the others?"

"Nothing from Levi, but Creek's kept me up to date. They're hedging all their bets on Levi busting into Avalon. I know it took me a while to come around to them all, but I trust them with her. I know they'll get her back. Levi is fucking terrifying with the things he's willing to do for my sister, and that's before the others even get on board."

"You're not wrong," I laugh, and he pulls me closer. He hugs me close, tucking my head under his chin. I've never felt safer than I do in his arms right now. He feels like home in a way I've never noticed before.

"So what did you want to talk to me about?" I ask, not moving from his warm embrace.

"I need your help finding someone. One of Nasari's trusted people has gone missing, and I was wondering if you'd help by scrying for him? I know we usually try not to ask for help, but with everything else we're juggling at the minute, resources are stretched a little thin."

"Of course I'll help. Get me what I need, and I'll do what I can."

"I can think of something you need."

I can hear his grin before I see it.

"I'm sure you could," I say, licking my lips though I pull out of his embrace, because I know if I don't we'll never actually get around to getting the job done. He's just way too distracting when he's this close to me, and scrying will require my attention.

"Where do you think you're going?" he asks, pulling me back toward him. I squeal when he lifts me, though my legs wrap naturally around his waist, and I settle my arms around his neck.

"Weren't you working before I interrupted?" I ask, laughing softly.

"Oh, I'm definitely still going to be working." He winks, and I laugh again as he cups my ass with his hands. "Or at least working out."

I don't think I'll ever be able to get enough of his many sides... The serious side, the protective side, and this happy-go-lucky, flirty side. I know there's still so much more to him than this, and I'm looking forward to learning even more about him.

Colt leans toward me, a heated glint in his eyes, and my breath catches in my throat. The kiss is soft at first, though he steals my breath completely as his mouth works over mine. Breathing isn't an option as his tongue dominates mine, and I'm only just aware of the sway of our bodies as he walks. Our lips tangle, and with each step he takes down the stairs, our bodies glide across one another. He carries me as if I weigh no more than a feather; and with the amount of my being that he's melding with his own, maybe I don't.

He kisses me as he walks down the hall. He kisses me as he carries me through the door. And he continues kissing me as he lays me out on top of his mattress. My chest heaves when he finally pulls his delicious mouth from mine, but he steals my breath again as he devours me with his eyes instead. His gaze is so intense I feel like I'm under a microscope. I feel his heated scrutiny travel across every inch of my skin, and it's exhilarating.

"I thought you were going to work out? Looks like you're slacking from here." I smirk, hoping to get a rise out of him. Because there is nothing hotter than Colt and his alpha asshole attitude when he flings me across the room and makes me forget my own name.

"I'll show you slacking…" he growls. There he is, all powerful and agile. He reaches over his shoulder, grabbing onto his signature black tee and dragging it over his head, granting me an unhindered view of his chiseled chest and abs. The glint of the metal through his nipples catches my eye as he hovers above me, watching me as I squirm and resist the urge to reach up to taste that metal. My mouth waters at the sight of him, and my skin prickles with anticipation for his touch. I clamp my thighs together as I take him in, already desperate for his touch.

His keen eyes see all of my tells, as if I'm a series of hotspots and he's watching them light up with every move he makes.

"Take it all off, Fallon. Except for the boots." The mischievous glint in the mesmerizing depths of his eyes tells me everything I need to know. He wants to play but only if I follow his rules. A shiver goes down my spine at the thought of it. I like playing by his rules, but I love pushing his buttons.

"But what if I want to take them off?" I ask, biting my lip as he stares down at me.

Colt ignores my question and instead takes a step closer to me, his need for me radiating from his skin like flames from a burning building. He doesn't have to say a word, his intent is clear. These boots will stay on because he's in charge right now, and I'm more than willing to let him be.

I shimmy out of my clothes, and his eyes never leave my body. I feel heat climb my spine in anticipation of what's to come. Unzipping the boots to remove my jeans and panties is a necessary evil, and my fingers tremble as he watches closely as I re-zip them. His Adam's apple bobs as the tops envelop my sensitive skin. A shiver crawls over my skin when I reach behind me to unhook my bra and his eyes flash with hunger.

Colt steps between my legs as the last of my clothing hits the floor, and I watch him, fascinated, as his tongue slides out of his mouth onto his bottom lip. He bites down on his lip, and a shudder of anticipation leaves me shaking. The move is sexy as fuck, and the way all of his attention is focused solely on me is fucking intoxicating.

He's not focused on his needs or wants. Not on his hard cock that I see pushing against the zipper of his jeans. Not on the creaks and groans of the old house.

All of his attention is on me. On my body and my pleasure. On my wants and needs.

It's heady, being the focal point of a man's undivided attention. But being Colt's only focus? It's like a direct line to my clit, and that space between my legs that longs to be filled by him and only him throbs with need.

"Are you wet for me, Fallon?" he asks, and when I don't answer, his piercing gaze shoots up from my pussy to my eyes. I nod, he's not okay with that.

"Words, baby," he says, grasping my chin with his finger and thumb. I gulp as I stare up at him.

"Yes," I whisper, and he nods.

"Hmm," is all he says before he releases my chin and his gaze slides back down to my pussy, seemingly happy with my answer.

With both of his hands on the backs of my thighs, he drops to his knees at the foot of the bed and pulls my boot-clad legs over his shoulders before leaning in and taking a lingering breath. His eyes close as he holds it in.

"Your scent is like a drug for me, Fallon. Do you know that?" He drags his tongue from one end of my slit to the top where my clit is very impatiently awaiting his hot touch.

"Do you know that every time I taste you, I can barely think straight? I can't imagine being anywhere else but right here?"

His teeth close around my clit, and my breath catches in my throat. There he goes stealing all of my air again. His tongue lavishes the swollen bundle of nerves with attention until I'm gasping for air and gripping the covers of the bed. It feels like my entire body is moments away from seizing.

He slows as my breath comes out in hard gasps. My gasps ring throughout the room as he fully stops his ministrations, but the sound of them aren't nearly as desperate as I feel.

Colt palms my ass, but before I can even register the change in angles, his mouth is on my pussy again. He feasts on me like I'm his last meal. He licks and nips and groans as he owns me with his tongue. His fingers dig into the soft flesh of my ass as he takes what he wants and refuses to slow down until he hears my cries.

The electricity of my orgasm fills every vein and artery in my body, making me feel like I've been electrocuted with shots of pure, unadulterated bliss.

When his mouth releases me and he pulls away, my

eyes pop open. I struggle to get a grip on myself as he resumes his monologue, acting entirely as if he hadn't just made me short-circuit from a body-numbing orgasm.

"The least I can do is share that feeling with you." He smirks down at me, and I close my eyes and struggle with my fried brain for a moment. What feeling? I don't know what he's talking about... Maybe my brain really *is* fried. As I reopen my eyes to look at him properly, I see him gently unzipping one boot, removing it, and slowly placing it behind him before repeating the action with my other boot.

He stands, watching me intently as he undoes his belt and unfastens the top button of his jeans. I fucking damn near drool at the sight of him lowering his zipper. He pulls out his belt and it cracks in the air, and I swear my pussy throbs at the sound.

Of course he's commando.

Because boxer-briefs are too mundane for the sexiness that is Colt.

I think I whimper when his thick cock springs free and stands proud against the happy trail that covers his lower belly.

It takes every last bit of strength I have not to groan as he pushes his jeans down before kicking them out of the way.

Fuck, he's hot.

As hot as the need that's boiling my every cell.

Leisurely, he takes his cock in hand, the metal bars in his dick making my mouth water as I remember just how they feel inside of me. He lets the corner of his mouth upturn into his signature cocky, knowing grin as if he can read my thoughts.

"What do you need, Fallon?" he asks, but he's just taunting me. He knows exactly what I need.

"You," I pant, staying where I am, because I know that's what he wants without him even breathing a word of an order.

"How do you need me?" he asks, his tone biting. I swear to fuck his voice makes my nipples pebble. They almost hurt with how hard they get in reaction to his commanding tone.

"Every. Fucking. Way."

"Good answer," he growls as he steps toward me and lifts me from the bed.

In seconds, I'm pushed against the nearest wall, and his pierced cock slams inside of me as his mouth descends on mine. Our tongues battle for control—we both know he's going to win, but I also know he loves it when I fight him a little.

With one hand on my ass, he uses the wall as leverage as he fucks me with deliciously vicious thrusts. I can feel him everywhere. His hand on my shoulder pulling me down onto him every time he pushes into me. His groin rubs against my clit with every fucking thrust, and it's fucking heaven.

His mouth explores every inch of mine as he pushes me closer to oblivion, yet his lips bring me back to where we are every time my mind blanks out from the pure pleasure of him fucking me relentlessly.

"Colt, oh Goddess—" My words are more moans than anything else. I can't control what comes out of my mouth because my body barely belongs to me.

Colt owns it.

He owns my voice. My movements. My pleasure.

All of it.

My body is like a violin, and he's the conductor making the masses cry from the beauty of its music. I love handing him the control; I love giving him this power.

"Fuck, Fallon, you're so fucking tight it makes me want to pray to all the gods that I never have to leave your magic pussy."

I laugh, I can't help it, but he shuts me up with a hard thrust that makes me see fucking stars. My breath catches in my throat as he carries me to the bed and spreads me out in front of him before slamming right back inside me and fucking me until another orgasm rips through me. I don't know how he's capable of controlling his own pleasure. He's like a fucking machine.

"Colt, give it to me, please." I practically beg, and he abides.

With both my arms held above my head and his cock pistoning inside me, hitting that magical spot over and over again, he grunts as the slick walls of my pussy tighten one more time.

"Fuck, yes—" He doesn't finish whatever he was about to say before we both cry out each other's names, shaking with unrelenting ecstasy.

I think I black out for a second because the next thing I know, he's cradling me in his big, strong arms and peppering soft kisses across my brow.

"Are you okay?" His voice is low, like a secret between us.

"I think you just fucked me blind."

I feel his chuckle across every inch of my skin.

"You're welcome," he laughs as I snuggle against him. We lie in silence for a little while, and I simply enjoy the feeling of being here in his arms. It's hard to not fall asleep after that, but I do my best to keep my eyes open and enjoy this time with him. I don't want it to end.

"What are your plans for tonight? Do you want to chill and watch a movie? We could cook together or something?" I ask softly.

"That sounds amazing, but raincheck? I have a patrol tonight," he says and I frown, rolling out of his arms and pulling the sheets up to cover myself.

"A patrol?" I ask, the words sparking a fire inside of me.

"Yeah, most of the Hunters are working on this whole Archer thing, and even with the factions working together, rogues still exist."

"Why are you going on a patrol?" I ask, and he looks at me like I've lost my mind.

"What do you mean?"

"I mean, you're an Elder. You have other Hunters for that shit," I snap, trying to not let my worry get the best of me. But apparently the part of me that was broken isn't quite healed, and this shit is triggering me.

"Fallon, I'm not the guy that sits on the sidelines. You know that."

"Well, why the fuck not? You're a leader now, you need to take a step back."

"Says fucking who? I don't see any of the other faction leaders stepping back from battle, and you haven't said a fucking word about that. I don't see your mom not heading into battle and she has you and Rebel to worry about. Don't ask me to not be who I am, Fallon. You won't like it."

"You're not fucking bulletproof, Colt. Stop acting like you are!" I shout, climbing from the bed, taking the sheet with me as I try to put space between us. This can't be fucking happening right now.

"I never said I was bulletproof, but I am good at what I do. I'm not about to change. I can't believe you of all people are saying this. After all the shit you gave me about a bigoted perspective because of who you were, and now you don't want me to be who I am? I'm a Hunter, Fallon. Before I'm an Elder, I'm a Hunter."

"And what if something happens to you?" I fling back at him, trying to stop my hands from shaking by gripping the sheet, hard. My knuckles ache as they turn white with my grip.

"Nothing is going to happen to me," he sighs, throwing his hands in the air before standing and tugging on his jeans.

"You don't know that! We didn't think anything would happen to me either and look what fucking happened."

"This isn't that, Fallon. I ask my Hunters to do this every day. I'm not going to ask them to do something I'm not willing to do myself."

"This is ridiculous," I screech, and even though I kind of hate myself for blowing up like this, the panic grips my throat and I know I'm not the one driving this train. I pull my clothes on hastily, stuffing my underwear in my pocket when I find them after my jeans are already on. "You obviously don't care about yourself, so why the fuck should I?"

I grab my boots and leave his room. Colt calls my

name, but I’m done. This isn’t something I ever want to feel again. This all-consuming panic isn’t something I can control or tamp down. Maybe after everything I’ve been through, I just don’t have the space inside of me to care this much about another person. The thought of loving him terrifies me, because losing him… Losing him will break me.

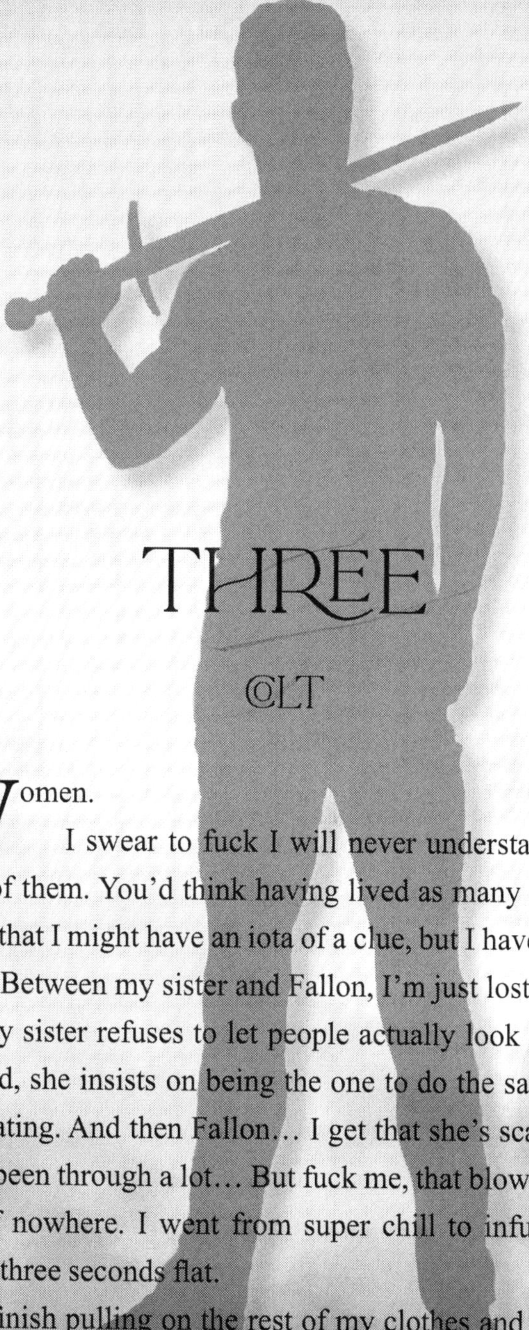

THREE

COLT

Women.

I swear to fuck I will never understand them. Any of them. You'd think having lived as many lives as I have, that I might have an iota of a clue, but I have fucking none. Between my sister and Fallon, I'm just lost.

My sister refuses to let people actually look after her. Instead, she insists on being the one to do the saving. It's infuriating. And then Fallon… I get that she's scared, that she's been through a lot… But fuck me, that blow up came out of nowhere. I went from super chill to infuriated in about three seconds flat.

I finish pulling on the rest of my clothes and slide my

feet back into my boots, not bothering to tie them. Elijah and the guys will be here in about an hour—there have been more rogue sightings, too fucking many, so I need to get my head on straight. Maybe a few rounds with a punching bag will help get out the frustration. I've never been wound so tight after blowing my load

Fucking women.

I make my way down to the basement, contemplating selling my apartment and Bauer's old house. Everyone died so fucking quick this time around, and I'm the only one left to handle it all. Sure I could ask Remy for some help, but fate knows she has enough on her plate at the moment as it is. I'm not about to drop a ton of legal bullshit in her lap, too. Considering we think the Hunter's curse is broken, we won't need to keep all of the properties like we usually would. Which means I probably need to go and empty out Bauer's house, too. I already dealt with his body, so I guess the house is just another thing to add to my ever growing to-do list. Not like being an Elder isn't keeping me busy enough on top of everything else we have going on.

Fuck my life. When did I get so weighed down?

I miss my brother some days, but mostly I wish he was still here so I could kick his ass all over again before he died. I don't blame Levi for what he did. Hell, I'd have probably done the same thing in his shoes. Bauer nearly killed Remy, and after everything else… well yeah, he deserved what he got. Knowing what Levi said about Michael, I don't think he's exactly going to allow my Dad and Bauer to live out their afterlives in Avalon either—which means Morgan and her guys will likely get them.

Being someone who fucked Remy over and then ending up with those guys? I shudder at the thought. It's glaringly obvious that they love her as much as I do, even from the reasonably limited time I've spent with them. Not that I'm surprised. My sister has a way of just making you want to love her without ever doing a thing.

I'm glad she's safe, even if I had to hear it from Creek rather than her... Granted he only heard it from Levi since she's still in Avalon at the moment. I don't want to think about how tied up she is now that he's there with her. Nope, no thank you. Not thoughts I need about my baby sister.

I kick off my boots as I hit the lights and pull off my t-shirt. I stomp to the bag. Fuck wrapping my hands today. I need some pain—such a sweet distraction.

My fist connects with the leather, and the sting in my knuckles grounds me a little. So I keep going, taking out every single fucking frustration I have on the bag until sweat runs down my spine. Still I keep going. Reveling in the simplistic bliss of beating the crap out of something and just letting go.

I haven't lost myself to this in way too long. It's one of

the reasons I'm going patrolling tonight. I've lost myself a little these last few months. Between everything with my family, and taking on a role with the Elders that I never fucking wanted, I barely know who I am anymore.

I need this patrol.

I'm know it's probably not healthy, but fuck it. I know who I am when I'm hunting—that's been my life longer than I care to think about. If I have a mission, I have a purpose. I'm good at what I do.

It's not like all the Elder shit doesn't give me purpose, but I've always been better as the guy getting my hands dirty. This stuff is bureaucratic bullshit, and I don't always have the patience for it. Who would've thought squabbles between grown fucking adults could be so childish? I mean, territory disputes I get, but who's leading a patrol? Sort your fucking selves out.

I smack the bag again and it splits, sand pissing out all over the floor. This day can suck my fucking dick. I sigh, pressing on the bridge of my nose, and the bag swings as it empties. I think I might be more wound up now than I was before I started. I really need this patrol tonight, and I'm really, really hoping someone has a death wish. And hopefully that someone knows how to fucking fight because there's nothing quite as therapeutic as using my bare hands to beat the shit out of an overconfident Lycan or Dracul.

The sand covers the floor, and I shake my head. I'll deal with that later. I need a shower before we head out, and time passed way too quickly while I was down here.

The bang of the door sounds as I'm stepping out of the shower. I hear the boys as they walk in, not needing an invite. It's nice that they're all around so much these days, especially since Creek is MIA now.

"I'll be down in a few minutes," I shout down from the first-floor railing.

"Yeah, alright, pretty boy. We all know it takes you longer than a few minutes," Elijah shouts with a laugh, and the others snort along with him.

"Fuck you, asshole," I shout back. "You wish you were this pretty."

"Hurry up! We'll attack your kitchen while we wait," Danny shouts back, and I groan. Those motherfuckers will wipe me out if I don't hurry. I dash to my room, towel wrapped around my waist, and wipe down my hair with another one. I hear them laughing as I grab my boxers, t-shirt, and jeans from the closet. Fates bless Maddie for having been here. I haven't had time for laundry and all that other domestic bullshit lately. She's a godsend. Hell, she's the only reason there's shit in my fridge for those assholes to pillage.

Once I'm dressed, I pull on my boots and strap on my shoulder holster. My guns and blades are downstairs already, so I can grab them before we go. I take in my reflection quickly, noting how jacked I've gotten these last few months. It's a little weird how quickly it happens without even really trying. I shrug it off and head downstairs.

"You assholes better have made me some food, too," I joke as I swing into the kitchen, finding them all sitting around the table. Elijah and Danny sit with a platter of lasagna between them while Joey and Emmett have a pizza.

"There's plenty to share," Emmett laughs as he lifts his beer to his lips and chugs down most of the bottle. I grab a plate and steal food from both parties, groaning at the Italian goodness as I shovel it into my mouth.

"You guys know the areas we're hitting tonight?" I ask casually as I sit back in my chair, more than a little bloated as I sip my own beer.

"Yeah, we were there a while back before all this shit started with your sister. It wasn't exactly a hive of activity then, but I've heard the recent reports, and it's been fucking insane there the last few weeks. Most of it's probably clear now, especially after all the patrols. You'd think they'd stop coming back to the same place, but stupid rogues are stupid rogues," Elijah says with a shrug.

"Well, let's hope they stay stupid. I could do with making something bleed tonight," I tell them, and Danny groans.

"Awesome, Colt's on a mission. Better take extra medical supplies tonight, boys."

"Fuck you." I flip him the bird and drain the last of my beer before asking, "You guys ready to head out?"

They let out a chorus of 'yes' and clear the table of their shit while I head toward the trunk I've moved near the front door and start gearing up. I slide on my jacket that Remy had made for me from the same material as her cloak, which means I'm safe from most weapons, but considering the new wave of angel glass we've seen... I might need to upgrade.

I'll deal with that later.

I strap on my sword and slide guns into my holsters, fastening extra ammo clips on my belt as the others appear, ready to go.

We roll out, and Elijah joins me in my truck while the others pile into the truck they arrived in. We always have two vehicles in case one is compromised. It's not an optimistic outlook, but the strategy has saved my ass more times than I want to think about.

I follow the other truck, driving without really taking in the direction we're heading.

"You okay, man? You seem fucking out of it," Elijah says, bringing me back to reality.

"Yeah, I'm good. Just chick shit."

"Fallon still adjusting after everything?" he asks, his concern evident. He knows everything that's been going on recently. There aren't many Hunters I'd trust with my life these days, let alone with my family's, but Elijah is one of the few that I do. He knows everything that's been going on, minus the Hunter curse shit. I can't tell anyone about that—I wouldn't even know where to fucking start. It's not like I can just casually drop it into conversation. Fuck knows how I'm going to tell the others about it if Remy finds out the curse really is broken.

"Something like that. We were totally chill, but when I told her I was patrolling tonight she went nuclear." I don't miss his wince.

"A nuclear Witch isn't something I want to witness. This is why I stay single, man. It's way simpler." He shrugs, and I scoff.

"Something like that," I say, noncommittally. "I just don't know what she wants from me. I know she's been through a lot, but I'm not about to change who I am. She's known me our entire lives; who and what I am are not a secret."

"Everyone changes in a relationship. Compromise is the key, or at least that's what my sister constantly blathers on about," he says with a chuckle. "Chicks are hard work, but apparently the right one is worth it."

I shake my head because talking about this shit isn't helping my concentration at all. "Just hope that we discover some asshole rogues tonight. I could really use the outlet."

"You should be careful what you wish for," he says as I glance forward in time to see Danny's truck slide to a stop. I slam on my brakes so I don't hit him when I spot what made him stop. Apparently the rogues didn't get the message that we're not going to stop clearing this place until they're gone. Whether they were working with Archer or not, rogues aren't welcome in Salem's Bay. I thought Kain and Roman had dealt with all the rogues, but it seems fucking never-ending.

There must be something here that they're after. Something other than my sister. Something they can't find, or something they're protecting. I fully intend to find out what it is and then fuck it up.

"Well fuck, looks like someone answered my wish—it's time to party. Let's go make some assholes bleed."

I lose track of how much time we spend hacking through the rogues. I lost my jacket in a scuffle with three Lycans sometime earlier, but I don't feel the cold. My arms ache from using my sword more than my guns, but the pain is the good kind. I hear gunshots, but it's not until I hear my name being shouted that I really focus. I take the head of the Dracul in front of me, instead of continuing to play with him, and spin to find the others running in my direction.

"Fuck, Colt, you're hit!"

I feel the blossom of pain in my lower back, and my vision blurs as they rush in my direction. It was Danny who shouted, I think, but my focus goes to my spasming muscles, and I lose concentration.

"Shit..." I groan, the white hot pain radiating from the spot in the small of my back. I grit my teeth, groaning as my knees give out from under me.

"We need to get him to a Witch," Elijah says as he and Danny stand me up and drape an arm over each of their shoulders. Joey and Emmett give us cover fire to escape the smaller group of rogues that seems to be growing again. I have no fucking clue where they're coming from, but the burning in my back keeps me from giving a fuck.

"Fallon," I groan, and Elijah pulls my phone from my pocket and dials. Danny throws me in the back of my truck, and I see Joey and Emmett jumping in the other one as Danny and Elijah jump in the front of mine.

"Drive," Elijah barks, and Danny peels out of the area. The squeal of the tires burning over pavement tells me the others are behind us. "She's not picking up."

"Fuck." I groan, trying not to worry about the amount of blood I'm losing from the bullet and hoping like fuck it's not angel glass. "Try Marie," I tell him, just in case. She's the only Witch I know with enough juice to heal me if it is angel glass. Even then, there's a very real possibility she'll be too late if it is.

"No answer there either. Fuck this, I'm calling Emma," Elijah says, and Danny grunts. Emma is someone I haven't seen in years. She's part of Fallon's coven, or at least she was once upon a time. She pulled away a while back, and the last I heard was that she was working for both sides these days—but a Witch is a Witch right now.

"Emma, it's Elijah. I've got a body heading your way. Multiple gunshots, unknown materials..." he pauses for a minute and practically growls. "Whatever you want, fucking woman. Just sort your shit, we're three minutes away."

The truck drifts around a corner, thank fuck for my new tires, I think with a wry laugh. Apparently blood loss doesn't suit me.

"I'm going to try Fallon again, just in case," Elijah snaps. I drop my head back down as I lay across the back seat, trying to not focus on the pain or the fact that I'm starting to feel real fucking woozy. I've been shot before, but they must've got me good this time. I haven't felt like this since… well, I can't remember since when.

I really hope it isn't angel glass. I don't want my last moments with Fallon to have been us arguing. Especially with the curse up in the air. I might be able to come back, but that doesn't mean I'm ready to die just yet. Who knows how long coming back will take?

The truck jolts to a stop, and I grit my teeth against the pain of the sudden motion. The guys jump out, coming around to pull me from the back seat because I couldn't crawl right now, let alone fucking walk. I have a hard time paying attention to anything as they carry me. I only notice we're inside when I can't see the night sky anymore.

They lay me face down, and I rest my head on my arms as they move about around me.

"There are five fucking holes in his back!" a female voice curses, and I assume it's Emma. Her words jerk my thoughts in another direction. Five? That's a new record even for me. "We need to get the bullets out and stop the bleeding."

"If this is angel glass…" Danny says quietly.

"It's not. With this many bullets, he'd be dead already if it was. Now shut up and help me. Put pressure on the other wounds while I start trying to get the bullet from this one," she says, and then searing pain rips through my body in the moments before I pass out.

I wake back up in my own bed sore as fuck. But alive, and that's better than I thought it was going to go for a minute there.

"Morning, sunshine." I look up to see Elijah standing in my doorway, a steaming mug in hand. "Glad to see you're up."

"How long was I out?" I groan. I feel like fucking shit.

"Little over a day. We were worried. There was a lot of blood loss, and Emma doesn't exactly have the same power punch as the Laveaus, but she did okay. We sorted a transfusion for you, thank the Fates for my universal blood." He winks at me, and I choke out a laugh.

"Thanks, man," I push myself to sit up, fighting a groan as I do. Getting shot really sucks.

"Nothing you wouldn't do for me. You going to be okay, or do you need me to stick around today?" He points at my phone on the table before looking at me with a frown. "Oh, and your phone has been going fucking nuts; I plugged it in on your bedside table so it didn't die."

"Fucking kill me." I scrub a hand down my face and glance at my phone. There are at least seven missed calls, and I know I don't even want to look at the number of messages on there. What the fuck happened yesterday?

FOUR

FALLON

It's been six days since Remy was taken, three days since I had my soul torn to shreds again, and two days since I've heard from Colt. Sure, I ignored a few of his calls after our argument, but I wasn't ready to talk to him, and he's been silent since. I don't really blame him, but I won't apologize for being fucking terrified of him getting hurt. Losing him isn't something I want to contemplate, especially now that I'm finally free again. But it's been a fucking week from hell.

My phone buzzes on my bedside table, and I groan as I roll over to check it. There's a new group text.

Creek: Remy's home. She's safe and okay, and she'll contact you both tomorrow. Just wanted you to know.

Colt: Thanks man. I expect details of exactly how Levi tore that Michael asshole a new one.

Creek: No doubt. We'll catch up in a few days, man. Take it easy.

Me: Thanks for letting me know.

I throw my phone back down on the table, half hoping Colt will text me directly, but I know he won't. He doesn't think he's done anything wrong, and he hasn't. I know that I freaked out, but I'm not sorry about being so fucking worried about him.

I spent most of the day yesterday somewhere between angry and sullen. Even Mama gave me a wide berth, sending me to the back room of the store to fill vials and do random jobs rather than dealing with customers. I could practically feel the worry emanating from her. Which reminds me, I still need to talk to her about that. Empathic abilities aren't exactly new to our bloodline, but it's definitely not what I was hoping for as my emergence power.

I still haven't tested my powers properly since having Azriel's soul torn from mine, either, so I probably need to tell her about that, too. Except, I don't want to worry her with that. Goddess knows she's had enough to worry about these last few months with everything else going on. It's not hard to see the toll that it's all taking on her, and I really don't want to add anything else to that.

Though, I do know she'll have my hide if she finds out I've been keeping things from her. Especially things that could affect the covens. Being an heir is more responsibility than I care to think about. I'll eventually have to come clean to the council about everything that's happened to me because it could ultimately affect my power. And that could also jeopardize my ability to take over Mama's position. The heirs are like sisters to me, but no Witch in our history has been through this. Our magic doesn't have a way to fix a ravaged soul, and I'm not sure they will want me to stand beside them once they know the truth.

Mama would probably say that not being an heir isn't an option for me, and she would be kind of right. Our coven has been around since the beginning. Power runs through our blood. The Dominance Coven will not let go of their heir so easily… But things are changing, and Rebel exists. If all of this has changed me irrevocably, the coven will do what's best for the coven.

Wow, I need to meditate today. My mind is all over the fucking place. Could be from everything that's happening, could be because my soul is missing pieces. Who fucking knows? But I seriously need to find some zen.

The sound of a knock on my bedroom door makes me want to smother my face with my pillow and scream. Instead, I climb off of my bed and drag the door open, finding Mama standing on the other side with an expectant look.

"Hi, Mama," I say softly, trying to sound more put together than I feel.

"I think we should talk…" She trails off, giving me that all knowing look of hers, and I sigh, nodding my head. I already know what this is about but I'm going to live in denial for as long as I can.

"What do you want to talk about?" I ask, smiling up at her, but she gives me that look of hers that brooks no bullshit. Well shit. I guess we're having this conversation now. She turns and walks away from me, expecting me to follow so I sigh, shutting the door softly before I head toward her in the living room.

"I think that you already know." She raises an eyebrow before handing me a mug of hot chocolate. With a groan, I plop down onto the sofa with her. This needs more than hot chocolate, but I guess we're having this conversation now.

I take a deep breath and then sip my drink, stalling as I consider the best way to answer. "Okay, so… I've noticed a new power. I don't think it's my emergence, but it's definitely new. I'm not sure why it's there or what triggered it."

"What new power?" she asks, and the concern from a moment before is replaced with a look of intrigue. I take the small win.

"It's empathic. If someone's emotions are particularly strong, I can feel them… It's almost overwhelming unless my emotions are crazy strong, too. That seems to nullify it," I tell her quietly, shrugging before taking another sip.

She's quiet for a few minutes, as if contemplating what this could mean before she turns her attention back to me. "You're right, I don't think it's your emergence. But it is strange for you to gain extra powers right now. Did you ever speak to Morgan about what might have gone wrong with the bond? Could it be linked to that?"

I gulp at her question and take a deep breath. It's now or never. "That was the second thing I needed to tell you…" I trail off, trying to find the words. It takes a minute, but she's patient while I try to figure out the best way to start. I don't want to have this conversation. Not with her. Not yet. But I guess this is happening whether I want it to or not.

With a determined breath, I dive into telling her everything I've found out in the last week... About Azriel, about what he did to me. About how Morgan removed him and the fact that the unknowns are still very real. She doesn't say anything at first. Instead, she stares at me, her lips turned down in a frown that looks somewhere between distraught and like she really wants to kick my ass. I'm not sure which one scares me more.

She stands up, taking my hot chocolate from me and putting both of our mugs on the table before turning back to me. "We're going to need something stronger than hot chocolate to finish this conversation."

Thank Goddess Mama got Misty and Renee to cover the store today. We stayed up way later than either of us meant to, talking about everything that's going on. A real shitstorm seems to be brewing, and one thing that we agree on is that we have to keep Rebel safe. She's already been through too much, so we spent a lot of last night talking about sending her to stay with my aunt, Erica, for a little while. At least until everything settles down. Plus side, Rebel will enjoy it, and it means Mama and I won't need to worry about her so much. Erica's place is a freaking fortress with wards for days. No one's going to get to Rebel while she's there—not even just to fuck with us.

My alarm clock reads eight, and despite the late night, I find myself awake and staring at the ceiling. Being up this early when I don't have to be, on top of so little sleep, makes me want to scream. But my mind won't get with the program. I tossed and turned all night after telling

Mama the truth of everything. It's like I can't settle. Like something inside me shifted and the turmoil of it all is a restless entity beneath my skin.

I need to speak to Morgan, to ask if she has any indication of anything being wrong with me even though nothing feels wrong. Then again, beyond the voice in my mind, nothing felt wrong last time either. That's gone now, obviously... Besides, speaking to Morgan right now probably isn't possible considering the state the Shadow Realm was in when I left the other day.

My phone buzzes, and even though I see Remy's name, I can't bring myself to pick it up. I know she's home and she's safe, but I can't deal with the whirlwind of Remy right now. Not when I feel like I'm barely keeping myself from drowning as it is.

The floorboards in the hall creak beneath the weight of someone's footsteps, and I sigh. I guess I might as well get up and be productive. Or at least as productive as my mind is going to let me be today. I feel more like myself than I have since I was taken, but something still doesn't quite feel right. But I guess that could just be me thinking about it all too much. Of course I'm going to feel different after everything. There'd be something wrong if I didn't.

Right?

"Fallon?" Mama's voice filters through my closed door. There's a quick, soft knock before the door opens.

"Hey Mama," I say quietly with a soft smile.

"The coven heads have called a meeting tonight. I'm going to take Rebel to Erica's this morning because I want her to get settled before school on Monday. Then I'm going to head to the store. I'll ask one of the girls to cover you tonight so you can be at the meeting. They're going to want the full story of what happened to you. We managed to skirt the majority of their questions before, but they're just going to keep prodding until we tell them."

"Do you think it will jeopardize the coven's position?" I ask, biting my lip.

"I doubt it. Our coven knows about everything you've been through, with the exception of what you told me last night. Our coven is like family. They won't think any differently of you for it. Power is what matters, and our bloodline has plenty of it. If the other covens want to cause trouble, I'll show them just how much power we have." She winks at me, and I can't help the small huff of a laugh that escapes.

"Thanks, Mama."

"I got you, baby. The Dominance Coven doesn't just discard power. There's a reason we're where we are in the hierarchy. Just remember it."

"What if my powers are affected?" I ask, voicing the question I haven't wanted to before now.

"If that happens, we'll deal with it. The Witch's Council

might try to force you out if they deem you as weak, if the change could affect the hierarchy, they'd need a unanimous vote, but they'll have to get through me first." She smiles at me reassuringly before she speaks, "I'm going to go get breakfast started. Do you plan on joining us?"

"Sure, if it's the last one we have together for a while, I don't want to miss it."

I take the day easy, trying not to focus on everything that could happen at tonight's council meeting. As we leave for the meeting, I find myself focusing on the Lunar cycle—it's almost halfway over, so the moon shines down brightly on us. I always feel happiest in the dark with a bright moon hanging in the sky above me. Maybe it's my ties to the moon, or maybe it's all in my head, but I'm going to take it. I can use all the happy I can find at the moment.

I go through the ritual of setting up the circle with Mama as we wait for everyone to join us. It's strange knowing Lizzie's coven won't be joining us, but they made their choice. It was the wrong one, and if they're caught, their punishment will likely be the most severe we have. Death is too good for some people, but stripping them of their power and making them human?

That's the worst kind of punishment for any Witch.

It makes me sick, thinking of our own kind turning against us, but I guess there are all kinds of casualties of war. This is just another one of them. It doesn't make it any easier to tolerate, though.

The anxiety of what will happen during tonight's meeting runs through me. The thought of airing out all of my shit to these people doesn't fill me with joy, even if they are basically extended family. I'm expecting a lot of questions, and some of them I know I won't have the answers to. I know this needs to be done because the covens don't have secrets, but fuck me.

Once Mama and I complete the calling ritual and everyone arrives, the round of welcomes happen the same as always, and I tune out a little as Mama and the other coven heads discuss Lizzie's attacks and the other intricacies of coven life. Mama will catch me up on anything I need to know later, but right now, I can't focus.

I feel a little guilty about it since I've been MIA for so long already, but I can't stop thinking about Mama's reaction and how differently the others are likely to react compared to her. I take a deep breath and tune back in. Luckily, no one seems to notice my absent-mindedness since heirs are expected to be seen and not heard unless called upon. It's a little archaic, but it suits my needs right now.

I take a few more deep breaths to steady myself as

the conversation about Lizzie draws to an end. My hands shake at my sides, and I curl them into fists, hoping to hide the shake. I'd rather face a horde of Demons than the angry Witch council… And they're sure to be angry. It might not have been my fault, but that doesn't mean I won't be blamed.

"Does anyone else have any other business they want to discuss?" Mama asks, and it's crickets. Silent as the dead.

"If no one else has anything to raise, I have one last thing," she says, taking a deep breath. I'm so glad Mama is the one explaining everything because I don't know that I could say it all out loud again. It was hard enough saying it all to Mama—I can't imagine saying it to all of them as well. I still feel a little dirty after everything, so I try not to spend too much time thinking about it. Unfortunately, there's no escaping it tonight.

I listen as Mama regurgitates everything I explained to her last night, though she leaves out the details about Morgan and the Horsemen, and my skin crawls. Even listening to it makes me want to stand in a scalding hot shower for a few hours. Anything to make me feel clean again.

Silence permeates the air once Mama finishes speaking, but I can feel every single set of eyes on me. I feel like I'm going to be sick. The judgement is pouring from them in waves.

"Are we sure that she is free of the Demon now?" someone asks, and murmurs start around the circle.

"Yes," I say, trying to sound more confident than I feel. "I'm free of the Demon, and his soul has been dealt with." I omit by whom, of course, because they don't need to know about mine and Remy's connections in the Shadow Realm. Either way, I'm pretty sure Morgan wouldn't just let him wander free. Totally not her style.

"How do we know the Demon isn't talking for you right this moment?" another voice asks.

"First of all, you could trust me. I have never done anything to betray my coven, even when I had a parasite inside of me. Secondly, you can scan me if you think you have the power to sense it," I challenge, not missing Mama's small smile before it disappears quickly. She told me last night I would have to defend myself, though I already knew that I would.

Power ripples through the air in response to my words, and I take every lash from each and every one of them until they feel confident they know their own truth. It's bullshit—if they could have sensed it, they would have before. But if it makes them feel better, I'm all for it.

Still, the questions don't stop. Time passes, and I feel like I've said the same thing a thousand different ways before Mama finally calls an end to it. I look at her, trying to convey my thanks, but I'm drained. Everyone says their goodbyes and disappears, but the looks I get from the heirs definitely say we'll be speaking soon. Yay, something to look forward to. I roll my eyes internally so no one sees my lack of joy. It feels like it takes forever, but once they're gone, Mama opens a portal for us.

"I'm very proud of you, Fallon. You handled yourself well tonight. The coven would be proud."

Last night with the covens was exhausting. Today, I feel like I'm dragging ass so badly. I'm tired all the way down to my bones. Being grilled so thoroughly about everything was intense. You'd think it was me who betrayed the covens, not Lizzie. I thought maybe they'd have more important things to be worried about... Like covens being attacked, but apparently not.

I mean, on one hand, I get it. I'm an heir and there are expectations, but still. It's not like I asked for any of this shit. Give me a goddamn break. All I wanted to do when we left was go and curl up with Colt, but I still haven't heard from him outside of the group text with Creek.

At least I know he's still alive. But there's no way I'm going to apologize for being worried about him—not a fucking chance. He was an insensitive jackass. Plus, I know I'll be seeing him soon. The Witches had Mama reach out to Remy and the Elders last night. And since the factions need to hash out everything that's going on, I have no doubt Colt will be there.

I lean back in the back porch swing and blow into my coffee to cool it down. It's unseasonably warm today, hence my little shorts and white bikini top, but I know I should probably change if I head into the store later on.

"Well, don't you look lost in thought?" The voice nearly makes me jump out of my damn skin, but I clamp my lips together before I let out a squeal.

"Goddammit, Deacon," I hiss. "Warn someone when you're bursting in. Goddess have pity on my poor heart. What are you doing here?"

"I just thought I'd come see my favorite Witch. Check in while I had some spare time since things back home have quieted down now that your bestie is back." He drops onto the swing beside me and pulls my feet into his lap.

I eye him as he rubs my foot, but he merely shrugs and continues doing what he's doing. "Deacon, I said last time..."

"I know what you said. We have shit to work through, but we're not going to work through it if I'm never around. And I know all about the Hunter. I'm here with an open mind, just wanting to be your friend."

"Be my friend?" I ask, looking at him suspiciously.

“Yes, be your friend. If an Angel can be friends with the Queen of the Shadow Realm, surely you and I can be friends.” He laughs.

“I’m not sure that they started off the way we did...” I trail off when he stiffens, but he quickly shrugs and continues rubbing my foot.

“All friendships have their rocky patches. Ours just happens to be a bigger hurdle than most.”

I sit quietly, sipping my coffee. That might just be the biggest understatement I’ve ever heard, but he’s not wrong. If I can forgive Colt for being a giant ass when everything happened with Remy, maybe I can try to move past the whole, ‘tortured me and kidnapped my little sister’ thing.

It’s unlikely, but I can’t deny that I feel some sort of kinship with Deacon. I went through a lot, some by his hand... But the rest? He was there for me as much as he could be, and he risked his life to save mine. Maybe I’m holding on to some of this too tightly. Mama always says that letting things go is the only way to deal with them.

“I told you once already, our story isn’t over yet. But where that path takes us, well, that’s for us to find out.”

“And if that path is us just being friends?” I ask quietly.

“Then you’ll be the best friend I have,” he says with a smile. “But that isn’t why I came here. I just wanted to check in with you and see how you’re doing since everything that happened.”

"I'm okay," I tell him hesitantly. "At least I think so. I told Mama what happened—that woman could make me confess to pretty much anything. We had to tell the covens last night about all of it, so now I have to hope no one loses their shit too hard. We have so much to worry about already, this is another thing we really didn't need to be dealing with on top of it all."

I blow out a deep breath, and he sits, hand on my ankle, looking out across the yard.

"I'm sure they'd be foolish to do anything to go against you or your bloodline. The power inside of you isn't something that should be thrown away. But if they do end up doing something foolish, just know I've got your back. Whatever you need. Even if that's to run away and come live with me." He winks, and I giggle.

"If only life were so simple that I could run away with no consequence," I tell him, my thoughts jumping back to everything with Colt. "But that is not the case."

"It could be. I could make it that simple for you," he says, the conviction in his voice almost makes me believe him.

"I'm almost sure you could, but for now, I'll fight my own battles."

"Just remember I'm here if you need me. But as long as you are actually okay, I'm going to head back. It's the middle of the night for me, and I should get some shut eye, but I just couldn't sleep without checking on you."

"Thank you." I smile as I pull my feet from his lap and stand. He hugs me tightly, as if he doesn't want to let go, and I can't help that my smile widens.

"I'll be back soon, and if you need me, don't hesitate to come find me."

FIVE

Today we're back at the witch's meeting place to call on the council, with the hopes Remy and the Elders are joining us so we can discuss all of this bullshit that's going on as well as the treaty Remy's been working so hard on. I hope no one mentions the shit with Azriel from the other night. I haven't shared any of that with my friends yet, and I'm honestly not sure that I'm going to. At least not until everything is over and done with. They have enough to worry about without worrying about my stuff, too.

Most of the Elders are already here, yet we find ourselves waiting on Colt, Remy, and her guys. I try to not be impatient, but I've barely heard from Remy since she got back. It's hard not to take offence, even if I did miss one of her calls, but I also know she has four surly guys to make feel better about her latest kidnap, so I'm not being overly pushy. Goddess do I miss my friend, though.

I miss when life was simpler.

I remember being so excited for her when she found out what she was—we could finally be open and honest about everything. But it's literally just been one thing after another since her awakening. I really miss the old days.

"Remy!" I hear Nasari call out and turn to see Colt as he weaves through the crowd. They might all be Hunters in their own right, but Colt and Remy's guys are easy to separate from the rest of the crowd here. They're the tallest, and widest in some cases too, guys here, but they just have this authoritative aura about them which makes them impossible to ignore.

I avoid Colt because we still haven't spoken since our blow out, and I'm not ready to deal with that here in front of everyone. Instead, I head straight for Remy, with my sassiest smile painted on my face.

"Remy, you better not be hiding from me, girl." I play up my drawl as I say it, and her smile is wide as she turns in my direction. I practically leap on her, wrapping my arms around her neck and shoulders to draw her in close. Feeling her here, real and whole in my arms, means the most to me. I really am glad she's back. "Girl, I am so glad you're alive."

"Me, too." She smiles as she hugs me back tightly.

"Mama is looking for you. I think she has some stuff she wants to talk to you about," I tell her quietly. Mama wouldn't tell me what she wanted to speak to Remy about, so when she opens her mouth to ask me what she wants, all I can do is shake my head. I hate being so cryptic, it seemed important, and I just wish I had a clue so I could give her more of a heads up.

"Okay, well we can hang out tomorrow, and if she's around, we can talk? Or you guys can come to the house?" she offers, and I nod.

"Sounds good to me. I miss you," I tell her, squeezing her hand.

"I miss you, too." This is way too much emotion for me right now, I need to pull myself together before I start crying or something. I look around the open field and notice Remy's guys glaring over at the Hunters here.

"Okay, now let's get this show on the road because your guys look ready to kill things, and I don't want to be here longer than I need to. I'll be back, though, I have to help Mama with the portals." I laugh before heading back over to Mama. When I look back, I see Remy heading over to her guys who are surrounded by the Elders. They look so fucking bored I could crack up laughing, but I force the laughter down and turn to face Mama instead.

"Ready to get started?" she asks, and I nod.

"I think so. If we get the Witches here at least, that should distract the Hunters enough from whatever they're gossiping about to get their asses over here." I smile at her, glad that she hasn't brought up the Azriel thing since the coven meeting a few days ago. It's not something I want to think about.

We begin opening the portals and the others head in our direction. I can just see Colt out of the corner of my eye motioning for everyone to stay a few feet back... I guess he really was paying attention the last time he was here. I turn my focus back to what we're doing.

As each of the Witches and their heirs arrive, they take their places in the circle. Once they all arrive, Colt moves the Hunters to stand between the covens, merging the circles. Remy and her guys move to stand with us, and I can't say that I dislike it. It just shows the strength of the relationships our coven has, and maybe that will stop any other covens who might have ideas about jumping ship with Lizzie.

Talks begin as the Coven heads start their treaty discussions with the Elders, and I tune out a little. The heirs are here by tradition only. We won't have any input at all over what goes into the treaty, but I trust that Mama won't let anything go astray. And as much as I'm not exactly Team Colt at the moment, I trust him enough to not let the Elders try to screw us either. Roman and Kain chime in occasionally, making sure their factions aren't fucked over in the treaty, and it's so strange to see them the way I do now. My entire life, they were these ferocious beings, and now, they're just my best friend's boyfriends. Sometimes I forget they're still rulers in their own right, but then something like this happens, and their power is unmistakable. Even the way they speak demands attention.

Overall, I'm just really glad this is finally happening. The previous agreement pretty much turned to dust after Archer's latest awesomeness revealed betrayers in almost all of the factions. It turns my stomach to think of how many people sided with him so easily.

"There's no sign of Lizzie or her coven," Ilaria tells the circle, and I sigh, ready for things to head south. We already discussed this at our coven meeting, but everyone else needs to know.

"How is that even possible?" Colt asks, his frustration obvious from the way he speaks through clenched teeth.

"Lizzie is a very powerful Witch," Ilaria's heir, Daniella, huffs, almost as if she's offended at the question. Not that I have any idea why she would be. Her and Lizzie were never exactly close. "She has more than enough power and talent to shield herself and her coven."

"You sound like you look up to her," Nasari chimes in, eyeing Daniella. In an instant, everyone starts talking over each other. I roll my eyes when it gets stupidly loud. When did everyone turn into toddlers?

"This isn't going to get us anywhere," Remy shouts as she steps forward, her voice booming across the clearing. Everyone else pipes down at her show of power. "Fighting amongst ourselves makes us weaker. If you can't fully commit to this new treaty and all that it means, then leave. We'll be better off without you. A chain is only as strong as its weakest link. I know that centuries of resentment isn't going to be fixed overnight, but goddammit. We're not children, it's not hard to be civil, so either buck up or fuck off."

She crosses her arms, watching everyone in the circle as she does so. I bite down on my lips to keep from laughing at the contrite expressions of a crowd of people who have been thoroughly told off. Colt smirks over at her, and I refrain from rolling my eyes at him. Remy waits a full minute to give people the chance to leave, and nods her head when no one does.

"Okay then, that's that. Can we not bicker like children and try to think of productive ways to pool our resources to find these people? We are four factions. Surely they can't hide from all of us." She takes a deep breath and looks back at me. I smile at her because I have a feeling I know what she's about to do. I don't envy her at all, but I do admire her strength. She doesn't have to do any of the things she does, her secrets are her own, but she's a born leader. And she always has been if you listen to the stories of her past.

"In the spirit of being open and honest, there is also something you should all know," she says with her head held high. She looks over to me again, and I nod. She moves to the center of the circle before looking back at her guys. I glance over my shoulder to see them all smiling back at her, except for Levi. He looks like he's ready to smite anyone who so much as looks at her wrong.

I can't help but smirk. He would be the villain in anybody else's story. The way he loves her has no limits. I can't stop myself from glancing over to Colt and wondering if he could ever love me that way or if that kind of love is unattainable for mere mortals, even magical mortals. Remy and Levi's love is something to behold, and while I don't think the others love her any less, she is his north. The others have other people they care about, others that they have to consider for their actions, but she is only the light in his darkness.

I turn back to Remy, struggling to contain all the emotion swirling inside of me as she crosses her arms, eyeing each person in the circle. I call on my power, just so it hums under the surface, ready to defend her should it come to that. My power might be a drop in the ocean compared to the people at my back, but she's my girl, and I'll fight to the death for her. Even against the covens. She takes a deep breath before speaking again. "Do not freak out."

I swallow down my laughter as she takes another deep breath and unfurls her wings. The gasps that ripple across the meadow are a mix of fear and awe. The emotion on their faces is as clear as the thousands of questions on the tips of their tongues. I smile at my best friend for facing them like this because attacking her here would have been just as easy as not.

"How is this possible?" Nasari asks. The wonder in his voice is evident. "You did not die?"

"Actually, I did. In the Shadow Realm. This was the result," she tells him, giving them all just enough information to understand what happened to her but no other details. They don't need to know the details.

Chatter starts up from almost everyone around us. They throw question after question at her, but everyone talks over each other and it's pure chaos. I laugh softly. Didn't she just tell them to not freak out?

I put my fingers in my mouth and let out a loud whistle. It screeches through the air, vying for the crowd's attention. I know I'm meant to be seen, not heard at coven meetings, but this is different. This is Remy. "People! Get ahold of yourselves. This is nothing but an advantage for us against an unknown enemy."

I smile at her, hoping she can hear how proud of her I am. I know she probably had some doubt about my acceptance, but she didn't need to. We've both been to Hell and back, fucking literally. I'm never going to judge her for being who she is.

Everyone around us grows silent, and I look back at Remy's guys, all of whom look fierce as shit, like they're ready to scorch the earth if someone steps out of line. I catch Colt smiling at me, but look away quickly. Not today. I need to deal with the coven shit right now. I can deal with him another day.

Remy walks back toward us. Mama and I smile at her as she passes us to go stand with her guys.

Mama steps forward and clears her throat, taking the meeting back under control. "Now then, back to finding Lizzie."

We accomplish a ton before the end of the meeting. We have a new plan of attack for Lizzie and her coven, some damaged relationships have been fixed, and thanks to Remy keeping her wings out, people seem to be coming to terms with the fact that she's changed. Again. The constant looks in her direction put me on edge, so fuck knows how she's dealing with it, but she doesn't look the tiniest bit bothered by it.

Once Mama draws the meeting to a close, the Witches begin portaling out, back to their own corners of the Earth, though they take some of the Elders with them to start the hunt for Lizzie. Once we're alone again, Mama pulls

Remy to one side away from the rest of us.

I look over in their direction, her guys' gazes barely leaving her despite talking amongst themselves. I notice movement beside them and I spot Colt heading over toward me. Goddess, take me away.

"Fallon, we should talk."

"We should, but not right now," I tell him, trying to listen in on what Mama is saying to Remy. I might be a little paranoid, but it's not the first time they've had a discussion about me behind my back.

Colt's face falls, but he nods and moves away to talk to Creek, giving me the chance to tune into Mama's words as Remy frowns.

"My vision, it's changed," Mama tells her, her gaze bouncing over to where Remy's guys are standing, but they're all talking and at least look like they're not paying attention. I look in the other direction, so it's not so obvious that I'm listening in. "I haven't told anyone else because I don't fully understand it, but it's changed. The war… the path has changed. There is no longer utter death and destruction on the battlefield, but someone who can get close to you is not what they seem. Their face is hidden from my vision, which makes me think they're working with a Witch to try and hide their intentions. It must be a very powerful Witch to block them from me. Be careful, Remy."

I turn back, trying to keep the fear and shock from my face.

Why didn't she tell me? I could have helped, or done something. Anything. I don't believe that anyone in our close circle could be working with our enemies…

Right?

"We haven't done this in forever." I laugh as Remy and I drop into the chairs at the coffee shop we used to spend more time at than at home.

"It's fun. Even if my poor plastic is feeling some pain." She drops the multiple bags from the morning of shopping we've done.

"This was way better than staying in with all those brutish guys of yours. What's wrong with them? You not putting out enough?" She laughs at my words the way I hoped she would, but I have no doubt that they've had her tied to a bed ever since she got back.

"Hardly, I just said something about going out with you without a chaperone, and they all went into overprotective alpha mode," she tells me, rolling her eyes as she picks up the menu.

"Girl, why are you picking up the menu? You and I both know you're going to order the same as always." I laugh at her, and she joins in. The whole day has been exactly what I needed, and I think what she needed too. Just some time to be who we are outside of everything we've been dealing with and the expectations that come along with being who we are. She drops the menu, still chuckling as the server approaches the table.

"What can I get for you ladies?"

"I'll have a pumpkin spice latte, extra whip, extra shot, with a cheese and ham croissant." I grin at her as I order the same thing I get every single fucking time at this time of year. There is nothing better than that latte, and I'll fight anyone who tries to tell me differently.

"I'll have a peppermint mocha with extra cream, with a chicken and bacon club." Remy smiles at the girl, who offers us a nod before turning on her heel and heading back toward the counter.

"I can't believe it's almost Christmas." I sigh. "I feel like it came out of nowhere this year." I shift in my chair, trying not to seem like I'm fidgeting, when I'm really just glad that this feels like something close to normal.

"Tell me about it. It's going to be weird as fuck this year. I don't know what we're even doing." She sighs and puts her head in her hands. "Do you think it would be weird if we just ordered Italian and spent the day watching movies?"

"Girl, after the year you've had, you can do whatever

the fuck you want, and no one can say shit. Though I'm pretty sure there are more than a few people who want to be with you guys that day. Including Maddie and Nate, though Nirvana will be home, so that could be interesting. And Colt will want to be there too… We could just do a big movie day? Goddess knows you guys have enough space to have everyone over. Everyone could bring their own dish, and we can just do presents, food, and movies?" I suggest, hoping she agrees, because that sounds like fucking heaven after what we've been dealing with since her birthday.

"That sounds like a perfect day. A day with nothing to worry about except how stretchy my pants need to be so I can eat all of the things." She sighs wistfully. Even just the idea of it makes me feel a bit lighter. It gives me something to look forward to, and I can barely contain my excitement over something so absolutely mundane.

"Then let's do it!" I squeal, but rein in my excitement as our coffee and food arrives. The server smiles at us as she drops our orders on the table and practically skips away. Oh, to be so oblivious and carefree.

We sit and talk about nothing but light and happy things as we enjoy our meal. Eventually, we head back to finish gift shopping, but it doesn't take us long before we're done and go back to the manor. Even though the day has been fun, the drive there feels a little tense. We haven't spoken about anything that's happened to either of us recently, and now that we're heading back, I know that's about to end. I'm still not sure I'm ready to tell her about everything.

It's not an uncomfortable silence, but when we pull up at the manor, I'm not sure who jumps from the car first.

"Oh, my girls are back, let me feed you. Too skinny you girls!" Nonnie fusses over us as we haul all of our bags into the house.

"Let us get this stuff to my room, Nonnie, and then you can feed us all you like," Remy says, omitting that we already ate. I don't blame her, Nonnie is fierce about food. Thankfully, I've always been able to eat. I'm not the girl who picks a salad over a burger, because damn, I love me a big, juicy burger. I'm definitely not about to turn down Nonnie's cooking, it's fucking sublime.

I follow Remy to her room, and she stuffs her bags in the back corner of her closet. I drop mine by her bed before we head back to the kitchen.

"Where are the guys?" Remy asks Nonnie, dropping a kiss on her cheek as we take a seat at the island.

"They were fighting in the gym, silly boys. They're fine, but look at you, you need to eat more." She fusses again and spoons what looks an awful lot like chicken Alfredo into two bowls, before placing them in front of us and pulling garlic bread from the oven. "Eat, eat. Do you like?"

I take a bite and groan around my fork as my taste buds burst to life, closing my eyes to savor the exquisiteness of the woman's cooking. Remy moans beside me too, and I smile as Remy speaks again. "Nonnie, I think you've outdone yourself."

She beams at the words and I smile. "I'm glad, yes, very much. I hid you a treat in the little fridge in the pantry for later." She winks at Remy, and then leaves us alone, heading toward the side of the manor where her room is.

"So…" I start before taking another mouthful, hoping if I distract her by talking about her, we can avoid the conversation turning to me.

"So… I nearly died, again," she starts, a sigh dragging from her lips before she launches into a retelling of everything she remembers happening with Bauer before she woke up in Avalon.

"Once I woke up, I spoke to Michael at length and realized everything I thought I knew about him wasn't exactly the truth. He is my friend, and he brought back my memories. Almost all of them, though I still have this black spot in my mind. He thinks I've managed to block it because of something emotional, but I have no idea how to overcome it. I remembered a lot more about my past too, which was nice, especially the bits of my life as Amantara. Seeing Levi in my mind from when I first met him…" She trails off and smiles like a goof. "Him and Michael have disliked each other since before the start of my existence, so the fact that they didn't destroy each other when Levi came to get me is pretty impressive."

She tells me more about Avalon, and my mind is kind of blown. It sounds like something out of a fairy tale.

"I also got dragged into an Archangel meeting, which was just as terrifying as it was awesome," she laughs. "I met some old friends, Gabe, the Archangel of Chaos is a fucking hoot, and he jumped to my defense against some of the others, so that was nice. It seems he's always been on my side, but then, he is the Archangel of Chaos, so I guess that makes sense."

I burst out laughing at that, and she joins me.

"I also saw my mom. I might have chewed her out when she tried to tell me that everything she ever did was for me." She takes a deep breath and tells me the rest, and though I can see the anger flashing in her eyes, I can see how much she's still hurting over it.

I lean back in my seat, unable to eat as she speaks, barely believing everything she tells me. "I mean… holy shit, Remy. If this was anyone else, I'd call them a straight up liar, but all of this could only happen to you." I sit, staring wide-eyed at my best friend and try to wrap my brain around everything. "I don't even know where to start. Michael, your mom, the Archangel council—Gabe sounds like fun, just a side note—but I swear to the fucking

Goddess. I have no idea how you even find the strength to get out of bed, I'd have quit on this shit way before now."

"Enough about me, what's been going on with you?" she asks, and I squirm in my chair wondering how and where to start.

"I'm okay. I've finally managed to get my power under control. Well, ish…" I pause, trying to think of how to tell her the truth, while not telling her everything. It's not that I don't think she deserves to know, but I can't pinpoint exactly what it is that makes me not want to tell her. She knows the truth about me, and while I know she won't look at me differently, there's still a little voice in my mind telling me not to tell her everything. I already feel like a burden to my best friend, saving me cost her a lot. I don't want to add to all of the problems she's already dealing with, and while I know some people might say that she's my ride or die, that I can tell her everything, the fear of hurting her again by not dealing with this myself is so real.

"Bryce spoke to me a bit after the whole Michael thing, once Levi confirmed you were safe. He gave me some tips for controlling the power inside of me, and they've been working. As for everything else in my life… Well, that's a whole other story. But not one I'm even close to figuring out right now." I offer her the basics, and I know she won't ask the others to confirm the truth about any of it. Besides, while I was in the Shadow Realm, they all agreed to keep my secret. Technically, none of what I've told her is a lie. I did speak to Bryce, and in a way, he did help me control the power inside of me. Leaving out the Azriel thing is just a small omission. I'll tell her eventually, but I'm just not ready yet.

"So that's your way of telling me not to ask how things are between you and my brother?" she asks, laughing softly.

"Pretty much." I shrug with a small smile, glad that she thinks it's that rather than anything close to any of the other stuff. I hate keeping secrets from her, but even the thought of talking it all out again makes me want to vomit.

"You know I'm here if you need to talk, right? I'm never too busy for you," she tells me softly, guilt painted on her face. My stomach clenches. I hate the guilt on her face.

"I know, and ditto. Once this madness is over and we get to the bottom of everything, I vote we go somewhere sunny, with white sand and hot boys to bring us margaritas."

"That, my friend, is a plan."

We spend the rest of the night avoiding heavy topics, and it's nice to just pretend we're normal people with normal problems that aren't more complicated than eating too much ice cream and deciding what TV show to binge next. The guys give us space, only dropping in to let Remy know where they are and when they head to bed.

She convinces me to spend the night rather than heading back home so late, and we drag blankets and pillows from her bed to the living room, so we can binge movies all night.

It's everything I didn't realize I needed all wrapped up in one day. Just one day of being a normal person, without the turmoil that's been haunting me taking over. I laugh at the cheesy romcom we finally decided on, enjoying the mindlessness of it all, and for the first time in a while, I drift off to sleep without my memories taunting and torturing me.

The next morning, I wake up alone in Remy's bed, no idea how I got here, because I know I fell asleep on the sofa. I frown since she rarely rises before me, or at least she never used to. I stretch out in her bed with a grimace. Sleeping in my clothes without doing my nighttime routine means I feel like shit.

I get up, heading into her bathroom and brushing my teeth with the spare toothbrush laid out by the sink. I look through my bags in her room and decide to shower, thankful that I have spare clothes, even if they are brand new.

It doesn't take long to get sorted and dressed, and since

I know I won't be here too long, I know I can deal with recycling my bra for the time being. It's a little weird not having panties on, but I can get changed as soon as I get home.

I head out of Remy's room, gathering my things as I go, and head for the kitchen. I just want to say goodbye and then head home. As comfy as Remy's bed is, it isn't mine. But yesterday was one of the best days I've had in a while, and I need to tell my best friend how fucking thankful I am for her helping me feel some semblance of normal again.

I reach the kitchen to find Nonnie there, but no Remy. "Hey, Nonnie, have you seen Remy?"

She looks up at me with a frown. "Isn't she still sleeping? She hasn't been through here today."

"No, the bed was cold, so I thought she got up ages ago," I say as Creek enters the room. He stills as he takes in the look on my face.

"What's wrong?" he asks, and I bite my lip.

"I don't know that anything is wrong, but I can't find Remy. I have only checked in here, but she wasn't in bed. She could've gone and climbed in with one of the others overnight," I say, knowing it's very possible.

"Maybe," he agrees, but he still frowns before heading back out of the room. I hear shouts as I sit down at the island and Nonnie puts a plate of eggs in front of me. I pick at them, not able to stop the worry churning in my stomach.

It doesn't take long before Creek returns with the other three in tow, the thunderous looks on each of their faces all directed at me.

"When did you last see her?" Levi barks, and I can't help but jump.

"Last night, we were watching movies in the living room and I fell asleep. When I woke up, I was in her bed but she wasn't there and the bed was cold. I guess she could've just never come to bed?" I try not to let my hands shake under his watchful eye. He looks like he's about to tear people apart.

Roman and Kain leave the room as Creek grabs a mug of coffee, though I can tell it's just so he has something to do while Levi glares at me. It's not long before the other two return, and Kain shakes his head as he looks at Levi.

"She's not here," Roman growls.

"Did she say anything to you?" Creek asks me, and I shake my head.

"No, everything was fine. We just had a human day; we spoke about Christmas and that's it. I have no fucking clue where she is," I tell them, trying to keep the shake from my voice as my concern for Remy ramps up. Creek pulls his phone from his pocket and hits the screen a few times, watching intently until it buzzes.

"She's not with Colt," he tells us all, and I gulp. What

the fuck's going on with my friend now?

"Fallon, you should head home. If she contacts you, let us know immediately," Levi commands, and I practically jump from my chair at the authority in his voice.

"Yeah sure," I say, nodding. "Can someone let me know if you find her, please?"

"We will," Kain agrees, his voice soothing compared to the harshness in Levi's tone. I grab my bags and head outside, Creek following closely behind me.

"I'm sure she hasn't gone far. We'll find her," he says, trying to reassure himself as much as me.

"I know you will." I manage a weak smile before I open a portal to head home. "I'm sure she'll be fine." I step through the portal, hoping to the Goddess that I didn't just jinx us all.

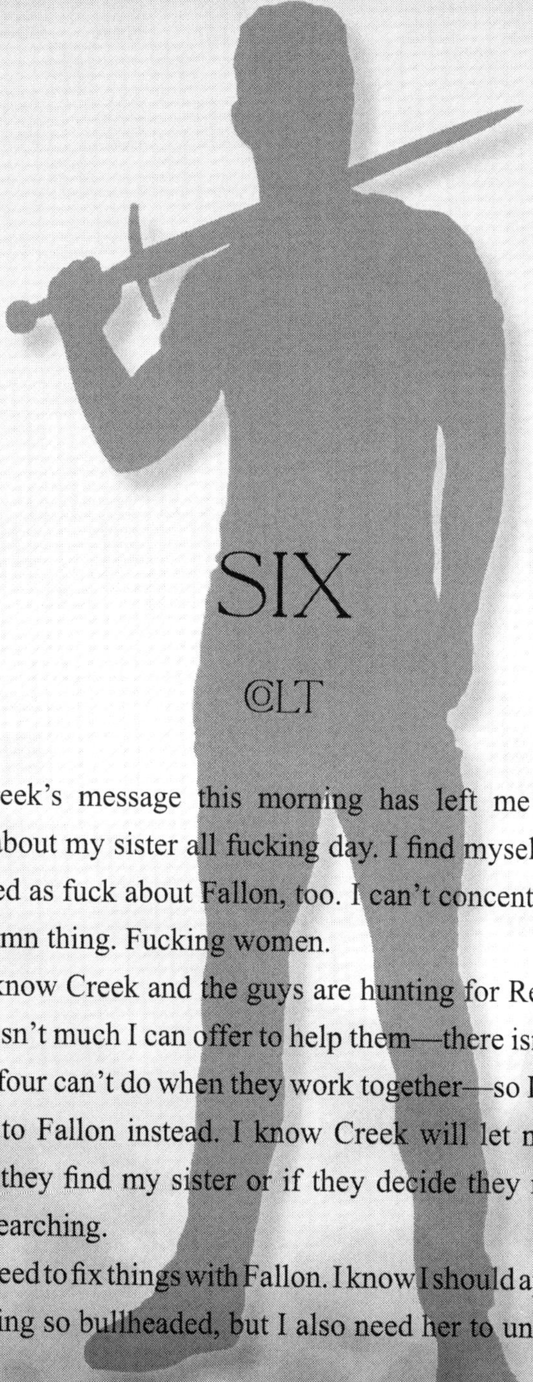

SIX

COLT

Creek's message this morning has left me worried about my sister all fucking day. I find myself feeling worried as fuck about Fallon, too. I can't concentrate on a goddamn thing. Fucking women.

I know Creek and the guys are hunting for Remy, and there isn't much I can offer to help them—there isn't much those four can't do when they work together—so I turn my focus to Fallon instead. I know Creek will let me know when they find my sister or if they decide they need my help searching.

I need to fix things with Fallon. I know I should apologize for being so bullheaded, but I also need her to understand that I'm not going to change who I fundamentally am. If she can't get on board with that, then all of this has been for nothing. I just hope she's had enough time to calm down and think shit through. She yelled at me once for not accepting who she is, so I like to think she wouldn't want me to change who I am, either.

I pick up my phone and put it down a dozen times before I man up and dial her number. I hold my breath as it rings, but it rings through to her voicemail. I groan as I hang up and drop my head in my hands. I'm not sure where my balls disappeared to, but I'm pretty sure I've permanently lost them.

I take a deep breath and pick my phone back up. Fuck this pussy bullshit.

Me: Fallon, we need to talk.
I'll be home all day, and I've cleared the day for us.
Let me know when you're free, and I'll head over.

I drop my phone and let out another deep breath. I hate waiting around. I'm a man of action. Normally when I want shit, I go out and get it, but this situation calls for finesse, which isn't exactly my strongest suit. So sitting around and waiting to see if she texts me back makes me want to crawl out of my skin. I hate feeling out of control, and that's exactly how I feel right now.

Running a hand through my hair, I decide that a workout is needed. I look down at my bare chest, gray sweatpants and bare feet. It'll do. I head down to the basement, starting up the sound system with rock blasting through the speakers. The angry beats soothe the beast inside of me. I climb on the treadmill and start running, building up to a punishing pace and enjoying the burn in my muscles as I push through, eventually raising the angle to push myself even harder.

I lose track of time and every other little thing and focus on the burn, blocking everything else out until the music stops. I nearly jump out of my fucking skin as I leap off of the treadmill, ready to attack, just to find Fallon standing across the room by the sound system rolling her eyes at me.

Women.

"I assume you can hear me now?" she asks with so much sass my hands itch to slap her ass and fuck it out of her. Goddamn, I love her attitude. "I banged on the door, hollered down here, and you didn't even blink. I thought you were meant to be hypervigilant?"

Her eyebrow raises, and I swear my cock twitches.

"I am, I was just distracted," I tell her as I cross my arms. Her eyes follow the motion, dropping to my chest and arms, and I see them widen before she gets control of herself.

Yeah, I know she wants me, even if she's still pissed at me. I'm more than willing to give her what she wants, but not until we air out this bullshit between us first.

"Have you heard from Remy?" she asks, and I shake my head.

"No, but that isn't what we need to talk about." I grab a bottle of water from the fridge down here, chugging it all in one go. "Let's head back upstairs and talk like civilized people, shall we?"

"I didn't realize you were civilized," she snorts, and I grin at her.

"I can be when I want to be, but I know you love the brutish side of me more," I tease, and she rolls her eyes, making my dick twitch again. I'm not sure if I prefer her sassy or submissive, but fuck, I'll take her any way she'll let me. I wave for her to head upstairs in front of me, and I bite down on my lip to stop myself groaning at the sight of her ass swaying in front of me all the way up the stairs. I need to calm my shit down so we can talk without my dick leading the discussion. I think that might be half our problem. Every time I'm around her, we end up fucking instead of talking.

Not that I'm complaining, but we really need to hash this shit out.

She sits at the kitchen table, and I watch her as she fidgets. "Coffee?"

"Something stronger?" she asks, and I feel the corners of my mouth tug upward. I glance toward the nearest clock and see that it's nearly three in the afternoon. I guess I punished myself longer than I thought on the treadmill, so I head to the freezer to pull out the bottle of tequila Remy stashed in there forever ago and grab a bottle of Jack for myself. I stop off for two glasses before I finally join her. She takes the bottle of tequila, and forgoes the glass, swigging it straight from the bottle. It takes everything in me not to focus on her lips around the mouth of the bottle because goddamn.

I take a few swigs myself, focusing on the burn of the whiskey down my throat to calm myself down.

"So, you wanted to talk?" she asks, her fingers drumming on the table in front of her.

I nod, taking another swig and trying to collect my thoughts. "The way you left here the other week was not okay, and avoiding me ever since then isn't okay either. We need to talk through our shit—all of it—or this isn't going to work. We've gone through too fucking much for it to not work, so we need to air it all out."

She blows out a breath and nods, taking another mouthful of the tequila before she starts talking. I sit in silence while she tells me how she panicked, how the fear of me getting hurt freaked her out, and I grit my teeth when she tells me she's been keeping secrets.

“What fucking secrets?” I ask, trying to sound calm but failing.

She twiddles her thumbs, and I clench my fists under the table, trying to stay patient. “When I disappeared for a bit after Remy was taken… It was more than I made it out to be…”

She trails off, but I don’t speak. I clutch the bottle of Jack, trying not to smash it while I struggle to keep my cool. I have a feeling I’m not going to like whatever it is she’s getting ready to tell me.

And fuck me if I’m not right. As the words spill from her mouth about what happened to her after she came back from the Shadow Realm, about Azriel hitching a ride on her motherfucking soul, and then about having to be torn apart again to remove him from her... It takes every piece of strength I’ve built over my several lifetimes to keep my ass in the chair instead of just losing my shit.

“Colt?” She says my name like a question, as if waiting for me to say something.

“Give me a minute,” I say, my voice harsher than I intend while I take a few deep breaths. Her face falls, and it guts me. “I’m not saying that because I think or feel any differently about you, Fal. I just need a minute so I don’t punch a hole in my just-fucking-fixed house.”

“Oh,” she says quietly with wide eyes, watching me as I close my eyes and try to shove that anger down.

"Okay, I'm good. And I understand why you freaked out, but, Fal, you cussed me out something fierce not so long ago when I wouldn't accept you for who you are. Every piece of you, the bits you couldn't and wouldn't change. So you can't ask me to give up who I am. I'm not going to change. I'm sorry for being insensitive to how you were feeling, even if I didn't have a fucking clue what was going on with you."

"I'm sorry, too. For keeping things from you, but I was afraid of losing you," she utters, and I reach across and take her hand in mine.

"You're never going to lose me, Fallon." I feel steadier now I'm touching her. "I'm not going anywhere. Who else knows about Azriel?"

She bites her lip again, so I use my other hand and pull it from her teeth with my thumb, making her look at me. "Mama knows, so does the coven and the Witch council. They had to know. Other than that, Morgan and her guys, obviously… and Deacon."

I growl at that motherfucker's name and she jumps, but I squeeze her hand. She has to know I'd never hurt her. "I hate that asshole. Everything he did to you, and then he thinks everything will just be okay."

"He didn't want to hurt me, Colt. He didn't have much of a choice," she says softly, and I growl again.

"Of course he did. He could've taken the punishment

instead. I won't ever forgive what he did to you, Fallon. Even if you do. Nobody hurts you and gets away with it. I won't kill him since you seem to want to forgive him, which blows my fucking mind by the way, but if he steps out of line even once more, all bets are off. I'll tear his head from his fucking body and bathe in his blood."

She puts her other hand on top of mine and nods. "That's fair, I guess."

Fair, I think it's more than fucking fair. The asshole deserves to fucking rot, but I'm not going to take that decision or that power from her. "Is there anything else you've been hiding?"

"No, but please don't mention this to Remy. I want to tell her, but not until I'm ready."

I don't like it. I hate keeping shit from my sister, and if it was anyone else asking, I'd refuse them. But I nod, agreeing, because this isn't my news to share.

"Thank you," she says softly. "Do you have any plans today?"

"No, I cleared my day, so we could talk," I tell her as my heart finally starts beating at a normal pace.

"Okay, well me, too. Want to watch a movie and order take out?" she asks, hope lighting her eyes.

"I can't think of anything better."

I watch Fallon as she moves around my kitchen after staying the night, and I picture a life for us. Living here, raising a family… She'd be a great mom. I love how at home she feels here, and watching her strut around in my t-shirt and her little panties makes my dick hard. I bite down on my fist as she reaches up into the cupboard and my t-shirt rises, showing me her ass. All I want to do is leave teeth marks on it.

Brand her as mine.

After I apologized yesterday, I kept my hands to myself, but I barely slept with her next to me because the heat of her in my bed drove me fucking insane. All I want to do is toss her over my shoulder and take her back to bed. Remind her that she's mine and only mine.

I can't think of anything but her, and I can't find it in me to care. The rest of the world can look after itself for the fucking day.

She finishes cooking, and I can't take my eyes from her as she sashays over and puts a plate in front of me. I take a bite, but I don't taste a thing, distracted as fuck by her.

"Is it okay?" she asks, looking up at me from under her lashes, and my dick twitches in my boxers. It's the only clothing I have on, but even the morning chill isn't enough to make my dick calm the fuck down.

"It's great." I smile and shovel another forkful in my mouth so she can't see just how distracted I am by her. I was a fucking idiot to let her go the first time, and I know I'll be fucked if I ever do it again. I'd fight to the death for her.

I groan as she bites her lip and closes her eyes, clearly enjoying her food. Fuck me, eating never looked so fucking good. I finish my plate, still not tasting a thing, and wait impatiently for her to be done. She's going to need some energy for everything I have in mind. Fallon's not leaving my bed for the rest of the day. If I have to fuck her into submission to make her understand that she's mine and I'm not giving her up, then I fucking will.

When she finishes, I clear our plates. The tent in my boxers is wholly obvious, and her eyes go wide as I stand. I can't help but grin as red creeps up her neck. I drop the dishes in the sink and move to stand behind her, leaning down and moving her hair out of the way as I whisper into her ear. "I hope you fueled up because you're going to need it."

My dick gets even harder as goosebumps rise over her skin and her nipples stand to attention. Fuck me, I will never get enough of her. I move beside her and lift her up and over my shoulder. She squeals but laughs as she says, "Colt, put me down!"

I slap her ass, and her protests change to a low groan. Fuck yes, I know my baby loves it a little rough. I say nothing, taking the stairs quickly as she continues to squeal and laugh.

"Colt, I swear—" She doesn't get to finish that phrase because I throw her on the bed. I stand back long enough to watch as she giggles and bounces off the huge mattress.

"Careful what you promise, baby. You gotta be able to live up to it."

My entire body feels like there's one massive fire burning across my skin as I watch her prop herself up on her elbows. She offers me a demure smile, but I lose my ability to think when I see my fucking t-shirt riding up her sun-kissed thighs.

My mind reels with the filthy scenarios bouncing around my brain. I'm not sure where to start. I want to fuck her fifty ways to Sunday and then go back for more. I want to make sure she knows she's mine. That she knows I own her orgasms and her sighs. I want her to feel me every time she takes a step and not be able to forget that I'm the one who put that soreness there. The feeling that even when I'm not at her side, she won't be able to forget me because her body is imprinted by me.

And I won't stop making her come until I've made that abundantly clear.

Taking a quick look around the room, my eyes fall on a belt and my grin grows in an instant.

Perfect.

I take a step away from the feast lying on my bed, and

Fallon's small frown at the action only makes my grin broaden. Knowing she has no idea what I'm about to do does something to me.

"Close your eyes and don't peek," I command, knowing she'll listen. She likes the games as much as I do.

I wait until her eyes are closed and stalk across the room. Taking the belt in my hands, I push my fists together and pull back quickly, making the leather snap. All the while, my eyes are on Fallon, and I see her entire body tremble with anticipation.

My dick is so hard, I'm afraid I'll blow my load as soon as I actually start fucking her.

"What was that?" Her voice is breathless. She knows me, she knows I wouldn't hurt her, but she also knows I'm capable of making her suffer on the edge of an orgasm. Make her ride that high and bring her back down before allowing her to actually come. She knows I like to tease her until she can't see straight.

"Make-up sex is a whole different ball game, baby. I'm just making sure I have everything I need."

When her little pink tongue darts out, followed by her perfect white teeth sinking into her plump bottom lip, I have to reach down and squeeze my cock to avoid coming all over myself like a fucking pre-teen.

Motherfucker, she's a temptress, and I love every second of it.

"Sounds delicious." My little vixen, she has no idea how true her words really are.

"Lie down on your back, keep your eyes closed." She doesn't even hesitate, just does as she's told. The image makes my dick want to say "fuck it all to hell" and just sink inside her for all of eternity.

But I can't do that. I have plans, and I'm going to execute every one of them. Patience is a virtue my dick is going to have to suffer today.

With the belt in one hand, I brace myself on the bed and lay an open-mouthed kiss on her collarbone, the tiny little space just below her slender neck left exposed by my t-shirt.

Fuck me, she tastes like heaven.

Concentrate, Colt.

"Give me your hands," I demand, and without question, she raises her hands and holds them out toward where I'm sitting on the bed. She trusts me completely, without a single doubt in her mind, and it makes me impossibly hard.

"Such a good girl." She shudders at my words, and her thighs squeeze together. So fucking delicious.

I take both of her wrists and pull them above her head, crossing them at the headboard and circling them with my belt. I secure the leather, making sure she has little room to move, and I groan as her back arches in response. Her pelvis thrusts into the air as though her body is absentmindedly searching me out.

She'll get all of me. I'll give it all to her, and she won't even have to ask.

"I wish you could see yourself. You're stunning when you're at my mercy." My heart is beating out of my chest at the sight of her, but her next words bring me to my goddamn knees.

"I feel beautiful when I'm at your mercy."

Fuck me, she's perfect.

Straddling her, I peel my t-shirt up her torso and leave it stuck around my belt. Now all I see is glowing skin and curves for miles. My only obstacle is a tiny piece of fabric covering her delicious pussy.

"Just how fond are you of those panties?" I ask, my voice little more than a growl.

"Does it even matter?" She chuckles, knowing damn well it was a rhetorical question.

"Not really." I don't wait before I push a finger through the flimsy material, making a small hole. A hole that tears easily apart with little effort, and I watch, enraptured, as her pussy comes into unobstructed view.

Beautiful.

Again, Fallon's hips lift into the air trying to connect with something, so I offer her a little relief. I run the pad of my thumb through her lips and groan as her juices wet my finger upon contact, her throaty moan in response is like a jolt down my spine, straight to my dick.

"I love how responsive you are. How much you want me," I rasp, mesmerized by the sight of her.

"Only you, Colt. Goddess, only you," she pants, and my dick twitches.

"Open your eyes, baby. Watch me play," I command, and she opens her eyes. My chest burns under the heat of her lusty gaze. She humbles me with her willingness to give herself so completely over to me.

"Please, Colt. Make me yours." My heart does something with those words. It swells and aches and beats inside my chest like a fucking gorilla marking its territory.

"Good answer."

I give her a little more by pushing a finger inside her pussy and curling it so I can reach her deepest, most secret, spot.

She moans, and I think I feel my dick leak out some pre-cum like I'm some kind of fucking teenager.

When I pull my finger from her heat and move my thumb to circle her clit, I swear I hear Fallon curse and then gasp. I give her a little, but only enough to leave her gasping for more.

"Colt—" She pants my name out like a warning, but I ignore it.

"Shh, I'm working," I tell her, laughing softly.

"You're playing!" she moans, and I smirk.

“Same thing, baby.”

A sheen of sweat covers her skin, and knowing it’s from the desire that I’m stoking in her makes it all that much sweeter.

Ripping her panties all the way off, I position myself between her legs and kiss her pussy like I would her mouth. Her moan is my drug. A sound I want to hear her make every fucking day for the rest of my life.

I lick her, my tongue running through her slit from bottom to top and then circling her clit. Her reaction is pure fucking gold. She whimpers, and plants her feet on the mattress, her knees bent as she reaches out for more of my mouth.

I place a palm on her lower belly and push her back down onto the mattress just as my tongue thrusts into her pussy. I explore every inch of her walls, lapping up her juices and swallowing her desire. She doesn’t just taste good, she’s the epitome of deliciousness. I want her for breakfast, lunch, and dinner for the rest of my life.

“You taste fucking divine, you know that?”

She doesn’t answer around her moans. And hearing her pulling at her restraints between her breathy groans only serves to make me hornier.

With one finger I gather her juices before running my finger down to her ass, circling her pink, puckered hole. I coat it before I push in just a little, watching Fallon as she writhes with desire, groaning even harder. She yanks at her restraints in the throes of her pleasure, like she's two seconds away from trying to break the fucking headboard to seek her release.

Goddamn, she's everything I could have ever dreamed of and so much more.

When my finger is pushed in all the way, I lower my head again and feast on her pussy while finger-fucking her ass.

That's when she comes for the first time. All over my face with her ass squeezing my finger in little pumps that are perfectly rhythmed with her orgasm.

I have to bite my lip until I almost fucking bleed to avoid coming in my fucking boxers. That's how gorgeous she is when she lets go.

But I can't wait anymore. I need to fuck her, but first…

Reaching over to the nightstand, I pull out a wipe and clean off my finger before I strip out of my boxers in record time and straddle her face. I pinch her chin, urging her mouth open.

"Open up, beautiful, I want you to taste what your orgasms do to me." She opens her eyes and glances up at me, a lazy smile on her face as she comes back down from her own blissful high. With her eyes boring into me, she opens her mouth, her chest still heaving from her orgasm, and licks right up the small slit on my dick, closing her eyes as she swallows the pre-cum.

"You want more of that, baby?"

"Yes," she moans, and I slide my dick between her lips as I grip the headboard. She opens up wider, and I touch the back of her throat as she takes me down.

"Fuck me." I groan as I slide in and out of her mouth. She looks up at me the entire time, and I'm fucking enraptured by her mouth. I pull out, giving her the chance to ask me to stop.

"More," she breathes, and I nearly come all over her fucking face right then and there. I take a deep breath and give her what she asks for, fucking her mouth until I'm so close to the goddamn edge I need to stop before I shoot my load without even having felt her pussy.

I need to be buried inside of her. I kiss her as my body slides over hers so she can taste herself on my lips. I massage her tongue with my own, swallowing her moans as she gets that first taste.

Sliding back down her body, I take my time to lick, nip, and suck her tits, making sure to leave a mark or three on her perfect skin, branding her as mine.

"Mine, Fallon. You are mine now, tomorrow, and for-fucking-ever. Do you understand what I'm saying to you?"

She only moans, her hips reaching out for me.

"Words, baby. Give them to me," I demand, and she doesn't let me down.

"Yes, Colt. I'm yours, always."

That's when I slide into her. With one hard, punishing thrust I'm inside her, buried to the hilt and begging all the Fates of the universe to give me the strength not to come within seconds of being inside her.

My entire body covers hers. We're chest to chest, stomach to stomach, and the urge to kiss the fuck out of her is stronger than anything else in the moment.

As my mouth molds to hers, I reach up with one hand and loosen the belt, unbinding her while pulling the stuck t-shirt off at the same time.

We're all lips and tongues and teeth clashing with the need to devour each other. My dick begs me to pump inside her, but I make myself wait.

Once her hands are on my back, nails digging into my skin, I pull out and slam back in with no apologies. Fallon's breath hitches, and I swallow her moans, my hips pistoning a little harder, a little faster. My entire body is devoted to one singular goal. Making my girl scream my name.

Reluctantly, I lift myself off her body, and with one hand wrapped around her throat and the other holding onto her hip, I fuck her like our lives depend on it. I fuck her like her breath depends on every thrust I give her. I fuck her like my heart beats for her every time the head of my dick hits her sweet spot. Our gazes don't waver, our bodies are primed for what's about to happen. My fingers squeeze just a little bit more around her throat, and as her nails drag down from my pecs to my stomach nearly drawing blood, I can't hold back.

"Now, Fallon. Together, baby."

I slam back inside her twice more before I feel her pussy squeezing my cock like a fucking vise, and then everything goes blank as she milks my dick.

White hot pleasure courses through my body, my balls aching with the need to empty themselves. Fallon stills, my name one long syllable spilling from between her lips and her name a cry falling from mine.

We come together, we shake together, we bond in a way I've never experienced before.

As it should be.

Forever.

SEVEN

FALLON

I wake up thrashing in my bed, feeling entirely disorientated. I blink up at the ceiling as the memories of my nightmare, the blood and the fear, disappear slowly. Nothing like starting the day on the wrong foot. I look around my room and confusion hits me… I thought I was at Colt's.

What the actual fuck?

I pick up my phone to see the date, and my heart nearly stops.

This can't be possible. Unless I'm totally clueless, which is entirely possible... But I could have sworn yesterday was... It couldn't have been, though, could it?

My phone isn't lying to me.

Maybe I should drink less? I mean, it's not like I drink a ton, but losing an entire day and feeling this disjointed about it—it's the only thing I can think of.

That's when I notice the dirt beneath my fingernails. I turn my hands over to find dried blood on my palms. What the actual fuck?

I climb from my bed and head for the shower. I need to get this off of me, hopefully that will help me feel more like myself. I can't shake the feeling that something is seriously fucking wrong. Biting down on my lip, I check my calls and texts. There's nothing there that I don't remember, but there's also nothing from yesterday.

I can't have lost a whole day. Right?

There's no reason I would have lost a whole day.

But none of this makes sense. Why would I have dirt and blood on my hands?

I wash my hands and scrub my nails before turning the shower on so the water can heat up.

I must be losing my mind, but the gnawing in the pit of my stomach tells me I'm missing something. Though, maybe what's on my hands isn't blood. I work with potions that are red most days, maybe it's that.

It has to be that. It just has to be.

I undress and stand under the hot spray for so long it eventually turns cold, trying to remember something, anything that will explain the emptiness in my mind. Mama will have my ass for using all the hot water if she's still here, but the house is quiet. I climb from the shower and wrap a towel around myself, chewing my lip as I wonder if I should speak to Mama about it. I wipe the condensation from the mirror and look at my reflection, trying to figure out if something looks different… Anything to give me a sign that I'm not losing my mind. Losing a whole fucking day isn't right, but I look the same as I did the last time I remember looking in a mirror. There are no physical signs of what might have happened yesterday, so I can't help but wonder if there is something inside of me fucking with me? Can I work this out on my own without Mama? Maybe this is a question for Morgan… it could be a consequence of what happened. Regardless, whatever it is, it's freaking me the fuck out.

What's weirder is the consistent hum of my power under my skin. It seems stronger somehow. I should definitely speak to Morgan. I haven't had much of a chance to use my power since she pulled Azriel's soul from mine, and I need to know if she took the power from me that he gave me or if part of hers might have been left behind after she separated his soul from mine.

It's not that I don't like the feeling of the strength of the power humming just beneath the surface, but with everything else going on right now, I don't trust it, which has me feeling off-kilter. I've always been one with my power, and not trusting it is like not trusting myself.

I take a deep breath and try to settle myself. I really need to try restarting my meditation, even if just to quiet my mind for a little while. Because right now, it's going at a million miles a minute, and the panic is winning. Panic doesn't get to win. I've survived way too fucking much to let the panic win now.

I clutch the towel and head back to my room, refusing to let this dominate my whole day. I'll deal with it, whatever it is, but first, I have shit to do. I have a shift at the store today, and I need to speak to Hayley about dropping my shifts at the restaurant. I can't keep up with everything, and I hate to keep letting them down last minute.

I get dressed, pulling my hair back in a slick ponytail to keep it out of my face before sitting to do my makeup. When I'm done, I feel more like myself—my painted red lips as much a part of my power as the hum under my skin. The mask I wear is as much for me as it is for the people around me. I add a little more bronzer, enhancing my already golden skin and making it look as if I glow when I smile, making sure that it doesn't look as fake as it feels.

My phone buzzes on my dresser, and I see Mama's name.

Mama: Please don't forget you're covering the store

for me today. I have to leave here in half an hour.

Me: I haven't forgotten. I'm leaving in five.

Mama: Thank you!

I pocket my phone and take another deep breath. The shadows in my eyes are present, but there's nothing I can do to hide those, so I have to hope the rest of my armor is enough of a distraction from them. Then tonight, once I'm alone and free of the responsibilities that come with being me, I'll try to figure out what the fuck happened yesterday.

It's officially been twenty-four hours since I woke up and realized I have a whole fucking day missing from my memories, and nothing I've done has triggered a goddamn thing to help me remember what I did or why the fuck it's gone.

It's infuriating.

Mama is at the store today, and Rebel is with Erica, so I'm home alone. I want to tear this entire place apart and build it back up from scratch, just to have something I can control. I sit cross-legged on my bed, my hands under my ass to keep me from doing exactly that, but I'm losing my fucking mind.

I need a distraction.

Fuck it. Mama keeps complaining that this place needs freshening up. We've had paint out in the shed for months just waiting for some time to use it, so that's exactly what I'm going to do. I'm going to distract and fucking exhaust myself into not focusing on those missing hours.

Maybe I should tell someone, but I'm so sick of needing to be saved. I want to figure this shit out on my own. Even if just to prove to myself that I'm not such a fucking drain on everyone around me. I just don't want to work it out today.

Yay, the self-deprecating part of this manic episode is starting.

I throw on an old, paint-splattered t-shirt and a pair of denim shorts and pull my hair back out of my face. I head to the living room, more than a little determined. I strip the entire floor of trinkets, my bedroom overflowing with the relocated ornaments and picture frames, then move all of the furniture to the middle of the room.

I frown at the burn in my muscles already. I've seriously let my stamina slip this last year. I need to get my fucking life together. Slipping on a pair of sneakers, I stomp out to the shed and pull out a ton of plastic sheets to cover the furniture and floors, then haul it all indoors with more cans of paint than I care to count.

It doesn't take long to cover the furniture in the living room, the counters in the kitchen, and then the floors through the hall. At least not as long as I hoped it might, but then I start to paint. I decide to do everything white first, and then once it dries, I'll go over it with color.

I lose myself in the work, focusing hard enough that my mind doesn't get a chance to wander or try to lead me down into the deep, dark pit inside myself.

"Fallon, what the fuck is going on?" I jump at the booming voice, and I squeal as I see Colt standing in the front doorway.

"What does it look like? I'm decorating," I tell him, dropping my hand on my hip, which is popped to one side.

"I've been calling you all fucking day, and I've been standing here trying to get your attention for at least five minutes. I wasn't trying to scare you, but you couldn't hear me." His eyes rake over me, his eyebrows pinched, and I can tell he's trying to make sure I'm okay.

"I'm fine, sorry. I got lost in this," I say, waving my arm around at the house as he moves around the room opening windows and propping the front door open.

"I'm surprised you haven't passed out from the fumes in here," he grumbles as he heads to the back door and props that open, too. "What are you running from?"

I gulp as he watches me with that predatory stare of his. He stalks across the room toward me, taking the paint brush from my hand and tucking a stray piece of hair behind my ear. "You know you can tell me anything, right?"

His voice shatters all the walls I thought I'd managed to build while losing myself to the burn of what I was doing, and I crumble. He catches me, scooping me into his arms and walking me out to his truck, just holding me tightly as I break apart.

"I've got you," he says softly before putting me in his truck and strapping on my seatbelt for me. He closes the door and pulls his phone from his pocket. But I can't do anything but sit and watch as I pull my knees up to my chest to try to keep everything inside of me from spilling out.

How the fuck do I explain this to him—to any of them—when I have absolutely no fucking idea what is actually happening to me?

He puts his phone back in his pocket after hanging up his call and heads back inside. I watch as he closes the windows, and then he locks the door behind him as he leaves. He watches me closely as he heads back to the truck and then climbs in beside me, taking my hand after he starts the engine and keeping it in his until we reach his house. It doesn't take more than a second after we stop for him to jump out, rush to my side, and take me back in his arms as he walks us into the house.

I don't know what it is about being here in his space,

but a weight lifts from my shoulders. It's like the darkness in my mind recedes, and my heart doesn't feel quite so heavy.

"You don't have to talk to me yet, but soon enough, we're going to talk about what's been going on with you since you got back, Fallon. I know you told me about Azriel," he says the name like he's chewing on nails, but he's still gentle with me. "But you're leaving something out. We don't keep secrets anymore, you hear me? Especially not ones that push you to the edge like this."

I laugh at his words. I don't know how he can see just how broken I am, but when he looks into my eyes, it's like he's looking right into my shattered and torn soul.

The day started off so well. Waking up with Colt, the darkness inside of me staying dormant with him at my side. But then I get a call from Creek, and everything goes to fucking shit as I listen to his hurried words before he drops the call.

I scurry from Colt's bed as I dial Mama, and he looks at me, bewildered that I just jumped from his arms while he was still half asleep. He watches me throw on clothes as I tear around the room with the phone pressed to my ear, hoping Mama picks up quickly.

"Mama," I screech when she finally picks up. "We need you. The Witches are attacking the Manor."

I don't give her a chance to respond before I hang up. When Colt realizes what the fuck I just said, he scrambles from the bed and quickly dresses.

We hurry downstairs, and I wait while he grabs his weapons, trying not to freak out about the fact that I have no idea what is going on with me and my power yet. But there is no way in hell I'm not answering the call. If Witches are attacking my friends, then I'm going to kick some ass.

I hope.

I just really fucking wish they'd managed to find Remy—I know they think she's with Morgan, there's literally no other trace of her, except for the blood they found in the manor gardens, but fucking still.

That is a problem for later.

"I'm good, let's go." Colt heads toward the door.

"Where the fuck are you going?" I ask as I start to open a portal.

"To my truck," he huffs as he turns around, spotting the portal. "Oh right. Much quicker."

I half want to laugh, but now is not the time. Rage simmers in my blood for the shitty hand I've been dealt recently, the fact that everything is still so fucking uncertain, and I think taking it out on some wayward bitches might just be the exact outlet I need for the darkness that seems to be growing inside of me.

We arrive at the manor and find Remy's four guys facing off against what feels like more Witches than just Lizzie's coven, but I don't have time to think about it as Mama portals in next to us.

A Witch rushes at us, and Colt darts forward, joining the fray. I have no doubt that Remy's guys could have handled the Witches themselves, but with the treaty in place, I guess slaughtering a ton of Witches with no one else here to witness it could've caused some tension.

I don't think, I just go into battle mode, letting the fire within me bubble to the surface as I attack. Mama sticks close to me as we work through the masses. I look around the grounds, realizing Lizzie isn't even here, and the fire inside me burns hotter.

Coward.

I'm not really that shocked that she isn't here, but man, it pisses me off.

I'm glad we didn't have time to call in anyone else to help. I want that bitch's head on a fucking spear for the shit she's done. Betraying her kind, betraying our ancestors… There's more coming her way than an easy fucking death. Because for a Witch, even in the afterlife, if you betray us and lose the battle, you're fucked. The ancestors don't exactly take kindly to that sort of bullshit.

But I will satiate that hunger for bloodlust later.

I lose myself to the madness of it, taking almost as many hits as I dish out and reveling in the depths of the power surging within me. I cover Mama as much as I can—she might be more powerful than me, but she's also a bigger target for the Witches. I don't know how long we've been fighting, but we don't seem to be slowing down their numbers. They're like a fucking hydra, for every person we kill, two fucking more appear.

I shriek as a bubble of shadow wraps around Mama and I. I pound on it, trying to get free until I notice the same bubbles around Colt and all of Remy's guys, too.

That's when I see her. My friend. The epitome of a dark fucking Angel.

She shoots into the sky, and unfurls fucking hell down onto our enemies. A sea of fire like I've never seen washes over the space, and then she drops down, blades in hand. She cuts through those who survived the flames and still try to attack her.

It's like watching an ancient warrior decimate her enemies—and I guess that's not far from the truth.

The screams are deafening as portals start to open but disappear before they can be used. The deathly smile on Remy's face tells me she did it, but I have no fucking idea how. And I really want to know.

I watch my friend in awe, wishing I could be out there at her side, kicking ass and taking names. Looking at the others, I know I'm not alone, but they don't hold my attention long. I turn my gaze back on Remy, and I watch with rapt fascination as she lets the last Witch alive jump through a portal before landing. She tucks her wings against her back and releases the protective, shadowy bubbles—she's covered in blood, and all I can manage is blinking at the sight of her as Colt starts laughing.

"Holy. Fucking. Shit. Remy, you're kinda of terrifying, you know that?" Colt says, his eyes wide and his voice full of awe. She shrugs at him but stays quiet. It's about to get awkward real fast. I don't know where she went or why; I'm just glad she's back and okay.

"You're back," Creek says softly as he takes a step toward her.

"Where did you go?" Kain asks, quickly followed by a growl from Roman.

"Why the fuck did you leave?" The anger on Roman's face is fueled by his worry, anyone can see that, but I can't help but flinch at the bite in his words.

"And, on that note, we're going to leave," I say, moving toward Colt.

"But…" Colt starts, so I glare at him until I reach his side.

"Call me, and we'll catch up later," I say, smiling at her because I feel bad for the shitstorm she's getting ready to endure. I tug on Colt's sleeve to make him leave with me and Mama. He grumbles an objection as we walk away, but he doesn't put up any sort of fight

"I will," Remy calls out, and I wave over my shoulder as Mama opens a portal ready for us. I might envy my friend's power, but I do not envy her situation right now.

EIGHT

"Well, that wasn't exactly how I expected today to go." I smile at Colt's words as he pads back into his room, a towel wrapped around his waist with water dripping from his hair onto his cut torso. I should not be drooling over him right now. These last few days should have me fully curled into a ball and rocking. But damn, that boy is a good distraction from all of my shit.

I'm still sitting in my own towel on his bed, my entire body aching after today's battle, especially since the adrenaline has worn away. I honestly don't know how the Hunters do it day after day. I mean, I know they're built differently, but still.

"So, are we going to talk about yesterday?" he asks, pulling me from my thoughts, and my heart stutters in my chest. I lift my eyes to his, realizing he's watching me way too closely as I try to swallow, suddenly dry mouthed.

Panic swallows me because I don't know what to tell him, or if I should even try. Especially since I have no fucking idea what's actually going on with me. It might just be a one off, a weird delayed after-effect of having my soul torn to pieces again. But there's a niggling voice inside of me telling me it's more than that.

I tried to convince myself before that Azriel's voice in my head was just my own trauma haunting me. Maybe that's what gives me pause—still not knowing exactly what's going on in my head. Because how do I explain something that I don't fully understand?

He's still watching me, waiting for me to say something, so I blow out a deep breath and try to explain it. "I woke up feeling so out of control. I think I lost some time, Colt. I have no memory of a whole day, and it freaked me out. So I tried to compensate for that, I guess, and I lost myself a little in the process."

He frowns at my explanation, and I look down at my hands in my lap, trying to escape whatever it is he's trying to see in my eyes. "We need to talk to my sister."

"No," I gasp. "Remy has more than enough going on without dealing with my crazy shit on top of it. It's probably a repercussion of Morgan shredding my soul to remove Azriel again. She'll likely be the only one with answers."

"Then I guess we better go see the Queen," he growls, striding across the room toward me. "I hate seeing you like this, Fallon. Please let me help you."

"I will… If it happens again. It's just a one off and it freaked me out. It was probably nothing. Please don't make this into a big deal. Promise me you'll keep it to yourself for now."

"Fallon…"

"Promise me, Colt," I plead, hating myself a little for making him promise. But I hate the thought of being a burden more. It's not like he doesn't have enough to deal with either, but I can't hide from him. Especially since he found me the way he did this time.

"Fine, but if it happens again, we're not keeping this between just us." I nod my head, knowing that if it happens again, I'll try my damnedest to keep it to myself so I'm not such a burden to everyone. They've all done enough and risked enough for me as it is. I'm more than capable of looking after myself.

I think.

"Do you think the Witches will attack again?" he asks me, and relief floods my being at the change of subject. I sigh deeply as I chew on my answer.

"Probably. They've turned their backs on the covens, on our ancestors. They won't give up unless they're beaten and they have no choice but to give up. The repercussions for what they've done are too great. They'll fight tooth and nail against us if that's what it takes." I stand up to start getting dressed, slipping into one of his t-shirts after I drop the towel. The shirt is practically like a dress on me, but it's my only option while my clothes go through the wash downstairs.

"You should wear my clothes more often," he smirks before strutting over to me. He captures my lips with his in a kiss that's almost bruising.

"If you kiss me like that every time I do, then maybe I'll make a habit of it," I pant, and he smirks down at me again, just as his phone starts ringing. He groans, but ignores it in favor of kissing me until I'm breathless. The ringing stops, and he grins until it starts again.

"Just get it, whoever it is, they're likely not going to stop trying if they called back that quickly." I sigh, and he nips my bottom lip before releasing me and answering the phone.

"What?" he grunts, and I laugh softly as he starts pulling clothes on.

"Fucking hell, I swear, this in-fighting has got to stop. I'm an Elder, not a fucking parent." The voice on the other end of the line starts up again, and I wander downstairs to see if my clothes are finished in the dryer. Whatever is happening on the other end of that call, I'm fairly sure it's about to cut our night short. It's probably for the best. All things considered, I should probably focus a little more on what the fuck is going on with me anyway.

As much as I told Colt it was likely a one off, the more I start thinking about it, the more I realize this isn't the first time I've lost time. It's just the first time I've lost a whole day, which is why I never put much thought into it before. My memory isn't that great, so forgetting what I did for an hour or so the day before didn't really faze me… At least not until now.

I need to see if there's a way to get in touch with Deacon so he can speak to Morgan for me. I'm not sure if I'll be able to talk to her myself, so I need an in. I bite my lip at the thought. Colt will be pissed if he finds out I went to Deacon about this, but I know I'm definitely right about one thing. This isn't something the Hunters can help me with.

I wake up, looking at my phone straight away, and let out a sigh of relief when it's the day I expect it to be. Having come to the conclusion that something is definitely wrong with me, I've been quietly freaking out since I left Colt's last night. I ended up covering the store for Mama, but she's hired two eighteen-year-old girls from the coven to start helping out so that we can focus on the shit we're dealing with around us, rather than the store.

I can't help but feel a little guilty about dropping the ball a lot recently, but Mama doesn't seem worried about our situation right now, so I'm not going to worry either.

I shower quickly, and once I'm sure Mama has left the house, I head to the herb stores so I can try to get a message to Deacon. It's not like I can just jump between Realms, at least not without Remy's help, and after the look on her guys' faces yesterday, there's a good chance she's tied to a bed somewhere, so she couldn't help me anyway.

I'm just hoping Deacon can help.

I go through the cabinet and pull out everything I think I'll need and head back to my room. I drop everything onto my bed and sit my ass down on the floor, drawing out the Dominance Coven sigil before grabbing the book from the bed. I read through it quickly, to find the other symbols required for communicating with the Shadow Realm.

I just hope I don't fuck this up. I find the symbols for greed, and hope it means the message will go straight to Deacon. I could totally fuck this up, but I don't know what else to do.

Once I finish drawing the chalk symbols on the floor, I pull the black agate bowl from under my bed and mix my blood with the herbs I grabbed earlier.

"Konekte m 'deyès ak sa yo ki sou bò a fè nwa. Kite yo

koute mesaj mwen an." I murmur the Creole from the book and repeat it until flames engulf the bowl.

I grab a pen and paper from my desk and scribble a note to Deacon, asking him to contact me as soon as he gets it, and drop it into the flames. They flare green and then extinguish.

I hope to the Goddess that that worked, because I really don't want to go to Remy and ask her for her help with this. I hate feeling like *that* girl. But I do feel a little lighter for at least trying to work this out. For taking the steps to sort my own shit out.

"What's wrong?"

I squeal as Deacon pops into the room before me. He looks like he's ready to go to battle, his rage barely contained.

"Hi," I wave at him from where I'm sitting on the floor, not feeling awkward at all. "Maybe tone down the crazy, angry Demon vibe thing to like a four?" I tease, and he deflates almost instantly.

"I thought something was wrong," he huffs before helping me to my feet. "Having flames appear on my desk followed by a note from you isn't exactly an everyday occurrence, but I'm glad to know you can reach me when you need to."

"Well, I mean, I took a risk, but it paid off…" I dust off my trousers and lead him out of my room to the back porch, very aware of just how awkward this feels. If Mama comes home and finds a Demon in her house, she's going to lose her shit. "But something is wrong, just not the type of rip down the world wrong thing you're imagining. I honestly didn't expect you to drop everything and come here straight away."

He shrugs at my words while watching me closely. "You called. Of course I came."

I smile a little at his words, and then spill everything on what I've managed to piece together about my missing time and when I think it started. When I finish, he's staring at me intensely, his rage back tenfold.

"This shouldn't be happening," he snarls. "Morgan said you'd be fine."

"And I'm sure she meant it," I say, trying to sound soothing. Even though I know that he wouldn't hurt me ever again, I can't help the shiver of fear that races down my spine at the sound of his snarl. "But something is going on with me, and it started after she removed Az's soul from mine. Can you help me speak to her? Or speak to her for me? I don't want to involve anyone I don't need to."

"I'll look into it for you. In the meantime," he says, pulling a journal from his back pocket. "Write down everything you've just told me in here, and keep it up to date if you lose any more time. The more detailed information we have, the better. Also, take this." He shows me a leather strap inlaid with black stones before fastening it around my wrist.

"The stones should help protect you from any Demons. I can only assume they're the ones fucking with you, all things considered. It isn't infallible, but it should help a little."

"Thank you," I smile up at him, but he doesn't release my wrist, his thumb stroking the sensitive skin between the bracelet and my hand. I lean up on the tips of my toes and peck his cheek.

"Anything. Always. I should get back, but I'll get in touch as soon as I have any information okay?"

"Okay," I breathe the words softly.

"Stay safe, and if you need anything, just call, and I'll be here in a heartbeat."

It's been a few days since Remy's been back and we've talked a few times, but it hasn't been as much as I'd like since her guys are keeping her so busy. Not that I'm surprised. I pick up my phone to send her a message but pause when I see a few unread messages on my screen.

Colt: Hey, you wanna hang out later?

Colt: Hope you're doing okay. I'm a little worried after

our last convo, just check in and let me know you're still… ya know, you.

Colt: Fallon, if you don't respond in the next ten minutes, I'm heading over.

Shit. That was like six minutes ago, so I texted him first.

Me: I'm here, I'm alive, and I'm okay. I was just lost in meditating. I'm definitely down for hanging out if the offer's still on the table?

I bite my lip as I hit send and hope to the Goddess he's not already in his truck. Patience isn't exactly his strong suit. I see those three dots pop up on the screen and let out a deep breath.

Colt: Thank fuck for that. Yes, the offer is still on the table… though right now I'm tempted to spread you out on the table and punish you a little.

Me: I mean… I'm not opposed to a little punishment.

I bite my lip harder as I hit send, but I can't help the little smile that threatens. Colt really is exactly what I need pretty much all the time. He feels like home, and after everything I've been through lately, he feels like my safe space. He's also always willing to distract me in the best ways possible.

My phone buzzes again in my lap, and a shudder of anticipation runs down my spine.

Colt: Then I suggest you don't keep me waiting.

I jump up from where I'm sitting on the floor and slip my feet into my boots. Checking my hair and face in the mirror before I dive from the room, I drop Mama a text to let her know I won't be around tonight and then portal into Colt's front yard.

It's like he knew I'd be here because he's standing in the doorway, arms above his head as he leans on the doorjamb, smiling down at me.

"You should hurry up and get in here," he says, the smirk spreading over his lips tells me that he's definitely in the mood to play. I scurry up the steps into the house and he slaps my ass as I dart past him. He points to the kitchen and I rush in, the brooding look on his face making me clench my thighs together.

I stand in the middle of the kitchen, waiting for my next instruction as he watches me from the doorway.

"Strip." His one word command makes my toes curl,

so I do as I'm told, right down to my underwear. He moves toward me, his fists clenching and unclenching at his sides as he stops a few steps away from me.

"Bend over the table," he commands, and I shiver before following his instruction and bending over. I'm forced on the tips of my toes because of the height.

"Are you sure this is what you want?" he asks as he stands closely behind me, heat rippling from him in waves.

I look at him over my shoulder, panting with want. "Yes."

I moan as he reaches forward, pulls on my hair, and growls, "Mine," before spanking my ass. I hiss at the sting, half embarrassed about how fucking wet I am over it, and half wanting him to do it again. He rubs the patch of skin before leaning down to whisper in my ear.

"Did you like that, baby?"

"Yes," I gasp, wanting so much more.

"Do you want me to do it again?"

"Yes, please. Colt…" I groan as he smacks my ass again before pulling on my hair and making me stand. He releases me and spins me around before picking me up and sitting me on the table. I sigh as the cool wood soothes the warm patches where he slapped me and look into his eyes. He is every part the predator right now.

"Lie down," he barks and I do, leaning up on my elbows, watching as he sinks to his knees. "I'm going to enjoy this."

I anticipate the warm, wet touch of his tongue but of course Colt isn't that predictable. With both of his hands holding my thighs apart and his head right at my center, he blows what feels like cool breath on my hot and needy pussy. The contrast in temperature is almost torture and, yet at the same time, I never want it to end. I feel him tracing air up and around my clit—it almost feels like he's touching me, like his fingers are dancing along my skin.

"Colt, please. You're killing—" I don't get to finish what I'm saying as I feel his playful bite on my right thigh. He doesn't need to say a word because his message is loud and clear. "I'm in charge, sit back and enjoy."

Who am I to disobey?

So I do as he wants. I lie back down on my elbows, my eyes trained on the ceiling above and my hair pooling on the table below. Without my eyes on him, his touch is somehow more intense.

A few strands of his hair tickle my bent knee as his whiskers scrape along my sensitive skin, his breath painting me with red hot need.

"I'm going to eat your pussy until you cry."

"Until I cry?" Raising my head, I let my gaze find his. The mischief written clearly in his eyes makes my skin sizzle with electric need.

"Until you cry. Until you beg me to stop. But I won't.

I'm going to eat this pussy until I'm satisfied, until I've had my fill. That's your punishment for making me wait and ignoring my messages." I squirm under his intense gaze, conflicted between pissed and excited over his words.

He doesn't wait for a response and just dives into my pussy like a starved man.

He's all lips and tongue, diving into the deepest parts of me, and I swear it's like he's touching my fucking soul. With every stroke of his tongue, he moans his approval like I'm his favorite kind of drug.

He ignores my clit, and I know it's on purpose. I want to reach down, for even the smallest amount of friction, but the thought of him stopping makes me hesitate. He's licking and nipping and kissing everywhere from my pussy almost down to my asshole. I cry out at the sensation of it all. His mouth is everywhere, devouring, taking everything I have to give him.

Fuck, I'm not going to survive this.

"Colt…" I whimper, unable to stop myself.

His teeth nip one of my lips, and I pant with need. It doesn't hurt, but it communicates his demands clearly.

"You're killing me, please, please touch my clit and let me come. Please." I can't stop myself from begging. I never thought I would, but for him, I'd do a lot I never thought I would.

At my pleading, he relents and brings his fingers to my

center. He spreads my lips and exposes that little bundle of nerves to the cool air of the room, and it's like ice on a burn.

I think, fucking damn near pray, that he's going to lick my clit, but of course he doesn't. His tongue runs all around it, circling it before he pushes two fingers inside me. The sensation sends my hips shooting off the table like a jolt of electricity has just hit me at full voltage.

"Fuck, Colt!"

"I promise I'll never make you wait," he murmurs as he pushes another finger into my ass. He fucks me thoroughly with his hand and I feel so fucking full. I'm no longer in control of my body. I think I'm speaking to him, but I might as well be speaking in tongues because my mind is fixated on one thing only: coming. I can feel it, just out of reach, and it's driving me fucking insane, being so close to the edge and not being able to free fall.

I know this is my punishment, him edging me and then bringing me back down, but I love every second of his sweet torture.

I have definitely learned my lesson.

"Colt, Colt, Colt…" His name becomes a chant on my lips, yet my voice is barely audible through my need for release.

I look down at him, and he must feel my gaze because he raises his piercing blue eyes my way. With that one glance, I know that he knows. The man fully knows just how fucking close I am, and I can see that he fucking loves teasing me like this.

All the while fucking me with his fingers, pushing in and out of my pussy and ass, he lowers his head back down with a glint in his eyes that clearly shows he's won this game and wraps his lips around my clit.

I lose all control as he sucks on it.

My back arches off the surface of his table, and all of my blood feels like it rushes to that one tiny spot between my legs. When his tongue flicks my clit in rapid succession, all of the built up pressure explodes and radiates throughout my entire body. I feel my orgasm in every part of me, every nerve alight with fire.

I think I scream, but I can't be sure. Everything feels muted for a brief instant, and just as I come back down from what the French accurately named la petite mort—the little death—I realize he's still fucking me with his fingers.

The devilish smirk on his lips is all I need to see to know that he isn't finished with me. I see the trademark smirk, and I know. He's about to ruin me for all others.

Curling his index finger so perfectly, he hits my deepest, darkest button and another orgasm rips through me out of nowhere.

When he finally gives me one last, achingly slow lap of his tongue. I can't contain the full-bodied shudder that comes over me and it's only when I feel his tongue licking up each side of my cheeks that I realize I'm crying.

"I always keep my promises." His words are profound, and though I feel like he's talking about more than just orgasms, my mind is too fried to analyze anything, much less his cryptic words.

His mouth reaches mine, and he makes love to me with a single kiss. When he gives me one last lick across my lips, my eyes flutter open, and I realize he's naked and standing between my open legs.

"This is my favorite part of the day." His mouth quirks up on one side, and he looks at me through long, thick lashes. "When I own you completely."

He keeps his eyes on mine as he slides his thick cock inside me from tip to root in one smooth glide.

He's right. In these moments when we're linked in the most intimate of ways, I feel whole. More than that, I feel like I'm his.

I'm his addiction, his drug of choice, and I love every second of it.

His movements are gentle, languid, smooth, and loving. With hands caressing my hips and thighs, hands massaging my breasts, and fingers pinching my nipples oh so lightly, I feel completely cherished. I feel like the most important person in his life. I feel loved.

Every thrust inside me is gentle, all the while

commanding. He's fucking me like he owns me yet caring for me like he loves me. That can't be right. It must be the adrenaline and the pheromones. I must be half-dead, right now.

I can feel the power of his body, of his thrusts, increase. The strain on his beautiful face is visible. He's trying to hold off his own orgasm. But why?

Wrapping his fingers around my wrists, he lays his naked chest right on top of mine, never missing a thrust, and pins my hands on either side of my head. He's watching me, his eyes boring into mine, his teeth sinking into his bottom lip and making my walls squeeze his dick so hard I see his reaction in the tic of his jaw.

"Come again, Fallon. One more time for me."

Holding me tightly against the table, his body creates the perfect friction against my clit. The tip of his cock hits my g-spot like it has its own GPS, and his mouth is suddenly on mine, stealing my breath with each push of his hips.

He swallows my cries as I come one last time, and I feel the exact moment he comes inside me.

I don't know how long we stay there, dazed and sated, skin on skin with heaving chests… Kissing like lovers. I've never felt more at home than in this one perfect moment.

"Next time I message you, I expect an answer."

"If my making you wait gets me three mind-blowing

orgasms, you are clearly adopting the wrong type of incentive."

If I weren't so damn exhausted, I might have laughed at his attempt at a growl.

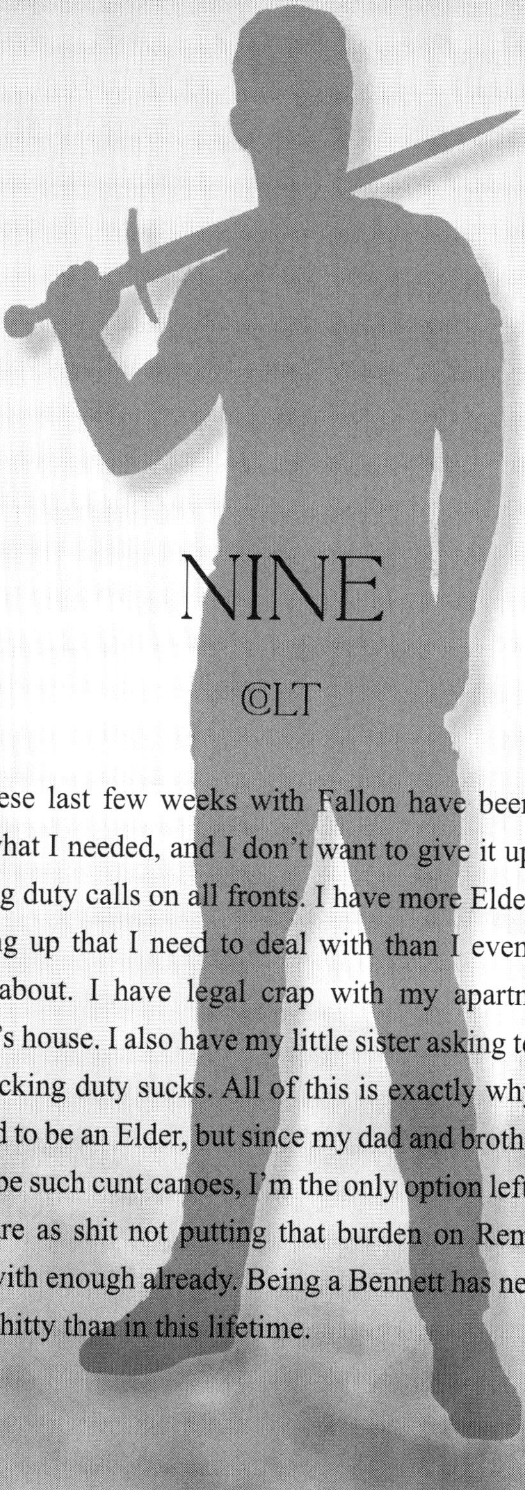

NINE

COLT

These last few weeks with Fallon have been exactly what I needed, and I don't want to give it up. Except fucking duty calls on all fronts. I have more Elder bullshit backing up that I need to deal with than I even want to think about. I have legal crap with my apartment and Bauer's house. I also have my little sister asking to see me.

Fucking duty sucks. All of this is exactly why I never wanted to be an Elder, but since my dad and brother turned out to be such cunt canoes, I'm the only option left because I'm sure as shit not putting that burden on Remy. She's dealt with enough already. Being a Bennett has never been more shitty than in this lifetime.

Especially with the Hunter's curse out of commission now. I might have made arrangements for myself should the worst happen and started getting my shit together, but fuck. All I want to do is go back to what I want. My girl and hunting. I was not built for this politicking shit. I'm just as likely to put a bullet in someone as I am work out what the fuck their backward riddles mean.

I scrub a hand down my face and jump in my truck. First things first, I need to go and make a start on packing up Bauer's house. I grab my phone and shoot a message to Nate, asking him to deal with the Elder shit for the day. It should've been him in my place anyway, but I've dubbed him my second. He deals with this shit much better than I do. Plus, I think since everything came to light, he's felt a little lost. Maddie and him have been suffering not just an empty nest since Creek moved over to the manor, but now their closest friends are gone, and I think they're still trying to wrap their heads around all of this crap that we've been wading through lately.

My phone buzzes with a message from Nate letting me know he's good to pick it up, so I start the truck to make the drive to Bauer's, music cranked up loud enough to make the entire truck shake.

Anger pulses through me like a living entity as I swing the truck out of the front drive and head across town to Bauer's place. I'm still pissed at him. For what he did, for betraying us, and for leaving me holding the fucking buck. I can't believe I trusted him—but if you can't trust family, who can you fucking trust?

We're meant to trust in each other, in the creed of the Hunters, and yet, this last year has knocked all of that on its ass. I wasn't just betrayed by my family, but by the entire institution I pledged my life to time and again. My entire fucking world has spun off its axis, and I've barely had chance to take a breath and make sense of what life is since then.

I pull into the drive of Bauer's house and turn off the truck, clenching the steering wheel, feeling fucking paralyzed. I haven't had time to grieve my brother, we've had so much shit going on, but sitting here is like having the breath knocked from my lungs. I know he was a giant asshole, and he did so much shit wrong… But he was also my brother, and for lifetimes over, he was the guy I could rely on. The one who had my back through thick and thin. I feel guilty about the grief pooling in my chest because he tried to fucking kill Remy. It's as if grieving him is a betrayal to her, which is the same reason I haven't really grieved my dad.

Fuck me. My heart feels like it's going to beat out of my chest. Why did my family have to be so fucked up? I know Remy isn't exactly sad that they're gone, not after everything, but now that I'm here, I can't stop the wave of agony threatening to pull me under.

I suck in a breath and climb from the truck. I let myself in the house and sink against the wall as a wave of grief crashes into me.

"Why did you have to do this to us all, brother?" I whisper as a tear slips down my face. I wipe it away angrily. He doesn't deserve my tears… And yet, I can't stop the pain that's threatening to break me. My gaze catches on a picture frame on his fireplace… Me, him and Remy. Taken on her birthday. The Three Musketeers.

I get up and pick it up, launching it across the room. Was any of it even real? Or was it all just part of the role he was playing?

I'll never get those answers, I'm more than aware of that, but there is so much I wish I knew. I clench my fists and leave the house. Fuck this shit. I'll hire someone to come and empty this place out, and put it all in storage for another time when it's not still so fresh. I can't deal with this right now.

I lock down the pain, letting my anger run free and jump back into my truck. I shoot off a text to Elijah about going for another hunt tonight. I need to feel the stain of blood on my hands to soothe my soul.

Nothing else will do.

"Glad to finally see you again," Creek laughs as I jump from my truck onto the driveway of the manor. After spending the last twenty-four hours beating the shit out of rogues, I look like absolute ass, but when Remy texted and asked me to come and train with her and Creek, I jumped at the chance. Beating the shit out of rogues is one thing. But a half Demon and an Angel? Now that's some real pain.

I grin at him, feeling the sting of my split lip as it tears open again. "I could say the same."

"You sure you're up for a beatdown today? You look like someone hit you with a truck and then backed over you again." Creek looks at me, his concern obvious, but I wave him off.

"Just a few overzealous rogues. The hunt never ends." I grin and he nods, knowing exactly what I mean. I shut down the anger I can feel simmering beneath the surface and follow him in the house.

"How's things been here since the attack?" I ask as we head through the foyer, toward the back of the house.

"About as well as you can imagine. Sometimes there are just too many egos in one conversation, but we're getting there. Remy seems more relaxed than I thought she would be, so I'm just trying to focus on her. It's not like I have a whole faction to split my focus." He shrugs, opening the door to the backyard where I spy my sister running laps. Apparently the Angel upgrade gave her a speed boost, too. I chuckle to myself about how the one person in our faction who didn't need a badass upgrade is the one who got one. She's been feared for centuries, this almost seems like taking the piss, but I wouldn't have it any other way. If she's a badass, she can keep herself alive.

"How is Remy coping after everything?" I ask, hoping that she's not feeling as fucked up as I am.

"She's surprisingly okay," he says, shrugging. "She's ready to kick your ass, though." I belt out a laugh because I bet she is. But I'm ready for her, today probably more than most other days. The burn of anger since I've felt since I left Bauer's hasn't lessened but I'm not that guy. I hate that he's still fucking with me from beyond the grave; I don't want to be this angry, grieving guy.

It doesn't take long before Remy runs toward us. She jumps on my back as soon as she makes it to me, pulling a laugh from me as I catch her. "Hey, little bit."

"Hiiiii," she practically sings. "It's good to see you." She drops down and hugs me properly, and the guilt over my grief churns in my stomach again.

"You, too. Creek says you need your ass kicking, so of course, I answered that call." I grin at her, hoping that the swirling emotions inside me aren't obvious. She looks at me closely, but whatever she sees, she dismisses it with a grin at me.

"Oh, big brother, we both know I'm going to kick your ass. It looks like you already lost a few rounds. You sure you want to risk the humiliation?"

"Pfft," I scoff. "I don't think it's me who has to worry about the humiliation—I assume wings and powers are off limits… then again you never did play fair."

The taunt hits where I wanted, but she laughs. "Fine, let's do this. We'll play with powers later so you get to learn something new, too."

"Sounds good to me." I smirk, rubbing my hands together. "Who's getting a beatdown first?"

"That'll be Creek. Fallon's showing up soon to reset some wards for us." Remy grins at me as I school my expression. Fallon and I might be back on the up, but I don't know how much Remy knows, and she isn't about to find out from me. So instead, I grin at her as Creek takes off his t-shirt, and I do the same.

"So be it. I'm happy to hand out ass whoopings to all."

I drop down on the ground, staring up at the darkening sky as I try to catch my breath. Training with my sister and Creek all day has been exhausting, but it's been the best kind of distraction. Even if I did get the wind knocked out of me when Fallon arrived and I got a little too distracted.

She's inside with Remy now—they went inside a while ago to do girly shit—so Creek and I kept at it. Holy shit do his new powers pack a fucking punch.

"Why are you on the ground?" I look up to find Remy standing over me, looking at me like I've lost my damn mind.

"Because the stars are pretty," I joke as she flops down beside me.

"Yeah okay, dork." She laughs. "Why are you really down here?"

"Just catching my breath and trying to get some perspective."

"A lot has happened this last year," she sighs. "How are you doing really?"

I pause, not sure how to answer her. She's all the family I have left. "Honestly?"

"Always, if this year has taught me nothing else, it would be that honesty is fucking key."

"I'm a little fucked up," I admit. "I went to Bauer's house to start trying to clear it out, get the ball rolling, and I lost my shit."

"I get that," she says, taking my hand in hers, the way she did when she was little. "You know it's okay to be sad that he's gone right? You two were thick as thieves. It would be shocking if you weren't fucked up about everything. Same with Dad. I've had a long time to come to grips with the fact that I wasn't like them, but this has been a fucking year of revelations, even for me."

"I just feel so fucking guilty for feeling any kind of grief. Granddad killed you, Dad allowed it, and Bauer tried to kill you. They're not small infractions, Remy. They all betrayed us, betrayed the entire fucking faction. The things they did to you… And I didn't stand up. I just… I'm so angry about it all, but it's also like I lost so much that I don't know which way is up." I let out a deep breath, feeling lighter just for having confessed.

"Colt…" she pauses, looking at me before glancing back up at the sky. "You have nothing, and I mean nothing to feel guilty about. You might not have stood up for me at the beginning, but you came around, and a hell of a lot quicker than I expected. You've had lifetimes of Dad in your ear teaching you one thing. It would've been a bigger shock if you just jumped to my defense instantly. As for your grief, feel it. Live it. And don't ever think it's wrong. We get real good at goodbyes living the life we do, but we never expect them to be final goodbyes. This time… Well that's not the case. We know it's pretty much done—so grieve them. Whether that's you feeling angry or sad, you get to feel whatever you need to and don't let anyone, even me, tell you that that's wrong."

I squeeze her hand as she finishes talking and swallow against the lump in my throat. Fuck, I never get this emotional, but damn this year has taken its toll.

"You're juggling so much, and I just kinda dumped the Elder thing on you too on top of everything. I'm sorry for that. I haven't made this last year easy for you. Between essentially causing a coup, throwing shit your way, bringing new enemies upon us, and then handing that burden to you too… I'm surprised you're even still speaking to me." She laughs, but it's rough, like she thinks I might just up and leave.

"Remy, you've carried more weight than I have for a damn sight longer. It's about time I pick up some of the slack," I say with a shrug.

"I was pregnant once…" she says, and my jaw drops, but I stay quiet letting her speak. "Back when I was an Angel. I lost it trying to escape a battle and a spear was thrown through my stomach. There was nothing I could do. That's why I left without notice for a bit. I remembered, and it washed over me, and I couldn't cope… That's not it, though. Everly… She was one of my descendants, too. From one of my early lives where Dad and Grandfather took away my choice to be a Hunter. I had a son, and so another Bennet line began, but they're human. Utterly human. Everly knew, and she loved me, without even telling me… And I failed her, too. Just like I keep failing everyone. So don't feel guilty to me, Colt. I have a lot of shit to make up for to a lot of people."

I have no idea what to say to any of that. Talk about fucking mind blown.

"You have nothing to make up for, little bit. You didn't kill them, you just trusted the wrong people. Their lives will be avenged. And maybe one day, now that you're immortal and all, you'll start another family… And I'll be the best fucking uncle that ever lived."

She laughs at my declaration, but I truly hope she gets that. Remy's always been so selfless, and she deserves her own piece of happiness.

"I have no doubt you will. Maybe I'll even name a kid after you, pump up that ego of yours a little more."

"Ha!" I bark out and roll onto my side as she laughs softly. "He'll be a little fucker, and you know I'm going to teach any of your kids all of the things a good uncle would. How to fight, the best cuss words, how to blow shit up."

"Oh, I know, but if you don't, I have no doubt their fathers would."

"Is that weird? There being four of them?" I ask, not wanting to know the inner details of how their family works, but I can't lie and say it doesn't bewilder me.

"Not even a little. It's like our souls are intertwined. We were always meant to be as we are now. I truly believe the Fates led us this way. Why, are you considering something like this?" She turns to look at me, and I can tell she's dying to know what's happening in my love life.

"I don't know that I'd ever say no one hundred percent, but I'm also pretty sure I'm not the sharing kind."

"You think Leviathan ever was? For the right person, you adjust," she says with a shrug, and I ponder her words, mostly hoping that's never a decision I have to make.

TEN

FALLON

I step out of the shower feeling so freaking relaxed for the first time in a while. After setting the wards around the manor, Remy and I sat and talked for ages. I told her a few things, mainly about Azriel, but kept a lot of it to myself still. She's dealing with enough right now as it is. Once all this crap is done with Archer and the Witches, I'll tell her. We have too much to focus on right now, and my issues are just that: my issues. They're not affecting anything else we have going on, so for as long as that's the case, I'm going to keep my mouth shut.

Remy steps into her room at the same time I do, and she smiles at me as we pad over to her bed. "Facials and pedicures. That's what this day needs."

"You okay?" I ask, because she looks somehow heavier than she did before my shower.

"Yeah, I'm fine. Just had a catch up with Colt." My heart stutters in my chest at her words, but I keep my mouth shut. Colt and I haven't really spoken about what we are, let alone the possibility of telling anyone else.

"Oh?" I ask, trying not to sound as invested as I feel in what she has to say next.

"Yeah, he's just going through some stuff. I think we just needed to get some shit out in the open. But it's done, I think it will help him. He stuffs everything down and doesn't let anyone help. I worry about him." She sighs as she drops down onto the bed. "Hopefully he's okay now, I just hope he feels more like himself at Christmas… speaking of which, are you guys still coming over?"

"We are. Mama didn't even bother going shopping. I think she's half excited not to cook." I laugh and pull on my pajamas before sitting opposite her on the bed.

"Makes sense," she mutters as she settles in opposite of me. "I think everyone is coming. I'm so excited."

"Me, too." I grin at her. "Did you finish shopping for the guys?"

"I did," she says with a smirk. "And Christmas Eve is all sorted out, too." I burst out laughing, knowing her usual traditions.

"Please, please, please take pictures." I giggle.

"I'll try my best. Now what do you want to watch? Chick flick or action movie?"

"What about the new John Wick? There is just something about that man that makes my thighs clench," I admit, and she laughs again.

"It's the head shots, that's what it is," she winks and grabs her remote. "But I'm never one to turn down a bullet fest. Lemme grab some face masks, and we can indulge in all the things."

I make myself comfortable as she heads into her bathroom before quickly reappearing with two packets, throwing one over to me. We both know her glowing Angelic skin doesn't need it, but well… It's fun anyway.

"Better get comfortable, this is a long-ass movie." She grins as she settles in beside me.

"Just don't drool," I tease, and she laughs because we both know how she likes a badass guy who's bloodthirsty.

"I'm not making any promises."

Christmas is always a strange affair in my house. We tend to celebrate it more for Rebel and the people around us than for ourselves, but today is extra special because Rebel came home last night, and it feels like forever since we last saw her. Plus with her around, Christmas still has some of its magic.

We spent the morning trying to decide what to do, and we finally came to the decision of opening some presents here, before heading to Remy's to celebrate the day with family because that's what this is really all about with us. Which is why we're now bundled up in the car, while it's still dark out, driving to Remy's with a ton of gifts in the trunk. We could have portaled over, but there just weren't enough arms to hold all of the gifts.

It doesn't take us long to get there, and Rebel is as excited as, well… a kid at Christmas. "Will there be chocolate and pancakes for breakfast like usual?"

I grin down at her and nod. "Probably, but I'm sure if you ask Nonnie, she'll make it for you special."

Mama presses the doorbell as Rebel bounces up and down between us, and I can't stop the smile spreading across my face. It doesn't take long before the door opens and Remy's face appears before us.

"Merry Christmas!" we shout and Remy laughs, ushering us in out of the cold. Mama floats in the bags we unloaded, and Remy giggles as she watches them pass by.

"I didn't know you guys would be here this early!" she gushes as she closes the door behind us.

"Well, we weren't going to be, but then we figured what is Christmas about if it's not about family? You're family, so here we are!" I tell her with a smile before bringing her in for a hug.

"What she said." Mama offers with a smile and hugs her quickly as I shuffle Rebel into the main room. "And I have a feeling more people are on the way. I hope you have enough space under the tree."

"Holy shit," I exclaim as I take a seat. "Mama, there is definitely not enough space under the tree."

Rebel gawks at the tree, and Remy giggles. "Yeah, the guys went a little overboard, I think."

"We certainly did not," Kain says sleepily as he appears in his reindeer onesie. I try not to laugh, because he looks so darn adorable, but also, the King of the Dracul is in a reindeer onesie… This is way better than a picture.

"You got them to wear them?" I snicker.

"Of course." Remy nods, giggling with me as she takes her spot in the corner of the sofa.

"There's coffee in the kitchen, but beware, it's mania in there," she tells us, and I don't need to be told twice. I head into the kitchen, and holy fucking Goddess, she wasn't wrong. The kitchen is piled with different dishes and Nonnie is a freaking whirlwind.

I rush to the coffee machine, staying out of the way as much as I can and grab a mug for me and Remy before rushing out of there. The kitchen is not a room I want to be a part of right now, and with everyone else heading in here, I'm glad to make my escape. I make my way over to hand one to Remy and sit beside her, snuggling into her shoulder. We sit in silence, enjoying the sounds of laughter around the house.

Colt is the next to appear, in his elf onesie, looking proud as hell as he struts into the room. "Merry Christmas, little bit," he says to Remy, before turning to me with a small smile. "Merry Christmas, Fal."

I look over at Remy, who's watching us closely, so I take another sip of my coffee before smiling softly at him. Remy looks away toward the kitchen where, by the sounds of it, the other three guys are now, too. I look back at him and snicker at him in his elf onesie as he just poses. It takes every bit of early morning willpower I have to not check out his dick in the fitted outfit.

Colt looks at the seat beside me longingly before heading toward the noise, and my heart drops a little. Maybe we do need to talk about exactly what we are and what we're doing. I know the others don't need to know, but it would be nice not to have to pretend in front of everyone else.

I sit and wait for them—because there's no way I'm giving up my primo spot—but it's not long before everyone files into the living room sipping coffee, or hot chocolate in Rebel's case. It seems everyone needs a little jolt to wake up properly before the unwrapping begins, but I'm having a hard time trying not to giggle at the others in their onesies. Seeing the Archangel of War in a reindeer onesie might just be the highlight of my Christmas this year. Not going to lie.

Levi takes charge and starts handing out gifts. Handing more than a few over to me, Mama and Rebel, which makes me especially glad that we brought all of ours over here for them, too. Thankfully, between ours and what was already here, no one appears left out. Even Colt has a decent pile in front of him.

Remy however, looks almost embarrassed about the amount of gifts left under the tree for her.

"Revel in it, it's about time you got shown the love you deserve," I tell her, remembering the fucking blender Jack got her last Christmas. What a jackass.

It takes a while, but we get through a decent amount, and Remy decides to finish opening the rest of hers later when the rest of us have gone. "Help me put this stuff away?"

"Sure," I say, snickering at her with the knives, the coloring books and Goddess only knows what else. I help her stash away her gifts, and while she gets dressed, I pull the bag I had hidden away for her out. When she reappears, I hand it over to her, grinning.

"What is this?" she asks, looking at me skeptically.

"This is something I knew you'd love. I had to get it

for you, but I didn't want you to cry if you opened it in front of everyone on Christmas morning." She looks at me warily, half worried, but I can tell she's just anxious about what's in the bag. "That makes it sound way bigger than it is, just open it, and you'll see."

I roll my eyes as she tentatively opens the bag, and pulls out a colorful sweater that reads *This is my ugly Christmas sweater.* She bursts out laughing, and I can't help but join in.

"I know this was like a you and Everly thing, but I saw it and knew you'd love it." I shrug and then she hugs me, and I feel some relief at having not overstepped. I knew today would be hard for her without Everly, and I figured with this, we could at least have a small piece of her here with us.

"I do love it. It's perfect, thank you." She pulls on the hideous green sweater, and I can't help but feel cheated.

"How is it you still look good even in that thing?" I ask, rolling my eyes. It's just not fair. Fucking Angelic best friends.

"It's a gift." She winks at me before linking her arm with mine, and we head back to the others for what is shaping up to be one of the best Christmases ever.

We got home pretty late from Remy's, and Rebel was wiped out from all the excitement, so I'm not at all surprised to find her still sleeping when I finally climb out of bed at ten in the morning.. Yesterday was amazing, and literally everything I didn't know I needed. I haven't really felt that relaxed since before Remy's birthday.

I grab everything from the fridge I need to start making a full breakfast and get to work on pancake mix as I heat the griddle for the bacon. I lose myself in the routine of it, taking refuge in how calm I feel doing something I've done every year for as long as I can remember. The day after Christmas, I always get up first and make everyone's favorite breakfast. So chocolate chip pancakes for Rebel, eggs Florentine for Mama, and then a breakfast burrito for myself. So simple and yet everything I need.

I start plating everything up as Mama and Rebel enter the room, still in their pajamas and yawning.

"Morning." I say cheerfully as I move the plates to the table.

"Yay, pancakes!" Rebel bounces over to her chair, practically singing. We all sit down to eat, and she talks my ear off about what her plans are with Erica for New Year's and how she's settling into her new school. She's with more of the coven at her new school, so it's probably better for her, but it doesn't make her being away any easier.

We pass the day away, playing board games and

watching movies. Once Rebel falls asleep, Mama puts her to bed, and I take a deep breath. There's nothing like a day with a kid running around to knock you off your feet.

"I'm going to pop out for a few hours," Mama says as she re-enters the room, now fully dressed.

"Okay, I don't intend on going anywhere, though I'll probably be asleep by the time you get back," I say and she leans down, kissing my forehead.

"Okay, well don't wait up for me." She winks and slinks out the door with a smile on her face. I wonder where she's off to. Not that she needs my permission or approval obviously, but I can't help but be curious.

Remy: I had the best day.
Thank you guys so much for yesterday. I hope you had a good day.

I smile down at my phone; she must have had some nectar. Remy doesn't do mushy unless she's a little tipsy.

Me: I'm glad you did, we had an awesome day, too. I've got some coven stuff and I wanna hang out with Rebel some more before she goes back to Erica's, but we'll hang out again soon?

Remy: Sounds good to me. I love you.

Me: I love you, too. Enjoy the rest of your night.

I drop my phone back beside me and snuggle into the sofa, smiling at the memories of the last two days. I flick the TV on and put on a cheesy Christmas movie, enjoying the warm fuzzy feeling, and finally feeling some hope for what's to come.

ELEVEN

I stretch out in my bed as I wake, groaning at the aches in my body.

Why the fuck do I ache so badly?

I pull myself to sit up and wince at the pain in my back. This isn't right. I grab my phone and look at the date as panic washes over me.

This can't be happening. Not again.

How the fuck did I lose two days?

I check my messages and call log. I've been responding to Remy and Colt with one word answers, telling them I was busy. What the actual fuck? Why can't I remember what happened?

I need to speak to Deacon. Throwing on the first clothes I find in my closet, I head out to the kitchen to find Mama making breakfast. I look around for Rebel, and my heart pangs. She must have gone back to Erica's while my brain was MIA.

"Morning, Mama." I try to keep my voice light and smile at her as I pour myself a mug of coffee, my hands shaking.

"Morning, sweet girl. Did you have fun with Deacon? I didn't see you for like two days, I was starting to worry." I let out a small sigh of relief. At least if I was with Deacon, I couldn't have gotten up to anything nefarious. At least I hope not.

"Yeah, it was good, sorry, my phone doesn't work in the Shadow Realm otherwise I would've gotten in touch. I have some errands to run today, do you need me to do anything for you?" I ask, half hoping she says no.

"I'm good, I went to the store on the way back from dropping off Rebel, so the house is stocked for a bit. The store is closed over the holidays, so I'm going to start prepping for the New Year celebrations with the coven. Are you still joining us?" she asks, watching me closely. I'm sure she knows something is off, but she also trusts me to tell her if I'm in too deep. I'm just thankful she's not prying too much, even if I do feel guilty as hell for betraying that trust a little right now.

"That's my plan, but I'll let you know if anything changes." I smile at her before taking a sip of my coffee.

The bitter taste helps me focus and clear my mind a little.

"Okay, well you know where I am if you need me." She shuffles over and kisses my cheek before heading back to her room, and I let out a small sigh of relief. I sink into the sofa and finish my coffee, waiting for her to get dressed and head out before I try to get in touch with Deacon. I drop a text to both Remy and Colt, apologizing for being so weird the last few days.

Colt: It's okay, I get it. You want to hang out tonight?

Me: Sure thing. Want me to bring pizza with me?

Colt: Sounds good. And maybe pack a bag, stay here for a few days while we both have a bit of time with nobody else around?

Me: I'm looking forward to it. Look at you being all domestic.

Colt: Oh baby, this isn't domestic, this is me looking forward to having you to myself to get reacquainted ;)

I can't help but laugh at him. That's one of the things I love about Colt. No matter what the fuck else is going on in our lives, he can always make me smile.

Me: Sounds good, we should probably talk, too.

Colt: *groans* Sure, but can we do that after I get my fill? (Angel emoji)

Me: And here I was thinking I'd be the one getting filled.

Colt: Oh yeah baby, that is definitely happening. I'm going to go grab a cold shower now. Drop me a text when you know what time you're heading over.

Me: I will do, enjoy your shower ;)

I laugh again, feeling a little lighter, even with the dark cloud of worry hanging over me. Mama reappears in a whirlwind, grabbing her keys before yelling out her goodbyes and leaving. Once I hear her car pull out of the drive, I head to my room and pull everything out from under my bed to contact Deacon from where I stashed it last time.

I go through the ritual and send him the note, telling him I need to talk and then wait on my bed for him to appear.

"We really have to stop meeting like this." I look up to see him standing in my doorway with a smirk on his face.

"You summoned me, my lady?"

"Idiot," I roll my eyes, waving him in until he sits on the bed opposite of me. "I don't suppose I was er, with you the last two days, was I?" I ask hopefully, but when he frowns, my heart sinks.

"No, why would you…" He trails off before the meaning of my question hits him. "You lost time again?"

"Yeah." I nod. "Mama said I told her I was with you, which is weird enough on its own, but I figured talking to you was the best place to start. My entire body fucking aches, and I have absolutely zero memory a-fucking-gain about what the hell I was up to. Did you get a chance to speak to Morgan yet?"

"I didn't, sorry. It's been more than a little manic, plus she was here with the Horsemen for the day after Christmas with Remy. I'll try to grab her as soon as I get back." He reaches out to take my hand, and a tingle runs up my arm. I manage to keep my reaction locked down, and when he smiles at me, I pull my hand back, feeling like I'm betraying Colt by even being in here with him.

When did my life get so goddamn complicated?

"You can come back with me if you like? I can keep you safe in the Shadow Realm. And with whatever is going on, it might not be able to reach you there," he offers, looking hopeful, but I shake my head.

"I can't just run away from this, whatever it is. Plus, I'm

needed here. I can't just abandon my mama and my coven at the first sign of trouble," I say, not wanting to mention Colt because things feel super weird right now. But there is a part of me that wants to go with him and maybe explore the excruciatingly sweet tension boiling between us. Fuck me, I'm a selfish bitch. I literally just made up with Colt, and I'm sitting here, practically panting over a guy who has done unspeakable things to me. But I can't deny that the thought he wants me too is something that I haven't thought about.

I shake my head, reaffirming my statement, because even if I want to run away, I can't. And I wouldn't without Colt either… But he'd never run away. He's not that kind of guy.

"I can maybe try to figure some stuff out back in the Realm so I can be here for you. You need someone who knows about all of this with you, making sure that nothing else happens," he says, frowning at me. "I'm worried about you, about what you might be doing, and what could happen to you during these fugue states."

"I'll talk to Colt," I tell him, letting out a deep sigh. "He'll keep an eye on me."

Deacon nods, but pulls away from me. "At least he's good for something," he mutters.

"Hey—" I start, and he waves me off.

"Sorry, can't help myself sometimes. I'm still a Demon,

and he has what I want. I haven't made a secret of that, and I won't ever hide it. I never said I was a good guy." He looks at me so intensely, it's like my skin is on fire. I rub my arms against the tingles, but they don't disappear

"You're not a bad guy just because you're a Demon. You know that, right?" I ask him with a fierce sort of grit in my tone, and he laughs.

"You know better than most that I'm not a good guy, Fallon," he says with a cold laugh and stands. "I'm going to head back if you don't need anything else?"

I frown at his sudden change from amenable to cold. My frown deepens at the realization of how much I don't like that sudden change either. My heart sinks because I don't want to lose him, but again, that makes me the most selfish bitch in the world. Especially since I keep telling him that I don't want him like that. I bite my lip to keep from telling him exactly the opposite of that and take a deep breath.

"No, but thank you, Deacon. I really do appreciate your help," I say, and he nods stiffly before disappearing before my eyes.

Well shit.

This last week has been so much fun. I've stayed at Colt's,

and it's like a little look into what life could be like if we got our shit together properly. Since we haven't had fires to put out, we've made the most of it. We've slept in, taken portals to go climb mountains, like when we went to Mount Fuji and watched the beautiful sunset. We went sightseeing in Tokyo, with Colt showing me some of his favorite places from when he lived there last year.

Today, we're going to the beach. It doesn't sound so fancy, but the thought of the white sands and blue seas of Australia, especially since it's their height of summer, appeals to me more than I'm willing to admit. I'm so freaking excited. Plus, Colt knows people there, of course, so he wants to go out on their boat and just have some fun like we haven't had in way too long.

"Are you ready?" Colt asks as he bounces into the kitchen where I've just finished packing a picnic basket. Apparently he knows about a little bay that's nice and private, so we can be as sappy and coupley as we want until we meet up with his friends.

He takes in the white bikini against my golden skin and I smile. "I am."

"Maybe we could just stay home," he growls as he wraps his arms around my waist, nuzzling my neck as I sigh.

"I don't think so, mister. I want some vitamin D."

"I'll give you some vitamin D," he whispers in my ear

and I burst out laughing.

"You are officially the worst."

He grins, letting go of me, "Yeah, but you like me this way. But if you're sure you can't be persuaded…" he trails off, his eyes sparkling as he sweeps his gaze over my entire body, intensely enough that I get goosebumps.

"I'm sure. Anyway, this is you we're talking about; I'm sure you'll find a way to improvise." I wink at him, and he bites down on his fist.

"Hell yes, baby. Let's get this show on the road. I can't wait to find somewhere new to corrupt you." I can't help but laugh at him again. I've laughed more this week than I remember laughing the last six months. It's so fucking refreshing, so I'm not going to overthink it. I'm just going to enjoy it because who knows how long this might last.

I grab my bag as Colt picks up the basket, and I open a portal for us, the grin on my face almost making my cheeks hurt. We step through the portal hand in hand and come out straight onto the sand. Fuck me, it is hot. But I miss hot, so I'm not going to complain. I'm just glad I have flip-flops on so I don't burn my feet on the blazing sand. I jump onto Colt's back as he finds his feet and squeal as he runs across the sand, not even a little fazed by my weight on him.

He runs with me on his back until we're so far down the beach all I can see are rocks and more beach. He drops the basket onto the sand and lets go of me so I can jump down. This place really is like a little piece of heaven.

"It's so beautiful here," I murmur, squinting as I look out over the vastness of the blue ocean.

"It really is. I knew you'd love it," Colt says as he drops down onto the blanket I packed and pulls me down to lie beside him.

"How did you find this place?"

"Well, before Creek went through his awakening, I spent a lot of time traveling alone—which is how I met so many people on this side of the world. I used to come here when the world got too loud. It was like my safe space. A place where no one knew to find me." He tucks me under his arm and kisses the top of my head, my heart swelling at his declaration. He brought me to his spot. It's his spot to escape the world, and he wanted me here with him.

We lie in the sunshine, talking about nothing, and take a dip in the cool water before eating the picnic I put together. We've had such a peaceful day so far, and I know that's going to change when his phone starts ringing. My heart sinks because his phone ringing usually means that something went horrifically wrong back home and we need to go back. I'm not ready to leave here yet. Goddess, I sound like a whiny bitch, but dammit, I've been enjoying our little bubble. I'm positive this is the calm before the storm, so I want to enjoy the fuck out of it.

Colt smiles when he looks at the screen and my fear

lifts a little.

"What's up, man?" He laughs as he answers the phone, grinning down at me as I lie enjoying the late afternoon sun. "Yeah, sure thing, let me get my girl, and we'll head down. You still docked?"

I guess this is the boat thing he mentioned. I start brushing off the sand now that I've dried off and pack up while he finishes up his call.

"You want to get out on the water, baby?" he asks, and I nod before he captures my lips, kissing me until I can't breathe. I gasp as he pulls back, touching my kiss-swollen lips. He smirks down at me, but the joy on his face is so infectious. I could literally lose myself in him and never really be mad about it.

"Let's get out of here then," he says, sweeping me up in his arms. I can't do anything but laugh. He puts me back down, though, and encourages me to jump up on his back again, so I finish packing up the basket and do. He crosses the sand in minutes, and soon enough we're at a much more populated part of the beach. I follow him as he hails a cab, tucking into his side as we drive to the dock his friends are waiting for us at.

We pull up to the harbor, and Colt exits the cab, holding out his hand for me. I take it and he pulls me from the car, paying the driver before he speeds off. The grin on my face is immovable. We head through the docks until Colt pulls me onto a boat slip with what can only be described as a small yacht. It's fucking beautiful. All long lines and gleaming white. I never realized I was a boat person, but apparently I am.

"Where are the others?" I ask as he helps me on board and starts untying the ropes.

"Oh, didn't I mention? This is my boat; the guys just prepped her for us. Today is all about us, baby. You don't think I'd want to share you, especially when you look good enough to eat?" My heart clenches at his revelation and the happiness I didn't think could expand does.

"I didn't know you could sail, let alone had a boat." I gasp as he takes me in his arms, kissing me quickly before leading me onto the deck where the navigation system is. He takes a hold of the wheel and starts the engine, grinning as he maneuvers the boat away from the slip.

"There's a lot you don't know about me, baby, so it's a good thing we have a whole lifetime to work it out."

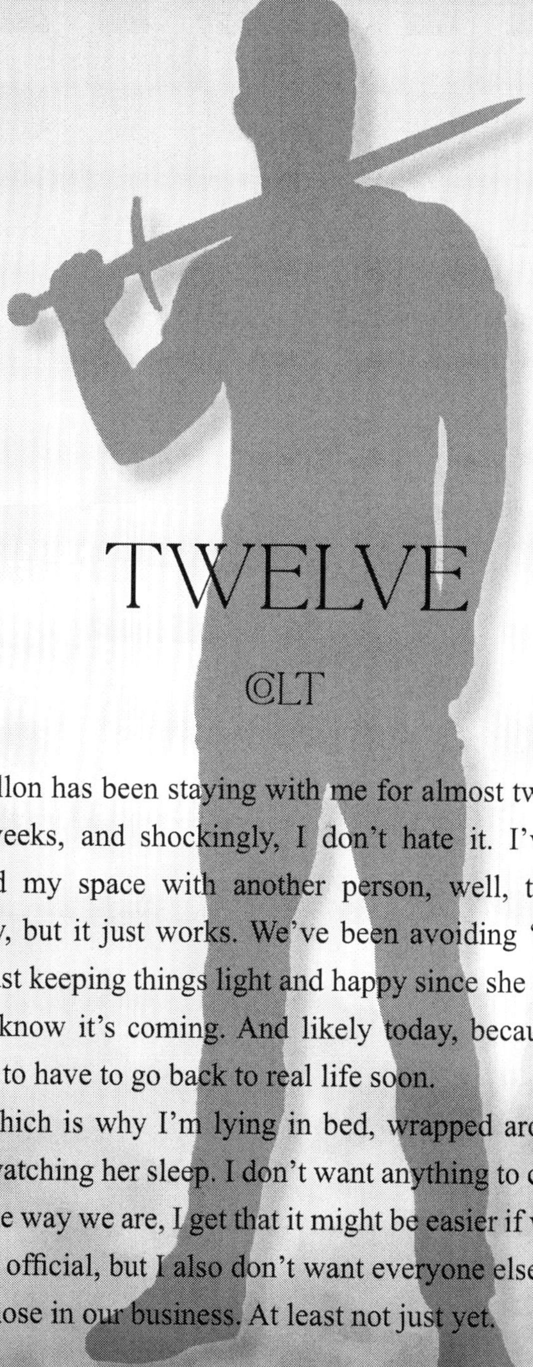

TWELVE

COLT

Fallon has been staying with me for almost two whole weeks, and shockingly, I don't hate it. I've never shared my space with another person, well, that isn't family, but it just works. We've been avoiding 'the talk' and just keeping things light and happy since she got here, but I know it's coming. And likely today, because she's going to have to go back to real life soon.

Which is why I'm lying in bed, wrapped around my girl, watching her sleep. I don't want anything to change. I like the way we are, I get that it might be easier if we made things official, but I also don't want everyone else to have their nose in our business. At least not just yet.

I pull her closer when she whimpers in her sleep. She was having nightmares again last night, but as soon as she tucked into my side, they seemed to disappear. I'm doing everything I can not to wake her with my extremely hard dick, but she just keeps rubbing up against me, and no matter what I do, it won't go down.

I don't know what it is about this girl, but I'm sunk. Hook and line. Totally whipped. I literally can't get enough of her, and apparently, neither can my dick.

She moans as she rolls over, throwing her leg over me, and my cock jumps at the sound as she gets comfy on my chest. I look down at her just as her eyes flutter open, still half asleep. Goddamn, she looks beautiful when she's carefree like this.

"Hi," she murmurs and smiles up at me.

"Hi." I grin down at her, and groan as she runs her nails down my chest, not stopping till she reaches the v of muscles that lead to my dick. Leaning down, I capture her lips with my own, taking my time with her, drawing out the kiss until she's panting and putty in my hands. "I could definitely get used to that sort of good morning."

"Oh, you haven't seen anything yet." She laughs throatily and moves so that she's straddling me. Fuck me, I could die a happy man right here, right now. She shimmies down until she's between my legs and wraps her hand around my cock before taking it into her mouth.

"Fuckkkkk." I ball my hands in the sheets beside me as she looks up at me and let her take control for a change.

Although, judging by the way she's toying with my dick, I may actually die from the pleasure of it all. At the very least, my molars will no longer exist because I'll have ground them to nothingness trying my hardest not to come right down her throat before she has time to swallow me whole.

I'm not exactly a small guy, my cock is not an easy one to deep throat, but Fallon seems determined. Who am I to try to stop her?

When she wraps her delicate fingers around the base of my cock, I can feel as her warm little tongue licks up and down my shaft, running over the metal bars of my piercing before circling my tip and dipping into my slit. It's slow and torturous, like she's trying to test my patience.

Silly girl, she knows I have none.

"Fallon," I growl like a man possessed, "you're playing with fire."

And then she growls against my skin, and I almost grab her by the back of the neck and fuck her mouth like a man on a mission.

I don't, of course, because I have fucking manners and shit. At least sometimes. But her teasing my cock is testing that theory. I mean, are manners even necessary when your dick is kissing the back of the throat, of the sexiest woman on the planet? I think fucking not.

"Careful, baby, I'm two seconds away from fucking your throat like a caveman."

She moans at my warning, the vibrations travelling from the root of my cock all the way up to the tips of my hair. I growl at the mischievous glint in her eyes, and just when I'm about to say fuck it, she does what every man loves most in this world. She turns her body around, my cock being sucked like a lollipop, and presents me with her pussy, all glinting with her juices, just begging to be devoured.

Alright, I can definitely get on board with this. She sits on my face and when her scent hits my nostrils, I turn into a fucking Neanderthal. My fingers latch onto her ass cheeks, pulling her pussy down onto my face so I can eat every single inch of her with abandon. Her taste is my salvation. She's fucking delicious, and when her sweet honey with a dash of tangy taste hits my tongue, I'm no longer in control of my actions. Not to mention she's sucking my dick like a Hoover, and I'm not sure how long I can last.

I circle her clit just as her tongue laps around the head of my cock, and I can't help the way my hips buck in response. My fingers dig so deeply into the flesh of her ass that I'm almost afraid I might leave a mark.

Well, afraid isn't really the right word.

Fucking proud is more like it. The thought of marking

her turns me the fuck on.

No matter what lies and excuses I tell myself, Fallon is mine. Now and forever. I just need to stop being a pussy and tell her without mincing my words.

I love this woman. And it has nothing to do with the fact that she's sucking my cock, practically swallowing the tip down her throat and moaning around it like she's tasting the finest chocolate on the planet.

It's way more than that.

What she's doing to me, though, is driving me fucking insane. So, I do what any man in my position would do. I reach up under her and pinch her nipple just as I'm biting down on her clit, and it's like I opened up the faucet to her orgasm. I'm lapping up her juices like they're fucking nectar, while the caveman inside of me beats his chest for getting her off and controlling myself, but Fallon isn't having it.

As she slides her mouth off my dick, she's like a fucking pro, making my balls tighten with the telltale feeling of an impending climax.

Fuck, I'm not going to be able to hold it off much longer.

Just as she gets to the head of my cock, she slides the tip of her tongue inside my slit and that's when I fucking lose my goddamn mind.

With my hands on her waist, I pick her up and throw

her down on the other side of the bed, then I'm on her in a heartbeat.

I'm a beast, a needy, horny, beast that can only be sated by her.

"Spread open, fingers around the headboard."

My entire being is centered on one thing, and one thing only.

Fucking the woman of my dreams. The perfect, most incredible being I've ever known.

My dick agrees wholeheartedly.

The thing is, Fallon has brought me to within an inch of my self-control, and if I don't fuck her like an animal, I may very well combust.

By the little naughty smile on her lips, she knows exactly what she's in for.

Spreading her legs for me as far apart as she can, she grabs onto the headboard and offers me her pussy like a silver platter of debauchery.

And I take it like the starved man I am.

Placing one hand on her hip and another around her delicate throat, I slam into her without another thought.

And then I'm home. Warm and wet, her walls hug me like a custom-made glove, and it calms the demons inside me. Her pussy tames me, and that's a scary as fuck thought.

Watching my hand around her throat as her eyes glaze over with unmasked lust, makes me piston my cock inside her at a bruising pace. I know I'm not hurting her because, luckily,my instincts when it comes to her are on point. My body knows exactly where the line between pleasure and pain is drawn for her. It knows where to stop to keep the lust floating without falling into the dark abyss of abuse.

Every muscle in my body is tight; my ass, my legs, and my abs are getting the best work out of my fucking life. My jaw tics with the need to keep my balls from surrendering to the pleasure of an orgasm. I won't give until Fallon comes on my dick one more time.

And I keep my promise.

I change the angle, just slightly, making sure my groin is perfectly aligned with her clit and bend my torso toward her until my mouth is just inches from her lips.

"Every. Fucking. Time." I grind the words out, my control barely holding.

I can see the question in her eyes, but I'm not sure I can say any more. I need to come, I need to let go between her lips.

"When I'm inside you..." I take a deep breath and punctuate my words with a deep, meaningful thrust. "Everything feels right."

I watch as a tear falls from the corner of her right eye and it does something to me. The protector swells with pride and the caveman in me roars as I continue fucking her like it's what I was made to do.

"Every fucking time I'm inside you, I feel like I'm home."

Those are the words that make her lose all her control and I know.

I know she's the one for me.

With my head thrown back and my body as taut as a tightrope, I let everything go. I come so deep inside her, I know for a fact I've marked her for eternity. Her cries as I release her throat fuel my own orgasm, and together we ride the train of bliss.

I fall down onto the bed beside her, panting, my body slick with sweat, and she takes my hand. "Don't think your distraction tactics are going to work on me, mister," she pants. I roll onto my side and grin at her.

"What do you mean?" I wag my eyebrows at her with about the last of my energy, and she laughs, pushing me onto my back and curling up into my side. Every single thing about this just feels right.

"You know what."

"I know I do. I get why you want to talk about it, I do. I just…" I pause, and she looks up at me, those amber eyes of hers like a window to her soul.

"I know. Defining whatever this is seems like a big step. I just want to do this for us, not for everyone else. I'm even good with keeping this between just us for now, but, Colt. I need you to know how I feel about you, even if no one else knows." She bites her lips, looking up at me expectantly. My heart swells, because I know how much of a big deal her keeping shit from my sister and her mom is. I don't want to have to do that, but I also know that if we tell everyone else, they're going to try to butt in. I'm sure they suspect already, it's hard not to. It's not like I was subtle when she was taken.

"I love you, Fal. That's all I need to know. If you want to tell people, we will. If you don't, we won't. But you're it for me. I've known it for a while; I just had my head up my ass for a bit. I don't want to hold back anymore."

"I love you too, Colt." My heart soars, and I capture her lips with mine. "We can work out the rest later. But I've never been happier than I am here right now." A shadow clouds her eyes, and I can't help but frown.

"What aren't you telling me?" I ask, not wanting to ruin the bliss of the moment, but there can't be secrets between us.

"I've been seeing Deacon… Not like seeing him, seeing him. We're just friends, but I feel like I need to tell you." I frown harder at her words. I hate that fucking asshole for what he did to her. I'd happily tear his head from his body, but if she wants him in her life… Well, I'm just going to have to get on board with that.

"Okay, well now I know. I'm not going to stop you from having people in your life, Fallon. I'm not that guy, but thank you for telling me." I kiss her again, and she relaxes against me. I pull away and lean back on the pillow, a thousand things running through my mind. I get lost until her breathing evens out, and I realize she's asleep again.

I might not like her decision to be friends with Deacon, but Remy is right. You do anything you can for the people you love. Especially if it makes them happy.

Fallon finally went home today, but now the house feels empty without her. It's weird as fuck, but it is what it is. She was here for nearly two weeks, other than spending New Year's with her coven. It's been two weeks of no craziness, despite having all factions out hunting for traitors. We had no attacks, nothing blew up, no one was kidnapped. Two weeks of pure fucking bliss.

But tonight, there's a coven meeting, which means I lose my girl for the day, and now I just feel a little lost. I mean… There's a ton of stuff I could be doing, just not anything I want to be doing. Which also means I should probably get on with the bullshit so I'm ready for when my girl is free again and we can have some more bliss.

I'm just glad we're on the same page about everything. It's like a weight off of my shoulders, knowing she feels the same way I do. While I'm not exactly overjoyed about her confession about Deacon, I know that it's just me and her. Hopefully for a long fucking time.

I tidy up the mess we left in the kitchen after our fun while cooking this morning. Who would've thought pancakes with cream and syrup could be so much fun? I chuckle to myself just thinking about it when my phone rings.

I see Remy's name on the screen and groan. There goes my chill day. "What's up, little bit?"

"We got a call… Roman's guys found the Lycan traitors. We have some people locked up here," she tells me, and I frown.

"Then why don't you sound happier?" I ask.

"Because I need you to gather the Elders. I finally heard back from Michael." I gulp at her words. Fuck, shit, and fuck again.

"It's official then?" I ask, my heart breaking for our entire faction.

"Yeah, it's official. So we need to let everyone know. How long do you think it will take to gather everyone?"

"Give me twenty-four hours? We can address them all tomorrow at the council chambers." I pinch the bridge of my nose, a migraine already forming just at the thought of it all.

"Yeah okay. I'm really sorry, Colt," she sniffs, and I let out a sigh.

"It's not your fault, little bit, don't sweat it. Life happens," I tell her, knowing I have shit in place in case this was the outcome, but fucking shit. "We'll face it together."

"Thank you, Colt. I love you."

"I love you too, Rem. I'll let you know a time once I've spoken to the others, okay?"

"Yeah sure, I'll talk to you later."

I hang up the phone and launch it across the room.

Fucking fuck.

Retrieving my phone, I dial Nate's number. Since he's acting as my number two, he should probably have some information. He doesn't answer, so I open the group text I started between all of the Elders not long ago.

Me: Meeting tomorrow at Council Chambers. Attendance is mandatory. Excuses won't be accepted. This shit is important.

I hit send and idly wonder exactly how I ended up in charge of the fucking council, but I guess some traditions stick. My grandfather and father were always the unofficial leaders, and so the mantle passed to me. I mean, realistically I know the seat was Remy's and she declined it, but it's not like we could both turn it down.

My phone buzzes as people let me know they'll be there. Once I hear back from all of the Elders, I shoot off another text. This time to Elijah and the boys, and Nate and Maddie, because I feel like I need to tell them first. I know Remy wants to be the one to tell the Elders, but these are my people, my family. We've been through a fuck ton of shit together, so I know I need to tell them myself.

Now I just need to find the words.

My phone buzzes again as everyone lets me know they're on the way to the house, so I grab a bottle of whiskey, and pour myself three fingers, ready to tell my friends and family the worst news I think I've ever had to deliver.

It doesn't take long for Nate and Maddie to arrive, and they thankfully don't ask any questions when they see me. Maddie just hugs me while Nate pours them both a glass, topping mine off, before we sit at the dining table while we wait for the others.

They arrive a few minutes later, and reading the room, Elijah grabs a bottle of beer for each of them. They join us around the table, but I still don't have the words.

"Okay," I finally start, my voice croaking. I clear my throat and take a swig of the whiskey, relishing the burn while I try to find the words to say. "So, I've known this was a possibility for a while, but Remy wanted to confirm it before we told everyone. I have a meeting with the Elders tomorrow, but I wanted you guys to hear it from me first. I feel like you deserve that more than anything."

"Whatever it is, sweetheart, you can tell us. We can see how hard this is for you," Maddie offers, patting my hand.

So I tell them, the looks on their faces breaking me as I keep speaking, and when I finish there's nothing but silence.

I broke my family, and there's nothing I can do to fix it.

I head down to the chambers first, refusing to tell anyone what's going on. Explaining the situation to those closest to me yesterday was hard enough on its own. I don't think I can say the words again. I find Remy pacing in the chambers, looking pale and like she's going to vomit.

I'm surprised the guys aren't here with her; she rarely goes anywhere without at least one of them. She doesn't see me, as lost in thought as she is, so I don't disturb her. If she feels anything like how I did yesterday, then I'd rather not fuck with her thought process. I head back up to the top and when I open the door, all conversation stops as everyone turns to look at me.

"You all might as well come down and get comfortable. But keep your shit to yourselves until we're finished talking," I demand, eyeing each and every person there. I know we're about to drop a fucking nuke on their lives, but I'm not going to let them beat on Remy because of it. She's not to blame here. The blame for all of this could quite easily be laid at Archer's feet along with every fucking thing else.

I lead them down the stairs, and they're dead quiet, not a whisper between them before I open the door and let them file in. Remy works her way through a round of hellos as everyone starts to sit around the boardroom style table she's set up down here. I move closer to where she's standing and take a seat nearby, proximity being the only support I can offer her.

She paces while everyone finishes getting seated, and the room goes quiet, stopping her in her tracks as everyone focuses on her.

"Okay," she starts, letting out a deep breath. "Thank you all for rushing here to meet with me, I know that it was, quite literally, the middle of the night where some of you were, but this is something we need to discuss face to face."

She pauses again, and I can see the indecision all over her. She runs a hand down her face before turning and looking to the room again.

"The Hunter's curse is broken." The room is silent, with people looking at her in confusion. I can't help the devastation that floods me, even though I already knew, it doesn't make this any easier. Last night was proof enough of that. It takes her a minute as she registers that what she's said isn't really hitting home with the people around us. As if it could be that easy.

"Okay, let me start at the beginning," she says with a sigh, and then explains the real history of the Hunters. How humans were only meant to be granted temporary Angelic gifts, to assist in the War of the Fallen. About the war from her own memories from her life as Amantara, and how without the curse, the war would have been lost.

"And then, I was dying, so Leviathan, in his grief, transferred my essence into a human form, essentially making me a Hunter. Except what he didn't know at the time was that in doing so, it would upset the balance of power. Of nature itself. And so, the Hunters, any families who had been gifted previously, became cursed to reincarnate each life. To be stuck in the cycles they were in, and for the curse to pass through the generations. It's why there are different time periods between lives because the loop has to reset. But someone's great-great-grandmother, is also their great-great-granddaughter… I swear that made more sense in my head. But essentially, the curse is why the Angels gave us the option of the true death. Because they found a loophole, should anyone want it." She shakes out her hands and takes another deep breath, before starting up again. I eye each person in the room, daring them to try to interrupt her.

"The curse is the reason for the cycles we've all been

living, and the link was cursed to my life. Except… I died, and I became immortal again. We weren't sure whether or not the curse would be broken because I was essentially still alive. We've looked into it extensively with Michael, and we've confirmed that the curse is broken. The Hunter cycles will no longer continue. We do believe, however, that as children have been born with the gifted Angelic powers, that the Hunter lines will continue in this manner."

It's as if the whole room held its breath, and then, in the blink of an eye, chaos erupts. Questions are shouted, some people are up and moving toward her, though others are still seated, dazed by the information she's given them.

I get it. All of it. The anger, the confusion, the sadness. Their lives have just been irrevocably changed, as has mine, though I've had the chance to process a little. But that still doesn't give them the right to attack her.

"Everyone shut the fuck up!" I yell across the room, and it's like a switch is flipped. Suddenly, there's silence. "I get that this is a lot to process, but if you have questions, you're not going to get answers by shouting over each other, so sit the fuck down and let's talk this out like civilized fucking people."

I sit down once everyone else has pulled themselves back together. I knew this would cause pandemonium, and I completely understand. This doesn't just affect them. They still have to pass this on to the people they represent.

That isn't something I'd wish on anyone. Just telling the guys last night was enough to make me want to vomit, we still have to tell everyone else.

I sit and wait with Remy while the others talk amongst themselves, but it's Nasari who turns to her first. "Is there any way to reverse it? Can the curse be reinstated?"

"Honestly, I have no idea, but it is definitely something we can find out before you tell anyone outside of the council. I understand that sitting on information like this is awful, but I think it would be better for me to get answers to any and all questions from you guys before we tell anyone else," she explains, and I can't help the little seed of hope that plants itself in my heart.

There is a murmuring of agreement around the table, and I feel a little calmer. At least panic isn't going to spread across the entire faction just yet, but I make a note to remind Remy to check with Michael as soon as we get out of here.

"Who else has questions?" she asks, and a dozen hands rise into the air. I groan internally, thinking back to yesterday morning when I thought of how happy this week was going to be. This is going to be a long meeting.

THIRTEEN

FALLON

It's been a while since I last saw Colt, but I know he's dealing with the fallout of the Hunter's curse being broken. My heart breaks for him. I wish I'd known what was going on, that I could've been there for him. It's causing repercussions throughout all of the factions. The Witches Council have been up in arms about it, some trying to find a way to break other curses, others trying to find out if there's a way to reinstate it. There are too many links with Hunter lines, and witches benefiting from those relationships for people not to try something.

I haven't seen much of Remy, either, and, I just hope she doesn't hold it against me. It's not that I've meant to be distant, but between spending time with Colt, losing time left and right, and getting no answers about why, I've been a little preoccupied. I lost another two days, on two separate occasions, since the Hunter shit has been going on. To say I'm terrified is an understatement, but Deacon said he's working on answers. I just have to trust that he'll find them before I lose myself completely to the darkness.

I pull my phone from my pocket and shoot a text off to Colt.

Me: How you doing today?

Colt: I'm good, just fucking exhausted. Creek's hanging here today. There's shit going down at the manor, so I think we're going to get pulled in soon.

Me: Thanks for the heads up. Let me know if you need anything.

I sigh as I drop my phone down onto the counter. The shop has been a ghost town today, and I'm losing my mind a little. I grab my tarot deck and decide to see if the ancestors want to give me any insight as to what the fuck is going on with me at the minute. I've been trying not to freak out about it all, trying to just stuff it down and keep my calm until we get some answers, but there's so much going on around me at the moment that everyone's just trying to keep their head above water.

So the ancestors it is.

I do a five-card spread, holding onto the question of where am I losing time, and flip the cards. They don't make any sense. It's almost as if someone is messing with my magic, or at least playing with the cards. I swear if there really is a ghost in here fucking with me right now, I'm going to banish that fucker from this plane.

I let out a huff and put the cards away, trying not to be as unreasonably angry as I feel right now. I should be happy. Colt told me he loved me. We're in such a good place at the moment, and I never thought we'd be here. But with every fucking thing else that's going on around us, our bubble was burst and reality is winning out.

I fucking hate it.

When we find out who is behind all of this, I want to watch them bleed out slowly. For putting my friend through this, for putting me through this… For everyone we've lost and the ones I'm sure we're still likely to lose. Mama's vision of war might have changed, but I have no doubt there is still more blood to be spilled.

I regret not staying in better touch with Remy; I feel very out of the loop with everything that's going on, which just makes me feel selfish. I'm as much a part of this as everyone else, but I've been slacking, trying to deal with my own shit. Guilt washes over me. Sure I've been dealing with stuff, but hasn't everyone? I really need to get my shit together.

The bell above the door chimes, and I paint a smile on my face for the humans giggling as they walk in, heading straight for the tonics and potions aisles. Goddess help me get through this day.

I have a final moment in my pity party for one and then vow to myself that from tomorrow on, I'm going to stop putting my own shit first and help out more. In whatever way is needed.

I groan as I roll over in bed. I slept in today because yesterday was just fucking exhausting, but my phone buzzing finally wakes me up. Relief floods me as it does every morning when I wake and it's the day I expect it to be.

I look down at my phone and see Remy's name, and I perk up. I was going to reach out to her today, so it's like she read my mind.

Remy: We need your help, like ASAP.

Me: I'll be over in a few,

just need to throw some clothes on.

No questions asked. I swore to myself I was going to pull my head out of my ass, and that's exactly what I'm going to do. I jump from bed and throw on some clothes, not giving a shit about what I look like, because they won't care. I dress as practically as I can because fuck knows why they need me.

"Mama, I'm going to the manor. Remy needs my help. I'll keep you up to date," I holler down the hall, and Mama pops her head out of her room.

"Okay, sweetheart. Let me know if you need me."

"Will do." I step out into the back yard and open a portal to the manor without another thought. My boots crunch on the gravel in the drive once I step through, and I let myself in with a quick knock. Remy finds me easily.

"Thank you for coming so quickly. The last few days have been fucking insane," she says as she hugs me quickly.

"Of course, what do you need?"

"So, I don't know how in the loop you are, but Emmett, one of Roman's wolves, captured a traitor. We've had him in the basement for a while trying to get some information from him. Finally, last night, we got what we needed. Laurent, the Lycan in the basement, told us that he wasn't the only Lycan working against us. Roman sent word to Theron, but we think that Aryna and the other Lycans he told us about will have already scattered and gone to ground."

"Wow, I really have been out of the loop," I say as I follow her through the hall to the library.

"That's only the start of it. So Michael had a theory about who could be pulling the strings with everything, since we know that Archer wasn't a grand mastermind… Anyway, he thought it could be an Angel who despises my very existence... and likely has since my life as Amantara..." She pauses as we sit down, and I simply try to follow it all, letting it sink in. "So when Laurent was spilling his guts, telling us exactly who has been working against us, he mentioned a name. Amelia, which is the name of the Angel that Michael suspected would have enough power to be behind all of this and want me dead."

"Holy shit, Remy… Since you were Amantara? That's a long fucking time to hold a grudge."

"Yeah, but apparently that hate ran deep. Anyway, what we need is for you to help us try to locate her. She disappeared after the War of the Fallen and hasn't been seen or heard of since. I know it's a big ask, but do you think you can help us find her?" she asks, and I bite my lip. This sounds like it will be hard. If she has enough power that she's stayed cloaked for this long, it won't be a walk in the park.

"I'll do my best. Do you have something of hers?" she nods in response.

"Michael slipped me this," she says, handing me a dagger. "It was hers, and it's all we have. I'm hoping it's enough. She has a Witch with her, too. We think that's who has been hiding her."

"If she's been hidden this long, I'm not sure my power will be enough to find her, but I'll try. Though it might be easier to track the Witch."

"If you need extra power, Levi and I can help with that," she offers, and I nod. I've seen those two power share, and it's fucking epic.

"That might just work. If you go get him, I'll get set up." I roll out the map Remy had waiting on the table, pinning down each corner as she disappears from the room. I have no idea where the others are—I didn't see or hear anyone when I got here—but I guess with all of this going on, everyone has enough to be doing.

It only takes a few minutes for me to fashion the dagger in such a way that I can use it to scry, and then Remy and Levi enter the room. "Hopefully this works," Levi grunts. "Creek and Roman aren't getting any more from the Lycan in the basement."

I'm sure he doesn't mean to be so fucking terrifying when he looks at me like the whole world is balanced on my shoulders, but I know he'll kill anything and anyone that stands between him and his mission.

"Okay, if you guys can channel your power and each

place a hand on my shoulder, I should be able to use the extra power to try and get through any protections this Angel has in place."

"Will she know we've broken through her spells?" Levi asks, and I shake my head.

"No, I'm too careful for that. It's not about smashing through, it's about peeling back layers. I'll put them back nice and quick so she has no idea we were even looking for her," I reassure him, and he nods sharply.

Okay, I guess we're doing this. I sit down by the map again, and they move behind me as I lift the dagger.

"*Atemis, Bondye fanm chache youn nan moun ki ap eseye kache pou nou. Moutre m chemen pou li. Devwale l 'ban mwen pou m' ka swiv wout la nan sò.*" The words slip from my tongue without thought, and their power smacks into me with such force it leaves me breathless. It takes me a moment to rein it in, but once I do, I use the dagger to slice my hand so the blood can lead us to her. I repeat the words of the trace until my blood pools together in the spot where the Angel has been found.

"We've got her," I whisper, unable to speak fully until they pull their power from me. Dizziness washes over me as they pull back, and Levi goes into full general mode.

"Serafina and Nevin will come with me, we'll scout the location tonight. Everyone else needs to prepare to go hunting. As soon as we're sure she's there and what reinforcements she has, we hunt." He strides from the room leaving me with Remy.

"He is intense as shit, girl." I laugh, and she nods.

"He is, but it's hot as fuck." I laugh harder at her as she drops into the seat beside me. "You should probably stay here until this all kicks off."

"Thanks, but no," I say, shaking my head. "I'll be here if we're needed, but with all of this going on, I don't want to leave Mama on her own if I don't have to."

"I get that…" She trails off with a distant look in her eye before shaking herself and turning her attention back to me. "And thank you again for coming so quickly."

"Always," I tell her, squeezing her hand. I hate that I've been a shitty friend lately. Before now, she'd never have even questioned if I'd show. "I'm going to head home, but keep me in the loop, okay?"

"Okay." She smiles up at me as I stand. Leaving doesn't feel like the right thing to do, but neither does staying.

Why can't anything be simple anymore?

I sigh as I drop down onto the couch, and turn the TV on for background noise. After I got back earlier, Kain and Luc dropped by and I created a portal for them to take Nonnie back to France while this shit goes down. They said something about a hunt after, but I wasn't paying too much attention. My main worry is about what might happen when this all comes to a head.

Sitting and doing nothing when so much is going on elsewhere doesn't feel right to me. I hate thinking about everyone else out there doing stuff with me just sitting here being useless.

I grab my crystals from the fireplace and center myself, drawing on the power in them. Even though Remi and Levi lent me their power for the search earlier, I'm still wiped out, and I don't want to be tapped out if I'm needed. I don't usually like drawing on the crystals, but earth magic is our higher power.

I lose myself in the power draw, the radiant light glowing around me as I take the magic in and feel more connected to the light and the earth than I have in a long time. I have no idea how much time passes, but I'm jolted out by my phone buzzing on the table. I frown when I see Creek's name on the screen. He literally never calls me with good news.

"Hello?" I say, hoping to the Goddess that the world isn't fucking ending.

"Fallon, Remy's been shot. She's not healing. We need you, now!"

"Where are you?" I ask as I scramble up from the floor.

"The manor." I jolt at the fear in his voice.

"I'll be there in thirty seconds," I say before the line goes dead. Thank fuck I still have my boots on. I don't hesitate before opening the portal in the middle of the living room, hoping to fuck nothing comes through with me, and step through to the back yard of the manor where all fucking hell is breaking loose. I find Creek and Roman bent over her, but the others are nowhere in sight.

"Just hold on, Remy. What the fuck did he shoot her with?" Creek asks Roman as I move toward them.

"Smells like salted iron. It's almost lethal to Demons, definitely fatal if you get them with enough of it. It must be because of her rebirth in the Shadow Realm. There's no other explanation."

"None of this makes any fucking sense," Roman curses violently as I reach them, drawing on my power.

"Out of the way," I say calmly, as my power glows softly, pulsing around me. Thank fuck I drained those crystals.

"Can you heal her?" Creek asks, his panic hurting my heart.

"I'm going to try, but I need you all to get out of the way." I give him my softest, most reassuring smile before kneeling down to Remy as they move back.

"Fal..." she croaks, and my heart breaks.

"Oh, Remy," I sigh "Look at the mess you got yourself into now."

"This is what I get for trying to exercise," she laughs, blood sputtering from her mouth as she speaks.

"No more talking," I tell her, and she nods as I place my hands on her wound. I push as much magic as I can into the wound; and I know this must be hurting like fuck, but I'm not going to let her die. I didn't even think it was possible for her to really die anymore, not after everything she's survived. I feel tears threatening to take over, but I harden myself and push more of the healing power into her, feeling as the bullet retracts from her and the wound starts to close as I work the bullet free.

She passes out for a minute, but I pluck the bullet from the wound and toss it on the ground before continuing.

"Is she going to be okay?" Roman growls.

"She will," I tell them, letting out a sigh of relief. I honestly wasn't sure if my power would even work on an Angel.

Roman leans over Remy's form lying on the grass—she's still out of it, but he picks her up carefully from the ground. Creek hugs me so tightly I can barely breathe.

"Thank you, Fallon. If we'd have lost her…"

"She'd have found a way to come back and haunt you, and you know it," I tell him, trying to relieve some of the fear on his face.

"You're probably right." He smiles, but it doesn't reach his eyes.

"Let's get her inside," I instruct, and Roman nods, moving toward the house with her cradled in his arms. I watch as Roman lays her down gently on the corner couch and then stands above her like a sentinel on duty. She stirs, but her eyes stay closed. I dash into the kitchen to wash the blood from my hands, and when I get back to the living room, she's awake again and trying to sit up.

Fucking stubborn, crazy-ass bitch. Creek puts his hand on her shoulder as he perches on the sofa in front of her.

"You should rest, it will help you finish healing." A tic in his clenched jaw gives away the anger he feels, regardless of the softness of his voice.

"I'll be fine," she says, her voice hoarse despite her reassurances, and I roll my eyes. Only she would think she'd be fine less than five minutes after nearly dying.

"You should listen to him," I tell her before sitting on the floor.

"She went to find Levi," Creek says as Remy looks around the room. I have no idea who the fuck they're talking about, but I just sit here with them, hoping that she can finish the healing process well enough on her own.

She pushes herself up so she's sitting, and I roll my eyes at her again. She catches me and grins, so I shake my head. She's literally the worst patient ever.

"Do you need something?" Roman asks, but she shakes her head.

"Have we heard anything from Kain about the Witches?" she questions, looking between them both.

"Nothing yet, but I've let him know what happened," Creek confirms, and she groans. I can't help but laugh a little. Because yeah, her guys were overprotective before, but now that she has an actual weakness, it's going to be hilarious watching them try to tame her.

"But I'm fine, and now he's probably going to come back here when he doesn't need to," she sighs, and just as she finishes speaking, a portal opens up in the living room and out walks the Dracul King, looking furious enough to decimate worlds.

"Is he dead?" are the first words he utters.

"Serafina dropped him before we even knew she was here. Apparently, Levi left her behind to watch the house. He was a Hunter. Not one any of us recognize, so he could be new, but we have no idea who he is," Roman informs him, his words clipped. So that's who Remy was asking about. I didn't even realize Serafina was here. I thought she went with Levi. I keep quiet, feeling like a voyeur in this moment between them.

Kain strides toward Remy, and Creek moves aside so he can see her properly. He crouches in front of the couch, looking her over from head to toe before standing and leaving the room without another word. The sound of glass smashing draws Creek after him, and I sigh. He's pissed.

Not that I blame him. I'm pissed, too. I really wish this shit would just be over and we could all stop worrying about losing even more people.

I'm just glad I got here in time. I head into the kitchen to grab a soda and a bar of chocolate for Remy. I need to do something to feel useful, and this will help. I head back into the lounge and hand them over to her. "The sugar will make you feel better, plus, ya know, chocolate."

I plonk down next to her and turn the TV on. I flick to a TV series about a mom and her daughter that we've watched a million times and snuggle up next to my friend. I've nearly lost her one too many times, and I just need to be close to her. Losing her would be like losing a piece of myself. Roman pulls a blanket from the chair and puts it over us before sitting down, too.

It's not long before Kain and Creek join us, finding their own spots on the sofa. I notice Remy smiling and smile myself. It's nice being surrounded by them like this, despite the circumstances. I've kept myself away too much. I don't know if I was punishing myself or holding everything that happened to me against Remy subconsciously, but I vow to sort my shit out right now. Being here, with family, just feels right.

A crash sounds outside and Kain heads out, followed by Roman. Creek stays on alert beside us, but I can feel the power rolling from him. That's when I realize the bearer of the storm that's picked up outside of the manor is Levi. My eyes go wide as I hear Kain's shout, "You need to calm the fuck down." Roman's growl accompanies it, and a shiver goes down my spine.

"You two need to get the fuck out of my way. Where is she?" Levi's voice booms, the power rolling from him so forcefully that I can feel it even in here. It takes a minute or so, but Kain and Roman must move because Levi finds his way in front of Remy, lifting her out of her seat and into his arms.

"You're okay?" he asks softly, looking down at her. I'm not sure he's even really asking, as much as reassuring himself, but she nods regardless and cups his chin in her hand. He still has static rolling from him—I can feel it from across the room—but he'd never hurt her. All you have to do is look at him to know that.

"I'm okay. I was healing, just slowly. Fallon got here quickly and helped me heal faster so I didn't bleed out," she tells him softly, her voice barely more than a whisper while everyone else in the room is essentially frozen in place.

The power rolling from him is intense, and I can tell that even what I can feel is restrained. He truly could wipe us from the Earth with barely a thought. Remy kisses him gently, and he visibly relaxes, the pulse of his static retreating. "I'm really okay."

He rests his forehead against hers. Serafina enters the room and clears her throat. “Sorry to break this love fest up, but Amelia escaped with the Witch.”

“She escaped? But you and Nevin were on her when I left.” Levi’s voice is low, and menacing. He’s beyond pissed, but he’s controlling himself. I hope.

“She had a few tricks up her sleeve, but I’m fine, thanks for asking. Nevin wasn’t so lucky, but he’s healing. He shouldn’t be far behind me,” she says, rolling her eyes.

“I’m glad you’re okay,” Remy tells her, as Levi visibly shakes with anger. “And thank you for everything.”

The guys all grumble their thanks, but Serafina waves it off. “I was just doing my job.” I’ve never really understood her whole ice queen thing, sometimes she looks so sad and lonely, it’s heartbreaking, but then she’s a dick, and no one really pays attention to the fact that she’s kinda broken. I see her, though, and she hates it.

She moves to the corner of the room, standing like she’s on guard while Remy’s guys shift around the room and get comfortable. I drop back to the floor on the rug, and Creek passes me a blanket before sitting down next to me. I smile at Remy as she snuggles into Levi, and we all sit, watching the TV, just enjoying our time together.

FOURTEEN

It's been almost two weeks since Remy was shot, and we've spent the entire time trying to get a track on Amelia and her Witch. We finally found her two days ago, which is why we've all been rallied by Levi into the library at the manor.

The whole gang's here. Remy, Colt, Mama, Serafina, Nevin, Remy's guys, some extra Lycans and Dracul, even Caleb. How they managed to get him here is beyond me, but well, everyone has similar goals. I'm trying to keep myself busy while the guys strategize, making everyone coffee. Nevin helps me hand out the mugs and then passes me my own.

"Thanks," I say, giving him a tight smile. The nerves are fucking real right now as we join everyone else at the table where Levi has the map laid out for everyone to see.

"So, we've scouted the area and confirmed Amelia and Clara are here. They have several people with them, stationed in the forest surrounding the cabin, so this isn't going to be an easy infiltration. With enough teams of three, we should be able to neutralize those threats quickly and quietly enough that Amelia doesn't notice. The only unknown is if there are any magical wards, which we should assume there are," Levi tells us as he paces at the head of the table.

"We'll be splitting into teams, so we can cover the perimeter easily enough. Roman, Theron, and Emmett. Kain, Luc, and Lysandra. Fallon, Nevin, and Serafina. Caleb, Colt, and Creek. Remy will be with me. Marie is going to stay here and track Amelia, staying in contact with us all to make sure we're updated. The rest of you will fan out between us to make sure there's no room for escape."

"There is no fucking way you're sticking me with the nerd," Serafina huffs. "Unless you want him dead, too, I cannot cope with his incessant worrying and blathering."

"I'll go with Nevin and Fallon," Remy volunteers, and it makes me feel a little better. Being with two Angels that I don't really know that well makes me a little nervous. At least if Remy is there, and I go all weird comatose person, she'll have my back. It hasn't happened for a while now, so I'm starting to feel better about it, like maybe it's passed.

But since I still don't know what caused it, I can't help but worry.

Levi looks at Remy while Caleb smirks at her. She raises an eyebrow, as if daring Levi to argue with her right now, and I see the moment he gives in. I duck my head to hide my smile because he really will do anything to keep her happy, even if he doesn't like it.

"Fine," he says sharply with a nod, before glaring at Serafina, who doesn't seem even a little bothered. "Everyone, gear up, we leave in thirty."

The gold glowing dot on the map moves a little, and I realize that must be Mama's tracker on Amelia. She used an old type of magic to keep the tracker on her, and I'm more than a little in awe of it. I'm also so happy I could burst. I can't believe we're here. That we're this close. That all of this insanity could be over by the time I go to bed tonight.

I feel a little giddy at the prospect, but I push the feeling down. I've never been the kind of person to count my chickens and all that.

Remy leaves the room and Colt slides up beside me, with both of us watching her as she leaves. The day he found out she'd been shot was not the most fun I've had with him lately, and he's been even more worried lately than he was before. I hate seeing how stressed he is, but I just hope that after today, we can all finally find some peace.

"Are you okay?" he asks, his fingers brushing against mine.

"I will be as long as we all make it back tonight unscathed. The thought of losing anyone else is fucking paralyzing, but I know that's a risk we're all taking."

"We'll all end up back here, you'll see. The end is in sight, and then we can start looking at what our life together looks like." He grins at me, and I smile back.

"That sounds really fucking good," I tell him, allowing myself to step into his arms and sink into him for a moment while no one is paying us any attention.

Remy re-enters the room with Creek on her heels and looks like a fucking badass with her leather pants, corset, and cape. Her hair is tucked back out of the way, and she's armed to the fucking teeth. I'm rarely jealous of how my friend looks, but damn.

"Remy," Levi says as they move further across the room. His hand clutches her hip as Creek leaves them and heads toward us. "Are you sure you're okay going with them? You're a conduit for my power, we'd be much better paired."

I tune out of their conversation and listen in as Creek and Colt start talking over the plans again. Creek nods and heads over toward Roman when Colt takes my hand.

"You be careful, okay? I know you'll be with Remy,

but if anything happens to you, Fallon…" He trails off, and I squeeze his hand.

"We're all going to be okay. You said it yourself. I'll be tucked up back in your bed before you know it."

We took off into the air not long ago, I have the map clenched in my hand thanks to Mama's genius, and I'm in Nevin's arms as he and Remy soar through the skies. It's exhilarating, terrifying, and uncomfortable all at once. I don't really know Nevin, and this is something of an intimate hold he has me in. Not that he seems bothered. Though in the few interactions I've had with the Angel, he doesn't seem to really be bothered about much at all.

Mama and Caleb help to get the others where we're going, but apparently we needed air visuals, so those that could fly are, and I'm just lucky enough to be along for the ride. Not that I'm complaining… Well not completely. This is freaking amazing. I'm going to have to tell Colt to persuade Remy to bring him up because it's so fucking cool.

Levi and Serafina are so competitive that they disappeared into the horizon a little while ago, but then again, they're covering the far side of the cabin, so they have a bigger distance to travel. Though if I had wings, I'd probably join the race, too.

My heart races in my chest. Today could go so badly, but I'm trying my hardest not to focus on that. No one really said much as we left the manor. No goodbyes—I don't think anyone wants to even consider the possibility that we might lose people today. It's a big possibility, especially if this is what we're all expecting.

I lose track of time as we head toward the cabin that Mama pinpointed Amelia and Clara to. We rise above the clouds to avoid anyone spotting us since it's not dark out yet, and it blows my mind that this is real.

"We'll need to land soon and move in on foot," I shout out to Remy after checking the map.

Nevin starts to descend, and I am rapt with awe at the sight before us. The large green forest in the distance must be the forest Levi mentioned. It doesn't take long until we land, and I wobble a little as I find my feet. Nevin shakes out his arms from carrying me for so long while Remy stretches out her wings before putting them away.

"We need to go this way," I say, pointing into the distance after looking at my map.

"I'll go first. Fallon, you stay in the middle, just keep on top of where we're going. Remy, you bring up the back," Nevin says, and Remy nods. He's been scouting the area, so I guess it's better for him to go up front, but I am glad that Remy has my back.

Once we land, we walk for a while, but it doesn't feel like we get very far because the foliage is so thick. I try not to get pissy about it because I love being outdoors, but still. Tripping on the undergrowth wasn't something I planned for today.

I walk through the trees, cursing under my breath when the wind is knocked from my lungs, and I drop to my knees. Pain rips through my head, and I clutch at my skull. Fuck, whoever this Witch is, she's fucking powerful.

"Wards," I groan, trying to warn the others. I hear Remy cry out and see her fall to her knees as she tries to get to me.

Shit.

"Fuck!" Nevin roars. "Fallon, you need to overpower them!"

His voice only just registers over the pain, but I look at Remy writhing on the ground as tears run down my face, and I nod. I take a deep breath but keep my gaze on Remy to help me focus. Stopping her pain incentivizes me. She's hurt enough for me already.

I focus on the wards and start chanting inside my mind, pushing my power against them, trying to bring them down with sheer force. I notice the glow that seems to emanate around me, it looks like the power from Az, but I don't have time to worry about that right now. I need every piece of power I can draw from inside of me as well as from the earth. I dig my fingers into the ground and pull the power into me that the Goddess offers, pushing it back out to break the bonds.

The pain starts to recede, and Remy inches toward me. If she can make it and add her power to what I'm already channeling, we might be able to just do it. Sweat trickles down my spine as I keep pushing against the wards, gritting my teeth as they fight back.

It's less than a second after she touches me that a pop sounds and my ears ring, but then Nevin is on us and pulling us backward.

When the ringing in my ears stops, the sounds of fighting intrude. So much for our stealthy approach. My heart jumps to my throat. How many of the others were trapped in wards? Is Colt okay? Shit. I know I broke our wards, but did I get them all? I touch the ground and send out a ripple of power, it'll give our location away, but I have no choice.

"Fuck, fuck, fuck!" Nevin creases the map in his hand. "Amelia is gone."

My phone starts to sound in my pocket, but I feel weird as I lift the phone to my ear. Almost like I'm not controlling my movements.

What the fuck is going on?

A male's voice comes down the line and I feel like I'm falling. Then I hear myself speaking, but it's not me. I try to move, but my body doesn't cooperate. I try to shout, but it's like I'm not in control of myself.

Help! Remy!

"Okay. Yeah, I got it," my voice says, but I have no idea what's going on. "Mama tracked her. I have the location, but we need to go. I'll text the others with the update in case Mama can't reach them."

Remy!

I try to use my power, something… Anything to reach her. Something isn't right. Why does Nevin look so nervous? What the fuck is happening?

Good little Witch, your job here is almost done.

I scream inside my mind at the male's voice in my head. It's the same one from the call, but I don't recognize it. My panic swells, and I start to freak the fuck out.

"Should we really leave without them knowing?" Nevin asks, looking between Remy and I. I try to move my arm again, but nothing. How is this even possible?

"Yes, there is no fucking way I'm letting her escape us again. If she's on the run, she won't have as many people with her, and it's likely she won't have time to set any wards. She might have a Witch with her, but so do we. I am not giving up, not when we're this close to putting an end to this bullshit," Remy answers, and I want to fucking cry. This has to be a trap. Is this why I was losing time? I can't be the reason she gets hurt. Not again.

"I don't know…" Nevin shifts, biting his lip, and I want to smack him in his face. He knows something. He keeps glancing at me like he knows, and I feel fucking sick. "Levi is going to have my fucking hide."

"You don't have to come with us. I can go with Fallon. She can portal us, and you can stay here and find the others."

"Are you kidding me? Levi might kill me for leaving here, but if I let you go alone, he'll skin me alive, wait until I heal, and then do it all over a-fucking-gain. I think not." He turns to me, smirking but quickly smothers it, and I notice the glow coming from me in the reflection of his glasses. "Can you portal us to where we need to go?"

"I can," I say, feeling myself nodding, but it's not me. My gut twists, this is all going to go horribly wrong.

"Are you sure? If you don't have enough juice left, we can fly. You just need to adjust the map," Remy offers, and I want to cry.

"No, I can do this," my voice says, and my body stands. Nevin catches me, eyeing me like he thinks I'm going to drop dead. I'll make him drop fucking dead, just as soon as I work out how to take back control of my body.

Oh, little Witch, you'll be dead before that happens.

"Are you sure this is a good idea?" Nevin asks Remy as the shouts continue in the distance. Fuck, Colt. If something happens to Remy, he won't survive it. Not after everything he's already survived.

"No, but it's our only shot. If we don't go soon, the guards we were here to find will find us, and that could give Amelia too much fucking time. I'm not risking it," Remy answers him, and I try again to gain control of my body.

"Okay, then let's do this." Nevin nods and then Remy turns to me, biting her lip, but I can see the hope, the trust all over her face.

"Open this portal."

We step out of the portal into another forest, but I have no fucking clue where we are. The voice in my mind has gone quiet, but I can feel his presence lingering. He has to be the one controlling my body. If I had any idea how he was doing it, maybe I'd have a better idea of how the fuck to fight.

If you don't stop fighting me, little Witch, you're going to regret it.

Fuck you, I answer the voice, and I feel like I'm falling again.

When it stops, I find myself in a cage of metal and glass. I scream again, but I still can't control my fucking body. I can see and hear every fucking thing, but I can't do a single fucking thing past that.

"Are you sure this is the right place?" Remy asks me as the portal closes behind her and Nevin.

"Yes, there's a building not far from here." I watch as I show her the map, it looks totally different from the one Mama produced for us. How the fuck is someone else controlling my magic? I can see the glamour over the parchment setting the new course, but it's just an illusion.

"Okay, well let's get moving because I don't want to give them any more advantage than they already have on us." Nevin nods at Remy's words and takes up the front again, pushing his way through the greenery. I stumble along behind him, and a wave of hopelessness washes over me. How the fuck am I going to get out of this? Remy doesn't even know anything is wrong, and I'm trapped.

Fuck. Fuck. Fuck.

"Are you okay, Fallon?" Remy asks quietly as we follow along behind Nevin, and I want to be sick.

"I'm fine," I tell her, my voice clipped, and I scream again as laughter rings out in my ears.

There's no escape, little Witch, it's useless to even try. You won't overpower me.

I don't know who the fuck you are, but underestimating me will be your downfall, I growl at the voice as I strengthen my resolve. I'm going to fix whatever the fuck is happening to me, even if it fucking kills me. I won't be the reason Remy dies.

For now, I stop fighting and try to focus on what's happening outside of my mind. Something to give me a clue as to who has me captive. My thoughts flick to Azriel momentarily, but I trust Morgan. If she said he's gone, then he's gone… But I wish I had an alternate explanation for this all. She wouldn't have betrayed Remy like that? Surely?

It doesn't take long for us to find the building on the map, but as we look up, I notice it's more than just a building, it's a fucking fortress. Panic claws up my throat again when I feel the power humming around it. That's my power… But I've never been here before.

"How the fuck do we get in there?" Remy asks, looking over at Nevin. He looks pissed off, but he's a good fucking actor. He knows what's going on with me. I just know it.

"I have an idea," he says before motioning that he's going to go ahead, and Remy nods. My body moves, and then I'm sitting. Everything goes dark as my eyes close. I can still hear everything, including Remy's footsteps as she moves around making sure no one sneaks up on us.

In a moment of weakness, I nearly break. Tears threaten, and I want to give up. How am I meant to save her when I can't even save myself?

I feel it as she sits beside me, so I push, just trying to even move a finger, but it's like my consciousness isn't connected to my body. This cage has cut me off from myself, and somehow, I just know that unless I can get out of here soon, I won't ever break free of this hold.

Nevin isn't gone long, but when he returns he looks happy and crouches down to where we're huddled. "I found a bridge. It's not the most inconspicuous of ways in, but it is the quickest. Is she going to be okay?"

"I'll be fine," I grumble, and then I can see again as my eyes open, and I notice the glow coming from my skin again. Why is my power manifesting like that still? None of this makes any fucking sense.

"Okay, well then, let's head out. It's not far from here," he says, getting to his feet and looking out into the distance. Remy helps me stand, and he takes the lead. I'm between them again, but whoever is controlling my body isn't paying much fucking attention because I stumble all around the fucking place. Remy catches me a few times as we follow Nevin, and I growl in my mind.

I might not know who you are, but if you hurt my friend, I start to threaten when his voice laughs in my mind.

Oh, I intend to do more than hurt your friend, little Witch. The most beautiful part is that without you, it wouldn't have been possible. You were the missing link all these centuries. But thanks to your help these last few months, I finally have the power to secure her and hide her from all those who might try to save her. Thanks to you, she is mine, and she will suffer for what she's done.

I slam my hands against the glass walls of my cage until my skin breaks and my blood smears on the glass. I sink to my knees, desperation rushing through me as I notice us coming up on a bridge. A fucking rope and wood bridge. Fuck my fucking life. Whoever is controlling my movement starts paying more attention as we cross one at a time, and I make it across in one piece, despite losing my footing a couple of times.

We reach the door, solid wood nestled amongst the sandstone. Nevin breaches it as quietly as he can, but I can tell there's no one here but us. Maybe because it's my power shielding this place, but I just know.

"You need to rein in your power," Nevin tells me, and I want to claw his fucking eyes out. "Just until we reach them. Your glow is going to give us away."

I notice the world move as I nod, and the glow dims before we move inside the building. Wards of my own making skim across my skin, and I notice another's magic intertwined with mine. I recognize the layers of these wards.

We're trapped.

Remy's hand stays on my shoulder as we move through the dark, damp hall, barely making a noise as we move behind Nevin.

We reach the end of the corridor, and it splits in two

directions.

"Which way?" Remy asks and Nevin shrugs, but heads to the right. We follow him until the corridor opens out to a huge, high-ceilinged room. Light filters in through windows close to the roof.

My feet keep moving, following Nevin as if I'm on a leash toward the middle of the room, and I try to work out where to go from here. When Remy reaches out for me, she misses and falls to her knees.

Remy!!!

"Fallon," she gasps. "Something is wrong."

She falls fully to the floor, and I start banging on the walls of my cage again as Nevin's laughter rings out along with the voice inside my head.

"Let's take them upstairs," I say, and Nevin nods. Why would he do what I say? None of this makes any sense. I knew he knew something, the fucking snake! He picks Remy's slack body up off the floor and throws her over his shoulder, leading the way through the destroyed building until we reach another hall where electricity lights the way. It looks like it's been revamped, and there are a ton of other people here. Witches, Lycans, and Dracul.

How is this even possible?

Was Nevin behind everything from the start? Is he the one who was pulling Archer's strings? Was he the one who Azriel told me about? My mind spins as he heads up a set of spiral stairs, me following along like a fucking lap dog despite my struggles. We go up for what feels like forever until we reach a top hall, and Nevin leads us to a large wood and metal door.

My feet carry me to the corner while Nevin fastens Remy to a wall with metal chains, clamping shackles on her wrists and ankles.

You can't do this! I shout, and the voice laughs inside my mind again.

Oh, I can do this and much more, little Witch. You're just here for the ride. I think I'm going to enjoy your pain as much as hers.

Once Nevin has her bound, he steps back, watching her closely. He moves toward her again, slapping her across the face.

I beat against my cage again, but my body does nothing.

Remy groans from where she's crumpled on the cold stone ground. She moves to sit up and hisses as she opens her eyes and sees me.

Fuck, she's going to think I did this to her.

She looks over at me, and then spots Nevin where he's moved into a chair, watching her with a slimy grin on his face.

"What's going on?" she asks, her voice hoarse, and Nevin belts out a laugh.

"You should've known better by now who to trust."

FIFTEEN

COLT

After a last minute change in teams, thanks to Remy's little switch around, I find myself teamed up with Serafina, working our way through this Fates forsaken forest. Getting trapped in a Witch's ward was not how I wanted to start this day. Or something I ever want to do again. That shit is excruciating. It knocked me and Serafina on our asses; I'm half glad the Angel went down so I didn't seem like such a pussy, but fuck me. My ears are still ringing.

I was worried that we'd be attacked while we were trapped, but thankfully, nothing happened. I'm sure not everyone was as lucky as we are. We haven't come across any scouts, and if Serafina's pissed off grumbling is anything to go by, I think we might have been given the 'easy' section.

Fucking Angel asshole.

I get he wanted me safe to keep Remy happy, but this is bullshit.

I keep trailing behind her, moving as silently as we can to not attract any unwanted attention. When Serafina lifts her fist, signaling for me to stop, I grind to a halt behind her. Then I see them over her shoulder. A group of six guys scouting the area.

I guess this wasn't the easiest section after all.

We move toward them, splitting up to come at them from both sides, and on her signal, I attack, sword out, and revel in the fight. I've been so angry lately, and the blood splatter on my face almost makes me want more.

It doesn't take long to cut them down, Serafina is a fucking badass, and I'm glad she's on my side. I'm not going to lie, though, it felt good to finally dish out some retribution for all of the shit that's been handed to us recently. I just hope Remy and Fallon had it as easy as we did.

I shake my head and try to focus on following Serafina toward the cabin. Thinking about Fallon will only distract me. The last thing I want is to be distracted and get someone killed. Someone including myself. I want this shit over so I can run away with my girl and worship her in the way she deserves.

That is what's getting me through this bullshit. Focusing on the future. One that has seemed too far out of reach for way too fucking long at this point.

Serafina signals for me to stop again. "The others are close."

Remy's team is holding the left with Creek's, with Kain's to the right. I know Levi and Caleb want to breach the cabin first. How the fuck the Archangel of War ended up friends with fucking Conquest… It literally could only have happened because of Remy. There is no other possible way that those two would be as close as they are, not without killing each other anyway.

The same could be said for us all. I snort quietly, thinking about how one woman managed to bring together some of the universe's most unlikely friends and make us family.

We inch closer to the cabin as a crack of lightning sets the roof of it on fire.

I guess that's one way to get the Angel bitch's attention. Gets us around the wards her little Witch blatantly had in place, too.

I hold my position while Serafina darts to the right, to make sure no one sneaks out of the back. I hear screams and desperately want to see what the fuck is happening, but I know I need to hold my ground.

Fuck my life, Fallon better be okay.

I bounce on the balls of my feet, ready to take down any motherfucker that comes my way. I'm on edge, and these fuckers are the reason my girl was taken. Today, I have no mercy.

"Amelia. Clara." I hear Levi's growl from here, but there's silence as the flames in the cabin extinguish. Hopefully that means people are getting some answers.

I fucking hate not knowing what the fuck is going on. I feel like I'm just standing here swinging my dick. I move closer to the cabin, pretty confident I'm not going to miss anyone by moving closer. I just want to know what the fuck is going on, so I move a little toward the front of the cabin.

"What the fuck is this?" a woman huffs as I get closer. "This is my home, Leviathan. We weren't hurting anyone, why couldn't you just leave me alone? It's been so long since the war, I hoped you'd all forgotten about us."

"You know why we're here," Levi says, as his static charge sweeps through the air. That shit is so fucking stifling I feel like I can barely breathe.

"No, I fucking don't, otherwise I wouldn't have asked," she snaps, and I wince. Fuck being on the other side of that.

"Amelia, maybe you should calm down a little, they have a lot of people with them. This seems like it's about more than us just running away," another female voice says, but I grow more and more confused. This isn't what we expected. This was meant to be carnage and bloodshed. A fight to the death.

Something isn't right.

"Levi," Caleb's voice reaches me, and I glance around wondering if I can get closer to see what the fuck is going on. I never said patience was my strong suit and usually I'd just bust right in and demand to know what the fuck is going on, but considering I'm the weakest link here right now - which grinds my fucking gears - I don't really want to get my ass lit up. "Something isn't adding up."

"What isn't adding up?" the first female voice speaks again, and I frown.

"She really doesn't know why we're here," I hear Roman speak just as Serafina drops in beside me, putting a finger to her lips. Apparently I'm not the only one who doesn't like being kept out of the loop.

"Why are you here?" the woman asks again. "And why the fuck did you just try to burn down our home? Do you have any idea how long it took to find a place as obscure as this, where we could build and no one would bother us?"

"Are you honestly trying to tell me you haven't been behind all of this?" Levi roars, and I fucking flinch. Fuck me, he's terrifying sometimes. Fuck being the woman he's talking to.

"Behind all of fucking what? We barely speak to people outside of the ones who help shield us. What on earth could we have done to bring your wrath down upon us, and why the fuck would we want to?" Her frustration is evident, and I start to wonder why Remy isn't weighing in. She isn't usually the strong and silent type.

"I don't think she's lying," Roman adds, followed by Kain.

"I agree with Roman."

"Maybe we should get Remy to look inside her mind, it's been a while, but I'm sure she remembers how," Caleb says, and I can't help but grin. These guys might be scary, but so is my fucking sister when she wants to be.

"Who the fuck is Remy?"

"Remy is Amantara."

"And you thought I talked in circles. What does that even mean? Where is your little pet Shadow Walker anyway?" the woman asks just before I hear Kain again.

"I can't reach her."

"What do you mean you can't reach her, she should just be behind the cabin," Levi growls.

"She's not here. Her, Fallon, and Nevin are all missing," Caleb announces and my heart fucking stops. I start to move, but Serafina keeps me fixed in place. Fucking Angel. That's my sister and my girl. What if something's wrong?

"I can't feel her," Roman shouts, and I swear I'm nearly

fucking sick. This can't be happening

"Where the fuck is she?" Levi roars, and my stomach flips again.

Please don't let them be dead.

"You need to let me go," I growl at Serafina. She rolls her eyes at me in response.

"Actually, I don't. We need to hold formation here. You think they can't find the girls without you?" she scoffs, and I want to punch her straight in the throat. I usually try to refrain from hitting women, but fuck me, this one's hard fucking work.

"Fine," I growl and start to pace. I can't hear what the others are saying anymore and that pisses me off, too. But she stands there like a sentry watching me to make sure the back of the cabin is still covered, even though it's obviously not a fucking issue.

I feel like we're waiting forever before Creek rounds the cabin and finds us.

"What the fuck is going on?" I ask, trying to keep my anger in check and totally failing.

"Fallon, Remy, and Nevin are gone. There's no trace of them. We've tracked through the forest, and their scents just kind of disappear. Roman and Kain can't feel Remy through their bonds."

"What does that even mean?" I ask, tugging at my hair. This can't be fucking happening.

"We don't know, Caleb has gone back to the Shadow Realm to see if Morgan has any answers. But they were pretty off track when we did find their scents. We have no idea why."

"Fallon wouldn't just disappear, neither would Remy. Something must have happened," I grunt, and Serafina huffs behind me.

"You think someone could have taken them both without a trace? Without them fighting back?" she asks, an eyebrow raised, and, again, I want to hit her in her smug face. This bitch is getting on my last nerve.

"We're hoping they've portaled home, but that doesn't explain a few things," Creek says, and Serafina rolls her eyes and heads toward the front of the cabin.

"I knew something was wrong. It felt too easy," I tell him, panic seizing my heart as the worst-case scenarios flick through my mind.

"If someone has them, we'll find them. We won't let anything happen to them."

"You can't promise that. They've both been through so much already."

"I know, man," he says, clenching his fists as he continues, "let's head back to the others so we can start searching properly." We head around to the front of the cabin, where Serafina is talking quietly with two women. I'm assuming the Angel and the Witch, and we head toward Roman and the others.

"Any luck?" Serafina asks as we reach them.

"Nothing. We're going to head back to the manor. Is everything okay here?" Roman barks.

"Yeah, they had nothing to do with any of this." She sighs and runs a hand down her face. "I've no idea how we got it all so twisted."

"We're sorry for the intrusion," Kain says to the two of them, and they smile at him with that starry look chicks get. Slick bastard. He could charm the pants off of a fucking nun. Even with the whole child of a Demon, blood sucker thing.

"Would…" the redhead starts, her voice so quiet. She clears her throat and then smiles again at him. "Would you like a portal to your home?"

"If you wouldn't mind, it would be much appreciated." He offers her another smile, and she blushes so hard she practically glows.

"Of course." She nods at him, and the blonde squeezes her hand before releasing her. She moves forward and everyone who was with us comes to stand together as she speaks to Kain about how to get the portal to open where we need it to. Roman moves to speak to Serafina and Amelia, while Kain finishes sorting out the portal with the Witch.

Fuck me, I hate feeling useless.

Roman is back with us in less than a minute as the Witch opens up the portal.

"Who's heading back first?" Kain asks as Roman moves beside him.

"I'll go back first, you come back with everyone else, and Creek can bring up the rear. It won't take long to get everyone through, but give me a few minutes to check the perimeter," Roman orders, while we all just agree.

"Okay." Kain nods and turns back to the Witch as Roman steps through the portal. Kain says goodbye and turns to Creek and I.

"Let's get back and find them, shall we?"

I nod, feeling like a fucking useless toddler and step through the portal in front of Creek. Roman is waiting for us on the other side; and once we're all through, the portal closes.

"All clear," he grunts and heads into the house.

Fuck, we need to tell Marie what happened, and I'm not looking forward to that conversation since I promised to keep Fallon safe.

I just hope she has some answers or can help us get some.

"What happened?" are the words that spill out of Marie's mouth once she sees us. The ground shakes a little as we reach her. I guess Levi just got back. The air fills with static just as she stops speaking.

I trail into the library behind Levi and Creek with Marie at my side, looking pissed off, but I'm so out of my fucking depth here. If these guys can't find them, then how the fuck am I going to be any use?

"Remy is gone." Levi's words are short and clipped, but they make me want to tear things apart. Marie, miraculously, remains calm, but that makes me crack a little more. "You need to find her."

"Where is Fallon?" she asks, and I start to bounce from one foot to the other. I feel like she's the only one here invested in finding them both as much as I am. I know they're all in love with my sister, but we need them both.

"We don't know," Kain tells her in that soothing way of his. Just the tone of his voice smooths some of my rough edges. "We were hoping you'd be able to trace her or Remy. Or even Nevin. They seem to have, well, vanished for lack of a better word."

Marie's eyes go wide, taking in everything he's saying. I get it. It's not just anyone that could take two Angels and a Witch. Something feels so fucking off that I can't keep still. I want to break things.

"Roman," Levi snaps, and I jolt, even though he's not snapping at me. "Will you keep fucking still!"

"Fuck you, Angel boy," he snarls. The rage rolls off of him in waves, and I keep my hand on the hilt of my sword. I'm pretty sure I'm outmatched here, but I'll step in if I need to.

"Guys, fighting between ourselves isn't going to solve fuck all." Creek sighs, but he's not as calm as he seems. He keeps clenching and unclenching his fists. He wants to pummel someone's face in. He's basically my brother from another mother; I know him as well as I know myself. He might seem like some soft and sappy guy with Remy, but dude has a temper, especially since the whole 'he became a Demon' thing.

"Gentlemen. If you'll stop arguing between yourselves, I'll try to locate them. Do you have something of Remy's? Something that she holds dear or that she recently touched?" Marie asks, trying to take control of the room, and I snap out of my funk to pay attention to what the fuck she's saying. Maybe she has a plan, which is a lot fucking better than what I have right now.

"Her necklace." Kain sighs sadly. "She didn't have it on when we left, I'll go and get it from her room." He stalks out of the library, and I swear I hold my breath until he gets back.

"Thank you," she says as he hands her the necklace. "I'll search for Fallon first, since she is easiest to look for. But after, I'll look for Remy too, in case they've been separated."

Levi nods at her but hovers close to the table she's standing by. Roman storms over to the windows while Kain stays between them, like the peacekeeper he seems to be. Creek stays by my side.

"Can I help?" I ask her quietly, and she nods.

"Help me lay out these candles around the room," she says, pointing me to the spots they need to go. "Make sure they're lit."

I do as I'm asked, the menial task making me feel a bit better, like I'm actually contributing. It doesn't take long to get the candles in place while Marie does the other half of the room. By the time I'm done, hers are all lit and she's back at the table with a world map laid out. I swear to anyone who's listening, if they aren't even in this country, I'm going to break shit.

Marie slices her hand, her blood dropping onto the page, chanting something I don't understand, but all of the hair on my body stands up, and I shiver. I respect magic, but sometimes it scares the shit out of me. I've seen it used against people way too fucking often. The candle flames flare, and she opens her eyes. Her face falls, and her heart races as she looks at the map and murmurs, "That can't be right."

My heart plummets at her words, and I close my eyes while I take a deep breath, trying desperately to cling to a shred of hope. She reaches over and picks up Remy's necklace in her bloody hand, and starts to chant once more. The candles flare again, but when she opens her eyes after her chant, I feel it in my gut before she even utters a word.

"I can't find them." Her words are barely more than a whisper.

"What the fuck do you mean you can't find them?" Roman snarls as he storms back over to the table.

"I mean, I can't find them. The spell can't find them. They're gone."

"What do you mean, gone?" Levi roars.

"I mean, it's as if their power is no longer on this plane. They're gone. Untraceable."

SIXTEEN

FALLON

I don't know how long we've been in here. My eyes stay closed a lot, and the presence in my mind dips in and out. No matter what or how hard I try, I can't break out of this fucking cage. But I have at least started to notice cracks in the glass the more I lose my shit and attack it.

A small part of me hopes that if I can break it, even just a little, that I can then reach Remy. I can help her. Sometimes I can see and hear what's going on around me, and others, all of my senses are locked from me. Like whoever is doing this only wants me aware for my own sort of torture.

I swear I'm going to rain down fucking hellfire on

whoever did this to me. I've always kept a lid on my rage, knowing what it can do to someone with the potential for power like I have, but fuck that. If the dark side of magic is where I have to go to punish whoever has stolen my freedom from me once again, then that's where I'll go.

I'm so sick of being the fucking victim. Of just surviving.

Not any fucking more.

Once I break free from here, and I will, that won't be my life. I swear it to the Goddess. I am going to forge my own path, and everyone else can fuck right off. I am so sick and tired of this bullshit.

The darkness lifts, and I watch as I move back into the room where Remy is still shackled. I move to sit, and Nevin chains my wrists to the wall before lifting a bottle of water to my lips. I want to spit it out, but I sip it down, easily tasting the poison in the water.

Is that how they're doing this to me? Keeping me like this?

I need to find a way to stop drinking that fucking water even if that's all I manage.

"What the fuck is going on?" Remy seethes, and my heart breaks for her. I hate seeing her so powerless. I've never seen her as anything other than what she is. A fucking badass. I wonder how they managed to subdue her… Even though my wards are masking her power, they wouldn't have taken it away entirely. I wonder if they gave her the same shit they're giving me.

"You'll see," Nevin tells her flatly before turning and leaving the room.

"Fallon," she calls my name, almost monotone; but it's like she realizes I'm not really here, and her face crumbles. A tear slips down her face as she gives into her tears, and I want to cry, too.

I scream out in frustration again, but my body doesn't even twitch.

She screams through her tears and tugs on her chains, hissing as the metal rubs on her skin. I notice the burn marks where the shackles lock around her and realize they must be salted iron.

Oh Remy, I am so sorry. This is all my fault. Again.

I can't help but wonder if the others have figured out what's going on. Whether or not they think I'm their enemy now. My heart breaks for Colt, too because if he thinks I've betrayed them after everything we've shared…

I scream and bang against the glass again until it splinters and a few shards fall away.

Holy shit.

"Remy?" I say, and I could fucking cry because my lips actually move. She looks up at me, and I feel the tears running down my face. But then the hole reseals, and I lose the tiny bit of control I had.

This can't be fucking happening. No! Remy!

I scream into the abyss again but nothing happens.

"Are you okay?" she asks, but I can't do any-fucking-thing else to let her know what's going on.

I am going to tear shit apart once I break free. I will decimate the souls of those who have hurt us all. I have had enough of being a pawn in their games.

It's time for them to realize that I am a motherfucking queen.

The darkness comes and goes. I'm not sure if I sleep or if only my body does, but when the darkness recedes, I can't do anything but watch Remy.

I feel so fucking useless. I've tried to shatter the glass again every chance I've had, but there's not even been so much as a splinter in it. Not that I'm giving up. If I could break through once, I can do it again.

I refuse to give in.

Every time I see Remy crying, my heart breaks a little more, but it also strengthens my resolve. I won't let them break her. Break either of us. This is not how we go out. Not after everything we've already survived.

"Do you know why he's doing this?" she asks, but try as I might, I can't respond to her. I watch the sadness creep over her face as she realizes I'm not going to respond, and her head droops.

Fuck this.

Whoever you are, asshole, know I'm coming for you.

I mean, you can try, little Witch, but surely you've realized by now that your power is nothing compared to mine. Good luck with your revenge plots because that's all they'll ever be. You are but a drop in the ocean, I am a god.

I roll my eyes at the ego on this guy. What a fucking bag of dicks.

The overwhelming feeling of helplessness drowns me as Remy sighs and shifts around on the ground, her chains scraping against the wall as she does.

"Oh goodie, you're awake." Nevin's voice filters into the room, but I can't see him. I try to move my head, but nothing happens.

"Hiding outside the room like the coward you are? How shocking," Remy sneers, and seconds later the lock clicks, and the door squeaks open. My head finally moves. Thank fuck for that! Nevin's scowl makes me laugh in my mind. I'd love to slap it from his stupid fucking face. He looks like a kid trying to be the big bad.

Remy grins at him, and my heart swells. He won't break her, no matter how hard he tries. He might be an Angel, but he's got nothing on my friend.

"You don't have all that much to be smiling about," he

spits as he moves to crouch in front of her. “No one knows where you are. No one is coming to save you.”

“Then why aren’t I dead yet?” she asks, the lilt in her voice giving me life.

“Because it’s not time yet.”

“You want everyone to think you’re something more than you are. That this was all you. But it wasn’t, was it? You’re nothing more than a puppet.” She grins, and I let out a whoop inside my mind. Thank fuck she’s working shit out. Even chained, they can’t keep her down. Now if only I could be of more use.

“You have no fucking idea,” he shouts, spit raining over her, and I want to gag. What a fucking jackass.

“Then why? Tell me why you would go through all of this. Why would you do all of this? What the actual fuck did I ever do to you to deserve this hell?”

“It was always you,” he mutters and stands, starting to pace between us. “I tried everything to make him see me, but you were always there in the way. Then I figured out a way to get rid of the problem. An arrow to the heart. Clean, simple, and done from far enough away that I wouldn’t be seen. I even aimed for him because I just fucking knew you would be the martyr and take the hit. But you even had him in fucking death!”

“You killed Amantara? You shot that arrow? For Levi?” she asks, and I sit here confused, wondering what the fuck she's going on about. I'm obviously missing something, but I pay as much attention as the host of my body will allow. If I see or hear anything that can help us, you better believe I'm going to hang onto that like the lifeline that it is.

"Yes, for fucking Levi. I've loved him since before he even knew you existed. I was his right-hand man. And then, then there was fucking you. The Shadow Walker filth. I knew the only way to win him was if you were gone. But even in death, you had his heart. He created a whole fucking race for you."

Holy shit. He's in love with Levi. That's why he's been terrorizing us all? It doesn't make any sense. Why would he try to keep the factions fighting if that was his goal? Something's still missing.

Fuck, I hate that I'm basically a bystander in this. I have so many questions. I rack my mind, trying to see if there's a way to access the memories that must be locked away from the days I lost. I assume I lost them to whatever and whoever has control of me now. If I can just remember, then maybe I can help her.

"Nevin…" she says, his name coming out as barely more than a sigh.

"Don't. Don't try to twist this. This is all your fault. If you'd never come along, he would have loved me."

This shit is bananas. How could he ever think that Levi

would love him? Why would he think hurting Remy would get him what he wants? Has he even seen them together? This guy is straight up deluded. I just wish he'd gotten a clue before we ended up shackled in here.

I try to tune them out, turning my focus inside myself, instead. If I can just remember, maybe I'll know who he's working with. Maybe I can work out how to get myself out of this cage and get us out of this fucking place.

I've pushed and pushed, and I've snagged snippets of my memories. Little bits of information about where we are but not why or who Nevin is working with.

But I've felt that presence in my mind recede a little, and the glass of my cage has become weaker. It's splintered, I just need to keep fighting to get free. If I can just take control of myself again, maybe I can tell her what's going on. Maybe we can work together to find a way out of here.

I've heard more activity outside the room we're in the last couple of times I've been awake, but it's all muffled words and banging, so I have no fucking clue what's going on outside of here. My stomach cramps from the lack of food and drink I've had since we've been here, but I try not to think about it. My body isn't my main issue, getting control of myself is.

I punch and kick at the glass, and a wall shatters.

Fucking yes!

"Remy…" My mind goes blank, and I panic. Where the fuck am I? Why am I chained up? "Remy, where are we?"

"Fallon. Thank fuck. We need to get out of here. Can you access your power?" I close my eyes and start to cry. My power isn't there. What the fuck is going on?

"I can't feel it, Remy." My voice breaks, and my tears turn to sobs. I feel like I should remember something, something just out of my grasp. Like it's on the tip of my tongue.

"It's okay. We'll get out of here," she says, and I grow frustrated. Why don't I remember anything? All I remember is flying to the cabin with her and Nevin.

"I don't remember… Remy, how did we get here?" I ask, maybe something she says will help me remember.

The falling feeling starts again, and I hit my ass as I'm back in my cage, my memories flooding back to me.

Naughty little Witch, thought I didn't have a failsafe in case you broke free again? Do you think I'm stupid? You'll work out soon enough that you won't win.

"No!" Remy screams, and I deflate. Maybe he's right. Maybe we won't win. Maybe I won't be able to get us out of here. I can't even save myself. Self-loathing floods me when I hear the voice from my mind, but it's not in my head.

"Why so sad?" the voice asks, and my body turns toward the giant man strolling into the room. "You look a little pale," he grins down at Remy, and she goes pale. Who the fuck is he?

She obviously knows him, but I don't even have a hint of recollection of who he is.

"You…" she starts, but she almost looks beaten. Whoever he is, they must have been close, because she looks truly defeated in this moment.

"That's right, sweetheart. Little old me. Bet you didn't see that coming, did you?" He winks at her as he saunters further into the room. With the click of his fingers, a chair and table appear opposite me and he sits down, still grinning.

"But why?" she asks, and I watch, rapt. Maybe I'll find a weakness of his, a way to overthrow his control of my body.

"You'll find out soon enough. But for now, we need to make sure you're nice and pliant." With another snap of his fingers, a syringe appears in his hands, filled with a black substance. He moves toward her, and she tries to move away from him, but there's nowhere for her to go. "It'll just pinch a little."

He wraps his fingers around her throat before plunging the syringe into the side of her neck.

"Soon, everyone will see you for what you are. They'll take my side. Even Leviathan won't be able to save you then."

Her eyes glaze over and then close, and she droops, falling to the floor and then he turns to me. "As for you, little Witch, if you try to break free again, I'll show you just how merciless I can be. Chaos might be my main game, but for you, I'll break my own rules. I'll show you what real pain is."

It hits me who he is. Gabriel. The Archangel of Chaos.

None of this makes any fucking sense to me. I am so sick of being a pawn in someone else's fucking game.

He clicks his fingers, and my eyes close. I feel my body lying down, the shackles moving with me. Then his footsteps echo off the stone, and the door closes.

I'm back in the dark abyss, but this time, my resolve strengthens. I won't let him break us.

I've spent the last few days, while having my body used as a punching bag for Nevin, trying to work out a better way to break through my cage. Gabriel's presence in my mind seems to be retreating, almost as if he's getting sloppy now he's revealed himself. Like he thinks he's unstoppable.

He's an idiot, but I'm glad for it. If he's not paying

attention, maybe I can reach Remy.

I'm constantly chipping away at the edges of the glass of my cage. I don't know if Gabriel stopped focusing so hard on me or if he simply thinks I won't be able break free, but he's not appeared in my mind again. His hold is loosening, and I'm going to take advantage of it.

Though that could be because of the poison they keep feeding me. I know it's going to hurt like hell when I finally take control of my body again, but that won't stop me now.

I've already started to remember some stuff. Being here before, the layout of the building. What they made me do.

Now I just need to get free of this prison inside my mind to let Remy know what I know.

I sit, banging against the glass when I hear Remy's voice. My eyes are closed, so I'm still shrouded in darkness, but I keep working at the glass.

"Fallon," she whispers, and I desperately want to answer her, but I haven't broken through yet. I start hitting it harder, losing the few fucks I have about Gabriel realizing what I'm doing.

"Fallon!" Remy shouts, and the glass shatters. I jolt up and open my eyes.

Fucking yes!

"Thank the Fates, you're awake."

"Everything hurts, Remy," I hiss as I push myself to

sit. My face is throbbing, from where Nevin used me to punish Remy. He's such a fucking dick.

"I know it does. Do you remember what happened?" I nod, a tear slipping down my face, but I swipe it away and steel my resolve. I will not be this weak.

"They're going to pay for this shit."

"They are. But first, we need to work out how to get out of here. Do you remember anything from before?"

I try to flick through my memories, relieved to find them still there, though a bit fuzzy around the edges. I take a deep breath before I tell her what I've started to remember.

"We're not that far from home. Just further north and inland a bit. This place is warded to the fucking high heavens, but it's also a twisted zone. The wards had to go on in the forest around this place, because magic doesn't work normally here. It's why they picked it, so that if anyone attacks, then he and his cronies have the upper hand because they know magic works differently. It's limited, dulled almost. The only reason they're keeping us drugged is because they don't know if it will affect you differently because well, you're you. And me… I think it helps the hold they have on me. It's like they have a door into my mind. I'm holding it shut right now, but even with them not here, it's like a battering ram on the other side of it, trying to bust through."

"So, there's no way to access any of our power?" she asks, and my heart sinks knowing that she's not going to like what I have to say.

"Not while they're doing what they're doing," I tell her, shaking my head softly, and I feel Gabriel's presence in my mind again. "They're trying to get back into my head, Remy. So I'll try to be quick, there's a back way in. There are tunnels underneath this entire place. A river to the south has one of the entrances. If you can get out, that's the safest and quickest way."

"I'm not going anywhere without you, Fallon," she tells me vehemently.

"Remy, if you get a chance to save yourself, do it. If you take me, and I'm still like this, they'll make me hurt you, and I couldn't live with myself if that happened." I can't help but sigh. "I love you, please just remember that."

The last word slips out, and my body starts to shake as if I'm seizing, as I try to fight the grip he has on me. I hate how weak I feel without access to my power.

"Better luck next time, Amantara." My mouth moves, but Gabriel's voice comes out. That shit is so fucking weird. But I'm glad he's not focusing on me so I can try to break this hold again. Even just a little more time would be good. Maybe I can help Remy escape. My body moves to lean in the corner of the room, so I can finally see the whole room without trying. At least I'll know what's going on, and when I break free next, because I fucking will, I can tell her what I've seen if she's not conscious.

"Hey!" She screams until she's almost hoarse, but finally someone opens the door. A small woman walks in. She looks meek as could be, but looks can be deceiving.

"At last. My friend needs to eat. If she doesn't eat soon, she's going to die," she tells the woman, whose eyes go round at my words. "I'm guessing people dying before they're meant to can't be good for business." Her panicked gaze bounces between Remy and I before she scurries away, the door closing behind her.

I don't want to think about the fact that the food will likely be poisoned, though with what I've remembered about the magic of this place, and Gabriel's hold on me, the poison seems a bit much. My body needs to heal so fucking bad.

The woman reappears with a tray in her hands. She places a cup and plate down in front of Remy with a sandwich, a pudding cup, and some chips on it then puts the same in front of me before scurrying away.

I watch myself eat, unable to taste the food properly, it's the strangest thing, knowing what I'm doing but being completely separate from it. Remy passes me her sandwich and cup of water too. I want to kick her a little because she'll need her strength, but she eats the pudding cup left out for her, while my hands pick up the sandwich she passed over.

I sit back in my cage and close my eyes, trying desperately to come up with a way to get out of this fucking cage once and for all.

SEVENTEEN

I've lost track of all time. Whatever happened the last time I broke out of this cage and got yanked back seems to have made it even stronger.

It doesn't seem to matter what I do, the glass won't break again. It won't even fucking splinter. I'm trying to not lose hope, but it's hard when I can feel my body being drained of its power; and as my body gets weaker, my mind gets weaker, too. The more fucked up my body gets, the harder it is for me to keep beating against the glass.

My eyes have been closed for what seems like a very long time, so I have no way of knowing what's happening with Remy, which makes me anxious as fuck, too.

Though all this time in the dark has given me time to take some perspective on my life. Shit could have been way worse. But it's only now, with the reality of the fact that I really could die before I find a way out of here, that I realize how little I've done for myself. The only selfish things I've ever really done are love Colt, and that's only selfish because I know I shouldn't. I know that the coven isn't going to be happy with their heir dating a Hunter. Especially with the potential ramifications of having my own heir. The other is being friends with Deacon, or whatever it is we are.

I'm aware that people don't understand how I cannot hate him, but I've seen the other side of him. Yes, I've seen him at his worst, but I've seen the gentle, caring side of him, too. Saving my sister wasn't something he needed to do, but I know he did it for me. He made sure she got home safely, and then he made sure that I knew, so I didn't have to worry anymore. It seems so small, but it really wasn't. Not with everything else going on.

I know I should be focusing on trying to get out of here. Being the savior. I shouldn't just lie here in the darkness and wait to be saved... But I'm tired. I am so fucking tired. Surrender isn't something I've ever considered. It isn't something I want to consider, but how do you fight back against something you can't see?

I might know who my enemy is, but I have no idea how he has this hold on my mind. How he created this cage inside of my head. None of it. I don't understand the magic, so I can't think of a way to break free from it.

Oh, little Witch. Your soul was a mess. It was so easy to slip in undetected. But I do like knowing just how broken you are. I mean, I already knew—no one's soul gets as shredded as yours has without being broken, but it's fun to hear nonetheless.

Fuck you! I shout into the abyss, and laughter rings inside of my mind. Except his taunts stir the fire inside of me. Fuck bowing down. I stand in the dark and beat against the walls of my cage with renewed vigor, his laughter ringing in my ears until I collapse with exhaustion.

I lay back down in the dark cage, tired but determined. I hear the rattle of Remy's chains, and I wish I could just speak to her. There's something about only having my own thoughts for company that gives me flashbacks to my time in the Shadow Realm with Azriel. Despite the physical torture, I think I'd almost prefer being back there. This mental cage is worse because he has control of my body, and I have no way to tell anyone what the fuck is going on... And no way of knowing if I'll ever get it back.

Azriel was an asshole, but he was right about one thing. He wasn't the worst monster out there.

I hear a pop, and what sounds like Remy sucking in a breath, followed by a few more pops. I have no idea what she's doing, but I really wish I was of more use to her than I am right now. Instead, I try to reach out to my power, maybe if I can reconnect with that, I can break free of this hell.

I hold my breath at the quiet sounds of footsteps in the room. I hope to fuck that's Remy somehow because the thought of someone else in here with us both chained, with my body this vulnerable, makes me sick with panic. I hold my breath, but nothing happens, and then I hear the squeak of hinges on the door.

I let out the breath of hope that means that Remy found a way to get herself out of here, even if she can't take me yet since I'm basically a zombie right now. But if she finds a way out, I know she won't just leave me here.

And just like that, the glass starts to splinter without me even touching it.

My eyes are finally open. I haven't managed to break through the glass yet, despite the spontaneous splintering; but I saw Nevin drag Remy back in the room by her fucking hair, and I wanted to scream. I guess she did get out, but maybe my directions weren't so great.

I screamed while he chained her back up and put a fucking leash around her throat. I want to wrap my hands around his fucking neck and see how he likes it! It's been an hour since they dragged her back in here, and I've just had to sit, unable to do anything as they check the room every few minutes to see if she's awake.

She groans, and I thrash against my cage. Her eyes open and relief floods me. Thank fuck she isn't dead. My eyes close, and I want to kick and fucking scream.

Gabriel is a fucking asshole. I get why he's keeping us separated—he thinks it'll be better for him if we feel isolated. It's the same tactic that Azriel used, but fuck him.

"Oh good, you're awake." Gabriel's voice fills the room, and I swear, even without being able to see him, I can hear his smug as fuck smile.

"Yippee for me." I cackle at Remy's snark. "A little overkill, don't you think?" she asks, followed by the clank of chains. Fuck my life, I want to be able to fucking see!

"I thought so, but Nevin is the one who has to deal with you, so who am I to object? As long as I get what I want, I don't care how we get there."

"What is it, exactly, that you want?" she asks, and footsteps move toward me. I swear I freeze even though I can't say or do a goddamn thing. So I sit and listen instead, hoping to catch some tidbit of information that might help bring back another part of my messed-up mind or might give me another clue about how the fuck to get out of here.

"Isn't that just the million-dollar question?" He chuckles, the scrape of wood on the floor sounds, and I have no fucking clue what's going on. "What I want is you and your abomination of a race wiped from existence. The magic and blood lines are so polluted, it's fucking with everything. Your kind was never meant to exist, none of the factions outside of the Witches were. Once I destroy you all, power will bounce back to where it was intended. A new world is coming."

"You're delusional. Is that really what all of this was about? Power?"

"Delusional? Your grandfather certainly didn't think so. And power will always be the best currency. When Leviathan 'saved' you, he fucked with everything. It was bad enough that the Lycans and the Dracul were created, but they would've destroyed themselves if they'd been left to it, disgusting animals, all of them. When Leviathan created you—created the curse—it fueled the other factions, creating an entire planet of filth."

"You really are insane. You think you can just wipe three races from existence without repercussion? The Fates aren't so kind. All that will happen is a power vacuum, and then something else will replace what was taken. It's not just going to snap back to Avalon because you demand it."

"I already broke the curse. The rest won't be so hard. Admittedly, it would've been easier with the Demons on our side still, but it's going to happen regardless. You can't stop it. The wheels are already in motion, the things that are happening out in the world right now, while you sit here like a caged bird… I don't know that I could be any happier if you were already dead."

"You really think the Archangel council won't intervene? That Michael won't stop this?"

"That would require those who aren't already on my side being aware, and most of them are so clueless and wrapped up in their own bullshit, they haven't been paying attention to what's happening outside of their little bubble. By the time they notice, it'll be too late. As for Michael, well, he has his hands full at the minute. A little chaos goes a long way.

"You can close your eyes, but you can't escape this. You will die, and they will all see just what we do to filth. We will hunt them to the ends of the Earth and extinguish every single one of you and the factions you love so much. Earth will belong to the ones who help us."

"And yet, you work with this filth you speak of."

"Every war has casualties. Friendly fire happens all the time."

Fuck my life, the guy is straight up delusional. I can't help but wonder if there's even a way to win against someone who doesn't seem to have any real sort of grasp on reality.

I hate feeling so helpless with this all. I feel like the world's whiniest bitch, even if it is just inside my own fucking head. I'm driving myself insane. It doesn't seem to matter how hard I try to focus on finding a way out, I get lost in a deep dark pit of suck.

I know there's a way out, I just need to find it.

The meek woman from before comes back more often, bringing regular food and water. I eat because I have to, but each time I do, I feel the poison in my body. My body always falls asleep again even though I can't shut my mind off.

I just wish I could manage to break free from this cage again so I could stop myself eating the crap.

Though I am quietly happy that my body is awake right now. At least I can see what's happening in the room. There's nothing quite like being nothing more than an observer in your own life. I am truly helpless, and it fucking sucks.

The creak of the door alerts me to someone's arrival, and I hiss when I see Nevin standing there with Lizzie, who's decked out in black, all the way down to the hooded robe that makes her look like every Witch cliché I've ever seen. I can't help but laugh even if she can't hear me.

"They really do look like filthy rats." The British accent fills the space, and I clench my jaw. I'm going to kill that traitorous bitch. Hers was one of the magics I felt intertwined with mine when we arrived here. She must be helping them keep me trapped in the cage of my mind, the one telling them which poisons to use most effectively. I swear, I want to slit her fucking throat.

"Still look better than you do," Remy snorts, and Lizzie hisses at her.

"Oh, it's going to be so much fun playing with the high and mighty Remington Bennett." The glee in her voice is unmistakable, though what she intends to do in here where magic doesn't work correctly, is beyond me.

"I'll leave you alone to get acquainted. Just don't break her, I'm not done with her yet," Nevin grumbles before stalking away. His footsteps grow fainter while Lizzie stands in the doorway, glaring at me. I swear she looks almost afraid. She fucking better be. She knows if she doesn't kill me, I might just deal her a punishment worse than death. It hasn't been done in centuries, but my bloodline has the power to strip a Witch of their magic. Destroy their connection to the earth. I'm not sure which punishment would make me feel best right now.

"This is going to be something to talk about for years. The day the infamous Remy fell. Bested by little old me." Her smile makes me want to tear her face off, and it's only the inability to control my body that keeps me still, because in my mind, I'm already clawing at her fucking face.

"What exactly is it that you're trying to do?" Remy

asks, her voice ice cold.

"You'll see soon enough." She claps her hands, and two of her Witches enter the room carrying blood-red candles, glass jars of black salt, and what looks like bundles of sage. Awesome, it's going to get real smelly up in here.

I can do nothing but watch as they draw a half circle around Remy that starts from the wall, but is far enough away that Remy can't reach it. They then draw a smaller circle which intersects with it, which Lizzie sits in, cross-legged. They place the red candles where Remy's semi-circle meets the wall, and again where the two salt circles join. Lizzie lights the herbs and smiles at me. And it hits me what she's doing.

Dark magic. The darkest kind. The sort that festers in your soul. The kind of dark magic that you don't come back from. It takes me a second, but I realize that she's trying to do to Remy what they've done to me. Breach the mind and then overpower it. I laugh maniacally, because if she thinks she can break Remy the way she broke me, she has another thing coming. I hope Lizzie shreds herself apart trying. I spot movement from the others in the room and practically hold my breath as the other two Witches I don't recognize head toward me. They undo my chains and walk me from the room while I try to fight back, but it's useless.

"Prissy little heir, she's nothing but a broken little toy

now," the first says, while the other cackles.

"I'm looking forward to playing with her."

EIGHTEEN

I blink and realize that everything seems heavier, like it's moving slower. "Stupid bitch isn't even trying to fight back. Maybe she wants us to end it for her."

I groan at the ache in my bones when it hits me. I have control back. I still can't reach my magic, but I can fucking speak!

Yes!

I look around the room, but I'm strapped down on a table of some sort.

"I'm going to cut the flesh from your bones slowly for what you've done to me. Or maybe I'll just strip you of your powers," I say, but it comes out far less harsh than I intended thanks to all of the fucking poison in my system.

They just laugh, and when Nevin enters the room he

smiles at me in a way that makes me feel dirty all over. I swear, I don't know if I'll ever feel clean again. My whole body shudders as his grin grows, and a shiver runs down my spine.

"I think it's about time you told us what you've been keeping from us." His voice is like ice in my veins. He tips the table, and it's like I'm standing, despite my restraints. What's worse is that I don't know what the fuck he's going on about. I mean, I'm likely keeping a lot from them, but they've had control of my body and my mind, if they haven't found what they're looking for on their own, I'm not just going to willingly offer them the information. Especially when I have no idea what it is they're actually after.

"I won't tell you a fucking thing," I spit. I might be weak, but my hatred is strong. "Why the fuck would I ever help any of you?"

"Oh I'm sure you could be persuaded… You've already helped us plenty, well me anyway." He looks up and down my body, licking his lips like he knows it better than he should, and I feel sick. Surely he didn't… While I was out of it… I don't remember anything, but oh shit.

Please, fuck no.

"There is no way on this Earth I'm going to help you any more than you've already made me. At least not willingly."

"Well, I suppose it doesn't really matter either way. Your usefulness is coming to an end, so you won't be with us much longer. I'm sure you can feel the drain on your power. It's a nifty little trick of Gabriel's, but once you've been without it for too long, being drained like that, you won't be able to get it back." My heart sinks, because he's right. Except I have no idea how long it's been going on, no idea how long I've been here, so I don't know if he's lying about my time nearly being up.

"We got what we needed from you, and soon you'll be too useless to help anyone," one of the Witches cackles, and I can't stop the sneer that appears on my face.

"I don't care if I die, but don't think you won't be far behind me," I snap at her. "Don't think for one second the covens will forget who betrayed them."

"It won't matter, those covens won't exist for much longer," she says, and I start to laugh uncontrollably.

"Shut up!" Nevin barks, and slaps me around the face with the back of his hand. It hurts like a son of a bitch, but I keep laughing anyway. It might hurt, but it's better than the non-feeling state they've had me in since I've been here.

He hits me again, and I groan through my laughter. "Is that the best you've got?"

"Oh, little Witch, you've already seen some of my best. I'm sure if you wanted to look through your memories properly, you'll find it." He winks, and I gag.

The two Witches start laughing as he wraps his hand around my throat, moving so close that I can't escape the stench of his breath before he licks the side of my face. "Oh, little Witch, you might not have much time left, but I'm going to have some more fun with you yet. Maybe Gabriel can make you nice and compliant again."

My stomach flips at his insinuation, but I refuse to flinch. Even if what he's saying is true, I won't let it break me. I've survived too much to break now. The time spent inside my mind has been a rollercoaster, but it's shown me how much I have to live for.

"Strip her," he commands, before stepping back and letting the Witches get close to me again. "We'll see just how much she can take before she starts speaking. You will tell us about the Queen and the root of her power. You might think you're saving Remy by keeping it to yourself, but I know you know. Everyone can be killed, and you're going to help us."

I make a vow with myself to never speak of what happened in that room. All that matters is I made it out alive. But Nevin and those two bitches are on my list. They won't survive my wrath. My only saving grace is that I seem to have been left as I was, able to control my body.

I've been awake a little while, trying to reach out to Mama, despite having little to no access to my magic, I am a Laveau. We are made of stronger stuff. So despite the aches and the pains that ravage my body, I continue to try and connect to her, either astrally or telepathically. It's not something I'm skilled at, but I'll be fucked if I'm not going to try now that I have some sort of control back. And I've noticed since they gave me control back that there is a small amount of magic still available to me, not much, since they keep fucking draining me, but it's something. If I can just harness it, maybe, just maybe, I can get us the fuck out of here.

My eyes flutter open, my body aches more than I ever want to think about, but I notice Remy pulling at the shackle around her neck.

"You won't be able to open it without the key," I mumble, my head feels like it's stuffed with cotton balls. The extra doses of poison they gave me are still working their way through my system, and despite having control, I feel like my bones are made of rubber.

"I'm so sorry, Fal," she whispers as I try to sit up, trying not to cry as I do. These fuckers don't deserve my tears. I just wish I had my magic, I could heal myself just enough to not want to curl up in a ball.

"None of this is your fault, Remy. You have nothing to be sorry for," I tell her, looking her in the eye. None of this is on her, and I hate that she might blame herself for everything that's happening. "All you've done is try to survive. We're getting out of here. I'm working on something, it's just taking time."

"What can I do?" she asks, but I shake my head.

"Nothing except what you're doing. Just stay strong. I've been trying to reach Mama, but between the natural shielding this place has and the wards laid down outside, it's practically impossible. That's without them draining me to fuel the wards and shit."

"What can I do to get you out of their grasp?"

"The hold they have on me? It's from Gabriel, I don't know what it is or how he's doing it. It takes a lot of concentration to push him back, and even then, it's only if he's distracted that I can push through the fog in my mind. It's like being a backseat driver in my own body. It's violating as fuck, but he'll pay for it, you best believe that, him and Nevin both." The venom in my voice is real, and I just hope she doesn't read anything more into it than she already knows.

"Oh, I have no doubt. Daydreams of making them pay for everything they've put us through are what keeps me going." Her smile matches my own as I've no doubt she has similarly sadistic dreams of how to make them pay.

"I tried to find the tunnels you told me about," she tells me with a sigh. "They found me, hence my new jewelry.

But I'm not giving up."

"I know you won't. The shackle on your neck is locked with magic, same as the others. I'm trying to hold on to enough each time they drain me so that I can undo the locks. The second I have enough power, I will free you. Don't worry about me, just get yourself out of here."

"There is no chance, in this life or any other, that I'm leaving you behind, Fal. Either we both get out, or we go down trying. Let's just hope for the former." She pauses and watches me, while the room spins and starts to fog. Shit, no this can't be happening again. Please Goddess no. "Are you okay?"

"He's trying to take control back. Remy, just remember what I said. Get out of here, come back if you must, but you need to get out of here. If you're not here, he won't get what he wants. I love you, just remember that, no matter what they make me do." I manage to push the words out before I start falling again, my ass hitting the ground as I find myself back in my cage.

I hear Remy's scream as she rattles her chains, her pain as evident as my own. "I will kill you, Gabriel. Even if it's the last goddamn thing I do!"

I lose track of time again while I'm banging against my cage. I was so close. There is no way he gave me power back to experience what I just went through for me to not fight with everything I've got to make sure it never happens again.

I notice loud voices from outside the room we're still kept in and scream again. I need to get control of my fucking body.

I hear Remy suck in a breath as the door handle twists and the door pushes open slowly. The voices stop when a woman I don't recognize enters the room. Remy hisses at the sight of her, and I just know I'm missing something yet again.

The woman grins between us both before turning her focus back on Remy, who snarls at the woman.

"Hello, Remington."

"Aryna," Remy's voice comes out as little more than a growl. "I should've known you were wrapped up in this bullshit. I guess losing your challenge to me was too much for your fragile ego."

"Oh, Remy, you think this wasn't already in play back then? Why do you think we challenged you both in the first place? It was an opportunity, and we took it. It didn't work out, but you weren't strong enough to do what was needed, and now here we are. Now you're mine to play with," she purrs as she lets the door fall closed and sashays toward Remy with all the swagger in the world. I swear I barely breathe, not wanting to miss a thing. She's obviously one of Roman's Lycans, but I don't remember ever hearing Remy talk about this bitch. I add her name to my list. It's getting long, but every person on it needs to suffer.

"I'm pretty sure you wouldn't be so confident if I wasn't chained up." Remy launches forward, pulling on the chains, and Aryna startles. She recovers quickly, but I laugh so fucking hard because I saw it. Her face reddens with anger, and she clenches her fists as Remy steps back to the wall and slides down to sit, looking not at all bothered by the woman's presence and threats.

Aryna crouches down to Remy's level, and though I can't see the Lycan's face from here, Remy doesn't look fazed. "It doesn't matter what you think, the fact is you're chained and powerless, and I am not. You don't have the upper hand here, and I'm going to make sure you feel every moment of our time together."

"Just remember, Aryna, that I will hunt every single person that hurts me and my family to the ends of the Earth. You will fear the shadows before I am done with you, and when I take your heart from your chest, my hands won't falter in the slightest. You will deserve every tortured minute that you experience." Remy's voice is cold, harsh, but I don't doubt a word she says. I am fully Team Remy.

"That's big talk for a girl in chains." She smirks and stands back up. "Let's see how big you talk when I'm done with you." She calls to someone outside of the room, and a guy, who I assume is a Lycan purely based on the sheer mountainous size of him, enters. He hands her a syringe with that fucking black goo in it.

Fuck, no! This can't be happening. I know Remy is strong, but if they keep dosing us both, there's going to be a line we can't come back from.

"Lowe, if you'll do the honors," Aryna says, and her eyes dance with delight. The monster of a man walks toward Remy, who climbs to her feet. I have little doubt that Remy could take him in a different circumstance, but I want to be sick. These people have no fucking morals, no rules that they go by.

I'll happily watch them all be eradicated from existence.

Remy grins at him as he approaches, and he looks uneasy. I guess he knows exactly who she is. "You know, if Roman gets ahold of you after you've done anything to hurt me, any pain I lay down on you now is going to feel like being tickled."

He hesitates and looks back at Aryna who scoffs. "Just get the fuck on with it. That's an order."

"Too scared to do it yourself, Aryna?" Remy taunts, baring her teeth. "A good leader would never ask her people to do something she isn't willing to do herself." Lowe slows at her words, glancing back at Aryna again.

Fucking yes! Turn on her! There's no honor amongst

assholes anyway.

"That pussy bullshit is why you're the bitch in chains, and I'm not," Aryna snarls. "Just fucking do it, Lowe."

The man steps forward again, his unease still evident, but an order from his Alpha is still an order. Especially when they've broken away from Roman's command, or so it seems. Remy moves back against the wall; the closer he gets to her, the bigger range of movement in the chains she's going to have and she just smirks at him.

Holy shit, she's going to fight him. Even chained up. I let out a whoop inside my mind, cheering for my friend as loudly as I can. Not that she can hear me, but fucking still. Hell fucking yes!

She waits until he's close enough and then pounces forward, throwing her fist out to connect with his face. I let out another cheer as she drops down and sweeps his feet out from under him.

Take that, motherfucker!

As he falls, Remy wraps the chain from her shackle around his throat and tugs him back toward her. He claws at her, but she doesn't even flinch as she tightens the chain and the syringe scatters across the floor.

"You can kill him, he's just a soldier, and apparently a useless one. Shouldn't let a man do a woman's job anyway," Aryna sighs, and Remy releases the choking Lycan from her grasp.

Yes! This bitch is going to lose her only ally. Come on, Remy, kick her ass, too!

"I suggest you leave here, really fucking quickly, and hope that Roman never finds you," Remy snarls at him, and he scurries from the room. I cackle with laughter until my stomach hurts at how quickly he scampers from the room. What a fucking idiot asshole.

"He'll never make it out of here alive." Aryna shrugs and picks the syringe up from the floor. This bitch needs to die already. I just hope Remy has enough left in the tank to be able to kick her ass, too. I hate not being able to help. Watching from the sidelines, useless, really doesn't fucking suit me. I bang against the glass of my cage again, hope filtering through as it starts to crack.

"He might. Guys like him tend to be really fucking squirrelly when they're running for their lives," Remy responds as Aryna paces around the room, her gaze bouncing between Remy and I.

"I wonder if you would sacrifice your friend to save yourself," she says, tilting her head as she watches Remy.

No, she doesn't get to use me against Remy. What a fucking bitch!

"No, you're right, you wouldn't. Far too much of a martyr for that. We've all heard the stories of the legendary Remington Bennett. Throwing herself in front of a sword to save her lover, the Alpha of Alphas." She spits the last words as if their very utterance offends her.

"Some of us love people more than power," Remy tells her, jutting out her chin, and I can't help but laugh.

"Only people with power say that bullshit," Aryna grunts and shifts toward Remy again. "You know, you were used as a story to keep young Lycans in check. You still are. The monster in the dark that will get you if you step out of line. It started about Hunters in general, but a few centuries ago, the stories changed to make you the monster. This was obviously before Roman fell for you. Stupid, weak men, always led by their fucking dicks. I would've made a much better Alpha than he ever could."

"Are you done yet?" Remy asks her, leaning against the wall and folding her arms. I can't help but bark out a laugh in my mind at the audacity of it all. Even chained, she's sassy as fuck. I'm so glad they haven't broken her, though I never really had much doubt. She's the strongest person I know.

"Oh, sweetheart, I haven't even started yet. Believe me, you'll be begging for me to stop before I'm even close to done with you. Seems like you've been holding back some information, and the supposed loves of your lives haven't retaliated the way we'd like either, so I think everyone needs a little bit of encouragement. A little push, as it were."

"You leave them the hell out of this," Remy snarls, and

my heart races at the thought of what she could mean. I hope Mama and Colt are okay.

"Oh, there isn't a chance of that," Aryna laughs, and then she zips toward Remy, using her Lycan speed. I scream as she plunges the syringe into Remy's neck with a laugh.

"I'll see you real soon, sweetheart. We're going to have a lot of fun together."

I whimper in my cage, trying to beat against the glass, but every time it starts to fracture, everything goes black, and it's fixed again. I've been trying to get through to help Remy because I can't stand watching this. The shit they're doing to her makes me want to vomit.

She's strapped to a table, and I'm opposite her, my body strapped to a chair and gagged, not that I could move or speak even if I wanted to. My eyes are open, and I can't escape the sight of it all.

I try to hold back a scream as Aryna drags her claw down the sole of Remy's foot, tearing the sensitive skin to shreds. They've been going at this longer than I ever want to think about. I have no idea how Remy is still conscious considering the blood loss. She hasn't screamed once, no matter what they've done to her, but I've screamed plenty for us both.

They threatened to torture me if they weren't torturing her, and I swear I cried at the steel look she got in her eye. She's kept her mouth shut throughout it all, no matter how much they taunt or threaten her.

They paused for a while, and I foolishly hoped it was over as they let her body start to heal, but they always come back for more. This is the fourth time Aryna's torn her feet to shreds, and each time hurts me worse than the time before. Watching her go through this rather than having them torture me is the worst thing I think I've ever been through.

I can't fucking stand it.

At least if they fucked with me, I wouldn't be able to feel it. She's swallowing every fucking cut without so much as a whimper.

"You know, if you'd just scream like your friend, maybe I'd stop. But it seems to me like you're enjoying this." Aryna's sadistic smile makes me sick, and I want to slap it right off her smug fucking face.

"I'm going to enjoy watching you scream as I flay you alive. It seems fitting, and we both know just how much Roman enjoys it," Remy says, her voice hoarse.

"Why do you think I know how to start at the feet? He had a life before you, you know."

"Ahhhhh, so it all makes sense. You're jealous. Alpha

wolf kicked to the curb for a Hunter. Poor little wolfy." Remy laughs, and I scream as Aryna slashes her claws down Remy's chest, slicing her torso to ribbons.

"See who's laughing now, you fucking bitch."

Remy growls, struggling against her restraints despite the blood spilling from her.

I feel like I'm falling again, but then I'm back in the room. It takes me a moment, but I realize I'm back in my body. My stomach rolls from the sheer amount of pain I've endured and the fear of what Gabriel has planned before he lets me have my body back completely. I try to pull against the restraints, but they barely give.

Fuck.

I lock eyes with Remy, and I can't help the tears that fall down my face, for her and what she's going through more than anything else. I know she'll hate that I'm here with her more than what she's actually going through.

"Fuck," Aryna mutters, and then calls in one of the Witches, who puts a hand on Remy's shoulder. Remy flinches against the woman's touch as she heals the damage Aryna inflicted on her. "Can't have you dying on me yet. We have a message to send to your boys, and it's more fun to keep you alive while you help us send it."

"Fuck. You," Remy wheezes, and I snort. I don't think anyone notices, but as the color returns to Remy's cheeks, I'm flooded with a sense of relief and dread. She looks healthier than she has in a while, but I hate to think just how much more they can do to her now.

I scream against my gag when Aryna starts shoving pieces of wood under Remy's toenails, lifting them, just to see if she'll scream. She doesn't, and Aryna shouts out her frustration. I think I'm going to actually be sick, and I'm going to choke to death with this fucking gag in my mouth.

"Fuck this shit. I'll just do what he asked. You stubborn asshole," Aryna grunts. "But you better believe this shit is going to hurt. And I'm not going to heal you, so you better stay still so I don't cut too deep."

"What the fuck are you going on about, you fucking psychopath?" Remy asks as my eyes go wide. Remy glances toward Aryna, who looks way too fucking happy.

"I wanted you to break, I wanted to see the infamous Remington Bennett cry. Maybe even beg. But I take my hat off to you. You're a strong son of a bitch, but that isn't going to save you. Or the ones you hold dear. We'll slaughter them, or we'll take control of them, the way we have your little Witch friend over here." Her glee is apparent in her tone, and it makes me fucking sick to my stomach.

"You know that isn't going to happen."

"You can think that all you want, but nothing is in your favor right now. You've been three steps behind this entire time, and Nevin is still there, with your guys, leading them in the wrong direction and letting us know if they stumble across anything that might fuck with our plan. It's all playing out exactly as he said it would."

"You mean Gabriel?" Remy asks, rolling her eyes. "If you believe him, you're a bigger fool than I thought."

"You can talk all you want, but at the end of the day, you're the bitch strapped to a table, and I'm not."

"He's going to wipe you all out. How do you not see his hate? His vitriol. I get Nevin, he's an Angel, he'll be allowed to side with Gabriel, but anything that isn't 'pure' is going to be exterminated. He told me as much."

"You expect me to believe your lies? I know all about you and what you're capable of. I know better than to believe anything that comes out of your mouth."

"Well, you best believe that when I get out of here, because I will, mine is the last face you'll see."

"We'll see," she says with a shrug. "Now scream if you want to. This is going to hurt."

She wraps a hand around Remy's throat and holds her in place, while I scream from across the room. Aryna extends her index finger, her claw sharp enough to cut glass, and grins down at Remy. "Time to collect our message."

She drags her claw from Remy's neck, down her shoulder, slicing down her bicep while I struggle against the restraints keeping me in this fucking chair. I can't just sit here. I reach for my magic, just that small drop I felt before, but they must have drained me again.

Fuck!

I gag as the skin lifts from Remy's arm. Aryna cuts down her arm to the elbow where her Leviathan mark ends, and then comes back up the other side. Remy looks like she's going to pass out while Aryna slices through her flesh, and I thrash harder, trying to get free to help my friend.

Aryna finally releases her throat before pulling back. She grins maniacally between us before ripping the cut flesh away from Remy's skin as her blood pours to the floor. I scream as she waves it in the air like a fucking trophy, and vow to kill this bitch the moment I manage to get my hands on her. Tears fall down my face, and I feel less than worthless. I couldn't save her.

"One Angel mark, as requested. The perfect message."

NINETEEN

I wake with a scream, the nightmares clinging to my consciousness even as I fight to wake up. I hear Remy's voice, and it pulls me into reality. Once I realize where we are, I burst into tears. I was dreaming about being in that room with Nevin and the two Witches. I wish I could just erase that memory like Gabriel has done with so many others.

"It's okay, you're here. I'm here," Remy says softly, but then I feel his presence back in my mind, and I start to fall again. I fight it, trying to keep control of myself, and he roars in my mind.

No! Fuck you! You've taken enough from me today!

I scream inside my mind as I fight back, and it's like he gives in because I'm suddenly back in the room. I'm panting from fighting him, and despite having done nothing actually physical, I feel drained. But I fucking won!

Hell fucking yes.

I don't know how I did it, or if I'll manage it again... And I can still feel him in the recesses of my mind, but at least I have control for now.

I look over and find Remy lying on the floor, staring at the ceiling. Her arm still looks raw as fuck and I don't even want to think about what's really going on in her head. I know she's been putting on a brave face.

"Remy? Are you okay?" I ask as I try to sit up. Fuck me, my body is a goddamn mess. I'm not even going to get started on my mental state. Watching her go through what she did, after what I'd been through, and not being able to help… It broke something inside of me, but it made me harder, too. I won't go down without a fight ever again.

"I'll be fine, Fal. Are you okay?" she says, and I sit there reeling.

"I'm not the one they cut up for hours," I say, my voice breaking as I try to speak, but the lump in my throat keeps me from continuing.

"They healed me, well mostly," she tells me with a shrug. I can't get over how nonchalant she is about all of it. How much must she have been through in her lifetimes for this not to break her. I feel broken, and I only watched. I wrap my arms around myself and shudder just thinking about it. The rawness of her arm is a stark reminder… Not that I'll ever be able to forget that particular mutilation.

"Your mark…"

"The skin has mostly grown back, and the mark is still there. It came back. Apparently the magic crap here isn't enough to fuck with that at least."

"Oh good," I whisper, blown away by her strength while I can't stop the silent tears running down my face. They're for her as much as they're for me.

"Talk to me, Fallon," she says softly. I take a deep breath and try to think of how to explain everything that's whirring in my mind.

"I wouldn't even know where to start. I feel so broken, Remy. Like I've lost a fundamental piece of myself in all of this, and I'm not sure that I'll ever get it back. I'm not sure that I'll ever be the person I was before I was taken to the Shadow Realm."

"I'm so sorry, Fallon," she says, shaking her head. I scoff, and decide to be honest with her about some things, things I've not really admitted out loud to anyone yet.

"You have nothing to be sorry for, Remy. I don't blame you, not even for a second. I know that none of this is on you. But I also know now that the hold Gabriel has on my mind is fucking with my access to my power. They keep draining me, but whatever happened in the Shadow Realm means that the well of power inside me is almost limitless, they drain me and I fill back up, but I can't quite reach it." I let out a deep breath, accepting that whatever Azriel gave to me power wise in the Shadow Realm is still inside of me, even if he isn't. But what he gifted me is cursed, and it's being used against us.

"It's the same for me! I think it's the nightshade they keep giving to us," she tells me. "Do you think they could've lied, and maybe it's just the nightshade fucking with us? Not this place?"

"I mean, maybe? They did set up all of those crazy wards around the place. I didn't do many of them, they basically used me as a power source. Though, all it would take to make this place a duller of sorts would be it sitting on a Ley line. But depending on the wards they used, that could be what's going on. I wish I knew more. You said they're using nightshade?"

"That's what Nevin said."

"Hmmm…" I tilt my head, wracking my brain, thankful to have something to focus on. "Nightshade would fuck with your power, you're an Angel, but it shouldn't mess with mine. It has to be Gabriel and the wards. It'd be such shit luck for us to be on a Ley line that dulls power, usually they're sites that increase power, but there's the odd occasion where nature likes to fuck with us."

"So if we can free you from Gabriel…"

"If I can break free of him, we have a decent shot of

getting out of here."

It didn't take long after speaking to Remy for me to get pulled back inside my cage. Gabriel's taunts and laughter have stopped now, but I haven't stopped trying to get back out. I won't quit, even if it costs me more of myself.

A win never comes without sacrifice.

I can't just keep sitting here, watching Remy swirl the drain of hopelessness that she's so obviously trying not to submit to. Anyone else would have broken by now, the least I can do is actually be there for her.

I suck in a sharp breath as magic settles over the room. I can feel it, even trapped inside my body as I am. Remy grumbles from where she's lying on the floor again, and then I scream as a dark-haired man appears in the room. I slam against the walls of my cage even harder because if he's as strong as he feels, there's no way I'm letting Remy face him alone!

"Remy? Are you Remy?" he says, standing over her like some pumped-up jackass. But all I want to know is who the fuck he is.

"Erm… who the fuck are you?" Remy asks, basically reading my mind, and he chuckles. He might be powerful, but laughing at Remy isn't exactly going to win him any points. I stop my barrage against the cage so I can hear what he says.

"My name is Prince Xavi of the Bronze City of Eteriya, Ferry's brother, but that isn't what's important right now..." He pauses, and I growl.

Keep talking, jackass! I know Ferry, she's a Fae in the Shadow Realm. Remy told me about her, but that doesn't explain why he's here. "I'm with your… Lovers? They've been having a hard time tracking you down, but we have your location now."

"You're with my guys? Wait no, you can't come here! Nevin is a traitor. They want you to come here. Please don't bring them to me," Remy pleads as he flickers in and out of the room, and I realize he's only here astrally. Holy shit he must have some serious power if he feels this strong astrally. And he's with Remy's guys! That means he's on our side. I try not to get my hopes up about what this could mean for us. "What the fuck is going on?"

"I'm not here physically. You can see my astral form. Fae magic is a little different to what you're used to. Speaking of…" he pauses and moves over to my body, placing a hand on my head. Holy shit… this is it.

I feel like I'm falling again, and I laugh as I hear the shattering of the cage.

I hear his voice, even as I keep falling. "That is that. Your friend is free. As for everything else, I'll let them know what you said, but a deal has already been struck.

I cannot change the terms of it. Stay strong, you won't be bound much longer."

I don't see him go, but when I'm back in my body, I can feel my magic. It's like he broke all of the restraints that were on me, ones I hadn't even realized were there.

I could fucking cry… Or kiss that guy.

"Holy shit," Remy gasps

"What happened?" I ask her, wondering if I missed something while I was trying to break my bonds.

"A Fae Prince…" she starts, and runs me through the bits I missed.

"Could it be one of Gabriel's tricks?" I ask because it seems almost too good to be true. Who knows what I told those assholes when they had my mind. They could've gotten most of my memories and plucked Ferry's name from there. I bite my lip hoping I'm wrong.

"It could be," she says, wincing as she shrugs. I stand and move over to her as closely as I can and hold a hand out to her. Placing her palm against mine, I close my eyes and smile. I have access to my magic, not all of it as I'm still not connected to the earth, but the power in me that was gifted by Azriel… That I can still feel. So I push my magic over her in waves, healing her, and I feel the heat from her hand push through me and heal all of the residual pain that I have.

"It has to be real…" I whisper, hope flooding through

me. “If it’s real, that means…”

Tears stream down my face, and the glow from my magic intensifies. I feel it building inside of me, like it’s angry that it was taken away and locked down. It floods my system until it feels like I’m going to explode and then pulses from me in a wave. Remy screams as she’s pushed back against the wall by the sheer force of the expulsion, but then the cuffs of her shackles fall from her body, and I grin like never before.

I’m about to fuck some shit up. Shouts start up outside as Nevin barrels into the room.

“What did you do?” he roars, and I smile at him, picturing every little thing I’m going to do to him once I get my hands on him.

“You should run. Now,” I say, my voice sounding not at all like my own, and glee floods my system as he pales. He runs from the room like the coward he is, and the darkness inside of me, gifted by a Demon himself, practically hums with the thrill of the chase. “He won’t get far.”

I look back at her as she moves to her feet, my memories starting to flood back from when Gabriel took me, and the bits I’ve missed while he’s had control since we got her. Fuck him and his self-righteous bullshit. I don’t cling to what I’ve been through, because right now, we need to get out of here. “Grab your boots and cloak, they stashed your weapons downstairs. You might be able to access your power. I don't know if I knocked out all of the wards or if this place is a nullifier, but I can't access all of my power just yet."

Remy starts to move and stuffs her feet into her boots. The power expulsion seems to have boosted her even more than the first bout of healing did. She practically glows in that Angelic way of hers. She pauses and then frowns. "I can't reach my power yet, so fuck knows. But I don't need my power to make some heads roll."

The air becomes charged, the ground shakes, and thunder rolls through the skies. Remy's smile is contagious, and I laugh at the realization of what this all means.

"I guess the cavalry arrived."

Sneaking from the room where they kept us isn't that hard, especially since my powers seem to be working somewhat. By the time we reach the ground floor, my heart is racing a mile a minute, but I stay as calm as I can manage. I refuse to be the reason we don't get out of here. Panicking and freaking out isn't going to get us anywhere but dead, and that shit is not on today's list. For either of us.

"I need my weapons," Remy reminds me and I nod, pointing down the hall in the opposite direction of us.

"The armory is that way, if I remember correctly," I

tell her, hoping this isn't just some trick or an implanted memory. My stomach flips at the possibility, but I shove it down. Panic is not going to win this time.

She nods and takes the lead, moving around the corner into the hall first, sweeping the rooms we pass as we go. Apparently, we weren't the only ones who heard the oncoming thunder. Nevin and Gabriel both know what comes with that storm, but I don't know if either of them are even still here.

Hell, I don't know who is here period.

Except for who's outside, of course. I'm not really surprised that Levi and the others didn't listen to the message Remy passed on with the Fae Prince. I don't know who's with them, and I'm conflicted about who I want to be out there... Not wanting people risking themselves for me. One, for them, but two, because between Remy and I, I think we can get out of here, fuck some people up, and be okay. My friend is a total badass, and with the power flowing through me at the minute, I feel like I could stop the world from spinning.

I'm trying to not get power drunk while we try to find the fucking way out of here.

Halfway down the hall, we find the armory, which is filled to the hilt. Fortunately, it doesn't take Remy long to find her weapons and strap them on. She grabs one of their bows and two quivers, slinging them over her shoulder before passing me a handgun. "You shot one of these before?"

"No, but I assume it's simple enough, point and shoot," I tell her, keeping my finger away from the trigger, I haven't used a gun, but I'm also not stupid. It feels heavier than I thought it would.

"Pretty much," she says with a tight smile that I recognize. Remy's shifting into battle mode.

"Okay, got it. Plus, I'll use my magic as much as I can anyway," I tell her, trying to reassure her, and myself, that I'm not going to be a burden.

"Sounds good, just try not to shoot our guys if you can help it." She winks at me, and I can't help but laugh. It feels so fucking good to laugh again!

"I'll do my best," I tell her as she pulls a few of the guns for herself. I try not to get bogged down in the fact that she seems to think we need this many weapons to get out of here.

"We should move. Do you know how to get out of here, other than the blocked tunnels?" she asks, and I bite my lip. Shit. I think so?

"Kind of," I tell her, hating that I'm the weak fucking link again. I swear once I'm out of here, I'm getting Colt to train me—tactical, defensive, all of it. I'm sick of being useless beyond my magic.

"It's fine, we'll follow the noise," she tells me, tucking

one last gun in the back of her pants after making sure the safety is on first. She lifts the hood of her cloak, while I double check the safety on my gun. She pauses, looking around the room and then pulls a Kevlar vest from the hooks and throws it at me. “Put this on, it won’t protect everywhere, but it’s better than nothing.”

“I can put up an energy ring,” I tell her, looking at the Kevlar like it’s poison. It feels wrong. How am I going to move around in that?

“I get that, but put my mind at ease and put it on?” she asks, and I roll my eyes. Of course she played that card, she knows I won’t say no. Stupid guilt.

“Fine, but only because I’ll feel guilty otherwise.” I pout a little, but she laughs, and it loosens the darkness inside of me just a little. I take a deep breath, steeling my reserve. We have to make it out of here. Both of us.

“Good,” she says, sticking her tongue out. “Now let’s get the fuck out of this hell hole.”

“Yes, ma’am. Let’s do this.”

“Keep it pointed down unless you intend to shoot and never aim it at me or you.” I nod at the instruction, and then she leads us from the room. The ground trembles again as we reach the doorway, and dust rains around us as the entire fucking fortress shakes. Holy shit, I guess Levi is more than a little pissed off.

Remy mutters under her breath before checking the

hall. "Okay, let's go. Keep one hand on my shoulder, and watch our six."

"Whatever we need to get us out of here, I'm up for. I'll walk on my hands if that's what it takes," I joke, trying to sound lighter than I feel.

"Yeah, let's not take it that far yet," she smirks. "Remember, gun down unless you need to shoot."

"Got it," I confirm, because yeah, I don't want to shoot her. She nods and heads into the hall, my hand on her shoulder as we sweep the rest of this stupid never-ending hall. An explosion from the right makes me stagger.

"Two guesses which direction people are in," she mutters, and looks back at me frowning as she takes in the sight of me with a gun. "Okay, new plan. Both hands on the gun unless you need to throw out some magic juju."

"Oh, good. This shit is heavier than they make it look." I roll my eyes, but do as she asks because it really is heavy.

"It really is. If you need to shoot, lean slightly forward, keep your elbows locked so you don't miss or break your own nose with the recoil."

"Awesome. Simple. But yeah, of course." I roll my eyes at her, of course that's her instruction. Simple as ever.

"Fine, just point and shoot, but hold on like fuck if you need to actually shoot." She moves my hands so that I'm holding it properly and frowns again, but we're running out of time. The clamoring of footsteps on stone tells me we're no longer alone, yet we're still inside this fucking fortress.

She puts her index finger to her lips and points in the direction of the footsteps before tucking me behind her. I hate how much of a liability I am right now. That I have to keep being saved. She stretches out her neck from side to side, like she's preparing herself to fight, and I brace myself, ready to use my power if I need to.

Two guys turn the corner at top speed, and if I had to guess, I'd assume they were going to the armory for reinforcements.

"Oh hi, boys, fancy seeing you here," Remy says with a smile. I don't recognize them, but I know they sure as fuck know who we are. Quicker than I can blink, she peels off two throwing knives. They slice through the air, cutting through their windpipes and spinal cords, and they drop heavily to the floor.

"Holy shit," I gasp, trying not to stare at the two bodies she just dropped like it was nothing. "I knew you were a badass... Like I've seen you in action, but holy shit, Remy."

She strides forward and plucks the blades from the two grounded Lycans, wiping them clean on their shirts before tucking them back away. "That was nothing, come on. Let's get out of here."

It takes some staggering around and running in circles, but we find the room we were in when Nevin drugged Remy the first time. Asshole. I hope to fuck he's still here because I want his death. That one is mine to claim. Though I'm sure a few people might try to argue with me on that.

The door from the room that leads outside opens, and Remy moves so she's covering me, but I recognize the three people blocking our way as Witches from Lizzie's coven.

"Mine," I tell her quietly, and then they see us. Fear flashes over their faces as I draw on my power and raise a hand, glowing with the soft golden aura I've had since I came back from the Shadow Realm.

"*Lanmò,*" I mutter, and their eyes go wide. I open my hand and flick my fingers out toward them. They grasp their throats, as if trying to pull away a hand, and I grin. Enjoying a little of the pain they inflicted on me and stealing their breath.

It doesn't take long for them to crumble to the floor and stop breathing completely. The second they're down, we head toward the door they came from. I'm not under any illusions, things have been too easy up to this point. I'm fully prepared for the fact that it won't be the same beyond this door.

Remy glances back at me as I look at the three bodies

on the floor. I always thought I'd feel differently after killing someone. But after everything they did to us, and everything they stood by and watched, they can rot in hell for all I care.

"Ready or not…" Remy's quiet words echo down the hall. As we reach the final door, the sounds of fighting grow louder. She squares her shoulders and looks back at me. I nod to let her know I'm ready, and she opens the door just a sliver.

"Shit." The curse echoes down the hall, and I stiffen behind her.

"What?"

"Something isn't right. There are a lot of bodies out there, but I don't see one fucking Angel," she mutters.

"What the fuck!" I hiss, pissed that neither of them are here to feel some pain.

"Exactly. Why aren't they here?"

"I have no idea, everything I've heard said this would be where they faced your guys. Where they tried to exterminate the factions," I tell her, trying to think back over everything I've learned, remembered, and heard.

"Unless that wasn't their plan," she counters.

"Or it could be exactly why there are no Angels here," I muse.

"It doesn't matter, we need to get out there. You good to cut through the masses with me, or do you need me to take a more stealthy route?" she asks, but I shake my head. Hell fucking no. I want them to feel some pain.

"Let's make them regret fucking with us. They picked the wrong side, it's time they learned it," I tell her, and she smiles wide.

"That's my girl. We'll make them bleed." She tears open the door and I run behind her out of the room. The second we pass the ward line, my powers hit me like a Mack truck. These motherfuckers are about to hurt a whole fucking lot.

I lose myself as I dive into the fray, using my power and reveling in the screams that come from those who try to stop me. I have no idea where Gabriel and Nevin got these kinds of numbers from, but anyone who sided with them... Well, they fucked up.

I try to keep alongside Remy as she decimates bodies across the way, mainly so I don't end up lost out here on my fucking own.

"Remy!" Levi's bellow reaches me seconds before he charges through the masses, bodies dropping in his wake. Watching him fight is like watching art in motion… Even if it is blood-soaked art.

Remy runs toward him, and he catches her. I look around for the others, half hoping Colt is here, a little jealous of Remy's reunion. Another part of me hopes that he isn't here because if he hugs me now, I might actually break. I can't afford to do that just yet.

"Where is he?" I hear the back end of Remy's question and turn to pay more attention to them and our surroundings. It's not the time to get lost in my own mind.

"He's back at the mansion, he wanted to sit this one out," he tells us. I move to throw out a blast of magic at the Lycan running at us, but Remy's knife plunges into his throat before I get a chance. I hear a war cry, and see Serafina flanked by four other Angels swooping down and raining down hell on the masses.

"Holy shit," I gasp, moving closer to Remy and Levi. "Any sign of Nevin or Gabriel?"

"Gabriel?" Levi asks.

"Yeah, he's kind of the mastermind behind this insanity," Remy tells him, while my simmering anger starts to rage again just hearing his name.

"That explains a lot. But no, no sight of either of them yet."

"Let's end this, shall we?" Remy asks with a smile, but Levi takes her hand and shakes his head.

"Morgan and the guys already requested the honor." Levi smirks as screams ring out around us, and Serafina and the Death Dealers rise back into the air.

"I guess you didn't bring all that many people after all, just the power houses." I laugh softly.

"Something like that, someone told me it was a trap."

He winks at me, and I laugh. "Can't let them have all the fun, right?"

"Absolutely not. We've got some retribution of our own to hand out," Remy says grinning at me, and I nod.

"Hell fucking yes, let's make them bleed."

It doesn't take long before Levi pulls us into the tree line, and Serafina, the Death Dealers, Morgan, and the rest of the guys obliterate anyone who wasn't fighting for us.

Mama arrives, and I crumble. She catches me, along with two other Witches from the coven. They take in the scene around us, the few left standing, and shake their heads.

"Do you need us here?" she asks Remy, who shakes her head and looks at me like she might cry herself.

"No, get her home, take care of her," she says, and Mama turns back to me.

"Why don't we get you home, baby?" Mama coos, wiping away the tears that fall down my face, before opening a portal and taking me far away from this place.

TWENTY

I've been home a day, but it feels like a blink of time. Mama got me home, helped me shower, and put me to bed. I've slept ever since, though it's been the worst sleep I've ever had. Some of my dreams were of Colt and were beautiful, but others… Others just keep shattering the already broken parts of me. Awake or asleep, it doesn't matter—I'm haunted. The memories start to overwhelm me, and I feel like I'm going to drown.

I feel manic. I bounce between feeling like my head is being held under water to being so angry that I vow to never let anyone make me feel this way again.

It's exhausting.

Mama has kept everyone away, though she did pass on the message that Nevin had been captured, which I'm beyond happy about, but today… Today I need to see Colt. It's like my whole body needs to be near him, so I pick up my phone and send him a message.

Me: Hey, are you around today?

Colt: Thank fucking Christ! I was losing my goddamn mind. Yes, I'm around for you. Always. Do you need me to come and get you?

Me: No, I'll get ready and portal over.

Colt: Okay baby, I'll be waiting.

I drop my phone and sigh, feeling a little lighter already. I don't want to tell him what happened, but I know I have to. Even if no one else ever knows what happened, I need to tell him. He'll know anyway. My body holds the damage of what was done to me. They healed me around the wounds so I'd be left with the scars.

Sure I could cut myself and re-heal, but I don't have the energy for that right now. All I want is to be in his arms, safe. Away from the loudness in my mind.

I climb from the bed, groaning with each step. I might have felt like a superhero the day we escaped, but a lot can be said for the after effects from a power surge coupled with adrenaline. Since that's all faded, all I feel is broken.

Body and mind.

I walk slowly to my closet to get dressed. I pull out jeans and one of Colt's hoodies I had stashed away in the closet. Not my usual clothes, but today, I need the comfort. I grab a t-shirt from my dresser and get dressed, trying not to wince as the clothes drag over my sensitive skin.

My door opens, and Mama's head pops through the gap. She frowns when she sees me up and dressed. "And where do you think you're going? You're meant to be resting."

"I'm going to go see Colt, Mama." She frowns a little harder but doesn't say anything more about it.

"The coven has Lizzie. We're passing judgement today. I thought you might want to be there," she tells me, and I heave a deep sigh.

"Honestly, Mama, if I never see her again, it will be too soon." I shake my head, not wanting to relive this twice today. "Strip her of her power. That's my vote. Let her live her life without a coven, without a family, and without her magic. Shun her. I can't think of a more fitting punishment for the power-hungry bitch."

"Okay, I'll take your proxy if you're sure." She looks me over, the worry evident on her face.

"I'm sure, Mama, I just… I need to see Colt."

"Are you sure it's a good idea? Forming attachments to

the Hunter?" she asks, and I pinch the bridge of my nose.

"Love is love, Mama. Factions be damned. Colt has been there for me through everything and never questioned me, even when the coven did. He won't care what I went through, for any reason other than that it hurt me. He loves me, and I love him. We weren't going to make a big deal out of it until we got more settled, but I need you to be okay with this."

"I just don't want to see you get hurt any more than you already have been."

"Colt isn't going to hurt me, Mama. He's the last person in the who would."

She smiles sadly but nods her head. "I know, baby. Just let me know that you're okay... Like daily, please?"

"Sure thing, Mama." I smile and hug her gently, before heading out to the back yard. I open a portal and jump through to Colt's. I'm barely through when I feel his arms around me and I sink into him, letting his scent envelop me.

"Thank the fucking Fates you're okay," he whispers as he holds me close and kisses the top of my head. "Let's get you inside."

He picks me up, his arm under my knees as I wrap mine around his neck. I let him carry me. I don't have the need to fight back, this right here… Being here with him, in his arms… This is exactly what I need. He carries me through the house and straight up the stairs before climbing into bed with me still in his arms. "I've got you. You're safe now."

And for the first time in a while, I fall asleep without memories chasing me into subconscious.

I've been at Colt's for the last week, and he has literally been perfect. He hasn't pushed me for details, though I did give him the basics. When I told him about what Nevin and the Witches had done to me, he lost his shit a bit, and the banging that came from the basement as he tore it apart after that was crazy.

We've done nothing but talk, eat and sleep for the whole week. I left the Lizzie bullshit to the coven, the bloodthirstiness I felt while we were escaping is gone. When I think back about the people I killed, I just feel hollow. Hell, I feel hollow most of the time now.

It's like the pieces of me I lost in that place are gone, and I don't know how to get them back. Being here with Colt has been helping, but I hate the sadness and anger I can sense in him. Like he knows I'm broken, and he wants to fix me… But he can't.

I know the only one who can fix me is me.

I just don't know how to fix myself yet though. Gabriel

stole a part of me away when he did what he did. I thought the way Azriel held me captive was bad, but I've had my whole perspective changed. Yes, what he and Deacon did to me was bad, though compared to Gabriel and Nevin… The torture wasn't nothing, yet it could have been significantly worse.

Except now… Now, I've lived through worse. I know I've survived it all, but I don't really feel like I did. Not fully. That dark pit inside of me calls out to me every day, and each day I fight not to fall into it. But the fight is exhausting, and sometimes I think giving into it would be so much easier.

But then Colt smiles at me, and reminds me I have something worth fighting for. His love helps me every single day. He's so gentle with me, so kind and caring, and I cling to it. I probably shouldn't put all of that on his shoulders, but he keeps telling me that he's here to share the burden with me, so I need to believe him… Because if I don't… Well, I don't want to even think about where I'd be without him right now.

"Hey," he calls out as he pops his head into the kitchen. I'm making breakfast, like I have the last few days. He saunters up behind me, wrapping his arms around my waist, and I lean back onto him. His heart beats against my back, calming my own. "You okay? You came down without me, you little sneak."

I laugh softly as he kisses the side of my head near my ear and wave him away. He really has been my rock. The calm in the storm of my mind. "I'm fine, I just woke up and didn't want to sleep anymore, so I thought I'd bring you breakfast in bed, but you ruined that by waking up, you big oaf."

He scoffs and spins me around, turning the stove down so the eggs don't burn and cups my face in his hands. "You swear you'd tell me if anything was wrong?"

"I promise," I breathe, barely more than a whisper, because that's what I swore to him at the beginning of the week. That no matter what, I'd be honest with him about how I was feeling. Especially after everything that's happened. He leans down and kisses me softly, just like he has all week. The dominating, playful version of Colt hasn't shown up this week, and I get it. But a small voice in my mind says he doesn't want to touch broken goods.

I try to push the negative thoughts away and lose myself in his touch, but he pulls back too quickly. "Let's get breakfast sorted out, and then we can start the defense lessons we talked about, yeah?"

I sigh, trying not to feel too disappointed because I get it. I'm all over the fucking place. "Sure, that sounds good."

I smile back at him over my shoulder, catching him watching me—looking at me like he thinks I'm going to break. He sees me, and his whole face changes as he smiles at me, like he alone is responsible for my happiness.

We spend the day training, and if I thought I was exhausted before, I was very fucking wrong. Colt is a beast when he trains, and while he didn't expect anywhere near as much from me, I got a big wake up call today about just how out of shape I really am. As a result, Colt decided we need to focus on getting my body in better shape before we start working on defense movements, but I'm kind of glad for it because working on strengthening my body, even just for a little while, helped me mentally. It gave me space to clear out some of the junk in my mind and just focus. The world fell away, and I realized that deep down I'm not completely broken. I just need to take my time to heal.

But with Colt by my side, I have no doubt that it's possible. After a quick shower, I finish dressing, and my phone starts to ring. I look to where it sits on my dresser, and frown when I see Creek's name, my heart sinking. Please let everyone be okay.

"Hello?"

"Fallon? Thank the Fates. We need your help. There was an ambush at the manor, Michael is hurt. Gabriel was here, he fucking attacked when we were distracted. Michael took a hit from Angel glass."

"Michael? As in the Angel? How the fuck am I meant to help him?" I almost shout, and Colt appears in the doorway, eyes wide.

"I don't know, but Remy asked me to call you… She needs you," he says, and my heart skips a beat. There is no way I can say no. Not after everything. I just don't know how much I'm going to be able to help. I haven't used my magic since I got back with the exception of portaling.

"Okay, I'm on my way."

"Thank you, Fallon," Creek says before hanging up. I pull the phone from my ear to see my hands shaking. Shit. I need to get a grip on myself. He didn't say that they were still being attacked. I'm going to be okay.

"What was that?" Colt asks as I stand and walk toward him.

"It was Creek, Remy needs me," I tell him, and he curses.

"My fucking sister. I love her, but sometimes I want to strangle her."

"I have to go, Colt," I tell him, hoping he'll understand.

"I know, let me grab my boots. Don't think for one second you're going without me. If they need you, then shit has hit the fan. I'm not letting you go alone." He darts from the room, and I hear his footsteps clamber down the stairs.

Thank fuck for him.

I make my way down after him and by the time I reach the bottom of the stairs, he's armed and ready to go.

"Let's do this."

We get to the manor, and it's a mess; but I try not to focus on the blood and the bodies. Instead, I rush to Remy's side and drop down beside her, a deeper part of me instinctually telling me how to help her with Michael, who lies prone on the floor before her. I guess the Goddess is with us today. I place my hand on top of hers, and my magic reacts to her touch in an instant, flowing through our hands and into Michael. It feels like it might be working for a minute, but then he screams beneath us, and my power snaps back to me, like it was rejected. It doesn't make any sense, every instinct in me pushes me to help him. I don't understand why this isn't working.

"It's not working. Too late…" he wheezes.

"No, it can't be too late," Remy cries, clutching at him. My heart breaks for her, she's lost too much. Too many people.

"It's okay, little bird. It is time." His words are barely audible, and I watch as Remy's heart shatters, her entire face falls.

"It is not time," she cries, shaking her head, and his

eyes close. A tear slips down my face, but I wipe it away quickly, feeling her pain as if it were my own.

"Angel, this is it, his soul is untethering, you need to heal him or let him go," Levi says as he drops down into a crouch on Michael's other side.

"No, no!" She grabs my hand and pushes her power back into him, mine answering the call of hers. "There has to be another way."

The power snaps back again, and Remy sucks in a deep breath before looking up at Levi, who looks like he's feeling her pain almost as keenly as I am.

"I need you to make him a Hunter," she begs him, and he blanches.

"Remy, I don't know if I can do that again. If I'm being honest, I'm not entirely sure how it worked the first time. I was just a man in love, broken and desperate."

"Please at least try," she pleads, and I see the moment he gives in. I get it. I'd save him for her if I could. She gives so much for everyone else. Her pain is a raw wound in my chest, and I just want to make it better for her.

"If it doesn't work—" he starts, but she interrupts him.

"If it doesn't work then we're exactly where we are now, it won't be your fault. It will be mine because I couldn't fucking save him."

He sighs and looks over at me. I gulp under his intense gaze, but steel myself. I can do whatever he needs. For

Remy. "Last time, I held onto her soul and placed it into a human body, one that was dying, knowing that she would be reborn. Once the soul leaves, our bodies are no different than yours essentially, but I didn't know that then. If you can heal him, I can try to re-tether his soul to the human form that his body becomes, since the way I did it before isn't viable right now. There will likely be different results, but we can't do anything but try."

"Okay, I've got you. I've healed Remy's Angel form, so I know I can heal him. It's just the angel glass that's the problem. If his soul leaving makes the angel glass wound no different to any other, then I should be able to heal him," I tell Levi, not feeling all that confident, especially since Michael's body keeps pushing back my power, but I'm going to give it all I've got. I know she'd do no less for me. I look back at Colt, and he looks fucking terrified. I try not to let it bother me, his worry for me, but I'm more than a little aware that the cost of saving Michael could be more than I have to offer.

I move back while Creek pulls Remy away. Roman extracts the dagger from Michael's heart, and then I jump back in, putting pressure on the wound. He lost consciousness about a minute ago, and that doesn't exactly fill me with hope for how successful this is going to be, but I push my fears aside.

"Ready?" Levi asks, and I nod. He closes his eyes and places his hands over the gushing wound in Michael's chest, and I put my hands back over his. His power hits me with so much force, it's like being struck by lightning. I suck in a breath and push my magic to merge with his, feeling as it wraps around the very essence that makes up the man beneath us.

"Are you really ready?" Levi asks quietly, so quietly I'm not sure anyone else will have even heard, but I nod and prepare myself. Levi's power retreats and takes Michael's essence with him. Quickly, I push every morsel of power I have into the dying body beneath my hands. The golden glow that comes from me lights up the room as I push harder, trying to heal the wound. I know I've healed angel glass before, but this seems worse than last time. Holy fucking shit. It takes almost everything I have, and I start to tremble, the toll of saving him sapping everything from me.

Colt rushes to my side, holding me up and giving me his strength as mine starts to wane. I'm so thankful for him being there, but I don't have the strength to say it.

It feels to take a lifetime, but the body slowly starts to heal, and after what feels like forever, the last of the wound closes. I sag back into Colt's arms and the glow dims around me as Remy heads back toward us.

I look up at Levi, and he's shaking. I can't even imagine how much skill and strength it takes for him to harness death right now. I know he did it before for Remy, but this… This is unreal. Remy places her hand on the curve of his neck, and he sighs. Skin on skin is the best form of conduit, and I watch as his shaking stops while he draws on her power. Watching them almost feels like intruding, but I couldn't move if I wanted to.

"Thank you," he says quietly, his focus never leaving Michael. He trembles as he kneels there, and I don't want to think about how much power this is taking from him.

Levi shudders once more and then pulls his hands away from Michael. His body healed, and his skin looks less bright than before. A burst of power cracks across the room, leaving everyone on their ass. Remy jumps up, as if preparing to fight again when Levi takes her hand.

"The curse has been reborn," he sighs. "The Hunters will cycle once more."

"Fuck!" Colt shouts from behind me, his body shaking with what I think is anger. "Are you kidding me?"

Levi shakes his head. "I'm not. It is the cost of offsetting the balance. It needs to be restored. I am sorry."

"Colt," Remy starts, and he shakes his head. I take his hand, and he squeezes it. I feel for him, he'd finally gotten used to the idea this was his last life. He stands up and starts to pace back and forth.

"You guys need to stop fucking with other people's lives. Did you even stop to consider what this would mean for me? For the other Hunters? The council have been working for weeks to work out how to break the news to people, the logistics. Do you know how many people were relieved that they would finally be able to rest? Of course you don't. You've been so wrapped up in how everything affects you that you've not given a second thought about us." My heart breaks for them both. Remy looks like he just put a knife through her heart.

"Colt, I am so sorry."

"Remy. Stop," he sighs. "Realistically, this is the better outcome, but… I had just gotten used to the idea. Things seemed to have more meaning again. We'll adjust. I just... Shit, this year has been a fucking lot." She strides over to him and hugs him, because he's right. It's been a fucking year. It's not that far from her birthday, but so much has fucking happened since her last one, it feels like a lifetime.

"I'm sorry I haven't been here for you. To help with everything you've been going through. That will change, I swear."

"It's fine, little bit. I just... It's been hard, especially with everything our family has been through. I'll be fine. I should get Fallon home. Let me know when he wakes." He motions toward Michael. "He's welcome in my guild, since this makes him practically family."

"There is one thing I should mention, before you leave," Levi pipes up. "I did alter what I did from the first time I started the curse. It is possible that because of what we've done, that Hunters will always get all of their memories back. Their life cycles could potentially be longer too, because of who the curse was triggered by—Michael's power level is substantially different to what Amantara's was when I tethered her soul. You might notice that you age slower than before. There are a lot of unknowns, but we will be here to help with everything as and when it happens. We'll face it together."

"Thank you, that's… A lot to process," Colt says as he helps me to my feet. Remy wraps me up in a hug so tight, I can't help but laugh.

"Remy, I still need to breathe," I joke as I tap her shoulder and she loosens her hold a little.

"Thank you, Fallon, for always being there when I need you. Even when these knuckleheads haven't always been. Thank you for never letting me down, even when it puts you in danger. You are the best friend I could have ever hoped for." Tears fill her eyes, and she hugs me again, so tightly I can practically feel her strain against me.

"Let's just hope things settle down soon," I say softly before pulling back.

"Famous last words," Colt chuckles.

It's been three days since the attack on the manor and Remy has checked in with us daily. I told Mama everything that happened and she wanted me to go home, but I told her no. I'm healing here, and while I know I should spend some time with her and the other witches, everything recently has shown me how short life can be. I don't want to fuck around not spending that time with the guy I love, the coven is important to me, but they've had years of my time without me ever really taking time for myself.

Something about what happened with Michael helped a part of me heal. It's like I realized I am strong enough to get through this, and I'm ready to start trying to live life again. With Colt.

He's still asleep, and it's been too long since he's touched me. I know it's because he wants to make sure I'm okay, but I've had enough of being treated like I'm made of glass. I want to live. I want to experience everything with him. I want to feel. I need to feel him on my body and show me that he still wants me. I need to erase the things that I went through, and I can't think of a better, more electrifying way.

So, I skim my fingertips down the hard planes of Colt's chest, down to his already rock hard cock and the metal pierced through it. He moans in his sleep as I slide down his body and crawl between his legs. I lick my lips, before running my tongue up the underside of his cock, watching his face as his eyes flutter open and he moans my name.

When I look up into his sleepy eyes, I feel wanton. I also feel powerful, like I hold the keys to his happiness. Especially when his pupils focus on where I am and what I'm doing. Colt goes from sleepy to highly alert in a nanosecond.

"Morning, handsome." I'm surprised to hear such a deep timber in my voice. There's a sultry, almost musical hint to it.

"Hmm, good morning indeed." He licks his lips and brings one of his arms up and tucks it under his head, a sexy as fuck grin making its way across his lips. His other hand comes to my head, his fingers digging into the messy strands.

"Come here," he murmurs, and I do as he asks after sucking the head of his cock and letting it go with a pop. Crawling up his body, I straddle his hips and lower my chest to his. We're close, our eyes saying so much, our hearts beating in tandem.

With a push against the back of my head, he brings our lips together for a sweet, demanding kiss. We moan into each other's mouths, my hips mimicking the act of fucking because that's what I need. I need him.

As quickly as it began, it all ends, and Colt, being Colt, gives me his sexy smirk and brings his other arm up behind his head.

"Are you sure?" he asks, doubt creeping over his features, so I kiss him again.

"I'm more than sure," I tell him, almost breathless. He stills for a beat, but then his cocky smirk that I adore so much returns.

"Then please, don't let me interrupt your breakfast."

Shaking my head, I bite his lower lip and crawl right back down to his cock and lick a long, wet path from root to tip, eliciting a groan from my cocky man.

"Hmm, you're quite the little vixen this morning."

I am. I'm horny, and he's been holding out on me.

Placing one hand under his balls, I gently fondle them as my mouth sinks onto his thick cock. I can taste his precum at the back of my throat, I can feel his arousal growing as his dick gets harder and harder, and it spurs me on. I want to swallow every drop of him.

Breakfast, indeed.

"Fuck, your dirty little mouth is gonna make me come so hard."

I love it when he talks like that. It's a sign I'm getting the real him. And if there's anything I love in this world, it's making Colt lose control.

"That's it, baby. Suck it, harder."

My pussy is so wet, I can feel it dripping between my legs. And because he hasn't told me that I can't touch myself, I place hand between my own legs and push two fingers inside, the sound of my juices pulling him back from whatever sex-induced stupor I'd managed to cause him to be in.

"Mine. That pussy is mine, Fallon. Your cum is mine. Only I get to have it."

Sensing that I'm too far gone for games, Colt places both of his hands on my head and fucks my face like a man on a mission. I'm practically choking on him, but it doesn't matter. I love it. I love feeling him use his power for our pleasure.

I love watching him lose it just for me.

Only for me.

The first spurt of his orgasm hits the back of my throat, coating it and sliding down as the second spurt fills my mouth. I swallow and moan at the dark and dominating taste of him.

"Fuck, so fucking good." His murmured words almost make me come as I try not to rub myself on the silk sheets of our bed.

"Goddamn, Fallon. So fucking good." He pulls me up and kisses my mouth, reverently, like a man in love, whispering his grateful words, thanking me for loving him so well.

"Breakfast of champions, right?" I chuckle at my joke, but it doesn't last long when I suddenly find myself flat on the bed, my legs hanging off his shoulders, with my hips in the air and his mouth eating my pussy like an extreme sport.

"Oh fuck… Oh fuck… Yes!"

He's not being gentle, he's licking me up like a melting ice-cream, using his tongue bar to hit just the right spot. Taking care to lick and suck every inch of me before pushing two fingers inside my pussy and fucking me within an inch of my life.

Or maybe within an inch of my orgasm.

"Give it to me, Fallon. Come on my face, baby."

With his fingers deep in my pussy and his face buried between my legs, I lose all semblance of control.

My fists clench the sheets, my hips push up toward his face, chasing his tongue, and my eyes close like I'm in pain. My orgasm ignites a fire I haven't felt in way too long.

I'm flying and falling all at once. My body is on fire and my limbs tremble with the electricity that's firing between each and every one of my neurons.

I'm crying out into the room, yet all I can hear is Colt telling me I'm beautiful.

"Yes, baby. You're so perfect."

"You taste so fucking good."

"I love watching you like this."

"I love you."

TWENTY ONE

COLT

Waking up to my phone ringing, and having my sister beg me to take in Michael was not exactly how I wanted to start my day, but that's exactly where I am. Thankfully, Fallon smiled and adjusted… I can't get over how far we've come in the last week or so. I still want to tear Nevin's insides out with my bare hands—if he wasn't already dead at my sister's hands after his capture, I'd happily be the one to watch him bleed. At least I know he suffered, that's the only silver lining for me. You don't hurt the ones I love and just get away with it.

I head back down the stairs, having set Michael up in Remy's old room for now until we find a better solution.

Michael has barely said a word since I picked him up, but I'm not really that surprised. Poor guy's world literally just shattered. But he's one of us now. He's family as far as I'm concerned, so whatever he needs is what he'll get. I drop down into my dad's old leather chair and lay my head back. As beat up as this thing is, it's comfortable as fuck, and I just need a minute to breathe.

These last few days have been an absolute mindfuck. I had to call another Elder meeting, and tell them that the Hunter's curse was reborn, but that it might not be the same as before. Having eleventy billion questions thrown at me and not having any answers was about as much fun as having teeth pulled. Sometimes, I swear I wanna strangle my sister for the shit she drops us all into. I get that she's only ever trying to fight for what's right, and fight for the people she loves, but goddamn it's hard running around after her trying to tidy up her mess.

I still haven't totally forgiven her for dragging Fallon into that whole mess either, but I do have to admit something changed in Fallon after that day. She seems lighter, like she let go of some of the darkness that was weighing her down. I mean, things are still pretty dark and twisty, but I have no doubt we can work through it. It's just going to take time.

Personally, I think she should talk to someone more qualified to deal with trauma than I am, but I'm not going to push her. If she wants me to be her safe space, then you can bet your ass that's exactly what I'm going to be. I just hope I'm enough, that I can get her through this, because anything else isn't acceptable.

I pull out my phone to let Remy know we're back home, and then fire off another set of messages to Nate and Elijah to let them know about the updates.

Nate: Talk about a fucking whirlwind few months, but keep your chin up. This is the best outcome we could've hoped for.

Me: I know, at least we don't have to break the news to everyone else now either. Just let me know if things seem to be going weird compared to normal.

Nate: Will do. Let me know if you need help with Michael. I imagine he's going to be pretty volatile right now.

Me: Yeah, I might take you up on that. He's staying here for now, but that's not a long-term plan.

Nate: Just let me know.

I let out a deep breath and drop my phone on the coffee table before leaning back in the chair again.

"You okay?" Fallon asks, popping her head around the door. She was out in the garden meditating when we got back, so I didn't want to disturb her.

"Yeah, Michael woke up. He needed some space, so Remy asked if he could stay here." She bites her lip, looking up the stairs like she's hurting for him. Her heart is so big, I know she feels responsible for the part she played in it all, but I also know she'd feel worse if she hadn't helped Remy when she asked.

"Do you think I should go speak to him?"

"Nah, babe, I think he just needs some time to process. His whole world just changed in an instant. It's going to take some time for him to adjust. He'll come and speak to us when he's ready, but I'm going to sort out some food and take it up for him. I imagine eating isn't something that's even crossed his mind, but he's mortal now." I shrug and stand up, taking her into my arms and holding her close for a moment.

We've seen way too much death recently, and I'm just so glad she's still here with me. It's come too close to the wire, way too many times.

"How about we sort him some food and then we put on a movie? We haven't done something so human in a while."

"Sounds perfect," I say, bending down and kissing her. I'm not sure what I would've done if I'd lost her, but I know I'm going to do everything in my power to make sure we have a long life together.

Even if it means a sacrifice.

The house has been almost a constant hub of activity since the insanity of the attack and pseudo-resurrection at Remy's last week. Michael has been out of the house most of the time, and having Fallon here with me has been fucking perfect. Since she's been back, I've had an almost insatiable need to touch her at all times. Obviously that's not entirely practical, but every time the house is empty, I need her.

I've been holding back, and my willpower was doing so well until the little vixen woke me up with my dick in her mouth. Just the thought of it makes my cock jump to life. She's in the kitchen, cleaning up after another whirlwind of a day, so I lean against the doorjamb and just watch her as she dances around the kitchen.

We haven't really spoken too much about what happened to her, but I'm not going to push, knowing she'll tell me eventually. I'm just glad that she seems more like herself than she has in months. I think she might finally be free of whatever was keeping her head under water after the Azriel bullshit.

“Oh shit,” she gasps as she spins around, dancing to the song playing on the radio and spotting me watching her. “Just how long have you been there?”

“Long enough, baby. I love it when you shake your ass like that.” I grin, and she sticks her tongue out at me.

“Do that again,” I growl, and her eyes flash. Fuck me, I need to feel her again. She sticks her tongue out at me, and I pace across the room, picking her up and putting her over my shoulder. “I always knew you were good at following orders.”

I slap her ass for good measure as I practically run up the stairs with her, and the sound of her moans after I smack her ass makes my dick twitch again. “If you need me to be gentle with you, tell me now.”

“No, I don’t want you to be gentle,” she moans as I drop her onto my bed.

I’m naked before the bed even stops bouncing. My clothes strewn all over the place and there’s not a fuck to be given in sight.

“There’s too many clothes on you, Fallon.” She knows what I want, and she’s quick about getting it done.

As she rips each article of clothing from her perfect body, I take every inch of her in. From her long legs to her succulent tits. From the golden glint of her skin to the dark mass of hair that adorns our bed. That tightening in my chest is back, the feeling that tells me she’s everything to me. My throat is suddenly dry, so I lick my lips and swallow my emotions, keeping my focus on Fallon and Fallon alone.

She's my focal point, the North Star that brings me home time and again.

"Open." She spreads her legs like a good girl and gives me an unobstructed view of her pussy. Wet, swollen, needy. And all mine.

Taking my cock in hand, I leisurely stroke myself as I try to imagine how to take her. I need to own her, every inch of her, but I also want to show her how much I love her.

I want my girl in every possible way.

I start with her mouth. It's the one part of her body that constantly defies me. I'll keep her smart mouth too busy to talk shit.

Kneeling between her legs, I glide my dick up and down her wet pussy. I make sure to gather as much of her juices as I can, watching as my precum mixes with her arousal. Then I straddle her chest and take her chin between my thumb and forefinger, telling her with a demanding yet love-filled voice that I need her to suck my cock.

Without hesitating, she opens her mouth and shows me her tongue. All pretty and pink, greedy and needy.

I can't wait to paint it with my cum.

Slowly, torturously, I slide the head of my dick along

her tongue and make sure she can taste herself before I thrust deep inside and watch as her gag reflex kicks in. Her eyes water and the image of her taking me even if she's struggling makes me even harder.

"You're so perfect. I love watching my cock slide in and out of your mouth. You're everything to me, baby."

Bringing her hands to my thighs, she squeezes my flesh and then runs her fingers to my balls, rubbing them together and nearly making me come on the spot.

She's trying to control the scene, and if I weren't already fucking her throat, I'd spank her ass for the sass.

"Tsk, tsk, tsk, Fallon. You're being a naughty girl. And naughty girls don't get to come."

She knows me. I'd rather die than deny her pleasure, but I love the game, and she loves playing it with me.

With one hand on the headboard and the other cupping her face, I thrust my hips at a slow, even pace, grunting every time the head of my cock bumps against the back of her throat. If I don't stop now, I'm going to come, and maybe that's okay. Just looking at her makes me hard, it won't take me long before the need to fuck her takes over every cell of my body.

"Do you want me to come in your mouth, on your chest, or in your pussy?"

I watch as her brows slant in confusion.

She wants it all, and I love that about her.

"Hmm, your mouth it is. Then your pussy."

Increasing my speed, I feel her hands on my ass cheeks, squeezing, her nails digging deep enough to almost break skin, and it turns me the fuck on.

"Fuck, your mouth is heaven. I'm gonna come, baby. You ready?"

Again with the nails, and I'm a fucking goner.

I come long and hard. I feel it deep within my soul. I watch as her throat works double time to swallow every drop, and that just makes me hornier.

Yeah, I'll be hard again in no time.

As I slide out from between her plump lips, my breath hitches and my mind reels with the emotions swirling inside me.

I need to kiss her, to have an intimate link with her. Tasting myself on her tongue doesn't bother me, it makes my inner possessive asshole all that much more like a caveman.

We both moan as I fuck her mouth with my tongue, and I feel her bucking with the need to have me. My fingers, my tongue, my cock. It doesn't matter. She needs to feel full, and I'm more than happy to deliver. Always.

Releasing her mouth with a pop, I give her one last nip on her lip and position myself between her legs once more. In one quick move, I get her turned around with her stomach on the bed and her ass in the air, her pussy ready to be feasted upon.

My mouth is on her in an instant, my tongue deep inside her, lapping up every drop of her juices like it's my last meal. Her scent and her taste do something to me. It's visceral, it's more than physical. Her back arches with the need to be fucked, and she mewls like a cat in heat. It's heady, and I can't wait to fuck that need right out of her.

"I love eating your pussy, baby. It's fucking delicious."

She moans at my words. My baby girl loves me when I'm dirty. Who am I to deny her?

When I know she can barely take it anymore, I reach around her and with just a pinch of her clit, she explodes in my mouth, her juices coating my tongue like a fountain of lust. I drink her in, hydrating my need for her, and it makes me instantly hard.

Fuck, only she can do this to me.

She's barely come down from her orgasm before I'm lowering her just enough to slam my cock inside her. We both groan at the feeling, the walls that surround me are so familiar and protective. It's home, and it's love. And I need to fuck it within an inch of its life.

With both hands on her hips, I impale her on my dick relentlessly. In and out.

I fuck her pussy, and I fuck her soul. I make sure she can feel me inside and out.

Reaching up, I put two fingers in her mouth and nearly

make her gag as I command her to suck.

She tries her hardest, but I'm fucking her furiously, and I'm sure it's no easy feat for her to keep up. But the selfish bastard I am needs to fill her completely.

So I do.

I hold her down by her mouth and without missing a single beat, I wet the fingers of my other hand with her arousal and slowly push one inside her puckered hole. She lets me, inviting me by slowly pushing out. I'm juggling the rhythm between my dick and my finger and she feels so fucking full like this, her pussy tight around my cock, but I need more.

I push a second finger inside her, and that's when I know everything is absolutely perfect.

Fallon is holding onto the headboard to keep herself up from falling with the force of my thrusts. Her mouth salivates, and her groans vibrate against my fingers as I give her everything I have.

"Fuck, so good. So goddamn good, baby."

I'm just saying random shit because my mind is blown right now. I haven't felt this good in… Fucking forever. She's the key. She's the reason that anything matters at all right now. And as I scissor my fingers in her ass and feel her walls tightening around my cock, I know without a shadow of a doubt that she's about to explode, and I'm right there with her.

Sucking my fingers with ferocity, she bites down hard as her orgasm squeezes my cock to the point of near pain.

My entire body succumbs to the pleasure.

I come so hard I'm afraid I'll never be able to come again.

The growl that escapes between my lips is a mixture between pleasure, pain, and everything I've ever wanted in my life.

It takes me a minute to come back to myself. My dick is still deep inside her, but I've taken my fingers out of her mouth. I bring them to her clit and enjoy the follow-up tremors she gives me as her muscles clamp my cock over and over again.

When she collapses, I fall on top of her and tell her exactly how I feel.

"Fuck, baby. I love everything about you."

Things are starting to finally settle down for me. And though everything with my sister, the Hunters, and this war of hers is still up in the air, I'm ready to start preparing for life after this. Having Fallon at my house all this time has made me realize I don't want her to leave. Ever.

I want the house to be a place for us, a place we can call our own, and maybe one day have kids. I know there's issues with the whole Hunter and Witch thing, but fuck it. We are the masters of our own destiny. There is always a way to make it work if you try hard enough.

Which is exactly why I'm emptying my shit out of my apartment. I only kept this place so I had some space away from the house, but I think this might be the perfect place for Michael, at least for the time being. This way he isn't too far away but can still have his own space.

I carry the last boxes down to my truck, unable to wipe the grin from my face. I met with the lawyers today to get the ball rolling to sell Bauer's place. Elijah emptied the place out yesterday and is bringing the boxes to my storage unit today, so that's one less thing for me to worry about. I'll worry about sorting out the storage locker once we get everything sorted with Gabriel.

For now, I think I'm going to head home and maybe speak to my girl about my plans for the future. I throw the boxes in the back of my truck and wipe the sweat from my brow as I jump in the cab. Cranking up Marianas Trench on my radio, I leave the parking lot, not even the tiniest bit sad to be leaving the apartment behind. I'm ready for newer things, and this apartment doesn't work for what I have in mind.

It doesn't take me long to get home, and Fallon is in the kitchen making lemonade with Maddie when I get back.

"Colt Nathaniel Bennett, it's about damn time I saw

your face again!" Maddie scolds me teasingly before wrapping me up in a hug when she spots me. I look over her shoulder at Fallon, who is practically beaming, and something inside of me settles.

We're actually going to make it through all of this bullshit. Once it's over, I have so many plans for my girl. We're going to fucking live.

"I'm sorry, Maddie," I say, kissing her cheek before pulling out of her grasp.

"Sorry," she scoffs. "I've barely seen you these last few weeks, and all you have to say for yourself is sorry. I thought I'd come and stock up your fridge, but I found Fallon here already on top of everything." Maddie beams as she says the words. Her opinions on relationships are very much like my Mom's always were. Love is love. You can't help who you fall in love with, and love is precious, so covet every fucking second of it.

"Yeah, she's been looking after me real good." I grin, and move over to my girl, kissing her cheek, too. "You good?"

"I'm good," she breathes back, her smile still on her face.

"Good," I say, feeling like a fucking school kid, but I don't give a shit.

"Well, if you kids don't need anything else, I'll head back home."

"Thank you for coming over and keeping me company," Fallon says, before hugging the older woman.

"Anytime, sweetheart. Remember, plenty of sugar and ice. That's the key," Maddie says with a wink before waving at me and heading out. I pour myself a glass of the lemonade, my face twisting as the taste bursts on my tongue, and Fallon starts to laugh.

"It's not finished," she says, laughing so hard she bends in two as I spit the drink out into the sink. I grab her and spin her around in my arms, her squeals and laughter filling the house.

"I love you," I tell her, looking down at her smiling face.

"I love you, too," she grins, wrapping her arms around my neck.

"I've been thinking… You should move in here with me," I say, my heart hammering in my chest, but her smile grows, and she nods.

"Yes! I'd love to." I grin so hard I think my face might split, but I don't remember the last time I felt this happy.

"Perfect! I'll start clearing space for you in the closet," I joke, and she slaps my chest gently as I put her back down on the ground. "We'll make this place a real home. A place of our own."

"I can't think of anything better."

It's been a few days since I asked Fallon to move in with me, but they've been fucking epic. We decided to keep it under wraps until everything is sorted out with this war her mom keeps getting visions of, but I honestly can't wait to just know she's going to be there when I get home.

For now, I'm at my sister's with Marie while Fallon looks after the store. Remy didn't exactly sound happy on the phone, so I'm just hoping this is nothing too fucking insane, but she demanded we come over straight away, so I grabbed Marie from the store when I dropped Fal off and rushed over.

I stuff another cookie in my mouth as Nonnie offers me the plate again, grinning at my love for her cookies. "Nonnie, you're going to make me fat."

"Pfft, I don't think you eat enough. Any of you," she scoffs as Remy enters the room looking like she's heading to the gym, and Marie chuckles softly opposite me.

"Hey," Remy says to no one in particular, the lightness of her tone not matching the look on her face. She slides onto the stool next to Marie and one arm hugs her.

"Hey, little bit." I smile at her from across the island. "What required our immediate presence today?"

"Colt!" Marie scolds me for my snark, and heat rushes up my neck. Damn, and to make it worse, Remy sticks her tongue out at me. Little shit.

"It's fine, I didn't really give any details when I asked you guys to come here. It's more for security than anything since no one has any idea where Gabriel is or what his plans are," she sighs, and Marie squeezes her hand. I'm already on edge, and she's barely started. I try to cling to my happiness from before, but I don't think it's going to work.

"It will all work out, I have to believe that. Especially after all that has been sacrificed," Marie says, anger and devastation evident in her voice. We've all lost a lot in this bullshit.

"That's the hope." Remy smiles at her.

"So…" I start, crossing my arms to try and hide some of my tension, while Remy rolls her eyes at me.

"Tone down the snark, I am pissy and armed. I'm not so feral that I'll just attack you without cause, but keep pushing me, Colt," she growls at me, my anger responding to her own as Creek enters the room from the backyard. His eyes go wide as he processes the scene.

"Woah, someone sounds a little hangry," he says looking at Remy intently. "Did you eat yet?"

"No, she did not," Nonnie tuts and hands her my damn plate of cookies. Though considering the look on Creek's face, I'm not going to argue about it.

"Did you tell them yet?" he asks, and she shakes her

head.

"I was trying, but dickhead here was being, well, a dickhead." She smirks around her cookie while I scoff and steal another cookie from the plate for myself. I swear she actually fucking growls at me. She never could share food.

She takes a deep breath, and sits up a little straighter, which just sets my teeth on edge. I wish she'd just spit it out already. "The attack on the other side of the country…"

"You mean the hospital bomb?" I ask, and she nods.

"Yeah that. It wasn't a bomb. It was Gabriel."

"Fucking shit!" I clench my fists, trying to rein in the rage. I saw it on the news, and my heart sank. So many innocent lives lost, for what seemed like a stupid human attack.

"He is no Angel, he is a monster," Marie says quietly. "We need to put a stop to his madness."

"That's the plan. Levi and I are heading to Avalon tonight to approach the council and speak to Zeph properly if we can. Try to work out what the fuck is going on over there and why they haven't wrangled Gabriel themselves." She picks up the last cookie and takes a huge bite, she knows I get snacky when I'm stressed.

Nonnie swaps out the plate for a slice of cheesecake and kisses Remy's cheek before humming as she wanders back into the pantry. Remy narrows her eyes at me as she catches me eyeing the cheesecake. "Try it, and I will stab you with my fork."

Marie laughs and shakes her head, "Oh, Remy, I do miss our family dinners. They always were entertaining."

"Me too. After all of this is done, we should try to start them again."

"I would like that very much. If that was everything, though, I have a coven meeting this afternoon, so I should head back. Keep us in the loop, and if you need anything, anything at all…"

"I know, I'll ask. We're not going to come out of this whole if we don't work together." She hugs Remy as they finish speaking, and I contemplate how to get a slice of that cheesecake. Anger makes me hungry, what can I say?

"How is Michael adjusting?" Remy asks, looking so uncomfortable that she looks like she'd rather chew nails than ask.

"He's getting there. It's a big change for him. I think he's a little lost. He's gone from having this huge purpose to being essentially a human with an empty path before him. I've tried to encourage him to get involved as my second with the council, which seems to be helping. And fuck knows I'd like to hand off some of the politics, which he seems pretty good at. I think it's just going to take him some time," I tell her. He does seem to be handling a lot of stuff well now that he's actually interacting a little. Maybe this won't be as bad for him as he thought.

"Okay… Tell him I asked after him?"

"I will, little bit," I say, before hugging her tightly 'cause she looks like she's going to cry. I can't stand to see her cry. "I know I'm an asshole, but you still love me, right? I'll try to be less grumpy next time I see you."

"I'll always love you," she says and squeezes me tighter. If nothing else, all of this has shown me just how important family is.

"Look after yourself," Marie says, squeezing Remy's hand before we leave her standing with Creek. I know something big is coming, I can feel it in the air. And even though I know I can't die for good now, it doesn't mean I want to die. I don't want to lose everything I've only just gotten a grasp on.

Yesterday I got the call.

It's finally here.

Today we go to Avalon to end this once and for all. I refused to say goodbye to Fallon this morning. We're not doing goodbyes. We'll get through this.

We have to.

She's staying on Earth with the Witches and the other Hunters to make sure that any overspill from Avalon doesn't affect the humans… Except for Michael and I.

We're going.

I wouldn't want to be left behind, and I know he wouldn't either. He geared up as soon as I told him what was happening and hasn't said a word the entire way here. I know he's struggling, but I also think he needs this. Sometimes the only thing to quiet the monsters in your mind is bloodshed. Adrenaline floods your system, and you realize that you can beat the monsters. Even the ones that live inside of you.

We head inside, and other than a nod to the guys, he heads straight outside without so much as a hint that he's happy with what we're doing. But I also get that, because going back to the place you've always lived and not being able to stay there… Yeah, he's got a lot to process.

The guys are all talking strategy when I walk up, and I slide in next to Creek to try to catch up on the conversation when I spot my sister standing in the doorway practically drooling.

"Little bit, you've got something just there," I tease, pointing to the corner of my mouth. She glares at the joke, but I don't miss her concern when she looks me over, I guess my anticipation to make some heads roll for what these assholes have done to the people I love is obvious. She never did like my thirst for war.

She pulls me to the side, just outside of the kitchen, leaving the guys to continue strategizing.

“What’s up?” I ask, trying to work out what’s going on with her. She looks skittish as fuck.

“I’m pregnant,” she says quietly, and I bark out a laugh before enveloping her in my arms.

“Oh, little bit, I’m so happy for you! That’s so awesome.” I give her such a cheesy grin before pulling back. “Wait, why the fuck are you geared up if you’re pregnant?” The fuck arc these guys playing at letting her go to war when she’s pregnant. I don’t give a fuck who they are, I’ll smash their stupid heads together.

She groans at me and squeezes my hands, drawing my attention back to her. “Not you, too. I’m more than protected, okay? Just trust that I’ve got this.”

“If you say so.” I roll my eyes because *goddamn*, and she swats my chest.

“I do say so, so look after yourself okay? Your nephew needs his uncle.”

“It’s a boy?” I ask, and I swear I get a fucking lump in my throat at the thought. “Don’t worry, little bit. Nothing’s keeping me from the life I’m building.”

I almost want to tell her about what’s going on with Fallon, but I bite my tongue. This is her news, and Fallon and I agreed to keep our silence for the time being.

“Where is Michael?” she asks, looking conflicted.

“He’s here, he’s just waiting out back. It’s hard for him, going back there today. For you.”

"I know." She looks down at her feet. I hate how torn up she is about this, but I'm not sure there's much I can say.

"But he doesn't hold it against you, Remy. He has his own debts to settle over there today."

"So, when are Morgan and the Horsemen arriving?" I ask, just as I hear 'Mara' hollered from the kitchen.

"Sounds like they're here." She smiles and we head back into the kitchen where we do another round of hellos. I extract myself from the group and pull up an app on my phone, searching for the perfect gift for my pregnant sister, and my soon-to-be nephew. I grin as I place the order, a bolt of excitement rips through me at all of the new possibilities.

It's when Serafina and Zeph arrive that the gathering is complete. I assume Zeph is Serafina's fuck buddy from the looks of it. I watch as Michael talks with them, and it's hard for him. That much is obvious. But I hold them in higher esteem when they don't treat him any differently. They approach the rest of us after a few minutes of talking, Zeph flanked by Michael and Serafina.

"It is good to meet you, I have heard many things about you all," Zeph says, addressing Morgan and her guys.

"It's probably all true, too," Caleb says cockily, and I laugh. "Now then, let's get this show on the road, shall we? I do love kicking Angel ass, and I have a little girl who asked me to be home to tuck her into bed."

"Being a little optimistic, aren't we?" Serafina scoffs, but he just turns his full grin toward her.

"Oh, sweetheart, you have no idea what's about to hit Avalon."

Between Zeph and Levi, they're able to transport us all to Avalon easily. Once we're there, gathered by Remy's cottage, Morgan and her guys go scouting. Zeph walked them through the best possible spots to attack, but we're hoping to draw Gabriel out to the field here by the cottage. It gives us a tactical advantage, since it's near where the Death Dealers used to train.

Serafina, Michael, and Zeph split off to gather their forces and set their plans into motion, while I sit with the guys and just take in Avalon. This place is fucking… Out of this world seems to be the only way to describe it. Even from a distance, the city gleams, and I squint against the light to fully take in the city that stretches far away from the cottage where Remy once lived. It looks like the buildings are all centralized around a massive white tower, which is interesting as hell all on its own. It splits into four sections, each spire jutting toward the sky in a way I can't wrap my head around from so far away. Looking from the outside in, it seems like the other buildings get bigger the closer they are to the tower, and I can just barely make out a huge stone bridge leading away from the city in the distance. I can't see where it goes since it seems to go on forever, but one day, I'd love to actually explore this place.

Creek looks as blown away as I feel, whereas Roman looks like he honestly couldn't give a fuck.

Those of us left behind move inside the cottage. Being out in the open, giving up the advantage of surprise that we might have, isn't the best idea. All we can do is wait as the others do their part.

It doesn't take long for Morgan and her guys to reappear, and between Caleb and Bryce, there's a lot of excitement crackling through the air. I suppose Conquest and War getting to do what they do best is a fun thing for them.

"It's been a while since I've torn some Angel wings off. Today is going to be so much fun," Caleb says, bouncing on the balls of his feet. His excitement is intoxicating, and it moves through the group gathering in the cottage.

"Gabriel is mine," Levi says, and the others just nod. I don't agree, but I'm not about to say it out loud. If I get the chance, I'm putting an end to the asshole who fucked up not only my girl, but my sister, too. The excitement builds to a crescendo, and adrenaline is just starting to pump through my veins when a boom sounds so loudly my ears ring. The ground shakes, and the adrenaline in my system spikes.

"The Death Dealers have started," Levi announces. "It's time to go."

"You guys should go first. Let him think you don't have the numbers. Force him to amass his numbers in the field to try to overwhelm you. Once you're there, the cavalry will come." Caleb winks at him, clapping his forearm with one hand as he pats his shoulder with the other.

"You heard the man, let's go," Levi calls out, so I follow along behind the guys with Remy. I crack my neck and prepare myself for what we're about to do. The very thing Hunters were created for.

War.

I spot Remy hanging back to look back at the others, so I wait for her. There's no way I'm leaving her here alone right now.

"Be careful, please," I hear her plead with her friends before catching up with us all. The Death Dealers soar overhead, and Zeph and Serafina appear in front of us with Michael.

"Let the games begin."

TWENTY TWO

FALLON

I've spent the whole day in bed. Mama refused to let me leave the house because I've been feeling off all day. I have the feeling that something bad is going to happen today but I just can't put my finger on it. Considering that Remy and Colt left for Avalon this morning, I don't really want to think about it too hard.

The thought of losing either of them is soul shattering. Mama pops her head in my room, where I'm curled up under the covers even though I'm fully dressed. "It all seems quiet down here. I think whatever's happening is being contained in Avalon."

"We should've gone with them, Mama," I tell her,

hating the desperation in my voice.

"We couldn't, sweetheart. The Angels don't allow Witches in Avalon, you know that," she says softly, and I think I might cry.

"We should've made them stay here then. We should've found a different way. Something bad is going to happen, I can just feel it."

"Let me make you some tea, it'll help settle your nerves." She closes the door, and I wait until I hear her footsteps fading down the hallway before I pull my map from under the bed. Maybe I can scry for them. Maybe see if they're back yet.

A soft knock on my door pulls me from the thought of scrying for my friends. Remy's head appears as if I'd manifested her just by thinking about trying to find her. A lump rises in my throat, making it impossible to speak for a moment. The joy of seeing her alive completely overwhelms me.

"Hey, Fal," she says, as she walks in and closes the door. Oh shit, it's written all over her face. Something really bad happened.

"Remy. What happened?" I ask, and she leans her forehead against the door for a second before kicking her boots off. She rolls her head on her neck before walking further into the room and climbing onto the bed next to me.

"We won," she says, her voice catching before she

tips her head back. I watch as her throat bobs around her labored breaths, and my heart sinks. "But we lost, too…"

"What do you mean?" I ask, my voice shaking. There's only one reason she would be here instead of with her guys… No, no. I won't believe it unless she says it.

I refuse to believe it's true.

No.

A lump fills my throat as my eyes start to water. Please Goddess no.

"Colt… He's gone," her voice cracks as she says the words. She clutches her chest as she speaks, and I feel my heart shattering inside of my own.

"No. He can't be… We didn't get… We didn't get to say goodbye. No, he's not gone," I rant, getting up and pacing the floor. It can't be true. I'd know if he was dead.

Right?

I should be able to feel it when the other half of me dies.

But she wouldn't ever lie to me, especially about something like this.

"I'm sorry, Fal. I wish it wasn't true." Her voice catches, and she has to clear her throat before she's able to continue, emotion thick in her voice. "He got separated from Bryce in the fight. Bryce found him after, but it was already too late. He was gone."

"No!" I cry, falling to the floor as my knees go weak

and give way beneath me. "He can't be… I didn't get a chance to tell him. Oh my Goddess. Remy, please. No." I wrap my arms around my knees, rocking on the floor and trying to hold myself together. There was so much we didn't say. I didn't even say goodbye. She climbs across the bed, sliding off of it to sit with me on the floor. The lump in my throat is impossible to swallow around, and my breaths puff hot and uncomfortably from between my lips. Remy wraps her arms around me, hugging me closely as we cry for the man we've both lost.

Sobs rack my body, and I can't stop the ache. Having my soul shredded has nothing on this pain. The weight of grief crushes me, and I gasp around my tears as my ragged breaths puff back into my face. I've been through hell and back, and yet nothing has ever felt as bad as this. My aching heart beats heavily in my chest as I lean into Remy's embrace. This hurts worse than anything I've ever endured.

"Fallon." Mama's voice reaches me, and I glance up, seeing her hazy form through my tears. She doesn't look as surprised as I feel by the entire situation.

"Did you know?" I ask through the sobs, heart breaking all over again. "DID YOU KNOW?"

"I'm so sorry, Fallon," she says as she hangs her head. The scream that tears from my throat is primal, and I feel my power rushing from me in a destructive wave. A slight cracking sound fills the room in the seconds before my window explodes outward from the force of my power.

"No!" I scream, clutching my chest against the tidal wave of grief and anger that's threatening to pull me under.

This can't be happening.

How am I meant to live without him?

Colt's memorial is today, and I am nowhere close to ready to say goodbye to him. I've cried myself dry, all the feeling in my body and soul escape with the tears and leave me numb. I'm going through the motions. Mama hasn't tried talking to me since she revealed to me that she knew Colt's death was coming. The more logical side of me knows that she couldn't tell me, but I'm not exactly feeling rational about any of this just yet. I can barely look at her. How can I be expected to talk to her?

I portal to the manor alone since Mama left earlier to prepare the body and the pyre. I am in no way ready for this. My mind keeps catching on our last morning together. On the cheeky kiss he gave me, the swat on my ass before he walked out of the door. I didn't even tell him I loved him.

How does that get to be our last moment?

It's not fair.

None of this is fair. He should still be here, and even though I know the Hunter's Curse is reborn and that this isn't the end for him, I'm even more aware of the fact that he won't be back in my lifetime. Even if he somehow does come back in my lifetime, our time is over. I just can't accept that; it hurts too fucking much.

The moon shines down around me, lighting the grounds as I round the corner of the manor. Candles form a pathway across the lawn, and I follow the path the flickering flames lay out to me. This doesn't feel real. How can he truly be gone? I don't know that I'll ever truly accept that I won't see him again.

I cross into the tree line, picking my way through the underbrush until I come to the clearing we used before for Everly's memorial. It's lit with candles, and a tall wooden pyre rests in the middle of the clearing with Colt's body laid across it. His eyes are closed, coins adorning both of them, and his arms are crossed over his chest. He looks like he's at rest. Peaceful, almost.

My eyes catch on the candles and flowers lining the base of the pyre, and a lump forms in my throat. I swallow thickly around the lump and shift my focus from the pyre.

It's only then I notice just how many people are already standing around the clearing. Hunters and Witches alike are mixed together to mourn the passing of a man who touched each and every one of us in his own way.

I pause, silent tears streaming down my face. I still don't know if I can do this. I'm definitely not ready to say goodbye to him. We didn't have enough time. We didn't have enough of anything. Gabriel had already stolen so much from me, and how the hell was it fair for him to steal Colt away from me as well? I don't care if Gabriel's dead—any death he had was far too easy compared to the pain and suffering he caused. I move to stand among the crowd of people, struggling to focus on any one thing long enough to really see the faces of those around until I spot Remy walking toward us.

I try as hard as I can to pull myself together. I try to remind myself that I'm not the only one suffering, that she lost him, too. Once she joins us, Mama moves to stand in front of the pyre.

"Today, we come here to celebrate the life of Colt Bennett. The man, the wonder, the joy. His light was one of the brightest I have ever known, and he will be missed by many."

I can't believe this is it. That we're actually saying goodbye.

"Colt was more than just a Hunter. He was a brother. A lover. A friend. He was taken from us in the worst of times and far too soon. But as is the Hunter's way, this will not be our last goodbye, unless the Fates agree to grant his final rest. Even if he is gone, he will still be with us. In our hearts, in our memories, watching over us as he did in life. I have known Colt since he was just a boy. He was fiercely independent, loyal, and he loved with every piece of himself. He gave himself to what he thought was right and fought for that belief until his very last breath. So, Colt, I will say this, with sadness in my entire heart. Until we meet again, my friend. Until Avalon."

"Until Avalon," the crowd murmurs, and I join in silently because I can't speak around the lump in my throat.

Others step forward and tell stories of how they knew Colt. Times when he saved them, others when he got into trouble with them, or, in some cases, dragged them into trouble with him. The laughter and the tears merge together until the moon is high in the sky. When there's no one left to speak, I move forward with Creek and Remy to stand at the pyre with Mama.

I work with Mama, wrapping his body in the white sheet laid over the pyre as we murmur blessings over his wandering soul. My hands shake as we move the fabric, and I freeze, holding the last corner. I need to cover his face, but it feels so wrong. He shouldn't be here like this. He was so full of life, so vibrant. This isn't him. Mama takes my hand in hers and helps me through the last little bit, until his face disappears under the cover of the white sheet.

"We send this soul to Avalon, and may he watch down

upon us in eternal happiness," Creek says, his voice thick, before he lifts a candle and places it at the base of the pyre. Remy and I follow suit. With only a few words, Mama and I feed the flames until they engulf everything—the pyre, the body… The love of my life.

Goodbye, my love.

I've spent the last two weeks in bed, barely able to breathe. I can't even count on sleep as a safe escape from the despair of my reality anymore. Nightmares of his death haunt me. But nothing haunts me as much as knowing that I should have done more. That I should have at least done something. That I should have stopped him from going. At the very least, I should have stopped him from going without me. Guilt and shame claw up my throat, threatening to steal my breath.

I haven't spoken to anyone since the memorial. My grief feels like a deep dark hole, and I'm so far down I can't see any light. It's suffocating, but I'm almost okay with the possibility of death if it means I'll get to see Colt again.

I know it's unreasonable—that he wouldn't want me to feel like this—but if he really didn't want me to feel like this, he shouldn't have fucking died. We had so many plans. So many things left to do with one another... But no one even really knew that I loved him, so who would I have to share my grief with, anyway? We were careful with our secret; and while I know Mama knew, I haven't found it in myself to speak with her yet.

"Fallon?" I pull the duvet down so I'm not completely submerged underneath it and see Deacon standing in the doorway. "Oh, sweetheart."

I break at his words, sobs racking my body painfully. He strides across the room and slides in the bed beside me, pulling me close and holding me as I cry.

"I can't believe he's gone," I sob, and he holds me even more tightly.

"I know. I've got you. Whatever you need, okay?" He rocks me back and forth while I cry the tears I didn't think I had left. I cry myself to sleep in his arms, and my subconscious is blissfully quiet for the first time in weeks.

I wake, still tucked in Deacon's arms. I pull back, guilt flooding through me for finding some form of respite in his embrace.

"Hey, it's okay. You're okay," he says as I push myself backwards and scoot away from him.

"You shouldn't be here," I say quietly, my voice hoarse

from tears and underuse.

"Fallon, I'm your friend, and you very obviously need a friend right now. I could feel your pain all the way in the Realm. I can't just ignore that. I'm not asking for anything. I just want to help you," he says softly.

What he says makes sense, but the words feel wrong in my heart. How can I find solace in his arms when Colt should be the one I'm lying here with?

I shake my head, but he stays where he is. "Okay, look, I won't get too close, but I definitely think you need someone. So I'm going to go and make some food, and don't you dare try to argue. You need to shower, and then we'll just sit here, eat, and watch a movie, okay?"

I nod because I'm not sure what else to do. Deacon taking control of the moment is a nice reprieve from constantly feeling lost among the feeling of not knowing what the fuck I'm meant to do next. So I move slowly to the bathroom and shower. Once I'm finished, I head back to my room to find clean leggings, a tank top, and Colt's hoodie laid out on the bed for me to change into.

Tears form in my eyes at the sight of the hoodie. I pull the clothes on before snuggling into my blankets and breathing in Colt's scent. I can almost imagine, just for a moment, that he's still here. That he's right here with me.

I move to the top of the bed and sit with my back against the pillows, ignoring the pain in my heart and focusing on his scent in the hoodie instead. I'm going to need more of his stuff if I'm going to get through this.

I lose track of how long I sit like this before Deacon re-enters the room, pizza in hand. "I figured no one needs to suffer my cooking, and pizza is good for the soul, right? I hope you like it. I also ordered ice cream. My sister always said ice cream could cure anything."

I can't speak, so I just nod and scoot to the edge of the bed. He sits on the opposite side, putting the pizza between us and turns WatchBox on my TV. He hits continue watching and takes a slice of pizza from the box, handing it to me, before taking one of his own.

"You can't stay here," I say quietly once I finish a few bites of pizza.

"I know. I'm not here to overstep. I just wanted to help however I could. But I'm here for you. If you need me, I'm here, but if you want me to go, I'll leave." I nod at his words and turn back to face the TV. I don't really pay attention to what's playing. I focus instead on trying to escape the swirling pit of despair inside of me that keeps threatening to drag me down.

After some time, Deacon stands with a long stretch. "I should get going," he offers as he glances around the room. "Don't worry about getting up. Just try to sleep again." He moves to the chair in the corner and picks up my big knit blanket, and my heart stops.

"No! Don't touch that!" He drops it, eyes wide. I scramble from the bed and clutch the blanket to my chest. It's so stupid. I haven't touched it because it's the one I slept under with Colt the last time we were together. Having Deacon even near it feels like a betrayal. Sobs rack my body as I stumble back toward my bed.

"Just go."

TWENTY THREE

Today, I'm going to be human.

Today, I'm going to get out of bed.

Today, I'm going to make it through the day without crying because today is Remy's birthday. She's lost so much, and I've barely spoken to her since the memorial. It's been two weeks, and I've been nothing more than a robot. But today, I'm snapping myself out of it. When I opened my eyes this morning, I decided to stop being a fucking zombie.

Rebel is coming home today, too, and I don't want to scare the shit out of her. I know how much I've been worrying Mama, but I haven't been able to get my shit together.

Today I have to.

I finish getting dressed and head toward the kitchen to find Mama already there curled up with a mug of coffee cupped in her hands. She looks so tired, and guilt pangs in my stomach over what I've put her through in the past couple weeks. She's been through more than her fair share the last few months.

"Hey, Mama," I say quietly, and she startles.

"Hey, baby, how you feeling today?" she asks, looking at me like she's scared that I might just run away again given the opportunity.

I shrug and move over to drop on the couch next to her. "I'm here."

"I understand that," she says, patting my knee. "You just have to take each day as it comes, and one day, you'll wake up, and he won't be your first thought anymore. You'll probably freak out when it happens, but it's okay. We all grieve in our own ways."

My heart races at the thought of it, panicked by the idea of forgetting him even though I know that won't ever be possible.

"Maybe," I croak, unable to say anything else for a moment. I take a deep breath before trying to continue. "But today is Remy's birthday, and I need to be there for her. She lost him, too."

"I know, baby. And we'll make it through today. I'll be there for you every step of the way. It might be good for you to get out of the house and be around the people who love you the most. Has your friend been by again?"

I shake my head and pull my cardigan more closely around me. "No, I just… I don't think it's a good idea for me to be around him right now." She frowns at me. When her eyes narrow to slits, I know I'm going to get some truths I'm not really ready to hear yet.

"Fallon, he's your friend. He cares for you. I might not like what he is or what he did, but you need to be around people who love you, otherwise you'll forget why you need to keep on living," she says with a sigh. "I know it's only been three weeks since he died, but you didn't die with him, Fallon."

Her words sting like a slap to the face. I know she means well, but I'm so not ready to talk like this yet.

"I'm very aware of that, Mama. But you knew he was going to die, so you've had more time to come to terms with him being gone." My anger rises, and it feels like I can't breathe.

"Fallon Laveau, don't you dare. I know you loved him, and you miss him, but I loved that boy like he was my own child." The hurt in her eyes is like a knife to the gut. Maybe I'm not ready for this yet. Maybe I should just stay home tonight. "Now get yourself some food, put on your face and paint on a smile if you have to. I'm going to get Rebel in an hour, and you are coming with me."

Her eyes flash, and I know her worry fuels her words, but that doesn't make them sting any less. I also know that if I don't get myself together, she'll pull me out of my personal pit of despair kicking and screaming if she has to. Mama is all about tough love. So I get up and pour myself a cup of coffee. I swore today I'd try to be human, and maybe she knows that. Maybe that's why she's being a hard-ass. So I swipe away the tear that falls as I take a sip of the coffee and try to process everything she said. She's right, I didn't die, but it feels like a part of me did.

She leaves me alone while I sit at the counter and drink my coffee. As soon as I'm finished, though, she walks over to me, looking much calmer than she did before my coffee break. "I love you, Fallon. Seeing you in so much pain hurts me. I just want what's best for you."

"I love you too, Mama," I croak around the lump in my throat.

"I just need you to remember that you have more in your life than just your grief." She pats my cheek before heading to her room, and I sit, staring at the wall while I try to process this entire morning.

Rebel has been bouncy as fuck since we picked her up this morning, but her excitement has been like a soothing balm on my soul. Her innocence and utter joy is exactly what I needed today. It's boosted me up, and I almost feel functional.

Which is good since we're heading to the restaurant that Remy has celebrated every birthday she's ever had in.

"Is everyone going to be there?" Rebel asks, bouncing in her seat.

"They sure are," Mama tells her with a big grin. I think she's looking forward to seeing everyone again, too. Me, I'm just anxious that I might finally break completely. Being around everyone means that the people who are missing will be more apparent. But I'm going to try my damnedest to keep my shit together for Remy as much for myself. I know I can't spend the rest of my life crying.

"You can do this," Mama says, squeezing my thigh as we pull into the parking lot.

"Thanks, Mama." I smile at her, and swallow around the lump in my throat. I take a deep breath before climbing from the car. We enter the restaurant, and the hostess leads us back toward the private room. Rebel skips through the restaurant, knocking into people as we go. Mama apologizes as we walk, but all I can do is smile. It feels good.

The smile drops from my face as we enter the private room, though. I close my eyes and take a deep breath... I swear I can feel Colt in the room. It's like he's here with us. A brush of wind makes the hair on the back of my neck stand up and a shiver runs down my spine.

"I feel it, too," Mama says as she takes my hand, leading me into the room.

Maddie and Nate are already here.

"Oh, Fallon." Maddie says my name with a sigh before pulling me into her arms, hugging me so tightly it's like she's holding all of my broken pieces together for me. I blink away the tears that threaten to fall as I hug her back. The last time I saw her was at the house when she was teaching me how to make lemonade just the way Colt liked it.

Shit, how am I supposed to do this?

She lets me go, and I give Nate a quick hug before retreating to the bar and getting myself a stiff drink. I throw the amber liquid back, taking solace in the burn before ordering another and heading back to the group.

Morgan and her guys arrive, saying hello to everyone as they step into the private room. Caleb pulls me to the side almost immediately.

"How you doing, kiddo?" he asks, and I can't help but laugh.

"I'm surviving," I tell him honestly, and he smirks.

"See, you smiled. I knew I'd make it happen. You can do this, and if you need anything, you know where we are, okay? I know Deacon has popped by to see you, but

I wanted to give you this." He puts his hand in his pocket and pulls out a long, thin box. I open it and find a silver necklace with a black crystal hanging from it. "Call it a thank you for the rings you arranged for us all. You can use this to come to and from the Shadow Realm at will. So if you ever need an escape, you have it. Morgan fashioned the stone herself, so there is literally nothing that will stop this from working. It will bring you straight to the Shadow Palace, and the room you stayed in before will remain yours. We'll always be here for you, Fallon."

"Thank you, Caleb," I choke out, and he pats my hand before moving back over to Morgan and the others. I clasp the necklace tightly in my grip, and I swear I feel a little lighter knowing I have somewhere I can go to escape from everything if I need to. I slip the chain over my head and move back over to Mama.

"She's coming," Morgan announces, and we all move into a semi-circle around the door.

Remy enters with Kain on her arm, and cheers of 'Happy Birthday' chorus through the room. I paint the smile back onto my face. She works her way through the others, and I chug down the rest of my drink to steel myself for the conversation I know is coming. I put the glass on the table right before she reaches me.

"Hey, girl, happy birthday," I say, pulling her in for a hug, my emotions running riot. "Thank the Goddess we made it, right?"

"Something like that," she murmurs, holding me so tightly I can barely breathe, but I don't care. We really did make it, kind of. "Thank you for being here."

"Oh come on, like I would miss this. This year took too much from both of us; not celebrating the good times isn't even an option. Colt would kick our asses if he knew we weren't living our best lives," I tell her as I pull back, laughing around the lump that forms in my throat from saying his name.

"That he would," she laughs softly. "He really did love birthdays."

"Which is exactly why we're going to celebrate this one the way he would've wanted." I take a step back from her as two servers enter the room carrying trays of shots.

I grab two glasses, shooting one back and grab another, handing it to Remy. She shakes her head, refusing it. "I can't."

"What do you mean you can't?" I look at her puzzled, but Kain taps a nail against his water glass and silences the room before she can answer properly.

"We have an announcement to make," she says to me, pausing before she takes a deep breath and announces loudly enough that those closest to us can hear, "I can't take the shot because we're pregnant."

Holy shit. A wave of excitement crashes over me and I

squeal. I'm freaking happy for her. I pull her into another hug. All I feel is pure joy for my friend. She deserves so much happiness in her life. The rest of the room bursts into excited chatter and congratulations as I release my grip on her. Remy is passed around the room, congratulations spilling from everyone's lips as she's offered countless hugs. I can tell she enjoys every second of it because this, this is what family is for.

I feel a pang in my chest for Colt. He would have loved her news, and he was always so great with kids. He would have made a fucking epic uncle.

I push the sadness down, refusing to succumb to it tonight, and turn my attention back to the room.

The night passes quickly, we eat and celebrate the entire time, taking time to think about those who should be with us and drinking in their memory.

"Don't be a stranger now, you hear? And if you or that baby need anything, you just call." Maddie fusses over Remy as we say try to say goodbye. Nate eventually drags her away, shushing her as they go. That drive home is going to be hilarious.

"What she said," Mama says with a giggle, and I think she might have had one shot too many. She hugs Remy before she and Rebel follow after Nate and Maddie, who are giving us a ride home. Mama and I are both way past the limit of being okay to drive. I set a reminder on my phone to come and get the car tomorrow.

"I miss you. We need to be better at the hanging out thing," I say to Remy as I pull her in for a hug. I mean it with everything inside of me. Mama was right earlier; I can't let my grief define me.

"I think, with everything that's happened, we can finally make time to do that." She laughs and I join in, the laugh turning into a snort when I start hiccupping. "I'll see you soon, okay?"

"Okay, night, Remy. I love you."

"I love you too, Fal."

I leave her with her guys and head to Nate's car, hoping like fuck I can eventually find a way to live my life without Colt in it.

It's been a week since Remy's birthday, and I've been exhausted the entire time. Just putting the mask on for her birthday party drained me enough that I could barely move for two days. I put on a brave face for her because I know she would hate to know how much I'm struggling. But it's even harder since no one really knew how close Colt and I had grown.

I know I said I'd try to move past it, try to live my life, but it's just so fucking hard. I can't help but wonder if my time with him was as good as it's ever going to get for me. What if the pain never lessens? Everyone says that time will help, but it just doesn't feel like it yet.

Remy texted me the day after her party, telling me that her and Creek were going to sort out the house. She asked if I wanted to go, and I've spent the last week going back and forth about it. It feels too much like a final goodbye, and I'm not sure I'm ready for that. But I also know I can't miss it.

I'm very aware that I'm not making sense right now, but I'm beyond caring. I just know that I was one of the last people in that house. That it was going to be my home. I should be the one to help put stuff into storage for when Colt returns for his next life.

I finish getting dressed and sit at my dresser, pulling a pen and paper from one of the drawers.

Dear Colt,

I know that by the time you get to read this, it's likely I'll be gone from this world, but I just needed to tell you how much you were loved. I miss you every single day, and I hate that you were taken from me too soon. We had so many plans, so much that we wanted to do, to experience, but now you're gone. I don't know that I'll ever love anyone the way I love you, but that's okay.

I just hope that in your next life, you find love again,

and don't let the experiences of this life taint the man you became. You bring so much joy to everyone around you, you brought so much light into my life. Please don't let that light ever be any less than it has been.

Maybe one day we'll meet again, in another place, and we'll finally get the chance for our happily ever after, but just in case we don't, I needed you to know that I will never forget you. Not in this world or any other.

I'll love you forever,

Fallon

Tears drip from my face onto the page, so I wipe my face and dab at the paper. I slide the note into an envelope and put it in my pocket. I'm not sure that I'll actually leave it with his things, but just writing down the words helps.

I've called his phone more times than I care to admit these last few weeks, simply to hear his voice again. Letting go feels wrong, even though I know he's not coming back. I shake my head and suck in a deep breath. I need to do this, so I drop Remy a text telling her I'll be at the house.

My phone buzzes in my hand, I lift it and see Remy's name on the screen.

Remy: Okay awesome.

We're heading there now, so I'll see you soon.

I take a deep breath and open a portal, stepping through before I can talk myself out of it. My heart hammers in my chest as I step out into the front yard. The last time I was here, Colt asked me to move in with him. The last time I was here, everything in my life was starting to make sense again.

Holy shit, I can't breathe.

I bend in half and put my head between my knees, trying to get a grip of myself as I hear the sound of tires on the gravel of the driveway. The car doors open and close, and the sound of approaching footsteps grows louder.

"Fallon, are you okay?" Remy asks, but I can't answer. I just focus on pulling air into my lungs and pushing it back out. She crouches down in front of me, and stays with me while I pull myself together.

Once I'm ready, I stand, noticing Creek still standing by the car. "Sorry, I just… I wasn't ready."

"You don't have to do this," Remy starts, her gaze darting over to Creek.

"I do… He asked me to move in with him," I tell her softly, and she sucks in a breath, her eyes wide with shock. "I spent a lot of time here before. We were… I just… I have to be here. It was going to be our home."

"I had no idea," she gasps and pulls me into a hug. "I am so sorry. Sorry that I didn't know, sorry that I've not been here for you. He'd kick my fucking ass."

"It's okay, you didn't know, and that was on us, not you. We were going to say something after… But then…" I suck in a breath, not able to say it.

"Oh, Fal." She holds me tighter. "Come on, let's head inside. And now that I know, don't think you'll be hiding any more of your shit from me. I'm pissed I didn't work it out, since my head's apparently been that far up my own ass."

"Hardly, you literally had the weight of worlds on your shoulders, and now you're pregnant. You're a badass, but you're not all-knowing," I say wryly as Creek joins us. He hugs me but then moves past us to open up the house.

"I fucking should be," Remy huffs and starts up the steps. I pause, one foot on the bottom step, when she turns back and comes to stand at my side. She takes my hand and waits. "We'll do this when you're ready."

I borrow her strength, having no idea how she stays so strong through everything. I let her lead me up the stairs to face one of the hardest things I've ever had to do.

"Let's do this."

We spent the entire day working through the house, packing things up—Remy finally emptied her whole room to take back to the manor. It was hard as fuck, and we cried more than a little. But we also laughed a lot and shared stories of Colt. Some that I never heard before from his past lives, some from his time away with Creek, and others that we were all there for.

It was both heartbreaking and healing at the same time. That's not to say I'm healed, not even close, but I think today was a good first step toward that.

I'm finishing up with packing a box of things I'd left here when I spot Creek in the doorway of Colt's bedroom. Just stepping in here was like death by a thousand cuts, but we had so many good memories, and that's what I'm trying to focus on right now. "You okay?"

"Yeah, I just… I think he'd have wanted you to have these," he says, and shows me the keys to Colt's truck hanging from his finger. A lump builds in my throat, I've already cried so much today, I don't know I have any more tears left.

"I don't know…"

"Remy and I talked about it. She doesn't need it, and we know you don't have a car to yourself. He loved that truck, and he loved you more than anything or anyone in all of his lifetimes. He'd want you to have it." He smiles sadly at me and tosses the keys over. "We know you'll look after it."

"Thank you, but honestly, I can't take it. I'd love to, but it's just too big for me. I'd need a ladder to get in it.

Take it to the manor, one of the guys can use it, I know you only have your truck and Remy's Mustang over there," I tell him and throw the keys back.

"Are you sure?" he asks, and I can tell he's torn.

"I'm sure. I portal pretty much everywhere anyway, and it really is too big. And this way, when the baby comes, you have something of Colt's. He would have liked that."

"Okay." He nods, his voice breaking a little. "Well, when you're ready, let us know. I texted Elijah, and he's going to come finish closing up the house tomorrow and move all the boxes into storage."

"I will, thank you." I swallow against the lump in my throat at the thought of this place being so empty when it was always so full of life before. At the thought of all the things that could have been.

"It was obvious he loved you, ya know. Even when we were away, before Remy became a Hunter. It was like he was a whole new guy. He didn't even look at other girls. I know he was an ass about it all, but I think he just didn't know how to reconcile what he felt with the pressures on him from Denny. But I could tell, even though neither of you said anything. He was just lighter when he'd been around you. He lit up when you came into a room. But he'd want you to be happy, Fallon. He wouldn't want you to stop living your life. I know you're still hurting, we all are, but just know that if something or someone else does come along, Colt would want you to have that."

I nod at him, unable to speak as tears fill my eyes. He smiles softly before heading back downstairs. I turn my attention back toward the room, and my eyes fall toward the bedside table. I take the picture frame from it, cradling the photo against my body. We took the stupid selfie one morning we were lying in bed, and he had it framed. It was so cheesy, but now, I'm so glad he did. I know what Creek said is true, that he wouldn't want me to be sad forever, so I swallow back the tears and clear my throat.

It's time to start trying to live, and honor him in doing so.

I head down the stairs, hearing a knock at the door.

"I'll get it," Creek hollers, and I see him opening the door. He leans down and then closes the door, coming back in with two packages.

"I guess he ordered some shit before…" he trails off, unable to look away from the packages.

"I guess we should open them," Remy says from the kitchen as I reach the ground floor, and I tuck the box of things I'm keeping by the stairs, ready for when I head home.

"Yeah, I guess," Creek says, looking between us, but I can't speak. It's not right that he isn't here for this.

We move into the kitchen, and Creek hands the packages to Remy. "You should open them."

"Okay," she nods and opens the first one, and she laughs, before tears fall down her cheeks. "That little fucker."

I feel my heart race and clasp my throat as I wait for her to lift whatever it is out. When she does, I start crying, too. She holds up a black onesie, that says 'My uncle is my favorite'.

"Oh man," Creek croaks, and then coughs trying to clear his throat. "He really would've been the kid's favorite, too. I just know it."

I didn't even know he knew, but of course he did this.

Remy opens the second package, and starts laughing again, even as the tears continue to stream down her face. My heart races as she shakes her head and clutches the package to her chest. "Oh, Colt," she sighs, and my heart breaks for her as her shoulders start to shake.

"What is it?" I ask in a whisper. She laughs and pulls something grey from the bag, and I realize it's a t-shirt when she slips it over her head. I can't help but laugh with her when I see the front, and Creek joins us.

There's a t-rex on the front with a bandana on its head and sunglasses on, and it says, 'Don't mess with Mamasaurus. You'll get Jurasskicked'."

"That is so fucking Colt," Creek laughs, and I smile through my tears.

Remy wraps her arms around herself, still laugh-crying. “It really fucking is.”

I wake the next day and find a note on my dresser from Deacon, asking how I’m doing. I guess after how I screamed at him the last time he was here, he’s giving me an out. So I pull out everything I need to send him a note back and tell him I’d like to see him.

Creek was right, I need to live, and Deacon is my friend. Remy has enough going on in her life, I need to branch out and start existing on my own again. I don’t want to be a burden to her, to anyone.

I send back the note, and jump in the shower, trying to wash off some of the sadness that still clings to me. It’s only been a month since Colt died, but Mama was right. I didn’t die, and I can’t keep going around acting like I did.

Once I’m washed and dressed, I feel more like myself.

“You’re looking a little better than when I saw you last,” Deacon says, and I let out a small yelp.

“Yeah… Sorry about, well, everything.”

“You never need to say sorry to me, Fallon. You were hurting, and I crossed a line. You’re allowed to hurt, to grieve. I just want to be your friend, to be here and help you start to live again.” He moves toward me slowly before sitting down on the bed facing me.

"I know." I let out a deep breath and offer him a quick smile. "I'm getting there. I thought we could maybe do something today?"

"Sure, what do you want to do? I hear rage therapy is what all the kids are doing at the minute." He winks at me, and I laugh softly.

"What the fuck is rage therapy?"

"It's beating the shit out of stuff to get rid of your pent-up emotions. Think a baseball bat on a washer." His eyes sparkle, and I know he's teasing me, but this almost feels good.

"I think I could use something a little like that," I tell him honestly.

"Well, then your wish is my command. Let's go beat the crap out of broken shit. And maybe we can get some pizza after?" he says, his gaze roaming down my body. He frowns a little, but it vanishes from his face so quickly I would've missed it if I wasn't looking at him, and I pull my cardigan tighter. I've lost some weight recently, probably too much, but that's okay, too.

"That sounds good." He stands and offers me his hand, pulling me to my feet when I take it.

"Well then, I guess we better get to it."

TWENTY FOUR

I can't believe we're here already. The last few months of me getting my shit together have flown by, and now Remy is only four months away from giving birth. We're finally throwing her a baby shower. Time has flown by in my return to normalcy, yet it was so easy to get caught up in going back to work at the store, in helping Rebel with school, in making time for Remy and everyone else, and even in spending time with Deacon—which has been surprisingly easy considering our history. I started healing before I even realized it was happening.

Today is the first day I didn't wake up and immediately think of Colt as soon as I opened my eyes. I cried once I realized that it happened, but Mama did tell me it would happen eventually. Of course I still miss him. Every fucking day something happens to remind of him—sometimes I just see something he would have loved and sometimes I hear a laugh that sounds exactly like his. But I'm finally able to function again, learning how to laugh and how to navigate the world without having him as part of my future.

He would have loved being here today.

I finish setting up the living room, we have so many freaking balloons and all sorts of decorations and activities. I can't imagine trying to set this up on my own, and I'm thankful that Maddie is bringing the cake and Mama is handling the snacks.

"How long till everyone heads over?" Mama calls out as I finish setting up the onesie making station.

"About ten minutes," I tell her before blowing my hair out of my face. I pull it back into a ponytail and belatedly realize just how much glitter I have on my hands. Awesome, I probably look like a stripper with this amount of body sparkle going on.

"Do you have plans for later?" she asks as she starts bringing the plates of food in.

"I'm going to see Deacon," I tell her, and she frowns a little, but it disappears as quickly as it appeared.

"Okay, don't forget we have the coven meeting this weekend and the meeting with the faction leaders in two days."

"I won't forget, Mama," I tell her with a sigh. I've

missed a lot of shit with the coven, and I know Mama's been getting some heat about it. I swear she's aged a few years these last few months, and I feel awful about it. I just haven't been of much use to anyone. "I know I need to come back and pick up the slack. I know people aren't happy with me, Mama. I won't let you down."

"I know you won't, baby." She kisses my cheek before leaving to set up the rest of the food while I set up the melted chocolate diapers for the world's grossest baby shower game.

"Hellooooo." I glance up to see Maddie trying to open the door, so I rush over to help her with the armful of presents she arrived with. We drop them on the gift table, and she huffs. "Good to see you, sweetheart."

"You, too! Are you excited about becoming a grandma?"

"Pshh, that makes me sound old. I'm going to be a Nana," she says, and I giggle.

"You'll be an epic Nana," I tell her, and she hugs me.

"I can't wait!"

"Wouldn't want to forget this," Nate says as he opens the front door, carrying the cake.

"Oh my word! Thank you, I'm such a scatterbrain at the moment," she says, rushing over and taking the cake from him and kissing him as she does.

"Let me know when you want me to come get you."

“I will, and don’t forget that Nirvana will be coming home tomorrow, so you need to clear your crap out of the house.”

“Yes, dear,” he grins before heading back out. She smiles after him with a sigh, and my heart pangs. I want that again one day.

The thought shocks me, but I shake it off.

Maddie moves toward the kitchen and says hello to Mama while I arrange her gifts on the table around the ones Mama and I already left there.

“I hope there’s more room on there.” I jump at the sound of Morgan’s voice and turn to find her in the middle of the room with so many gifts around her I can’t help but laugh.

“I think you might need your own table,” I tell her, and she laughs, too. She clicks her fingers, and another table appears next to the one I’ve set up, her gifts arranged on it in a heartbeat.

“Problem solved,” she grins, and I shake my head. It is weird as fuck having the Queen of the Shadow Realm in my living room. I know that she’s more than that. She’s Remy’s friend, hell, she’s my friend, but it’s still weird. “How long till the guest of honor arrives?”

“She’ll probably be here any minute. You know how she is about being early.”

“Oh, don’t I. Hopefully that kid of hers doesn’t have

the same tendencies as his momma. He needs to cook for as long as possible!"

"Let's hope so!" I say, and we both laugh.

My phone buzzes in my pocket. I grab it to see a message from Creek.

Creek: We're here!

"She's here!" I call out, and Mama and Maddie haul ass into the room, confetti in hand. I groan at the thought of the clean up later, but fuck it. Baby showers for my best friend don't happen every day!

The front door opens, and we shout "Surprise!" Remy bursts into tears, and I get a bit weepy when I see she's in the t-shirt Colt bought for her.

"She's been a little emotional today," Creek says, wincing when she turns on him.

"How about you cook a baby and be a giant ball of hormones and don't be emotional all at the same time? I am never doing this again!" she growls and throws her hands in the air before turning back to the rest of us. "But this is so freaking awesome, you guys! Thank you!"

She says her hellos while Creek quietly leaves, waving to me before he disappears.

"Hey, you," she says as she pulls me in for a hug. "How are you doing?"

"I'm okay," I tell her honestly because each day is getting easier. I have my friends, I have work, and I have my family. "How are you?"

"I'm fucking huge and always hungry, that's how I am," she groans. and I laugh.

"Well, it's a good thing we have enough food to feed an army."

"Hell fucking yes!"

"Morning!" Deacon calls out, and I look up from the book in my lap. Yesterday was exhausting, and I ended up calling a rain check on our movie night. We've been doing them at least once a week since… Well, since Colt's death.

He's been a rock for me, never faltering when I lose my shit, and always helping me get back up on my feet again. He's been such a good friend, and I'm not sure I'd have made it this far without him. There were mornings where I'd wake up alone, but I knew he'd snuck in and slept with me to help keep my nightmares at bay. I could still feel the heat of his body when I woke. I know he was using his powers to stop my mind going to the worst places while I slept; and while we've never spoken about it, I'm so fucking grateful for everything he's done.

Mama hasn't been exactly thrilled about our friendship,

especially since the coven has been on her case about me not being at meetings and everything, but she also hasn't said anything against it. I know she's seen how much he's been helping me.

"Morning!" I call out before taking a sip of my coffee.

"You feeling better?" he asks as he drops onto the porch swing beside me.

"Yeah, yesterday was just a fucking day. I forgot how exhausting stuff like that is."

"What are you reading?" he asks, nodding to my book, and I grin.

"A book about a girl in rehab. I'm not too far in yet, but she hates her dad, and the guys she's in there with… Let's just say they have some history and well, there's been some hate sex." I laugh, and he joins in.

"Sounds like a fun book," he says, plucking it from my fingers. His eyebrows rise when he reads the passage I was reading, a super hot shower sex scene.

"This is… Different. You like that sort of thing?" he asks, and I shrug. I've always been a little submissive.

"Maybe," I tell him and stick my tongue out at him. "Anyway, do you want to come to the market with me today? I need to grab some things for the house, and it's such a human thing to do. I thought you'd enjoy something new."

"A market?" he asks, looking at me like I'm speaking

a different language.

"Yeah, a farmers market. Come on, it will be fun," I plead, and he shakes his head.

"You just want someone to carry your bags while you shop, don't you?" he teases, and I giggle.

"Maybe, but I also think it will be fun." I flutter my lashes at him, and he barks out a laugh.

"You're such a brat; but okay, let's go." He stands and holds out a hand for me, which I take as I jump to my feet. I hurry inside to finish getting ready while he talks to Mama. I watch them from the doorway as she hands him her list and laugh at how stern she looks.

"Don't fuck up my list. I need everything on there," she tells him, her arms crossed, and I can tell he's trying not to smile.

"Yes, ma'am."

"Ready?" I call out as I enter the room, and Mama frowns again as her gaze bounces between us.

"Ready and willing," Deacon smirks, and Mama scoffs.

"Then let's head out!"

"This is probably the most human thing I've ever done," Deacon says as we weave our way through the throngs of people to look at the different stalls.

"You should do more stuff like this. Broaden your horizons." I wink at him. "Plus, you're friends with a human now, you should learn some more about our culture."

"Yeah, yeah. I'm sure I do, but learning how to carry all of your heavy things somehow doesn't seem culturally relevant," he teases, shaking his head.

"Possibly not, but you're so very good at it," I joke, and he nudges me with his shoulder.

"Yuh-huh," he grunts, but he's smiling, so I know he's enjoying it really.

We eat so much food as we walk around, trying samples every chance we get. We eventually manage to get everything on Mama's list, and we find everything I wanted as well before we head back.

"This was fun," he says, smiling down at me. "Maybe I should do more human shit."

"Yes!" I pump my fist "I told you you'd have fun."

"Helps that the food here is amazing," he groans.

"Yeah, I love it here. Let's head back and get this back to Mama, she seemed more on edge today than usual." My smile has barely left my face tonight, so much so that my cheeks ache.

"I noticed, is everything okay with the covens?"

"I think so," I tell him as I strap on my seatbelt. "I haven't really been… Participating with the coven since everything happened. It's causing issues, which I feel bad about, so I'm going to start making more of an effort."

"They should chill out with their shit. You've been dealing with a lot," he practically growls, his eyes flashing red momentarily.

"It's okay, I get it. I'm an heir, and the coven is meant to come first. Even over my own shit. They have every right to be angry."

"Do you ever wish you could live a different life?"

"Sometimes." I sigh before starting the car. "But I know that if it wasn't me, it would be Rebel, and I would feel so guilty if she had to deal with the weight of everything that comes along with being an heir. It's a lot of responsibility."

"What would you do? If you weren't an heir, I mean."

"Honestly? I don't know. I've always wanted to travel, to explore the world. But I have to stay close, to be available for the coven. I have to settle down eventually and produce my own heir. My path has always been very clear, so I thought about the road not traveled too much."

He goes quiet when I answer, so I turn the radio up, listening to Sam Hunt as we drive back home.

"The fair comes here in a few weeks, that's a super human activity. You should come with me," I tell him, trying to break the silence and the weird atmosphere in the car.

"It sounds like fun. I have no idea what a fair is though." He grins, but it seems forced.

"Oh, you are in for a treat!"

Mama and I woke up early today, and she dropped Rebel off with a friend first thing. We're on our way to the meeting with the other faction leaders at the Hunters' chambers. I can't help but feel on edge. Today isn't even really about me, but as an heir, I have to be here. It's part of my duty.

The car ride is short, and I can't help but feel antsy. I'm not sure why I can't settle, today shouldn't be too crazy.

I follow Mama into the Hunters' chambers and walk down the dirty steps, shocked at the state of the place. I've never been here before, but I know the Hunters usually take more pride in their shit.

We head into a domed room with a large, round stone table that has fourteen seats around it. We're the last ones to arrive, and Remy smiles at me from where she's sitting next to Levi, with her other guys standing behind them. Michael and Nate are to their right with Morgan and Caleb on their left. Tobias and Theron. Luc and Emrys. Zeph and Serafina. They're all sitting around the table, so Mama and I take the last two seats. There are tons of people, hovering around the edge of the domed room. So many people from every faction, since we're gathered here to try to come to an official accord between us all.

“Thank you all for coming,” Levi says as the stone door closes, sealing us all in the room. “You are all aware why we are here. War has existed between our kinds for far too long, and while some of us are born enemies, there is no reason that we can’t try to reach some semblance of an alliance. Each of you sitting here represents your kind, their options and their wishes, but also by being here, you take responsibility for your kind and their actions. Make no mistake, the actions of all will be vital…” He pauses, making sure he has everyone’s attention, and as I look around the table, I’m relieved to see that all focus is on him.

“What we are proposing is a time of peace. For us all. For too long we have fought, lived through a time of unrest. It is time for that to end, so that we all might find our own piece of happiness.”

I sit beside Mama, tuning most of the discussion out while they deal with territories and authorities. I know I should pay more attention, but my heart just isn’t in this right now. I know this is what Remy has worked toward for lifetimes, and I’m happy for her, but being here just makes me think of Colt and how he should’ve been a part of this.

Levi’s hand cracks down on the table, pulling me from my thoughts. “What happens if anyone steps out of line?” he says, and I’m not sure who he’s addressing, but I’m glad it's not me he's leveling with that glare. "If anyone steps the fuck out of line, they have me and my family to answer to, and none of you will fucking enjoy it if we have to deal with your fucking bullshit. Do you understand me?"

Static ripples out across the room as his power slips beyond his grasp as he's challenged, and fuck me, he's kind of terrifying.

"I second his statement," Caleb adds with a grin as he leans back in his chair. "Any of you fuck with my Mara, and I'll take this pretty pendant off and show you just what the Four Horsemen of the Apocalypse really fucking look like." His threat is so casual, but I can't help but smile. I look down at my feet to hide it while the rest of the room practically holds their breath in fear of pissing him off. I think Levi's almost a little put out that he's not the biggest, baddest threat in the room.

"So, do we have an agreement?" Morgan asks. There are whispers around the room, each set of people talking to the rest, but I know pretty much everyone here. No one is going to have an issue. And no one is going to want to fuck with Levi. Or Caleb for that matter. With a wave of her hand, an old looking parchment appears on the table with the terms of the accords laid out. "Mara, do you want to do the honors?"

Remy smiles at her and nods, and the paper floats across the table toward her. She pricks her thumb on her nail and presses the bleeding digit to the paper, signing her agreement. Each of us sitting at the table do so too, binding the agreement in blood. Once the last person has put their blood to the parchment, it disappears from sight.

"Well, that should just about do it," Caleb says, jumping to his feet and rubbing his hands together. "Let's get out of this dark little hole, shall we?"

I stand, and Mama follows suit as I move toward the stairs. "That was less… Explosive than I thought it was going to be," I say quietly.

"That it was, but I have no doubt there will be many things to discuss at the coven meeting in a few days."

"Oh, I'm sure," I snicker as I follow her back up the stairs. "But we'll handle it like we always do. Together."

She nods, but looks down at me, almost like she's worried.

"I'm sure we will."

I glance back to see Remy heading off into the distance with Michael, and my heart hurts for her. "I'm gonna wait for Remy. I'll see you back at home?"

"Okay, baby. I'll see you later." I kiss her cheek and watch as she climbs into the car and drives away. I sit on the ground, with my back against a tree, waving to Creek as the guys leave and settling in to wait for Remy. It takes a little while, but Michael eventually heads back this way and gets into Nate's waiting car. Less than a minute later,

Remy appears, and I jump to my feet, trying to catch her eye. When she notices me waiting for her, she changes directions and heads toward me instead of the parking lot.

"Hey, are you okay?" I ask her and she nods, despite her glassy eyes.

"Yeah, there's just so many goodbyes these days," she says, and my heart breaks a little for her. "It's for the best, we all need to move on with our lives. It's just that so much is changing."

"It is, but you know I'm always going to be here for you, right? Well, as long as my mortal body lets me." I laugh, and she smiles sadly at me.

"I'll always be here for you, too. Are you okay?"

"Yeah, I'm okay, just taking each day as it comes," I tell her with a smile, and we both settle back down on the ground.

"I get that. But life keeps moving, and we all have to learn how to heal."

"I'm getting there."

"You know he'd want you to find love again, right? Moving on is a part of life. He wouldn't want you to be alone."

"I know," I tell her with a sad smile. "It's just hard. Sometimes I feel guilty just about being happy."

"Same," she huffs and winces as she cradles her bump. "This kid is going to kick straight through my ribs I swear to the Fates."

"He's kicking?" I ask, and she nods, taking my hand and placing it on her small bump. I jump when I feel it, and we both start laughing.

"New life is coming. The world keeps turning, and we don't have a way to stop it. But I mean it, Fal. Be happy. Find love. It'd be more of an affront to his memory if you stayed sad and alone for the rest of your life. He might come back, but it won't be in this lifetime. I don't want to see you waiting around for a memory of him."

"I'll try," I tell her with a sad smile.

"Good," she says, smiling and climbing to her feet. "Now let's go get some cake, this kid wants all the sugar."

I laugh as I stand and nod. "Who can say no to cake?"

TWENTY FIVE

I stand with Mama and open the circle, calling the Witches to our meeting spot. It feels strange being back here, with the weight of all this responsibility back on my shoulders. But I promised Mama I'd be here—that I'd try, so that's what I'm doing.

The Witches appear one by one, but no one really looks at me. It's a little weird, but I get it. They're pissed off that I haven't been here. You'd think they'd be more understanding, but I guess the death of a man, even if he was a hunter, isn't deemed as important to anyone else in this matriarchy as it was to me.

"Welcome, sisters, to the circle," Mama starts, and I listen as she jumps in and begins speaking about the new accords we signed a few days ago. There are some bitchy comments thrown around, but overall, nothing worse than I expected. Of course they think parts of it are unfair, but accords require compromise on all sides. I'd love to see them try to raise their objections to Levi and Caleb. Hell, I think I'd pay to see that shit.

"We shouldn't be making deals with Demons," someone says, and my gaze whips around the group. I see Ilaria sneering right at me.

"The Demons are as much a part of this world as we are," Mama tells her. "If you have a problem, I'm sure the Shadow Queen will see you."

"It's not surprising you're so willing to make deals considering the company your daughter keeps." Murmurs start around the circle at her snub, and Mama glares at her.

"We have discussed working with the Demons already. A decision has been made, and we will not be discussing this again," Mama says, as if daring someone to question her.

"We know the decision was made," Ilaria says, her chin jutting forward. "But we've all discussed it, and we believe that Fallon's association with the Demons makes her no longer suitable for the role of Heir." My ears pop at her words, and it's like I'm in a bubble. This can't be happening. This just isn't done.

"You don't get to decide who my heir is!" Mama roars, and while some of the coven heads look subdued, others look even angrier.

"Then maybe you should be removed from your position, too," one of the Witches says, and I stumble backward.

"No," I breathe. I can't be the reason Mama loses everything she's worked for. This coven, this Witch council… It's everything she's ever worked for.

People shout back and forth, and even some of the other heirs look uncomfortable, no one catches my gaze, despite me trying to get their attention.

"Enough!" I shout. I can't take this shit. "Vote on it. If you truly find me unworthy, each and every one of you will need to vote me out. It will have to be unanimous and to my face."

"Fallon, no," Mama gasps beside me, and my heart starts to crumble.

"Mama, I don't want this. For me, for you, or for Rebel… But if they don't have faith in me, then the council won't work. If they won't follow me, then I'm useless. If I have to make this sacrifice for the coven, I will. It's not like I haven't already lost enough this year. If they want to take this from me, then they will. Whether we oppose it or not," I tell her, feeling defeated already.

I might have been getting tired of my duties and responsibilities, but this is the last thing I ever wanted. More for Rebel than for me. She's so young, and since she didn't need to be taught the ways of the coven the same way that I did, she's had a relatively normal childhood up to this point.

"Fallon," she says, and I shake my head. I don't want this, but nothing I said was wrong. If we fight back at them, just because this is something that isn't done, it's going to cause more problems. We'll have more issues than we've ever had, and considering everything the covens have just been through, solid leadership—a solid council—is more than needed.

"All those who wish to see Fallon stripped of her title and position as Heir, raise your hand," Demetera says, giving me a sad smile as she raises her hand. I don't hold it against her. She's been Mama's closest ally, but she knows just like I do that if this is for the good of the covens, it must be done.

Mama grips my hand in hers, and her hand grows tighter around mine as every other hand raises around us.

"It is done," Demetera says, and my knees shake as a tear slips down Mama's face.

"This meeting is over!" Mama shouts, and the covens begins disappearing.

"I truly am sorry, Marie," Demetera says before disappearing with her heir.

"Not as sorry as I am," Mama says softly. "I am so sorry, Fallon. I had no idea."

"It's okay, Mama," I tell her, trying not to cry. What the fuck does my life look like now? My whole life has been about the coven and the council. It's been my entire purpose. And now I feel like the string tethering me to the earth has been cut. I'm just floating around with nowhere to go.

"It is not okay, Fallon," she snaps before portaling us back home. She slams the door after she enters her room, and I hear glass smashing. I wince, glad that Rebel isn't here right now.

Shit.

We need to tell Rebel. Her entire life is about to change, too, and it's all my fucking fault.

Telling Rebel was easier than I thought it would be. Since the coven meeting two weeks ago, she's been tucked away with Mama starting to learn everything she never should have needed to know. I've done my best to hold down the store for Mama. Between that and spending time with Deacon, I haven't had time to think about what this actually means for me. I haven't even told Deacon or Remy yet. Saying it out loud just makes it too real.

Like, who even am I without it?

I've tried not to think about it in the few moments I

have had because it hurts, and I've spent too much time hurting already these last few months.

"Hey," I jump at the sound of Deacon's voice as he walks into the store. "You lost inside your head again?"

"Something like that." I smile a little, and he frowns at my lackluster response.

"What's wrong?"

"It's nothing," I tell him, waving it off. "What are you doing here?"

"That can wait. What's wrong? I thought we were through hiding shit?" he says, crossing his arms in front of his chest, pinning me with his stare.

"I…" I take a deep breath, preparing myself to say the words I don't really want to say. "The Witches council stripped me of my title as Heir."

"They did fucking what?" he roars, and I wince. "When?"

"A few weeks ago. That's why I've been covering the store so much. Mama needs to bring Rebel up to where she needs to be with everything so she can step into the role when she's old enough."

"Why?" His voice is one hundred percent Demon right now, but I'm not scared. Not of him, even after everything we've been through. I know he'll never hurt me again.

"I was gone too much after Colt died."

"That's fucking ridiculous. Let me talk to Morgan,

there has to be something we can do."

"There isn't," I shake my head. "But thank you."

"What aren't you telling me?" he demands.

"They didn't like that the Demons were part of the accords… Or my friendship with you guys. It was part of why they took my title and the extra power that goes with it."

"They took your power?" he growls.

"They did, but it wasn't much. I hadn't come into my extra power as heir yet, so I didn't really notice the difference."

"Fucking petty little Witches," he grumbles as he paces back and forth in front of the counter.

"I'm coping. But only just. It's weird, but I'll be okay. I'm more worried about Rebel," I tell him with a sigh.

"Why?"

"The expectations from her are going to be so great after this. She'll have to deal with the fact that, in the eyes of the others, I've tarnished the Laveau name. It means she loses all of the freedoms she should have had," I tell him, my hands shaking. I hate all of this. He walks around the counter and hugs me, tucking me under his chin.

"What does this mean for you now?" he asks, not letting me go.

"Honestly, I don't know. It means my life is wide open, but I have no idea what that even really looks like," I admit.

"Well, whatever happens, you know I'm here for you, right?" he says, tipping my chin up so I'm looking up into his eyes. I blush at the intensity of his gaze and pull back a little.

"I know. Thank you," I say a little awkwardly. "What are you doing here anyway?"

"Well, I mean, I'm not surprised you forgot, but you promised me a human experience in the form of a fair," he smirks, and I clasp my hand over my mouth.

"Shit, I totally forgot!" I laugh, the awkwardness thankfully evaporating. "Misty will be here to take over in about twenty minutes, you cool to just chill until then?"

"When am I ever not down to just hang out with you?"

"Hold on," I say as I really look him over for the first time since he stepped into the shop. I can't help the smile that takes over my face. "Your hair... It's different." I laugh. Who knew Demons dyed their hair? The new darker look suits him, though, more so than the blond ever did.

"I'm a Morph," he smirks. "This is my true look, but I didn't want you to associate me with Az before, so I changed myself. We've come a long way since then, so I figured why not?"

I can't remember the last time I laughed this much. The

concentration on Deacon's face is priceless as he tries his hand at the ring toss to win me the giant black unicorn stuffie. I cheer as he gets the third ring over the glass bottle and he picks me up, spinning me around.

"YES! I AM UNSTOPPABLE!" he shouts, and I can't help but laugh. It was only like his seventh try, but who am I to remind him of that?

"Which prize did you want, man?" the bored teenager in the booth asks as Deacon sets me back on my feet.

"My girl wants the black unicorn, so the black unicorn is what she gets!" he says, and my heart skips a beat at his words. I know he didn't mean it like that, but even just hearing it… It feels a little strange.

Not bad, strange, but still. Strange.

The guy hands over the giant stuffie and I laugh because it's nearly as long as I am. "Maybe I should hold onto this?" Deacon jokes, shaking his head at me cuddling the giant unicorn.

"But she's mine!" I laugh.

"Fine, fine, she's yours. So, what next?"

"The Ferris wheel! I haven't been on one in years!" Really, I haven't done anything like this in longer than I can remember, but I'm having way too much fun to dwell on that.

"Then the Ferris wheel it is. What exactly is a Ferris wheel?" he asks, and I wheeze a laugh, pointing to the giant light-up metal contraption. “I see. Well, at least I know I can keep us safe if it comes off its stand.”

I shake my head at him but he takes my hand and walks me over to the Ferris wheel, stopping to get some cotton candy on the way. The whole night has been amazing. I almost don’t want it to end, but we’ve been here for hours, and it’s going to shut down soon.

Though as long as I get a ride on the big wheel, I’ll be happy enough. We join the line, and he feeds me cotton candy, taking in the whole experience.

“Humans know how to have fun.”

“I guess that’s part of being mortal,” I say grinning. “You take more joy in what’s around because time is so precious.”

He frowns at my words, as if he hadn’t really thought about the fact that I’m mortal. But it disappears, and he takes a giant bite of the cotton candy. I bark out a laugh.

“You’re an animal.”

“Oh, I know,” he says with a wink. “You haven’t seen anything yet.”

By the time it’s our turn, the cotton candy is gone. We climb into the chair, and the girl supervising the ride closes the gate, offering to look after my unicorn while we ride. And then we start to move.

“This is slower than I thought it would be based on your level of excitement,” he says as the chair sways back and forth.

"Yeah, but the movement isn't the best part of the ride, it's the view from the top. You can see the entire city from up here," I gush, way too excited for what's coming.

Once we reach the top, I gasp, and the wheel stops. "It's so freaking beautiful."

"It really is," he says, and I turn to find him looking at me. He strokes my cheek, and a shiver goes down my spine. I lean into him, but the Ferris wheel starts again, and I jolt away from him, blushing. Did that really just happen?

I know he always said he wanted more, but I thought we'd settled into being friends. I can't deny that there was something between us at that moment, but it feels too soon.

He doesn't say anything, but puts his arm across the back of the cart and lets me lean into him to enjoy the rest of the ride. When we climb off, he grabs the stuffie for me and takes my hand again. We just walk around the fairground talking about nothing until the lights start shutting down.

"I guess I should get you home," he says, and I sigh.

"Yeah, I guess. Did you enjoy your time pretending to be human?"

"It has been one of the best nights I've ever had," he tells me while smiling down at me.

We walk back to my house in a comfortable silence, and he walks me to the back door of the house. "I guess

I'll be heading off."

"Okay, I'll see you again soon?" I ask and he nods, placing the stuffie down on the porch swing.

"Yeah, I've got a few things I need to handle at home, but you know I'm always here for you," he says, tucking my hair behind my ear.

I smile and he pulls me in for a hug. He's so freaking warm against the cold chill of the air, and I almost don't want this night to end. I pull back and look up at him, our eyes catching.

"Night, Deacon," I breathe, and before I can overthink things or try to stop myself, I lift up on my tiptoes and go to kiss his cheek. But he moves, and then my lips are on his, and I'm breathless. Lost entirely in him as he makes me feel again.

I pull back quickly, my hand against my lips. "Deacon…" I say, trying not to panic about the guilt swirling inside of me. I can't believe I kissed him back.

"I'll see you real soon, Fallon," he says, kissing my hand before disappearing in front of my eyes.

What the fuck did I just do?

I toss and turn in bed, my conflicting emotions running riot and not letting me sleep. In the end, I pick up my phone and call Remy. I know she barely sleeps these days, so she'll probably still be up.

"Hello?" she says as she answers the phone, and my stomach twists again.

"Remy, it's me."

"I know that, dummy. Are you okay?" She laughs, and I hear one of the guys grunt. I guess she was in bed after all.

"I'm okay, it's late. I can just call you back tomorrow."

"Don't be silly, you never call unless it's important. What's up?" I chew my lip, trying to find the right words, but ultimately decide to just blurt it out.

"I kissed Deacon."

The line is quiet for a minute, and then I hear a male whoop in the background followed by more voices. "Idiots, every single one of them. Sorry, Fal, let me move into another room."

I hear her tell her guys to grow the fuck up and then her footsteps as she moves around the house. "Okay, I'm back. So… How was it?"

"I mean… It was… I just feel so guilty," I confess. "Colt's barely…"

"No," she says cutting me off. "Colt is gone. Fal, I love you, but he's gone, and he's not coming back. Not in this lifetime. Maybe not for a good few. If Deacon makes you happy, then be happy."

"But…"

"No buts, Fal. Happiness isn't all that easy to come by. If you find someone who brings you joy, who makes you laugh, then you take hold of it with both hands. You guys have a lot of history, but if that's something you can look past, then I'm not going to hold it against him. He came for you when it mattered. He's been there for you these last few months, every time you've needed him. I can't believe I'm saying it, but he's a good guy."

"The kiss was good," I tell her, wringing out my hands.

"I bet it was," she cackles. "I need to hear everything."

So I tell her about the whole night, and about the kiss all over again. She laughs and coos, and we giggle like we haven't in a long while.

"I haven't heard you this happy in a long time," she says wistfully.

"I haven't felt this happy in a while," I tell her honestly.

"Then follow your happiness. Fuck what anyone else thinks. This has been a suckfest of a year. You deserve happiness more than anyone else I know."

"Thanks, Remy," I say, smiling softly.

"Just speaking the truth. So what happens from here?"

"Honestly… I have no fucking idea."

TWENTY SIX

It's been a few days since The Kiss, and I haven't heard from Deacon. I'm beginning to think I read things wrong, and that I overstepped.

Fuck my life, how did I get this all so messed up? First, I felt guilty about what I did, but now I just feel sad that I thought it might be something after I spoke to Remy. Obviously, I misjudged it all.

Maybe I'll just quit men forever. It seems like the simpler option at this point.

But really, that isn't an option at all. Remy was right, and despite the lingering guilt I feel, this thing between Deacon and I isn't new. He's been there for me through so much, and he's the reason Remy found me all those months ago in the Shadow Realm. Who knows if I would've even survived Azriel if it wasn't for him.

So I opt to make the decision for him.

I wrap my hand around the necklace that Caleb gave me—I haven't taken it off since that day—and I transport myself to the Shadow Realm. It feels so weird traveling like this on my own. I guess Deacon has a stone like mine because this is how he's been getting back and forth between the Realms since Morgan and Remy sealed the main portal. My ears pop as I land in front of the palace. I'm unsteady on my feet for a moment, but then the world rights itself, and I feel okay again.

Man, that is going to take some getting used to.

I head into the palace, feeling a little awkward coming here just to find Deacon, and run smack into Bryce as I reach the entrance hall.

"Woah there," he says, catching me before I fall on my ass. "Someone's in a hurry."

"Sorry." I blush. "I wasn't looking where I was going."

"It's okay. What brings you down here?"

"Caleb gave me this," I say, showing him the necklace, and he laughs a little.

"Oh I know. I was asking what you need?" His eyes crinkle with his words, and it's strange seeing him so light. He's usually much more dark and broody.

"I was er, looking for Deacon, but I know this only brings me here and…" he interrupts me, lifting his hand.

"Say no more. The necklace will default to bring you here, but if you just picture where you're going in your mind, it will take you there instead. I imagine you haven't been to his place since all of the changes, so I'll take you there now, but you'll know for next time."

"Really? Thank you. I don't mean to interrupt."

"Really, it's not a problem at all. You're practically family, and family gets all the help they need," he says with a wink and takes my hand. Bryce whispers us away before I have a second to object, and then my feet touch the ground again. We're outside the palace on level six, I recognize the architecture, but it does look different. Less dark and gloomy than before.

"If you head in, I'm sure he'll find you real quick."

"Thank you," I tell him, and he nods before disappearing from sight. I try not to feel too embarrassed about how I got here, knowing that they'll all know where I am, and head inside. It's so weird being back here. My memories of my time in this place aren't exactly the best, but as I walk through the halls, it's obvious a lot has changed. It looks completely different. If the layout wasn't the same, I'd believe it was a whole new building.

"Fallon?" I hear Deacon's voice, and look up when I reach the main hall with the giant staircase.

"Hey," I call back with an awkward wave. He moves down the balcony hallway, and down the stairs quickly till he's at my side.

"What's wrong?" he asks, looking me over almost frantically.

"Nothing, I just wanted to talk," I tell him with a small shrug.

"You wanted to talk?" He eyes me skeptically, and I nod.

"Yup!" I pop my P and smile, feeling more than a little silly.

"Okay then, let's go somewhere that's not got the eyes of the masses, shall we?" he says, waving me down the hall to the right, when I look up and see just how many people are watching us. So freaking weird.

We walk silently until he ushers me into a small room that has a giant TV, a leather couch, and a mini fridge. This room is like the ultimate TV chill room. It's so snug, I kinda love it. "This is cozy."

"This is my nook," he tells me, blushing a little as he scratches the back of his neck. "So you wanted to talk?"

"Yeah," I tell him, still looking around the room at all the trinkets and pictures that line the walls.

"What about?" he asks, almost looking uncomfortable having me look at his personal space.

"About the fact that I kissed you, and then you ghosted me," I say, trying not to laugh because this is so freaking weird.

"I didn't, or at least… I didn't mean to ghost you. You looked so freaked out. I wanted to give you some space, some time, and then the renovations here stole every second of my focus and well… Now you're here."

"So you didn't mean to ghost me?" I ask, turning back to face him, and he moves forward into my space. So close that I can feel the heat from him without him actually touching me.

"Fallon, I told you a long time ago that I wanted more from you, but you had other things going on. I've been your friend because that's what you needed me to be. That's all I thought you wanted. But if this is you telling me you want more, then know that I'm in for this. I have been for a while. I told you once before that our story wasn't over yet." He reaches up and cups my cheek before leaning down and kissing me. The kiss is so fucking hot that my toes curl. I wrap my arms around him, and he picks me up. Wrapping my legs around his waist so I don't fall, I lose myself in his touch.

Remy was right. Happiness really is worth chasing with everything you have.

"So what does this mean for us?" I ask, reminding myself I'm allowed to be happy.

"This means that we take each day one at a time," he says, before kissing the top of my head. "I know you're still hurting a little, even if you don't admit it, and that's okay. But know that there's no rush here. We have forever. You're mine now, and that's not going to change."

It's been six weeks since 'The Kiss'. Since I went to the Shadow Realm and told Deacon that I wanted more. And what a six weeks it's been. I have been wooed within an inch of my life. Dinners, dates, movies, and his unwavering attention. I've felt like a princess. Except that beyond kissing, he's been the perfect gentleman, and frankly, I've had enough of his gentlemanliness.

I want more.

So I've decided that tonight is the night. Mama is away at Erica's with Rebel, and these last few months have been… Well they've been fucking agony, but Deacon has helped me through that. And after bouncing back and forth after speaking to Remy, I've decided she's right.

Colt would want me to be happy. He might not exactly jump for joy that it's Deacon who makes me happy, but I'm not going to turn happiness away. Not ever again.

We've been skirting around this thing between us, and he's been giving me space to navigate all of it with zero pressure. And while that's been amazing and exactly what I've needed, I want to control my own destiny. So I've invited him over tonight.

I pull out the lingerie I bought specifically for tonight. That particular shopping trip with Remy was beyond awkward, but she made light of it all, and I am so thankful to still have her in my life. The fact that she's supportive of whatever I choose to do means so much to me.

I shimmy into the white lingerie set, with matching stockings and garter, then slide on the white leather body harness that crisscrosses over my chest before circling down around my waist and accentuating my curves. If he pulls the gentleman card when he sees me in this, then I might just quit this whole path because this is my last card. I don't know what else to do to show him that I'm ready.

I slip on the white silk robe that's been hanging on the back of my door and check my phone. He should be here any second.

Filled with nervous energy, I jump when I feel his energy reach out to me, and I turn to find him standing at the door to my bedroom. When I turn around, my breath catches at the sight of him. The brute masculinity that emanates from his every pore. The square jaw that is, at this very moment, ticcing with reined in power. Those deep, soulful, blue eyes that rake over my body, oh so devastatingly slow, until they reach my own wide gaze. That seemingly laid-back stance he's faking as he leans against my doorjamb, arms and ankles crossed.

Everything about him screams sex. Every. Fucking.

Thing. And his mere presence gets me instantly wet.

As though my thoughts are written all over my face, Deacon's gaze goes straight between my legs where I know he can sense just how badly I need him.

The silence between us isn't suffocating, it's foreplay. We're not at a standstill, we're anticipating the moment this spell breaks and we're on each other like wild animals.

Blinking once, then twice, Deacon straightens and takes two steps toward me. He's close enough that I can smell the soap and cologne he's dabbed on himself, but too far away still to feel the heat from his body.

"Are you sure about this?" he asks, his hand almost shaking as he stops himself from touching me.

"I'm more than sure."

"I don't just mean this thing between us, Fallon. I mean this, everything. I'm not like other guys you'll have been with. I'm a Demon, I am quite literally Greed, and I have a lot of darkness in my past that you don't know about yet… The things I like… That I need. They're not for everyone."

"What is it you need?" I ask, practically panting. There's an aura around him right now that calls to me, and I don't think there's anything he can ask for that I won't give.

"I need control. Of you, of this. And not in that crazy, I'm going to ruin you and abuse you kind of way. I just want to take care of you, but I need you to let me do that.

Submission is… Well it's a trade of power. You hand that to me, but you have the ability to take it back or stop anything, everything, the instant that you want to."

"Are you going to hurt me?"

"Never," he says with so much passion, I swear my heart skips a beat. "I want to care for you, look after you. If you do something that goes against that, then I might have to punish you, but I will never truly hurt you."

I nod, taking it all in. This isn't exactly what I expected from him, but if I look back, even just at how he's taken care of me the last few months, this all makes sense. The thought of handing him that control almost feels like a relief. Like something I didn't even know I wanted or needed, but hearing him say it out loud, it's like something falls into place.

"I'm sure," I tell him, biting my lip, anticipation flooding me. My fingers practically tingle with excitement. I am so ready to walk this path.

"This is how it's going to go." Did his voice get deeper? Somehow, he feels bigger, more powerful. I'm caught in his web, unable to move or speak, but I know that this is exactly where I want to be.

"In our bed, I call the shots. Every single one of them. I tell you when and where you can touch me. When to speak. Where to sit, where to lie, and how to present yourself to me." His words turn me on more than I could have ever imagined, but it feels right. I don't dare say a word and that alone makes me feel like all responsibility is off my shoulders. This is what I've needed. To feel the weight of my life, my grief, my doubts all lift from my shoulders. I had no idea that this was a part of who he is, but I am more than excited to see where this goes.

Deacon's gaze pierces into me, assessing, weighing the situation, and when he sees that his demands are my desire, he continues.

"When you're mine, you're all mine. I control it all. Every single inch of your skin. Say yes if you understand." I blink because I feel like I'm in a trance, his voice is that hypnotizing. But when he brings an arm back and pulls his shirt off in one smooth move, my mouth waters. I know I'm supposed to do something but apparently, I'm too slow to follow his command.

Deacon's hand shoots out so quickly I have no idea how he got this close so quickly. But he's here, close enough that I can feel the burn from his skin next to mine. His fingers are in my hair, pulling my head back so our eyes are fixed on one another. "You don't hesitate when I ask you a question. Is that understood?"

I nod.

"Words, baby girl." Fuck, I'm wet.

"Yes."

The slow grin that makes its way across his lips is

deadly sexy. Like he knows a secret, and I just gave him permission to do whatever he wants with me.

It's not just an impression. I want him to take me in any way he needs. Any way he knows I need.

"Now, be a good little girl and drop to your knees."

Holy. Fucking. Shit.

My brain doesn't contemplate any other action, and I don't hesitate. My knees bend, and my body follows as though his commands are wired into my synapses.

"That's a good girl." His fingers in my hair loosen as he massages my scalp and looks at me like I'm his entire world. Right now, he's mine. My sun and my moon. My pleasure and my pain.

"Now, open that pretty little mouth of yours and show me your tongue."

Again, I follow his orders. I open my mouth and stick out my tongue, trying my best not to drool all over my chin. Deacon brings his other hand to my mouth and holds my tongue between his index and thumb.

"Like velvet. It'll feel so fucking good against my cock." He pulls a little, like he's testing it, testing me. "Are you ready to suck my dick, baby girl?"

I nod because speaking is impossible.

"Good girl. Now put your hands on your lap, shoulders back, head up. This is how you present yourself to me when you're about to swallow my dick. When I tell you to get on your knees, this is how I want to see you. Understand?"

I nod and position myself exactly how he asks. It's not the most comfortable position, but as he lets me go and brings his big, strong hands to his black jeans, I suddenly couldn't care less about the position I'm in. All I want is to taste his cock. To feel the power of it in my mouth. To please him.

In that moment, my only focus is his pleasure, knowing damn well that his pleasure will mean mine tenfold.

Agonizingly slowly, Deacon unbuckles his belt, and it doesn't escape me that he meticulously places it at his feet that are somehow bare. When did that happen? I'd been so dazed at his arrival that I hadn't noticed him taking his shoes off. And fuck, the sight of him so comfortable and in command is sexy. The thought makes my pussy clench, my fingers digging into my thighs as my muscles tighten with need.

I expect him to drop his jeans once he unzips them, but he doesn't. He unfastens just enough to allow his monster cock to spring out, framed by the vee of his jeans. Deacon is not just gorgeous, he's sex on legs. Everything about him emanates power and sex. Dirty, filthy, sex.

With my mouth still open and my tongue still out, he carefully places his feet on either side of my thighs and takes his shaft in hand, pulling it down just enough to tap his tip against my tongue. I'm salivating, my saliva dripping from the sides of my mouth but I don't dare move. I wouldn't survive him stopping this right now. I wouldn't do anything to jeopardize this intimate moment between us.

As his tip slides up and down my tongue, getting him wetter and wetter, he looks at me like I hung the moon, the stars, and the sun in his universe. He looks at me like I'm love incarnate. Like I'm his reason for breathing, for fucking, for coming.

"You are the most beautiful thing I've ever seen. You make me so happy when you dress like a naughty little slut. When you present yourself all clean and ready for bed." He pushes his dick all the way inside my mouth until I gag and then pulls out as though nothing happened.

"I can't wait to ruin your makeup. I want to see your tears while you choke on my cock. I want to feel your cries in my black soul when you come all over my face." His eyes turn from a deep, calm ocean blue to a category five hurricane about to destroy everything I've ever known about sex.

I can't fucking wait to live through it.

"Are you ready for me?"

I nod, knowing my life, from this very moment, will never be the same again.

With his dick settled on my tongue, Deacon places both of his hands on either side of my face and pushes his cock inside my mouth. At first, he uses a lulling rhythm, in and out. Tip of my tongue, back of my throat. It's not uncomfortable, in fact it's quite satisfying knowing that my entire mouth is pleasuring him.

"If it's too much, I'll know. I'll feel it. I'll sense it because I can sense anything when it comes to you. I know your needs better than you do, baby girl. I feel your desires every time your mouth sucks on my flesh, but if you want me to stop, tap twice on my thigh. You're not going to be able to speak." Every time I swallow around the tip of his cock, I can hear the slight hitch in his voice. The tiny bit of loss in his control. The human part of him that feels the pleasure I'm giving him.

"Look at me, baby girl."

I do, and what I see there is overwhelming. So much lust, so much need. His stormy blues are like an open door to his very soul. He might think it's dark but it's not. It's blood red, filled with passion and heat.

But then his rhythm speeds up, and I'm grateful for his hands. They set the pace, they keep me stable, and they hold me as he fucks my face like the Demon he is. His hips thrust with singular determination, and I think he's about to come when he suddenly pulls out and looks at me, panting as his eyes flash with his reined-in control.

I can see that he's assessing the situation, that he was close enough to exploding but it's not what he wants. I don't dare ask or move or twitch, even. I patiently wait for him to decide how he wants to do this. If this is how he wants to play, I'm more than willing to go on this ride.

With his chest heaving and his top teeth digging into his bottom lip, he lets go of my face.

"Close your mouth and relax."

My jaw feels the soreness now that I'm relaxing the muscles there, and I revel in that comfortable pain. I hadn't even really thought about the whole pleasure-pain thing, but I think this is something I can totally get on board with. Especially with him.

His right hand reaches down to the leather straps of my lingerie and as his fingers wrap around the white material, he pulls me up from the kneeling position to standing.

"I want to know what you look like when you come. You were such a good girl, sucking my cock like you were born to do it."

Fisting my lingerie, he pulls me in and slants his mouth over mine, his tongue demanding entrance, his lips soft but dominant. His free hand grabs the flesh of my ass and squeezes, making me moan as one finger lands right beside my hole.

God, I want him. Here, there, everywhere, and he must see it, too.

"Don't worry, baby girl. I'll be fucking that hole, too. Maybe not tonight. But soon."

Then he kisses me again. We're all lips, tongues, and teeth. At one point, I taste the coppery tang of his bite and feel my pussy clench as he licks the drop of blood right off my lip. His eyes flash red. There one second, gone the next, but I know. I know his Demon is basking in this moment. Loving the control he has over me, knowing he's about to fuck me.

Then his mouth is at my ear and I practically melt at his words.

"I hope you're not too attached to this contraption because I'm going to rip it off your body, and then I'm going to eat your pussy until you come all over my face. That's your reward for being such a good girl and sucking my cock just like I want it."

Fuck. Me. I could come from his words alone but I know, without a doubt, that if I do, he won't be happy, and I want him to be happy.

As though he knows, he leans back, smiles his deliciously sexy grin and says, "Good girl."

In the next second, my lingerie is ripped into pieces and lying all around our feet.

I wish I could say I was upset about that. But I'm not. Not even a little bit.

"Get on the bed, legs spread open so you can present your pretty little pussy to me."

I take the two steps back needed for my knees to feel

the mattress. Then I sit, slide back, and lean down on my elbows before I bring my legs up, folded at the knees. My hair falls behind me like a dark waterfall, my thighs aching from the position, and my pussy hungry with the need for him.

He licks his lips, his eyes scanning me from toes to eyes before he kneels on the bed, bringing his hands to my knees and pulling my legs up to his shoulders. I let myself fall on the bed, my arms at my sides as he lifts my hips and brings my pussy to his mouth.

The only smell I can register is that of sex. Pure, unadulterated sex. Filthy, taboo, and fucking irresistible sex.

But when his tongue parts the lips of my pussy, all thoughts of anything except him vanish into an abyss of nothingness. With my legs on his shoulders and his hands planted firmly on both cheeks of my ass, I'm nothing but a meal. The lingering lap of his tongue soon turns to melding of lips. He eats my pussy with abandon. Fucking me with his tongue and sucking my lips into his mouth like I'm his dirty little lollipop. I'm shaking, my entire body aching with the need to come.

But I don't dare.

He calls the shots. That was the deal, his first words to me. If I disobey, he will be furious.

And as much as I want to defy him, see what a

punishment feels like at his hands, right now, my biggest need is to come and make him happy. To bring him pleasure through my own.

"I could eat you all fucking night. Just devour this pussy until you can't see or think."

Then his mouth is back at it, going deep inside me, licking up every drop of my juices as they run down my walls.

But my control is tested when he brings his mouth to my clit and sucks on it without even trying to control himself. It's like he's testing me. Flicking the hard, sensitive bud with his tongue. Biting and licking. Adding two fingers to the mix, he slides them in from behind, and it takes every single ounce of my hard won self-control not to explode all over his mouth.

He's doing everything he can to see how far he can go before I defy him.

Testing my boundaries. Silently begging me to disobey him so he can show me what a punishment is.

I hold it all in. I prove to him that I can be a good girl. I can obey.

But fuck, it's hard. A battle rages within me. I feel a yearning so strong pulling me in both directions.

Finally, he stops. My chest heaves, my eyes are shut tightly, and my hands are strangling the sheets in hopes of holding my orgasm at bay against his pleasurably destructive mouth.

"You are fucking perfect. You can come now."

His words are heaven. Every single muscle in my body relaxes as he buries his fingers deep into my pussy and engulfs my clit in his hot mouth.

At the single flick of his tongue on my battered nub, I go off like a bomb.

Lights flash in the back of my eyelids, sound no longer exists because I know I'm crying out his name, but I can't hear myself.

My hips thrust against his mouth as the orgasm sears through me like a runaway train. He moans against my pussy, and I can feel it in my chest, my throat. My soul.

When the tremors die down, he gently puts me back down on the bed and covers my naked body with his, immediately kissing me and sharing my taste with me.

It's heady, tasting myself, knowing that he's been swallowing me this entire time.

"Keep your legs open. It's my turn to come all over you."

I'm still in a daze when he effortlessly slides inside me. I'm so wet, I can hear the sounds of our fucking, and it's turning me on all over again.

His thrusts get harder, deeper. His kisses are more demanding. His fingers digging into my scalp give me that bite of pain that reminds me that I love the mixture.

"Mine. All mine." His words punctuate his every move. Every time he hits that secret spot deep within me, he reminds me that I'm his. That he owns me. That he will always take care of me. That he will destroy me oh so beautifully.

Without thinking, I bite down on his lip as my need to come overpowers me all over again.

I expect him to be angry, to lash out with a spanking or denying me my next orgasm. What I don't expect is for him to lose all control.

What I don't expect is for him to be even more blindingly gorgeous as his orgasm takes over his entire body.

"Come, baby girl." His words are tight, coming through clenched teeth as he waits for me to let go.

And Goddess, do I ever.

Pulling himself back into a kneeling position and bringing me up with him, he puts both hands on my shoulders and buries himself so deep in my core I can't imagine him ever not being there. We're face-to-face, lips-to-lips, eyes hypnotized and caught in each other's gazes as our heavy, climax induced breaths mix one into the other. We share our oxygen as our bodies share an orgasm.

In that moment, we are one. I can see the emotions running through the depths of his eyes as he takes my mouth one last time. His demanding kiss stokes the fire within me, but we fall to the bed in a heap of limp, sweaty limbs before the inferno consumes me entirely.

TWENTY SEVEN

The day is finally here.

I got the call yesterday from Creek. Remy went into labor. Elysiel was there with them, helping her with the birth. Pretty sure the hospitals wouldn't know what the fuck to do with the birth of an Angel, and I can't help but laugh at the thought.

Then this morning, I got the text. They had a little boy, who looks just like his daddy, with his mama's beautiful violet eyes. I am literally over-the-moon happy for them, and I can't wait to meet him.

Raziel Michael Bennett.

Who knew Levi would cave on the middle name, cause I sure as shit didn't think it would happen! Though, he never has been able to deny Remy a thing.

Today, we're all heading to the Shadow Realm to celebrate the little guy's birth.

It's also the first time Deacon is joining all of us in something like this. We've kept our relationship pretty low key the last few months, just enjoying our time together and getting to know each other. But we decided it can't stay like that forever.

These people are our family; and it's not like they don't know that we're together, they just haven't seen it. I've been a little nervous, truth be told. I know that Remy and Creek both gave me their blessing, but they were also both the closest to Colt. While I still carry him in my heart, and I always will, I don't want them to hold anything against Deacon. I know our history isn't exactly sunshine and roses, but we've moved past it.

I just hope they can, too. Hearing about it is one thing, but seeing it is another.

We've told each other everything. He knows every little thing there is to know about me, the good, the bad, and the ugly. I'd like to say I know everything about him, but he's lived a substantially longer life than I have. Sometimes I wonder if I'll ever know everything, but what's important is that I know who he is now.

"Mama, I'm heading out now," I call out to her from my room. Her and Rebel are going to a council meeting; and while that's something that still weighs on me, Rebel is handling it better than I ever could have imagined. Mama still isn't jumping for joy about my relationship, but I keep it out of her sight as much as I can while she adapts to it.

"Okay, baby. Congratulate Remy and the guys again for me."

"Will do! Love you, Mama."

"Love you, too, baby."

I close the door to my room and clutch my necklace, closing my eyes. We told everyone we'd meet them at the palace, and I know I'm going to be late. I took a little longer than I thought I would getting ready and curling my hair. I haven't dressed up like this in front of everyone in a while, but today deserves the effort.

The whoosh still fills my ears as I cross over into the Shadow Realm, but I'm getting way better at it these days. I've had a lot of practice. I drop into the courtyard where everyone is already gathered around Remy.

"Hey, baby girl," Deacon says, kissing the top of my head as he reaches me. He takes my hand, and we walk across the lawn to where the others are.

"Hey there, Mama," I say when I reach Remy; my eyes fill with tears when I see the sheer joy on her face. I look down into her arms, and the little boy with a head full of hair captures my heart in an instant. "Oh Remy, he's so beautiful."

"Thanks, it was worth all the pain and the hormones.

He is just fucking everything, Fallon," she says, the boys moving away to leave me with her and Morgan.

"She says that now, wait till he starts talking." Morgan laughs, and we both join her.

"I'm sure he'll be a perfect delight," Remy says, making me laugh harder.

"Not if he's anything like his mom," I tease, and she pokes her tongue out at me. "How are you feeling for real, though?"

"Honestly, I'm a little tired, but he's been so good. He's slept so much. I was a little afraid, but Elysiel tells me that's normal. So I'm going to try to not freak out."

"And by that, you mean, freak out every other second," Morgan adds, and Remy nods enthusiastically.

"That's exactly what I mean. Though if you think I'm a wreck, you should see Levi. I don't think he's blinked since Raze was born," she says, and I look over to the group of guys and find his gaze still on us all.

"Poor guy, he loves with everything he has. At least you know this kid is going to know true and pure love." Morgan sighs. She snaps her fingers, and a garden lounge set appears with a table full of food and drink. "Let's have a toast, shall we?"

The others move back to us, and Deacon stands behind my chair, one hand on my shoulder. We each take a glass as Malik pours the champagne.

"To love, to family ever growing, and ties that will bond us forever," Caleb says, lifting his glass. I lift mine and take a sip of the bubbles, Deacon squeezing my shoulder. I look up at him and find him staring at the baby, a far off look on his face.

"Are you okay?" I whisper to him, squeezing his hand.

He looks down at me, coming back to us, and smiles.

"I honestly don't think I've ever been better."

We left the others a little while back. Mireya was being introduced to Raziel, and things were getting very family orientated, so we decided to give those guys some space and head back to Deacon's.

He's finally let me loose in his kitchen, much to the disgust of his cook. She kicked up a major fucking fuss about having me in here, but I'm so excited. It's a full chef's kitchen, and it's totally stocked.

"So, what are we eating?" he asks, grinning at me as he sits on the counter, enjoying watching me as I explore the space.

"How are you with spicy?" I ask, and he barks out a laugh.

"Oh, I think you already know I'm good with spicy." I laugh at him, and he wags his eyebrows as I head back to the refrigerator. I spot the crawfish and everything else I need to do a proper low country boil, and smile over my shoulder at him.

"Oh, baby, you are about to experience a proper New Orleans wonder, just the way my grammy taught me to make it."

I work around the kitchen, loving the space, walking him through everything as I do it. He watches, and even helps me at times, never minding about getting his hands dirty. Once everything is finally cooking, he keeps an eye on the crawfish, making sure they're turned every few minutes while I focus on everything else. Once the sausage, potatoes, and corn are in the pot, I can't help but just stand and watch him when he isn't fully paying attention to me.

It's fun seeing him like this. Even in his shirt and jeans, he's barefoot and happy. I think this might be the most relaxed I've ever seen him.

Once everything is done, he helps me plate everything up, and then he carries it down to the nook, not letting me carry a thing. I try not to swoon at him sometimes, but I usually fail. We've added a table in here, since we spend so much time in here, so he puts everything down and pulls two beers from the fridge. I'm not usually a fan, but it's the perfect drink with this food.

"Time to get messy." I wink at him as he rolls his sleeves up.

"Oh, this is just the beginning," he chuckles before joining me on the sofa and we tuck in.

It's so comfortable being here with him like this. We sit with the TV on, playing the show we've been binging when we've had the chance and just enjoy each other's company.

I eat way too fucking much and groan as I lean back. "Holy shit, that was so good, but I should've stopped ages ago."

He grins at me and my still half-full bowl. "More for me!"

"Well, I'm glad you're enjoying it," I chuckle, and his grin widens.

"Baby girl, if you keep cooking like this, I'm never going to let you leave," he jokes, and I swat his arm.

"Funny."

"Have you ever thought about having kids?" he asks, biting into the food once more, and my heart stops momentarily.

"I mean, yes and no," I say, wondering where he's going with this. "It was always expected I'd have an heir to continue the line, but now that's not a requirement of my life. I honestly haven't really thought of it much beyond that. You?"

He shakes his head. "I never used to want kids. My childhood was… Well, it was beyond fucked up. I've experienced a lot of bullshit in this long life of mine, and I never thought bringing another person into the world was a good idea. But after today, I think I might have been wrong. Seeing everyone, how happy they were… That kid… I swear he stole my heart. So I don't know. Maybe one day."

I nod, lost for words.

"But not anytime soon," he adds on, and I let out a deep breath. "Doesn't mean we can't practice plenty though." He gives me a wolfish grin, and I laugh. He pushes the table away from himself and crawls over the sofa toward me until I'm lying beneath him. "And maybe we can practice right now."

The last few days have been a whirlwind. Remy's back home with Raze, and I've been over there more than once, cooing over his newborn smell. I literally just can't get enough of it. But because of how crazy everything has been at home, it's been a week since I've seen Deacon.

I miss him.

So I use my necklace to take me to the Shadow Realm, making sure to focus on his place, so that I end up there rather than the palace. I picture it in my mind, and my ears pop as I move between Realms. When I open my eyes, I'm in his bedroom, and he's standing there in dress pants, his shirt unbuttoned and bare footed.

Hot damn, I think I'm drooling. His hair is all messy on top of his head, and in the dark colors of the room, he's like a shining light. We've come so very far since I first met him, and I never thought we'd end up here. But I'm finally happy, and while I still miss Colt every day, I know that he'd want me to be happy.

"Hello, Princess," Deacon says, his wolfish smile making me shudder. "Have you been a good girl?"

I sigh, feeling the stress of life falling from me just being in his presence. He really is my rock, my fiercest protector, and my safe place. I know I can feel anything and everything, and he'll catch me when I fall. "I've been bad."

I smile as he stalks toward me, practically holding my breath with anticipation. We've both been busy recently, so it's been a hot minute since we had time to let the shackles of life off, and I need this surrender as much as he does.

He reaches me in no time, stopping inches in front of me and then bringing his hand to my chin, pinching it between his index finger and thumb.

"Let me take care of you." Those six barely whispered words hold the power of a nuclear bomb because together, they form a promise. One I need so desperately right now.

"Yes, please."

In that moment, everything else evaporates from my mind. I let it all go. All of the stress, all of the questions, all of the planning. I leave it all at the door and focus only on him. Deacon, with his masterful dominance capable of destroying even my shittiest of days, lifts my chin and brings our mouths together in the softest of kisses. Just barely there, a ghostly swiping of lips against lips. And then he's gone. The Dom back in position, ready to play our favorite game.

"Clothes off, ready for inspection."

I don't think, I just act. Under his watchful eye, I shed my clothing and begin to pile them neatly on the chair against the wall. He expects it. I should be neat and tidy or else face his punishment.

Goddess, though sometimes I just need his wrath.

Like now. Right the fuck now.

Just as I'm about to carefully fold my jeans, I decide I need more of him. Instead of bending at the waist so he can see my pussy as I place my clothes on the chair, I act carelessly and throw them over without even looking to see if they land on the chair.

I watch him, my defiant gaze telling him more than any words could. His eyes turn hard, his spine straightens at my brattiness. His fists are at his side, clenching and unclenching, like he's itching to grab me and fuck me into submission.

Yes, please!

“Fallon.” One word, my name, which he only uses outside the bedroom or when he’s about to unleash his punishment, echoes off the walls like an omen.

It’s so fucking hot.

I don’t respond because I’m not stupid.

“Are you sure you want to do this?”

Fuck. He’s just turned the tables around against me.

I can feel my bravado waver as he takes one, then two, steps closer to me. I’m naked and at his mercy which would normally be ideal, but right now, I have no idea if my plan is even going to work.

“Present yourself to me.”

I hesitate but decide that if I want the scene to last, I need to do as I’m told.

Sinking to my knees, I sit on my haunches, place my hands on my thighs and keep my back nice and straight. My eyes trained on him.

“That’s my good girl. I thought she’d left the room.” He makes a circle around me, and I don’t have to look at him to know he’s inspecting my position. I know I’m sitting perfectly, he’s taught me well.

“You want to tell me what that stunt was all about? You may speak.” He’s asking, but he already knows. He’s testing me, seeing if I’ll lie, or if I’ll go back to being good.

But I’m feeling a little rebellious.

"I don't know what you're talking about." Fuck, I'm wet just watching his eyes flash and his cock push against the fabric of his slacks.

"Is that so?" Staring at me for a second longer, I almost cave under his scrutiny. Instead, I do what every defiant girl does, I lift my chin and stare straight at him in a 'whatcha gonna do about it' pose.

And oh yeah, it has the desired effect. The tiniest twitch at the corner of his mouth is the only indication I have that he's enjoying my defiance as much as I am, but then the arch of his brow reminds me that he always wins at this game of give and take.

"Very well," is all he says as he turns away from me and walks to his dresser drawer. I'm expecting a flogger or a paddle. Maybe a cat o' nine. But it's none of those things.

Hanging from the tip of his middle finger, taunting me, is a blindfold. Dark and thick, it promises to hide everything from my sight. I almost want to backpedal and beg him for forgiveness, but that would never work. Besides, I'm too stubborn to give him the satisfaction of giving up.

He knows damn well how much I love watching him undress, how I yearn to devour his body with my gaze. How his every move is a step of foreplay that leaves me hotter than Hades.

He knows all of this so well that my punishment is not what I was hoping for. It's not a good lashing or a hard spanking.

It's deprivation, but knowing him, it will be the sweetest kind.

"Bad girls don't get what they want." His words are laced with dark humor, and my only response, unless I want him to also put a ball gag in my mouth, is to take my punishment like a good girl.

Fuck, he's infuriating when he uses his ability to read me like a map against me.

"What do you say to me when you disrespect the rules?"

Dammit.

"I'm sorry."

"And?"

"I won't do it again." I have to bite my bottom lip because he and I both know it's a blatant lie.

"Good girl, you almost sound truthful."

Then I'm blinded by the blackout fabric that he ties around my head. It's exhilarating in a whole new way as every other sense is heightened. Maybe I'll enjoy this after all.

"Bend over, forehead on the rug, thighs open so I can see your pussy."

I don't hesitate; I move instantly.

"Hmm, you're so wet, baby girl. Is all that arousal for me?"

“Yes.”

“Good answer.” I jump slightly as he runs a thick finger up the seam of my pussy lips. “Why are you so twitchy tonight?”

“It’s the blindfold.” My words are just barely whispered.

“Do you think I’m being too harsh with you?” There’s a right answer to that question and there’s a wrong answer.

“No.” And that was the wrong one. At the same time, it was a trick question. My other choice would have been a lie, and that’s a worse offense.

I almost fall over as he sinks two fingers inside me and hooks them just right, sending shivers running across my skin. He’s fucking me earnestly with those digits, trying to get me to come.

Holy shit, this feels so much more intense. His breath on my skin, his touch. It’s like every nerve in my body is alive. My nipples pebble so hard they almost hurt as they brush against the material beneath me, but it’s a good kind of hurt. The best kind.

He pushes me so fucking close to the edge, so much quicker than usual, and I know that’s because of the blindfold. I may feel defiant right now, but I’m not an idiot. I will never come without his permission. I handed him this power, so this is on me.

Then his fingers are gone, and in their stead I feel something cold penetrate me. Gasping, I try my best to keep my position and not fall to the side as the sensation of it almost overwhelms me.

Not seeing might just be a new favorite of mine.

When the object slides out then back in, I think it's a dildo but then he slides it out one more time and guides it to my ass, letting it penetrate just a little. My juices have lubricated it a bit, but it's not enough to be pushed all the way inside.

"Don't move." His voice is pure restraint as he moves away for a second, and the next thing I know, I can feel the gel of the lube he's pouring onto my skin. The cold of it against the heat of my skin makes my entire body shudder.

I'm guessing this is less a punishment and more his reward. Because what's not to like about anal?

After using his fingers on my ass a few times to open me up slowly, Deacon finally slides the butt plug in and then slaps my ass. Hard. Twice on each side. Every time it jostles the plug and makes me moan for more.

"Up."

Carefully, I climb to my feet and feel him close to me, ready to catch me if I lose my balance.

I don't, but I wish I had so I could feel the strength of him around me.

Once I'm up, I hear the shuffle of fabric, and I'm guessing he's undressing, depriving me of seeing him in all his glory. I sigh at the loss of his little strip tease. I know

I asked for this yet I can't find it in me to regret one second of any of this.

Then his hands are on either side of my cheeks, and his mouth is gently gliding over my lips in a reverent kiss that leaves me aching for more.

"It's my job to take care of you and protect you. Even when your own worst enemy is yourself." His words are breaths against my lips, and then his tongue demands entrance as his hands position me at the perfect angle for his kiss. I don't fight it, I let him take the reins and enjoy the satisfaction of letting it all go.

I'm hoping my compliance will give me back my gorgeous view of him.

A quick slap to my ass cheek is my answer.

Obviously, I'm not going to get what I want quite yet. But I know he'll never truly deny me the things I want. That isn't the kind of dominant he is.

"I would have let it go at the negligent folding. But you just had to keep on going, didn't you?"

Walking me to the bed, he bends me over and taps my ankles on the inside to make sure I spread them further apart.

"Hold on to the bed spread for leverage. It's time to remind you who's in control here."

Bunching the fabric up with my fists, I position myself exactly as he wants me. Face turned to the side so I would usually be able to see him, with my chest pressed against the mattress. Except, I can't see him, and I really want to. Damn this double-edged punishment. I bite my tongue because I'm enjoying this so much, but I also love watching him with me.

"I'm sorry," I blurt out the words without permission, hoping he can forgive me. I bite my lip because while I'm sorry I purposely pushed him, I am not even a little sorry at what happened because of it.

"For what, baby girl?"

"For pushing you."

His only response is his hand running from my neck to my tailbone. It's an intimate caress, a loving and understanding touch. It's forgiveness. But I know he doesn't start something without seeing it through.

So, I take it. I let it all go and allow him to give me back my strength by taking away my power in these intimate moments.

"That's my good girl." His words are true, they vibrate throughout my body as he pushes his dick inside me and stills. With the plug inside my ass, I'm feeling incredibly full. Almost too full, but not quite.

A moan escapes me, and he squeezes my hips in response. He loves it when I tell him how good he feels without using words.

Once I adjust to the combination of his girth and the

plug, he starts to fuck me in earnest.

I see stars as he pounds my sweet spot over and over again with abandon. I try my damnedest to hold on to the comforter and keep my feet solidly planted on the rug, but his thrusts are demanding and brutal. Skin slapping skin every time he pushes inside me, the sound of sweat and cum evident every time our flesh meets.

"My favorite part of the day is sinking inside you, baby girl. Do you know that?"

"Yes."

"And when I sink inside you, I love having your gaze on me. Speaking to me with your big, bright eyes."

I can feel him losing a semblance of his control, I can hear it in his voice, but I know he's enjoying this just as much as I am.

"I'm sorry," I gasp, hoping that he's ready to give me what I want and let me see him. He growls as he fucks me harder and I feel myself teetering on the edge.

"I know. I forgive you."

Then he's out of me and I feel myself being turned around, my knees coming up to my chest as he sinks back inside me.

The light of the room attacks my eyes as the blindfold is ripped off, leaving me blinking and disoriented.

"Now, look at me while I fuck the defiance right out of you."

And he does.

His thrusts are devilish, hard and fast, pistoning into my pussy. He wraps his fingers around my wrist and holds me against the mattress like a prisoner of his lust.

And I am more than okay with that.

It's when he kisses me that I know he's forgiven me for being a brat, his tongue like a balm to my soul. His lips a bandage to my wounded heart.

"Let me take care of you, Princess. It's what I live to do."

"Okay."

Fucking me like a lover who's just returned from battle, Deacon whispers gently in my ear.

"Come for me, Princess."

And on his next thrust, as he grinds against my clit, I explode like a thousand suns. Stars and light flashing behind my lids, electric surges running through my bloodstream. It's heaven and hell all at once, and I love every single moment of it.

As his name flies out of my mouth with the desperation only he can bring out of me, I watch in awe as he allows himself to explode right along with me.

Lesson learned.

"I've been thinking," Deacon says to me as I sip my coffee in his nook.

"Did it hurt?" I tease, and he scoffs. "Sorry, I couldn't resist. What have you been thinking?"

"Well, obviously, you're mortal. I'm not. And I don't know if anyone told you, but when you're here, you essentially stop aging." I blink at him, trying to process that. Azriel mentioned once that I would be able to stay here forever, but I figured that was the bond and nothing more.

"Nope, no one ever told me that."

"Okay, well, now you know… But what I was thinking is that you're here all the time. I'm in this for the long game, you're it for me. I've known that since the moment I saw you." He pauses and comes to sit beside me on the sofa, pulling me onto his lap.

"I love you, Fallon Laveau… And I want to be with you forever. I want you to move here, with me." He kisses me till I'm breathless, and when he pulls back, it takes a minute for me to pull my thoughts together.

"I… Don't know what to say. This is all still so new realistically, and while I know I love you, too, this seems like a big step. I still have Mama and Rebel…"

"You don't have to answer me now," he says cutting me off and tucking me against his chest. "Just promise me you'll think about it."

I chew on my lip, both freaking ecstatic but also torn about leaving my family behind. I feel the same way he does, and honestly, I never thought we'd get here. I didn't think I'd ever feel like this about another person ever again.

But sometimes people have more than one soulmate. I have no doubt that Colt was my soulmate, but Deacon is, too, and I don't want to waste any time pretending otherwise.

With the coven having stripped me of my title, my life is now my own to do with as I please, but is this all moving too fast? I know I'm mortal, and staying like this with him forever sounds more than a little appealing, but I just don't know. I take a deep breath, and I look up at him, kissing his cheek before I nod.

"I promise I'll think about it."

TWENTY EIGHT

ONE YEAR LATER

This last year has been a whirlwind. So much has changed, and yet, I couldn't picture my life any other way now. I still miss Colt every day, but I also love Deacon with my entire heart. After the whole come to Jesus conversation with Remy, I realized she was right. Colt wouldn't have wanted me to be miserable. He wouldn't want me to waste my life mourning him. And I'm starting to get over my guilt at finding happiness with Deacon. Sometimes, it still gets me when I first wake up, stealing the breath from my lungs, but Deacon is there to help me through it.

"Fallon, are you okay to cover the shop for me this

morning?" Mama calls out from the kitchen, and I sigh. There goes my quiet day of pampering myself. Dammit, I had an entire spa day planned.

"Sure thing, Mama," I call back to her, trying not to be too disappointed and finish fixing my hair. I head into the kitchen when I'm done, and Mama kisses my cheek when she sees me, wrapping me in a hug. I smile back at her after she releases me, we've all learned just how short life is recently and started taking more time for the small things. How long it'll last, I don't know, but I'm going to enjoy it for every single second it does.

I've finally started to forgive Mama for not warning me about Colt. I get why she didn't but still… Sometimes being a slave to the Fates fucking sucks. But she's also been massively supportive of me since the fallout with the coven and having my heirship revoked. She's even finally starting to come around to the fact that I'm dating a Demon. It's been an interesting time for sure. We still don't rub it in her face, but each time she sees us together, her frown gets a little less intense than the time before. It's part of the reason I still haven't taken Deacon up on his offer to move in with him. I think Mama needs some more time before I spring that on her, and I don't want to miss too much time with Rebel, either. She's growing up so quickly.

My heart pangs as the image of Colt flits into my mind, and a small sad sigh escapes me. It's a very confusing time to be me. Rebel bounces over to me and hugs me. “Love you, Fallon.”

“I love you too, sweet girl.” I stroke her hair before she bounces back to the table.

“I’ll need you to take Rebel to the store with you this morning. Misty will be there, too. I have an errand I need to sort out, so I’m hoping it won’t take much time, I shouldn’t need you there too long to cover for me.”

“No worries, Mama. I got it covered for however long you need.” I smile as she hands me two plates of food for Rebel and I. I take them and sit at the table with my little sister, glad that the events of the last year haven’t corrupted her or taken away that childish innocence of hers. She’s too young to be corrupted. It would break me if she was forced to endure the crap my friends and I have been through.

Once we’re both fed and ready for the day, I drive us over to the store. “Why don’t you go into the back with Misty and help her sort out the herb vials?” I say to her, and she nods eagerly before skipping to the back room where Misty is already all set up. I still feel awful that the mantle has passed to her since my fall from grace with the coven, but as is everything in my life at the minute, it’s not so simple. Because I also feel happy as fuck that I’m free to live my life how I see fit, but I find myself feeling guilty about that, too.

Working through my emotions is a full-time fucking

job, but luckily, I have people around me that help me every day and support me no matter what. Remy went fucking postal when I finally told her about what happened, but that was the same day she asked me to be Raze's Godmother, so I can't help but have only good memories of the day.

I work for a few hours, reading more than a few tarot decks and dealing with some really naive humans before Mama breezes through the doors with a wide smile on her face. "Hey, baby, I hope it's not been too chaotic in here. You can head out now if you want to."

"Thanks, Mama, but I can stay if you need me to. It hasn't been too bad, just a normal Saturday." As I finish speaking, the bell over the front door sounds again, and I see Deacon standing just behind Mama, looking serious as shit. My heart sinks. I haven't seen him look like that since… Well since I told him that I was hearing voices in my head. Goddess, that feels like an entire lifetime ago.

What the fuck is going on?

"Fal… Babe. I need you to come with me. It's important," he says, his voice flat, and my panic spikes.

"What's wrong?" I ask, moving round the counter to stand by him.

"I can't explain… I just," he pauses and takes a deep breath, looking up like he's trying to find the words or the patience. "I really just need you to come with me. Right now. It'll take too long to explain, and I don't know that you'll even… Please, we should go quickly."

I turn back to Mama who is frowning at us, coming to terms with me dating a Demon is one thing, seeing it is another thing altogether. "Will you be okay if I go? Really?"

"I'll be fine, sweet girl, but whatever this is, you let me know as soon as you can. I don't have a good feeling about any of this," she says, eyeing the Demon at my side, but he looks like his world is breaking in two.

"Sure thing, Mama," I say, moving to kiss her cheek before turning back to Deacon. "Okay, let's go."

I can't get a read on him as I take his hand. He seems angry and sad; he's practically shaking. A shot of fear runs down my spine at whatever the fuck it is he needs to show me. At least I'm assuming he needs to show me something since he can't explain whatever the fuck is going on. I want to say something more, but then he whispers us to the Shadow Realm before I have a chance to open my mouth.

I land unsteadily as the marble of the throne room floor of the Shadow Palace comes to life beneath my feet.

"Why are we here?" I ask, looking from him and spotting Morgan and Caleb in front of us. I move toward them, wondering what the actual fuck is going on since Deacon won't say a word. I repeat my question once I reach them to see if they'll tell me what this is all about. "What's going on? What was so urgent?"

My gaze bounces between them, when they look over my shoulder, Caleb's somewhat wary smile turns into a frown. I don't understand what is going on.

"Fallon?" My heart stops at the voice calling my name. This can't be real. I take a deep breath and turn around, but all the air is sucked from my lungs when I do. Shit. My knees go weak, and I think I'm going to fall, but I'm fucking paralyzed. Even my heart stops, and I can't work out which way is up. This isn't possible. No, no, no. He's meant to be dead. They told me he was dead. I blink at the man opposite me, not quite believing what I'm seeing.

This can't be real…

ABOUT THE AUTHOR

Sloane Murphy is the author of the international bestselling series, The Immortal Chronicles, as well as a range of other paranormal and contemporary romance. Sloane lives in Peterborough, England, with her husband & fur baby and over the years, she has developed an unhealthy appreciation for cheesy YA Films, cupcakes and bad pop music. She adores fairy tales, ballet and all things supernatural, drinks far too much coffee, and watches an ungodly amount of Netflix. When she's not busy writing, she can be found exploring the world with her husband and chocolate Labrador.

If you would like to send Sloane an email, you can reach her at sloane@authorsloanemurphy.com

Want to sign up for her mailing list? You can sign up HERE

Or come join her reader group on Facebook, Sloanes Little Monsters

facebook.com/sloanemurphybooks

twitter.com/SloaneMurphyBks

instagram.com/sloanemurphybooks

bookbub.com/authors/sloane-murphy

ALSO BY SLOANE MURPHY

THE SEVEN REALMS SAGA

The Shadow Walkers Saga

(Reverse Harem Paranormal Romance)

A Crown of Blood and Bone

A Crown of Smoke and Ash

A Crown of Shadows and Secrets

A Crown of Thorns and Lies

A Crown of Fire and Wrath

A Crown of Pride and Ruin

The Shadow Weaver Series

(Menage Paranormal Romance)

Witch's Curse

Hunter's Heart

Demon's Blessing

The Shadow Queen Series

(Reverse Harem Paranormal Romance)

The Shadow Queen

The Shadow Legacies Series

(Rejected Mates Romance)

Luna Rising

THE IMMORTAL CHRONICLES SERIES

(YA Paranormal Romance. Complete Series)

Descent

Crash

Soar

Rapture

BLACK WATER ACADEMY SERIES

(Upper YA/NA Paranormal Romance. Reverse Harem)

Marked

Chosen

Hunted

DARK FAE DUET

(Paranormal Romance. Dark Fantasy)

Summer Princess

Winter King

OTHER AUTHORS AT HUDSON INDIE INK

Paranormal Romance/Urban Fantasy

Stephanie Hudson

Xen Randell

C. L. Monaghan

Sorcha Dawn

Sci-fi/Fantasy

Devin Hanson

Crime/Action

Blake Hudson

Mike Gomes

Contemporary Romance

Gemma Weir

Elodie Colt

Ann B. Harrison

Printed in Great Britain
by Amazon

79493212R00294